Lénobe Bosquet

The Exploits of

Lénobe Bosquet,

a Virtuous Young Atheist, & of

Monsieur Wagnière, His Fellow Librarian

an historical novel by

Roy Luna

professor of French Language and Literature
at the Key Largo Campus of the
Florida Keys International College,

with historical notes provided by

Dr. Theophilus Ralph

professor of History at the University of Münster,
Thunder-den-Drang Campus, Westphalia, Germany

SOL U TION HOLE PRESS

SOL⏝TION HOLE PRESS

Copyright © 2018 by Roy Luna
First Edition.
First Printing: 2018
ISBN: 978-0-9967031-2-3
Solution Hole Press LLC.
www.solutionholepress.com
Book Design: Jorge Saury.
Mise en Place painting by Trish A. Jesselli. Photograph, and sleeves, by Marie Zurenda. Author's picture courtesy of Mark P. Young.

Introduction, acknowledgments and dedication

I wish to thank, once again, my dear friends who trudged through the manuscript of *Lord of Reason,* the first novel of the trilogy, *A Revolutionary Education,* and then had the fortitude to come back for this second part. My heartfelt gratitude goes to Cheryl Clark, Maureen O'Hara, Viktor Prokofiev, Robert Vitale, and Marie Zurenda. Together we unite and continue the battle begun by Voltaire: *Écrasez l'Infâme!*

Once again I wish to thank Professor Theophilus Ralph, historian, biographer, academician extraordinary, for having returned to the further adventures of Zénobe Bosquet. He continues to explain the esoteric peculiarities of the late-Eighteenth-century milieu and the particular contemporaneous circumstances with which the modern reader may be unfamiliar. I realize that in the past, *Herr Doktor* Ralph and I have had moments when we didn't see eye to eye, but dissent and controversy are the indispensable apparatus of change and progress. *Dix-huitièmistes* we may both be, and we may also contemplate at the altar of Notre Dame de la Méthode, but we retain our idiosyncratic disparities. This is a good thing. Enlightenment happens in fits and starts, attended by fracas and frays, down in the dirt, or up in the skies. Differences of opinion, secession from conventionality, contempt for entrenched traditions, passionate altercations in full view of the public, and even quibbles about picayune details, all serve to direct the reader's attention to what has not been established as fact, or to differences in the interpretation of that which may be a fact but which remains fraught with contention.

I.e.: Voltaire's death on May 30, 1778. Was it calm and peaceful as I portrayed it in the first volume of this story? Or was it agitated and macabre as Voltaire's detractors have described it, multifarious variations of which can be found plastered on many an Internet page today? What dismal scenes! Nothing stoic or heroic about Voltaire being philosophical when facing his coming demise. We encounter a Voltaire we've never seen before, with the old man eating the contents of his chamber pot, frightened out of his wits at the approaching final judgment of god, recanting every single sentence he ever wrote against the church, and gazing in horror from his deathbed at the ghastly spectacle of hell that appeared in front of him. Dr. Ralph opts for the first alternate reality, basing his logical selection on the rational historical evidence of the testimony of credible eyewitnesses. I, however, also base my choice on the first alternative, fully and fearlessly, simply because I know that there is no hell. There is an immediate corollary to this: I know for a fact that religious zealots have been known to lie, cheat and swindle in order to maintain their dominance over the belief systems of the gullible. They use the idea of hell to frighten the incredulous, to threaten them, to manage them, and to coerce them into desired behaviors. The only proof they can come up with is what has been printed up in their sacred texts, which is no proof at all. Their texts only prove that these wild and fearsome stories have been around for eons, and that the fearmongers continue to alarm little children in the hopes that they tread a moral path. Wouldn't it be better to convince those children to follow the ideals of morality simply for the love of humanity, for the esteem of virtue, for the respect of justice?

Dr. Ralph would like to quote from Joseph de Maistre, the diplomat and political writer who straddled both the French Revolution and the Counter-Enlightenment: "Every nation has the government it deserves."[1] I would like to add that, then as now, the faithful who blindly and unquestioningly maintain their faith in view of blatant malfeasance by the clergy, also deserve the religion that they get. If their religion is repressive, reactionary and recalcitrant, it is the fault of all of the people who prop it up, by giving it money, by attending its services, by paying attention to it, by giving credence to it. But there is a slight glimmer of hope, and it is this: it is beyond the powers of Reason to accept people's piety in the face of the wrongful, wanton dishonesty of the ruling clerics. It might be an admirable case of Christian charity when parishioners show clemency towards the sins of priests, but it is clearly illogical when they exculpate the bishops for having relocated the guilty clerics in order to foist them onto new unsuspecting congregations. That is clearly a case of stupidity, or cruelty, or sheer wanton blindness, or complete disregard for the well-being of the parishioners. Those who turn, albeit slightly, albeit weakly, to reason, to logic and thus to reality, will begin to see the sins of religion and the errors of its ways.

It is unreasonable, illogical and incredible to accept injurious practices that religious leaders impose on believers: circumcision, clitoridectomy, honor killings, faith healing, forced marriages of children, repression of sexuality, suppression of science and education, the caste system, the discarding of widows, the prohibition of birth control, slavery, the isolation of believers from their families, the appropriation of a believer's finances, the imposition of biblical mythologies as justification to meddle in the socio-politico-cultural realm, the psychological trauma done to children by stories of the everlasting torture of fire and brimstone, etc., etc., etc.

It is beyond the ken of Logic to understand the hatred and intolerance fomented by those eager ecclesiastics with which they target those outside of their religion and, indeed, sometimes within their religion. It is almost beyond the Hope of Mankind that such prejudice against other religions and discrimination against freethinkers be quelled, and consequently the flow of blood occasioned by such enmity be staunched. Peace on Earth is but a mirage, an empty, impossible dream, unless the priestly class in all its echelons and in all lands refrains from deprecating other religions and from pretending to their own superiority.

Dr. Ralph wishes now to leave the final word to Voltaire. "If there were in England but one religion, its despotism would be fearsome; if there were but two of them, they would cut each other's throats; but there are thirty of them, and they live happily in peace.[2]

There are more that thirty religions in the world. Why don't we live in peace?

---

1   In a letter to M. le Comte de Vallaise in 1816. The exact quote is: «[...] *c'est un axiome capital, aussi sûr qu'un axiome de mathématique, que toute nation a le gouvernement qu'elle mérite.*»

2   In Voltaire's *Lettres philosophiques,* published in 1734 after the philosopher visited England and observed how the different sects of Christianity had learned to live in (relative) harmony. «*S'il n'y avait en Angleterre qu'une religion, son despotisme serait à craindre; s'il n'y en avait que deux, elles se couperaient la gorge; mais il y en a trente, et elles vivent en paix et heureuses.*»

For Mark P. Young

Contents

Part 1:
Following the Scent of Sulfur

Prologue
June 1, 1778 2
    The Machinations of the Church

Addendum to the Prologue, ... 5
    The Man of Two Sins

Chapter I
June 2, 1778 7
    The Man of Two Foils

Chapter II
June 3, 1778 14
    Exploring Farming Techniques in Champagne

Chapter III
June 3, 1778 20
    Desperate Times

Chapter IV
June 3, 1778 23
    Falling into Danger

Chapter V
June 4, 1778 26
    Letter to a Lover

Chapter VI
June 4 to 7, 1778 32
    Flouting the Laws of God and Nature

Chapter VII
June 8, 1778 35
    Waylaid

Chapter VIII
June 8 & 9, 1778..39
    Traveling Companion

Chapter IX
June 10, 1778 42
    Arrival into Chaos

Chapter X
June to September, 1778 48
    Work Staves off Boredom, Vice and Need

June to December, 1778 51
    Fragments of letters of people who have nothing to
    do with this novel, yet shed some light on its context

Part 2
Expedition to Save a Library

Chapter XI
August, 1778...59
    Secret Convocations

Chapter XII
Beginning of October, 1778 62
    Meeting the Creator of Figaro, and His Publisher

Chapter XIII
Mid-October, 1778 66
    Villette Arrives to Oversee His Domain

Chapter XIV
Received mid-October, 1778 69
  Letters from Loved Ones

Chapter XV
October 31, 1778...84
  The Eve of All Saints' Day

Chapter XVI
November 1, 1778..86
  Going Home

Chapter XVII
November 2, 1778..94
  Dead to the World

Chapter XVIII
November 2, 3 or 4, 1778 97
  Inquisitional Stratagems

Chapter XIX
November 4 or 5, 1778..108
  Bolt to Freedom

Chapter XX
November 8, 1778 111
  In the Land of the Protestants

Interstices Addendum, between Part 2 and Part 3
The centuries leading up to 1778 119
  Fragments of ancient kingdoms and their dispersed monarchs

Part 3
Safeguarding a Legacy

Chapter XXI
November 10, 1778 122
  Off to Russia

Chapter XXII
Third week of November, 1778 125
  Visits to Historical Places

Chapter XXIII
Last week of November, 1778...129
  Books in Danger

Chapter XXIV
December 1, 1778 136
  Librarians in Danger

Chapter XXV
First week of December, 1778 139
  In Sans Souci with the King

Chapter XXVI
First week of December, 1778 145
  The Intimate Guest of the King

Chapter XXVII
First week of December, 1778 149
  What Did They Talk About?

Chapter XXVIII
December 9, 1778 161
  The Sources of Poetry

Chapter XXIX
December 10, 1778 167
   A Detail Slips Out

Chapter XXX
December 11, 1778 173
   Last Stop in Germany

Interstices Addendum, between Part 3 and Part 4
December 12, 1778 178
   A Response to the Letter from Diderot

Part 4
Sailing on the Baltic

Chapter XXXI
Days following December 12, 1778...185
   Discussing Morality

Chapter XXXII
Days following December 12, 1778...189
   A Storm at Sea

Chapter XXXIII
The Day after the Storm, circa December 13, 1778 192
   A Discussion on Free Will over Breakfast

Chapter XXXIV
The Days after December 13, 1778...196
   Dead Calm

Chapter XXXV
About a Week after December 13, 1778...198
   The Captain Relates His Story

Chapter XXXVI
Around December 20, 1778..202
   A Medical Emergency

Chapter XXXVII
The Days before Christmas, 1778..207
   The Patient Worsens

Chapter XXXVIII
Christmas Day, 1778...209
   Arrival in Saint Petersburg

Chapter XXXIX
Between Christmas and the Festival of the Epiphany, 1778-1779 ...212
   Letters Written to an Empress

Chapter XL
January 6, 1779, Festival of the Epiphany.....................................222
   Letter from the Empress

Interstices Addendum, between Part 4 and Part 5
January, 1779 223
   A Word to Certain Readers about Catherine and Zénobe

Part 5
The Throne of the North

Chapter XLI
January 7, 1779 226
   An Audience with Catherine the Great

Chapter XLII
January 8, 1779 ....**233**
Discussing Literature with Catherine the Great

Chapter XLIII
January 9, 1779 ....**240**
An Empress Impressed

Chapter XLIV
January 10, 1779...**244**
An Expensive Gift

Chapter XLV
January 11, 1779...**249**
A Simulated Circumstance

Chapter XLVI
January 14, 1779...**253**
Absconding to the Summer Palace

Chapter XLVII
January 15, 1779...**261**
The Difficulty of Historical Novels

Chapter XLVIII
January & February, 1779 ....**272**
An Empress in Love

Chapter XLIX
January 16, 1779...**275**
Temptation

Chapter L
January 16, 1779, evening, & the following morning **279**
The Queen is Not Amused

Final Addendum
Last Days of January into February, 1779 ....**284**
Departure

Part 1:

Following the Scent of Sulfur

June 1, 1778

The Machinations of the Church

The appropriate letters had been sent, the official documents lodged at the highest levels of the hierarchy of the bishopric of Paris, a bevy of priests chosen—some borrowed from the Holy Office of the Supreme Sacred Congregation of the Roman and Universal Inquisition[3]—and the hunt was on for one Marie-Jean Joseph Zénobe Bosquet, nineteen years of age, native of Savoy, and quite possibly the revolutionary bastard scion of Victor-Amédée, by the grace of God, Duke of Savoy, Prince of Piedmont, King of Sardinia, of Cypress and of Jerusalem. More recently, Zénobe Bosquet had flagrantly flouted holy laws to become secretary, protégé and adherent of Voltaire. Now he was a dangerous outlaw, a gentleman run amuck and armed to the teeth, and a threat to all that was good and holy in the Christian realm of Louis XVI.

For more than fifty years Voltaire had been the most antagonistic of all the enemies of the Holy Catholic Church. As the oldest of the *philosophes*, a band of despoilers and degenerate humanists whose influence grew like a cancer, Voltaire had corrupted a succession of generations of the youth of Europe and produced new apostates in droves, including Bosquet, who was caught in the old man's snare while both were residents of the *hôtel* de Villette in Paris. But—finally!—God had seen fit to remove this blight upon the world. Voltaire was deceased! Voltaire was no more! The head of the serpent had been cut off! The bells of all the churches and cathedrals would have pealed out the happy news had Louis XVI not proclaimed that no one should mention or even allude to the philosopher's death. While the King wished to pass by these happy tidings in silence, the Church would have preferred to celebrate the death of a monster, to praise God for His glorious determination to reestablish equilibrium in the world. But the King in his wisdom counseled reticence, and perhaps that was best in order to quell the movement that Voltaire and his accomplices had initiated. Nobody wanted Voltaire martyred for then he could regain even more power and influence in death.

---

3   This administrative office, in 1542 founded, was in 1908 and 1965 renamed, in order to cleanse its name of so many terrible connotations. Today it is as the Congregation for the Doctrine of the Faith known, and it still actively searches for "unacceptable doctrines" that might endanger Christian tradition. For instance, in 2007, six nuns in Arkansas were excommunicated for believing the heresy that one of their number is the Virgin Mary reincarnated. It is to be hoped that the CDF no longer heretical people for years in prison keeps; it is to be hoped that it no longer tortures, maims and executes them.

The end of Voltaire could not be commemorated but, luckily, Voltaire's followers were not off limits. Zénobe Bosquet no longer had Voltaire's protection to count on, and the ecclesiastics felt that his apprehension was only a matter of days, perhaps weeks at the most. It was known that he had accompanied the dead Voltaire in a secret nocturnal carriage ride from Paris to Scellières, in Champagne, where the philosopher had been given sepulcher in direct opposition to the directives of the archbishop of Paris, Christophe de Beaumont. It had been Voltaire's nephew, *l'abbé* Mignot, who, as the commanding monk of the abbey in Scellières, had allowed this aberration to take place. The Church would deal with him later.

Voltaire had been buried. Masses had been intoned for his pathetic soul. It was too late to undo the sin of having granted him a Christian burial, and nobody wanted to exhume his mortal remains, including Beaumont who was afraid of opening a hornet's nest. He was still miffed that the Paris police lieutenant Lenoir had not been on his side when Voltaire was still alive and desperately looking for a grave. Still, the descendants of St. Peter through the centuries had learned to be patient. This abbey in Scellières where the old man had been interred was an old, decaying monastery that was no longer of any use to the Church. The walls would soon collapse on the grave of the most irreligious of heretics this side of hell. Voltaire was dead; the Church now wanted to take possession of Zénobe Bosquet as the next best thing. The young man was an enthusiastic follower of the Enlightenment, the intellectual movement of the moment that the Church was crusading mightily to destroy, for it brought forth independent thinking contrary to the teachings of Christ and was anathema to the doctrine of the Holy See.

The charges against Zénobe were numerous and grave, and growing: pertinacious heresy, irreverence, falsehood, impiety, irreligiousness, blasphemy, profanity, sedition, and treason, all calculated to lead others to perdition. Zénobe had been stigmatized with the name of innovator, rebel, perjurer, schismatic, heretic, and apostate. His heresy was tantamount to a social leprosy that would insidiously undermine the faith of others, and thus Zénobe had to be eliminated. Before that, however, he would have to be held up to the highest scrutiny that a society can give, identified as the miscreant that he was, and given a widely propagated indictment, followed by a very public punishment, in order to show the world that such wanton godlessness would not be tolerated. The Holy Office of the Inquisition was trembling in anticipation of making an example of the young sinner. After his trial and execution, all such young people would think twice before emulating any of the tenets of the Enlightenment. Think for one's self? Impossible! The Church offered the people centuries of well-honed principles that provided peace for the soul and temperance for the body. Embrace science as the harbinger of knowledge to mankind? Incongruous! Science only brought confusion and dissatisfaction among the populace, and allowed people to act in direct contradiction to established dogma. Think that there is no God? Unthinkable! One might as well let anarchy run rampant over the earth and society dissolve into barbarian confusion where the law of primitive appetites would rule over men, if they could still be called men. Animals, was more like it.

Zénobe was an animal on the run and as such, he would be caught and a splendid public spectacle made of him. A marvelous auto-da-fé, with accompanying carnival, would be organized, with Zénobe in the middle of the bonfire, for the edification of the faithful who needed reminders once in a while to keep the faith. Along with Archbishop Beaumont, there were also *l'abbé* Jean-Joseph Faydit de Tersac, the *curé* of

Saint-Sulpice, the parish church of the neighborhood where Zénobe had been living; and *l'abbé* Louis Laurent Gaultier, the Chaplain of the Hospital of the Incurables, who had spent the last weeks of Voltaire's life trying to make the old man recant for a lifetime of sinning against the Church, to no avail. The old man went to his grave as unapologetic an apostate as he ever was, and from there directly to hell. With this triumvirate in liaison against him, Zénobe had no hope to escape ecclesiastic discipline. He would be caught, put to the Question, and duly delivered, with purified soul and repentant heart to the gates of heaven, another wayward soul gathered unto Jesus Christ and saved from the clutches of Satan.[4]

As soon as the Paris bishopric heard of Voltaire's midnight burial ceremony in Scellières, emissaries were dispatched forthwith to Champagne and the surrounding provinces to intercept the young man who had accompanied Voltaire's corpse on its macabre ride to the tomb. Zénobe Bosquet knew nothing of the ecclesiastical machinations that were at that very moment being orchestrated for his capture. In spite of his intelligence, he was being rather blithe about the dangers emanating from the Parisian bishopric. He would not be able to escape the vast net that the Church was casting out for him, and that was by the hour drawing tighter and tighter in concentric circles around him.

---

4 Allow me at this junction a word about the Church and its lexicological practices place. A sinner "put to the Question" meant none other than being tortured until the unfortunate agreed to the questions being put to him, that he was indeed guilty of the sins with which he was charged. The sooner he agreed, the sooner the torture would cease. In the rare cases where the sinner did not agree, the flames of the auto-da-fé (in which the victim was burned alive) were thought to be sufficient to purify the soul and render it in a shape pleasing enough for God to be accepted into Heaven. Kind reader, please keep in mind that in those unenlightened times belief in Heaven and in Hell was real, and that those two places were daily in people's thoughts. Stealing a piece of bread brought one closer to Hell, as was thinking lasciviously of one's neighbor's wife. Tithing to the Church, which was mandatory, brought one closer to Heaven, as did identifying a fugitive from justice. Zénobe had much to fear from anyone faithful to the Church, especially those whose sins would be absolved if they pointed the finger at such a valuable prize as he.

The Man of Two Sins

Had Zénobe been *just* a heretic and apostate, the catholic church would have apprehended him, put him to the Question, and burned him alive in great pomp and circumstance on the Place de Grève, in front of the Hôtel de Ville, where all infamous religious and political enemies were dispatched into the next world. But the fact that Zénobe was guilty of another sin, one that was at this time unknown to the clerics, was just by itself capable of landing him in the same predicament. For Zénobe Bosquet they would have lit in their exuberant glee a double bonfire, starting off on either side of him and orchestrated to link their flames in one mighty conflagration. This second sin was perhaps even more abhorrent than the first, for those who were found to be guilty of crimes against Nature, of the unnamable wickedness of transgressing God's laws, of going beyond what was the purely criminal and into the realm of iniquity and vice, those heinous miscreants truly deserved to be roasted alive in the flames that, while incinerating the wicked flesh of the offender, could never be hot enough to purify his soul, could never blot out the deviant offense, because such evil flouted both civil and sacred principles. Such an offender could never hope to have his soul saved by Jesus, and with Jesus bypassed, the luckless sinner would forever be plunged into the fires of Satan. The virtue of society demanded that such degenerates be obliterated, for the Sacred Text had taught true believers that everyone died in Sodom and Gomorrah, both the debauched who brought on the wrath of God, but also the innocent who had stood by and done nothing.

The last such transgressor in France who was burned at the stake for the sin of sodomy was Étienne Benjamin Deschauffours, who met his fate on May 24, 1726, for many transgressions, not just sodomy, but also pimping and child abuse. Another man arrested with him, a painter called Nattier, cut his own throat while in the Bastille. Still a third, the *abbé* de La Fare, bishop of Laon, was locked up in a seminary, and a fourth, the *comte* de Tavannes, was exiled. The last homosexual couple who met the same fate were Bruneau Lenoir, carpenter, 18 years of age, and Jean Diot, pork butcher, 20 years of age, in 1750. They were caught in flagrante delicto by a night watchman at the intersection of rue Montorgueil and rue Saint-Sauveur at 11:30 at night. He observed them in what he called an "indecent posture" and he had them promptly arrested by his fellow officers. Depending on one's sources, there might have been, or perhaps not, a passerby who later lent his own eyewitness account, saying that the two men had been committing crimes that "propriety does not permit to express in writing." On the strength of this one, perhaps two, testifiers, Lenoir and Diot were burned at the stake on July 6th, 1750.

Zénobe would have laughed had he been accused of sodomy. Strictly speaking, he and his friends had never engaged in that particular practice, for neither Zénobe nor his partners would have wanted to take on the so-called passive, or womanly role. They were proud of being men, and would not have wanted to demean the other by making him take on that role. Exploration of the other man's body by means of the hands and mouth was not considered to be humiliating, but, again, fingers and tongues did not go anywhere near that rear exit, for it was an exit, not an entry. But most heterosexual people, ignorant as to what practices the "anti-physiques" performed, assumed that buggery was the essential procedure that was routine among all of these "inverted" deviants. In turn, these deviants, continued the erroneous analysis, by committing such a heinous act, mocked the very Nature who, in her benevolence, had allowed these monsters to exist in the first place. It was Nature, then, who cried out to humanity and conventional morality for vengeance. Humanity came rushing to her aid, and in all countries where the Word of God, or Allah, or Jehovah, or whatever name was given to the deity, the slaughter of wicked perverts was encouraged, in the name of that God, and in the name of Nature whose perfection under the creation of God must prevail. Zénobe would have denied, without lying, even under the pain of torture, being a sodomite. His attackers would not have delayed their assault on Zénobe for even a minute in order to reflect on and then to clarify the fine distinctions of nomenclature. A man who had kissed another man was sufficiently evil in their hostile minds, and they meant Judas. To the zealots, Zénobe, in his own way, was a Judas, for he had betrayed Nature, and Nature was the creation of God. Against the religious mob, Zénobe wouldn't have had a prayer.

And while we are at it, let us mention that neither Zénobe nor any of his sexual partners ever took a prurient interest in young boys. Even though most heterosexual people, then and now, assume, for some strange reason, that all homosexual men feel it their mission to befriend, seduce, or assault young boys, in order to "turn" them, i.e., act as a vector of contagion to transform them into future pederasts, this is patently not true. Zénobe would have laughed at that assertion, too. There might be a small percentage of homosexual men who do prey on boys, just as there is a percentage of heterosexual men who prey on girls, but Zénobe would have found both cases to be disgusting, immoral and criminal. Zénobe had turned out to be a healthy, mentally stable, masculine homosexual man, and his sexual interests made him look for similarly built men. The fact that Zénobe was handsome and graceful afforded him the chance to attract the same. Many men, even those who would never come near to confessing to such concupiscent behavior, were attracted to Zénobe in a way that would have been surprising to them had they exercised the habit of self-analysis. But Zénobe would never have bothered to claim comradeship with those, for he wanted his lovers to feel comfortable in their skin, to harbor enough insight about themselves to have shed the shame that society flings on them, and to be enlightened enough to realize that these so-called sins were entirely invented by religious idiots who had so much dogma in their brains that there was no room for anything else, not even common sense.

The Man of Two Foils

Romilly-sur-Seine could have fit onto the quai des Théâtins, the neighborhood where he had been living in Paris, with plenty of room to spare. Zénobe could see it in the distance as he traversed the flat marshy area of the spring floods of the Seine. He realized that he was just south of the river again, like in Paris. There his heart had been full, as he worked and learned beside the most famous author in the world, and every time they had stepped out onto the streets, they were mobbed by hundreds of people who appeared as if by magic. But here in these hinterlands, where he could see not a single person walking around, he felt an ache in his heart and an emptiness in his stomach. He realized he hadn't eaten since the preceding day in the afternoon, his lugubrious solitary repast during the carriage ride from Paris, in the presence of his dead philosopher friend. His friend was now underneath one of the flagstones of the crumbling abbey of Scellières, and Zénobe hoped that the spring flooding would not reach the level of the tomb. Voltaire underwater was a terrible image upon which his mind would focus in spite of his will to fight it. As fresh tears ran down his cheeks, he underwent a sensation that was entirely new to him, and which he witnessed clinically as if it had been happening to Condillac's statue:[5] he felt like dropping into one of the ponds of the marsh and giving up on life. For over a day he had held a cover over his emotions to suppress his dejection, but now, surrounded by pools of mire and river muck that slowed his steps, he stooped over as he gave vent to his overwhelming grief. He crouched into a fetal position to make himself small although there was nobody on the marsh to hear him mourn. He saw widening circles forming in the water, interfering with each other, and he drew consolation from the fact that his tears would eventually make their way to Paris, although he didn't have the science to tell how long it would take them. These parallel arms of the Seine had a current, although the reeds and water lilies did their best to dam the flow. Zénobe's eyes, twin pieces of Sèvres glass submerged in teardrops, followed the sluggish rivulets and trickles around the leaves and stems. He learned a lesson from the current, however lethargic it ran: the flow would not be staunched; it managed to find a way around obstacles, perhaps underneath them. So, too, would Voltaire have wanted Zénobe to find a way to Ferney, for there was work to be done.

The library was sold, as easily as one sells crates of Normand apples, but there was nothing to do about that but catalogue the inventory. However, the most salient idiocy of all the idiocies in the world, the manuscripts were also to be sent to Russia.

---

5 In Condillac's *Traité des sensations* (1754), his statue is allowed to experience only one sense at a time, which indeed quite a sensation created, especially on sensitive souls like Zénobe. This book explores the incipient conceptions of psychology.

All those writings that Voltaire had carefully put away, in locked drawers and in false books, with the instructions that they not be published during his lifetime, those writings that existed only in single manuscript form, were more precious than treasure, for those were the writings that the philosopher deemed as too dangerous to publish while he still lived. Voltaire's philosopher friends understood this, for they all had a collection of their own, ensconced in secret compartments at the rear of desk drawers or under clandestine quoins behind garden trellises. Diderot and Condorcet had even allowed Zénobe to read some of their confidential manuscripts, proof of their trust in him. By deferring their publication they succeeded in avoiding the troubles that their unorthodox books would have brought to them. Being flag-ellated on the steps of Saint Sébastien was not a fate they wished to experience. In truth, their contemporaries were not ready for much of their revolutionary thoughts. The *philosophes* intended to target their works directly to posterity, bypassing their contemporaries altogether, for they were not yet worthy. It was this attempt to influ-ence the future in a sort of posthumous impact that induced them to keep their secret stash of papers in a safe place, away from the authority of the government, the prying eyes of the priests. The church would have liked nothing better than to make a huge bonfire of these writings, so that nothing would come to trouble the peace and the power of undivided devotion that came upon man with the presence of the holy ghost on earth. These revolutionary writings threatened the dominion of this holy ghost, whatever the hell that was. Zénobe had never completely understood this one tenet of catechism that was forced on him in his childhood. Apparently, it represented god's spirit, or it *was* god's spirit, or perhaps it was the soul of god, maybe his mind as manifested to humans. In any case, the way Zénobe understood it, *le saint esprit* represented the benevolence and charity of the almighty, his gifts to his flock. It also represented, Zénobe thought, the unquestioning and unceasing worship of the lord the father god, and the unwavering belief in the primacy of the son god, whose body was the one holy catholic and apostolic church. To this young atheist, catholic doctrine felt tenuous and makeshift, as airy as the original Greek word for the soul, *pneuma*, or perhaps like the ground around the Seine in the spring, over which he now walked: uneven, soggy, turbid, hiding deep pools and maybe even quicksand. But no matter the inconsistency of religious tenets, or perhaps because of them, the church would not, could not, brook the existence of any rivals or counterfeit pretenders, forgetting that the son god never instructed his followers to reduce his teachings to belligerence and hostile ultimatums; that is, Jesus never coerced his listeners to follow him or die. The perverse church (but all religions were the same in this) sought to destroy all thinking that demonstrated how absurd and convoluted were the precepts of the priests. These were priests who waged war, Zénobe thought, for they spared no foe who sought to document their irrationality, and destroyed all treatises and manuscripts that declared war on their priestly class. Destroyers of truth, Zénobe called them. Annihilators of justice. He was on the side of truth because it opposed blatantly factitious dogma, and he was convinced, as the *philosophes* were, that justice needed to be based on truth, and not on tales saturated in prejudice and superstition, and that both truth and justice were ideals worth fighting for.

This last thought brought Zénobe up from his knees. He stretched to his full stature like a soldier, squaring his shoulders and jutting out his chin. His left hand fell on the pommel of his foil, the right sought the pommel of André's foil, which he wore on his right side. He had a duty to perform, he had made promises to Voltaire, and he was wasting time. He needed to be in Ferney as quickly as possible.

He took a step forward and his foot landed in water. He looked down and saw that his shoe had stirred up eddies of mud and silt from the bottom of the puddle, and he broke out in laughter. Not a promising start to his noble cause. As he directed his walk to higher ground, his shoe squished, but Zénobe hardly gave it a thought. His mind was already elsewhere, into the future, taking up the defense that would protect Voltaire's ascendancy into that future, for someone had to continue his work to undermine the absolute corrupting power of the tyrannical forces that sought to obliterate all conscientious objection to its rule. Every man had a right to liberty of thought, and if that thought led the man to doubt the existence of god, no other man should think it his right to meddle with him. No one should come between a man and his conscience, even a priest. Especially not, a priest.

Zénobe was energized, although still hungry. Finding a place to break his fast in Romilly was effortless, for there was only one establishment in town that took care of traveler's needs, albeit in a modest way. This included fresh post horses for those who lost their way from Paris to Troyes, but at any one time there were only four of them, and consequently they were not for sale. Besides, as Zénobe eyed the wretched beasts, he felt embarrassed for the whole village that they should foist these unsound animals on unsuspecting travelers. The man who served him his meal told him of a farmer not far away who sold horses, and as soon as Zénobe had eaten and administered to his daily ablutions in a barely adequate room, he set off to find himself a splendid steed commensurate with his objectives.

The servant at the Romilly inn and his fellow workers had noticed that their guest was a gentleman, but he had been seen coming into the village alone and on foot, without trunks or any possessions save for a small rucksack. He wore two foils, highly unusual. He called himself Bosquet de Voltaire and didn't speak much. He didn't even say grace prior to eating his breakfast, and he seemed to devour it rather gluttonously. Sinisterly, his fork was placed in his left hand, and he used the same hand to pick up his bread and to drink from his glass, both of which he had placed to the left of his plate. The serving wench, who had experience with boats on the Seine, thought the table itself was listing to the left. She reported to the kitchen staff that the traveler said he was from Paris, but there was a strange lilt to his accent that announced his origins elsewhere. One of the women in the kitchen, who out of curiosity came out to stare, called him "the foreigner" and she crossed herself three times when speaking to the others about his otherworldly eyes, which she was convinced could see through objects, including her bodice and inner garments, so that he could ogle her breasts. She was so struck by the beauty of the strange man that she subsequently refused to come out into the dining hall and stayed in the kitchen until the foreigner had left. Even then, as she reported to the authorities later, she felt nervous about touching his plate and cutlery, and instead of washing them as usual, she boiled them in a pot of water. What she didn't tell the priests who came later on that day looking for the stranger and asking all sorts of questions, was that she did manage to drink, without anybody noticing, the remains of his glass of ale.

Christophe de Beaumont, Archbishop of Paris, Duke of Saint Cloud, Peer of France, Commander of the Royal Order of the Holy Ghost, Principal of the Sorbonne, etc., etc. was known throughout Europe for his courage and for his tenacity. Having received from destiny the onerous task of fighting against the godless *philosophes* and their so-called humanistic concerns which threatened the altar, the throne and everything that was sacred to men, he had providentially received a head stronger than those of his enemies, a head of diamond, brilliant and hard, and, as sentinel of Rome, he defended the faith and the monarchy with unshakeable determination and ardent zeal. With a noble character and the compassion of a charitable Christian, this saintly prelate, whose ancestor Joffrey de Beaumont in one of the early Crusades brought to France from the Holy Land the relics of the martyrs Saint Côme and Saint Damien, also provided to France an incommensurate service to her well-being: through his patient administrations, his undying philanthropy, and his personal moral principles, he sought indefatigably to rid the homeland of apostates and heretics. The Devil was afoot all over France, and good, conscientious Christians had to do their utmost to pry his claws away from the people whose souls he sought to infect. Christophe de Beaumont was not one to rest easy while the Beast claimed more and more victims. Through the energetic exhortations of his sermons, he informed the faithful that the ascendancy of Lucifer had to be squelched, for the Beast from the bottomless pit had risen and was busy abroad reaping souls for his chthonic abode. The Day of Judgment would be swiftly upon them, and the war between good and evil had to be fought and won. There would be no one left standing in the middle, for all had to take sides. It was either God or Satan; all had to choose their Master, and all had to choose well.

Beaumont's emissaries were ubiquitously occupied. Many were now grouping in Champagne because the word was out that a dangerous apostate was lurking there after the burial of the antichrist himself, Voltaire. It was believed that the old philosopher had corrupted the young man, and he in turn was seeking to infiltrate other unsuspecting Christians in order to turn them into soldiers for Satan. The Christians had to fight back. Told to look for the infidel, Zénobe Bosquet, half a day after Voltaire's funeral had taken place in Scellières, they were instructed to fan out into the surrounding countryside. They were given the helpful advice of sniffing the air periodically to follow the scent of sulfur. Similarly, they knew to look for smears of yellowish-gold on the path. Polyglots were accosted and interrogated to find out if one of the languages they spoke was ancient Aramaic. The priests spread the word that anyone who brought forth information that led to the apprehension of said criminal, would receive for himself and for his family five years of indulgences worth at least a thousand *livres*.[6] It was only a matter of hours until the priests discovered that the outlaw had been to the inn in Romilly, and had asked for instructions to a nearby farm where horses were sold.

---

6   Indulgences were an important money-maker for the church: for a fee, catholics could collect and save them for a rainy day of exceptionally abundant sins. Rather than let them pile up, they could use the indulgences to reduce the number of sins, and the severity of the punishment. The church, which admitted it had a treasury of indulgences that were amassed from the so-called merits of Jesus Christ and all the saints, promised reduced stays in Purgatory, and for substantial users of indulgences, perhaps no stay at all. St. Peter's Basilica in Rome was almost entirely on the profits of indulgences built. Every once in a while, indulgences were by the British captured on French ships bound for America. George III made full use of this commodity, selling them back to the French, or to his country's own catholics. Indulgences were too precious to squander.

The horse farm was close to the Seine and therefore Zénobe was back in the marshes. The horses, according to the farmer, were of a rare race bred for the great Spanish Queen Isabella, the one who had finally rid her kingdom of the wicked infidels and the Christ killers, and who had sent the holy word of God to the other half of the world. Zénobe almost walked away after hearing this peasant speak in such a manner about muslims and jews, and about Columbus spreading the contagion of catholicism to the New World, but then he caught sight of the horses galloping on the sloughs amidst the sprays of water they left in their wake, the sunlight glinting off their golden flanks and sharp white manes and tails. They were magnificent, and Zénobe was spellbound. He had never seen such horses, and these looked healthy and powerful, and fast. Such a horse would get him to Ferney in four or five days, he was sure.

But Zénobe could not help commit blunders that did not help him to keep secrecy and normalcy in his transactions. Asking for a stallion was not unusual, but insisting on buying one of the farmer's studs offended the peasant, who subsequently raised his price to an unheard of category. This he had done after having seen Zénobe's stock of coin, which the naïve boy neglected to keep out of sight. Besides the librarian's salary that he had received from the *marquis* de Villette, he also had the remorse gold that the *marquis* de Thibouville had slipped into his pocket, the lucre that the *marquise* de Polignac had packed into his chocolate, the coins that *monsieur le maître d'hôtel* Maurel had given him, and the heavy sack that the three philosophers Diderot, d'Alembert and Condorcet had provided for him, all of which were still in their original leather (and silk) pouches and were all tied together in tangled knots. The tintinnabulation of this treasure was prodigious, especially to the musical ear of the farmer. Zénobe did not barter, another blunder which gave the peasant the freedom to charge doubly for the saddle and harness. The farmer also espied the books that were in the young gentleman's rucksack, thick books that looked out of place and suspect. But any misgivings the farmer may have had, and his dismay at selling off his best stud, were eased by the handsome sum he received.

Those very same misgivings, and that dismay, of course, emerged anew when being interrogated by the clergy. Of course he had not wanted to sell his horse to this strange gentleman, and of course he did not want to give aid to this foreign person who looked odd in both his appearance and in his transactions, but he had feared for his life in view of the fact that he was wearing two foils, one on the right side and the other on the left. Besides, he looked at you with an unwavering stare, and the farmer was afraid of falling victim to the evil eye, for this gentleman had a malevolent gaze if he every saw one, and the farmer believed that he had experience in this domain. He told the priests everything he had observed, the money, the books, the rough simplicity of the rucksack which did not match the magnificence of the gentleman's attire, even the objectionable manner in which the man had sat astride the horse as he galloped away. He looked more like a yokel hanging low over the horse's mane than a refined cavalier trotting elegantly off.

The priests, of course, were disappointed in this latest incident. Their suspect was now fleet. In their favor, however, was the fact that this horse was exceedingly rare and thus easy to identify. Palominos were unheard of in France. Zénobe would have done better to buy himself an inconsequential bland-brown mare. But only if he first bought himself a dark cloak to hide his patrician apparel.

Zénobe arrived in Troyes in four hours with his beautiful new horse that could have easily extended the day's travel. The old mare that had taken him to Paris four months ago could go no faster than a trot, and needed frequent periods of rest. Four months ago, thought Zénobe. It was hard to believe that he had gone through so much in just four months. It was hard to believe that in the same time Voltaire had gone from the apogee of his career to being no longer, from being applauded and praised by all to being forced out of Paris and relegated to an unmarked grave, forgotten by the very people who had lionized him. Destiny was indeed strange, mused the young man who had yet to experience the full extent of the violence and miseries that the mad Furies could bring. For the time being, he felt no need to press on, his horse notwithstanding, and he certainly didn't want to be caught on the road after dark, so he decided he would remain in Troyes for the evening to rest.

As he passed the town's cathedral, a religious procession was returning from taking their statues and relics out for an airing. Zénobe, remembering the *chevalier* de la Barre, the young man who had been imprisoned, tortured and executed for not having shown respect for such a religious procession, turned around as fast as he could before he could be observed.

It was, of course, too late, for he had been observed. The report that Zénobe's cleric trackers heard the next day was that a man on a strange horse did not stop to admire the procession and did not make the sign of the cross. Instead, the report went, he quickly crossed the plaza, cringing in fear of the holy relics the marchers held high above their heads. It was their patron saint, Saint Lupus, whom they held aloft, physically as well as spiritually. He had saved their city in 451 from Attila and his rapacious Huns, by offering himself as hostage if the barbarians spared Troyes, which had no defenses. They also carried Saint Joan of Arc who, in 1429 helped the Dauphin recover the town from the English. There followed a hagiographic inventory that was sure to keep the town safe from evil catastrophes, including the known calamities of flood, fire, pestilence, drought and military invasions, but also those that were rarer and that the Devil might bring on for his sport and diversion: invasions of frogs, lice, flies or locusts, sickness of their livestock, water changed to blood, boils on all men and animals, thunder and hail, darkness falling throughout the land, and even, perhaps, the death of their firstborn. Troyes had it under control: after Saints Lupus and Joan of Arc, they worshiped a panoply of saints who were all born locally and would intercede for them in times of trouble. Saint Leo, Saint Sabinian and his sister Saint Sabina, Saint Patroclus, Saint Maura, and Saint Prudentius, all had a statue in the cortège.[7] They were the first among many who made up the body of Christ, the church, and the body of Christ was made up of men and women, of young and old, of rich and poor, of sinners who became saints; and on every Sunday when the faithful came together to adore Christ, the saints became the temple where Jesus renews his sacrifice and where

---

7   Patroclus, or Saint Parre as he is in France known, had an effigy that differed from the rest: his is the headless one. But this was not due to an accident or to willful defacement of church property. Saint Parre is depicted as carrying his own head on a gold-encrusted replica of the Book of Gospels, since he was by being beheaded martyred.

God is present. Gaze upon them, with their faces tired or radiant, their tears or their smiles, and you will know you gaze upon the face of Christ. They are the body that Jesus promised to resurrect from among the dead.

But the stranger fled when he gazed upon these saintly visages who wept real tears. He could not rejoice at the sight of these sacrificial lambs who gave up their lives to protect the people and protect the town. He could not approach the altar of God and eat from the bread of the Realm to receive from the Lord a foretaste of Paradise. He–

The interrogators interrupted the witness's prattle. They had an important question to ask. Where did he go? Twenty people gave twenty different answers, thank God, so that Zénobe was safe for the night. What saved him was that he had indeed fled from the religious procession, not because it offended or frightened him, but because he remembered the fate of the young *monsieur* de la Barre in 1766, who for not having removed his hat and for not looking pious enough in front of a procession had suffered an outlandishly severe punishment, having his right hand and tongue cut out, then decapitated, then his body and head thrown onto a pyre, burned to ashes, and the ashes thrown to the wind. Into the pyre also went the copy of Voltaire's *Dictionnaire philosophique*, which had been found in the twenty-year-old's bedroom. Like his hapless predecessor, all Zénobe saw was a troop of raving lunatics venting their delirium and moaning selfish demands to a dilapidated collection of upthrust effigies made of wood and wax. Among his own books, there also was a copy of the *Dictionnaire philosophique*, which was his Bible. He got the hell out, indeed, and crossed the town at a gallop. It wasn't until he rejoined the farmland south of Troyes that he started inquiring as to lodging for the night. He found satisfactory shelter just as the sun was setting behind a beautifully arrayed vineyard, the vines following the contours of the land and trained on sturdy trellises. Zénobe had never seen such a geometric disposition of plants. The farmer, Jean Blas, turned out to have a disposition just as rational, and was friendly, too. The farmer's wife, Marie-France, was hospitable, the champagne was excellent, and the fare even better. From the looks of it, the vintner used modern methods to make his wines, since he praised «*la science botanique*» and spoke of fertilizers and seasonal pruning and well-timed grafting. The farmer also had a son, a strapping youth with a bright face and a helpful disposition, who explained the methodology of cultivation as coming directly from the recommendations given in Diderot's *Encyclopédie*, and who managed to stay most of the night in the guest's comfortable room as a means to explain more fully the marvels of new science and to continue tasting, all alone with the handsome traveler, the consequences of enlightened viniculture.

June 3, 1778

Exploring Farming Techniques in Champagne

The priests who were closing in on Zénobe were already in Troyes and asking about him before he had even left the farmhouse, late in the morning. While the clerics converged, conferred and scattered anew like black ants sweeping across the terrain, Zénobe was completely ignorant of the extent of the power from Beaumont's bishopric. The priests had finished interrogating the witnesses of the procession of the previous day, all of whom, by the way, had proved to give willing and able testimony. Back at the farm, the farmer's son continued to be engaging by tending to Zénobe's ablutions; then Marie-France unhurriedly served Zénobe a copious breakfast while Jean Blas himself carefully attached a double pouch to the back of the traveler's saddle to balance the six bottles of Chablis he wanted him to have for the road. The farmer decided against champagne because that might have proved too explosive for the skittish Palomino. The farmer's son, Gil, would have liked to kiss the handsome traveler one last time, but with the whole family bidding adieu to their guest, he thought such an act inappropriate. All he could do was squeeze his new friend's calf after he was mounted on his horse.

Zénobe thanked them for the wine, but also for the lessons in viniculture, which he promised to study and observe as he traveled through the region. He was happy that science was helping in the production of so necessary an industry, and he regretted not having had time in Paris to get to the letter V in volume 17 of the *Encyclopédie*.[8]

He thus slowed down his pace considerably, as he surveyed the vineyards that dotted the small farms of the area south of Troyes, and, as he stopped for samples of the products of these farms, he could not help but marvel at the effervescence of this heavenly wine. These grapes produced a natural gas that lightened and refreshed the taste, so that one felt ethereal and buoyant while drinking it. He wondered what the gas was and hoped it was oxygen, for that would be a retort to those who thought of champagne as the Devil's wine, in view of the habit it had of every once in a while spontaneously bursting out of the bottles it was kept in, blinding and maiming those

---

8   Volume 17 of Diderot and d'Alembert's *Encyclopédie* has several articles under «*Vigne*», mostly on its horticulture, but notably on the pharmaceutical benefits of the grape vine's sap.

who where nearby. Oxygen was necessary to human and animal life, therefore it was beneficial.[9] It was part of Nature, and the Devil had nothing to do with it.

When the marauding priests finally caught up to the Blas vineyard later on that day, their black cassocks billowing in the wind and their black skullcaps, or tonsured pates, instantly indicating their identity as hostile troublemongers, the family nevertheless welcomed them amicably, offered them drink and sustenance, but remained steadfast in their ignorance of a traveler on a strange horse, an aristocrat with a foreign accent, who obviously didn't belong in the region. *Monsieur* Blas scratched his head, *madame* Blas scrunched up her face while trying to remember, and the young mischievous Gil Blas tried not to smile at the pleasure of confounding the ministry. It was difficult to get back at them, but when these small ways to block their progress presented themselves, it gave him an unmitigated thrill. The Blas family was emancipated, although secretly so, for they were surrounded by bible-thumpers. They went to church on Sunday and tithed monthly, for there was no way to get around that, but the rest of the week they functioned free of the influence of mythology. They were clandestine atheists, and thus liberated to investigate fully the allure of science. Their vines were superior to those of farms around them, and their wines were unequaled in the region. All the more reason to remain reticent about what happened in the privacy of their conscience.

Zénobe had learned more in one night and one morning about the cultivation of vineyards than he had in his entire life. He observed, for the first time, truly closely observed, the cultivation of grape vines. What better place to do this than in, according to the farmer Blas, one of the best terroirs of white wine in France. If the leaves were too light a green, then they needed a dose of fish emulsion. If the ends of the vines looked shriveled up, then the chalky soil needed to be amended with compost. If there were scions growing beneath the graft, they needed to be pruned out. If there was no graft, the whole harvest could be in jeopardy. Zénobe was ecstatic to be able to identify problems with the crops as he ambled by them, and to possess the knowledge of solving them. He rode on in zig-zags, studying the vineyards as he, for the most part, headed south.

One of the farms he crossed had huge plants, as tall as he was, with sword leaves radiating out from a central core, and from the middle rose a tall stem that ended in a bulb a little bigger than the size of a man's fist. He had to stop and admire this plantation of exotic vegetation for it was nothing that he'd ever seen before. A farmer wearing a big straw hat walked up to him and told him that the name of the crop was artichoke. Nothing on it was edible, he explained, except for a tiny portion at the base of each of the leaves of the flower bud and its heart that provided just a mouthful. It was a plant grown solely for the aristocracy who were the only ones able to afford its profligate use of land and the extraordinary care it took to cultivate it. Indeed, answered Zénobe with a sardonic smile, it was a perfect metaphor for the aristocracy itself, living off huge tracts of land, taking for itself most of the nutrients available for all, and in the end rendering but a morsel that was useful to society. Being that Zénobe had grown unaccustomed to curbing his speech, let alone his thoughts, he happily shared with

---

9   Joseph Priestly had already in 1767 carbonated water created, after he had water in a bowl above a vat of fermenting beer suspended. Also known as soda water, its science was by him in 1772 published, in a book entitled *Directions for Impregnating Water with Fixed Air*. Unfortunately, it still had not to Zénobe's attention come, otherwise he would have known that the gas in champagne was carbon dioxide. By 1783, a Swiss of German descent, Johann Jacob Schweppe, had a company in Geneva founded to manufacture carbonated water which was advertised as having medicinal qualities.

the farmer all his opinions of the artichoke, including its similarity to the aristocraps. Both the vegetable and the nobleman cast huge shade, beneath which hardly anything else could grow. Artichoke leaves looked frilly, but were really prickly, just like the effete patricians he encountered in life. The farmer didn't know whether to laugh or to run away, but he quickly decided that scoffing at the aristocrat on horseback hovering over him might prove to be dangerous. Especially given the fact that the *chevalier* was wearing two foils. The result was that he stood transfixed with mouth agape in front of the stranger mounted on a ghost horse. Zénobe remembered that he was an aristocrat in camouflage and that perhaps he had said more than what was wise about the social class he was representing. The conversation had stopped cold and he thought it wise to bid the farmer a good day and retreat in silence.

Thank the gods or the Fates, or perhaps the blind powers of providence or destiny, Zeus, Thor, Vishnu or Quetzalcoatl, the Almighty Winged Serpent of the Guatemalas, for with this detour, Zénobe chanced upon the road to Tonnerre instead of the primary road to Dijon. He knew he was going south, but it wasn't until he entered Chaource that he realized he had strayed from the main road. Had he maintained his original course, a group of riders in black cassocks would have caught up to him that very afternoon. A blithe negligence to the dangers of the world made Zénobe a brother to Candide, who would have fit right in as a companion on this picaresque quest. Zénobe thought often about Voltaire's hero during his own journey, enjoying the similarities, except that he, Zénobe, had a nobler crusade other than looking for his Cunégonde. He knew André was safe and, if not exactly happy in Normandy, at least he was content; therefore Zénobe was released to follow the venture of safeguarding Voltaire's manuscripts in Ferney. He had a quest to fulfill, a reason for which to strive, a crusade to undertake.

He could not believe the stupidity of Voltaire's niece who had sold the sage of Ferney's library in one huge lot, the manuscripts along with Voltaire's books, to Catherine, Empress of all the Russias. The philosopher's personal books, with his marginalia and notes and comments, sent to a feudal potentate who bought libraries wholesale and thought that these acquisitions meant an automatic aggrandizement of her dominion! Catherine might be smarter than most monarchs, but her accumulation of the Enlightenment's best libraries meant that Voltaire's books, as well as Diderot's, would be forever more unavailable to French scholars. Contrary to the tsarina, *madame* Denis was an idiot, a foolish biddy who had not even realized that she was sitting on a grand fortune, had she known enough about publishing to sell the manuscripts to the printers of Europe. The publishers would have fallen all over themselves to possess those manuscripts. They would have paid lucre enough to satisfy that foolish, grasping woman until the end of her natural fatuous life. The ecclesiastical censors would have had apoplectic convulsions to see these manuscripts appear in Holland, Switzerland or England. In France as well, if the publishers were clandestine enough. But the brouhaha would have made the publications even more desirable, thus raising the price further. And in the end, Voltaire's posthumous publications would have overrun Europe with their message of humanistic enlightenment, in order to throw off the shackles of tyranny and oppression. Blood of christ, exclaimed Zénobe to himself, but the church was a tough nut to crack! But crack it must, so that men could live in total freedom, so that entire populations would be liberated from the deceptions and the threats, from the guilt and fears perpetuated by religion. The Reign of Reason was nigh, and Zénobe was one of its defenders.

But first he had to stop for a meal. In Chaource, too small for an inn, he had to use a *louis d'or* at a farmhouse for he had no small change. The farmer had to make change with the help of some of his neighbors even though he charged the traveler triple for a plate of scrambled eggs and bacon, accompanied by some cheese and wine. He was later to remember that the traveler removed his wig while at the table, releasing a mane of straight black hair that fell to his shoulders. He also told the priests who came the next day asking about this very same traveler that in his presence he had felt a twinge of alarm, a frisson up his spine that made him think that perhaps it had been a mistake to offer this stranger hospitality. The strange gentleman had asked him about the cultivation of his land, which no aristocrat had ever asked him about, and had also mentioned grafting and fertilizers and other nonsense that was as incomprehensible as the cackles of his hens. When he heard him mention the Encyclo-something-or-other, and Diderot, the farmer quickly ordered the members of his family out of the dining room and into the kitchen. The stranger was not offered dessert, and the farmer brought his queer horse around as quickly as he could. He didn't want the stranger to stay one more minute. He had done right, to react like that, hadn't he, he asked the clergy. That's why they were looking for him, wasn't that so? The man was guilty of something, wasn't he? That's why he had felt the man was no good, that he was up to something, something devilish. He couldn't allow such a man around his family, could he? Oh, before he forgot, the farmer added, he wanted to mention something else the stranger said. "He had talked about Voltaire, yes, here in my house, with my family within hearing, and had asked me if the people in the area had heard about his death. I told him that no such news was come, and that no one here would be interested in the comings and goings of Voltaire, anyway, even if we had heard something, which we hadn't, and that we preferred to know nothing about such people, and that I didn't want nobody stirring up no devils on my farm."

The man's final comment was so curt that Zénobe realized he had overstayed his welcome. The problem with the payment came up, and the farmer had to send one of his children to make change with the neighbors. As soon as he came back, the farmer gave Zénobe back his change, which the young man didn't even glance at.

Zénobe thanked the man and, under the influence of some sort of intuitive suspicion, he headed due west away from the farm. The farmer's vituperation against Voltaire was not to be trusted, and giving him a false lead seemed like the intelligent thing to do.

Where the young man remained in total ignorance was in the domain of ecclesi-astical punishment. Of course he had read about autos-da-fé, and would even laugh about Voltaire's portrayal of one in *Candide*, during which the heroes in a huge public ceremony are tortured and hanged. Their crime? They were the foreigners who had caused the earthquake that had razed Lisbon to the ground. Getting rid of the culprits was in keeping with heavenly retribution, only that as soon as the victims were dispatched, to the rhythm of appropriately solemn music, there was a new earthquake, aftershocks, as they are called in modern times, that caused many ruins to fall on the heads of those who had been lucky enough to survive the first earthquake. It was Voltaire's way of making fun of those who mistook Nature's destructive powers as being manifestations of God's disapproval. So Sodom and Gomorrah were annihilated along with the wickedness of their sinners. But what about the innocent children who were too young to know anything about the depraved behavior of their parents? Why did they have to be terrorized and punished as well?

Zénobe knew nothing of the tortures done in private. Deep underground, in cells beneath the apse of ordinary churches, in the dark, dank recesses shared by crypts and sarcophagi, lit by smoking torches and long tapers guaranteed to last all night, were strewn about the instruments of torture used by the Inquisitors. Most of these devices were made of ungiving iron, and their purpose was to make people taller or shorter, or to make parts of their body longer or wider, perhaps truncated or condensed. A thumb could be flattened to caricatural dimensions; a young woman could grow two or three inches in a matter of hours; the iron pear could increase an aperture to a phenomenal degree; a common length of rope, tied to a body part, with gravity doing the rest, could quickly alter the look of a limb or a penis. The body resisted at first, of course, but with the patient application of the priests, flesh would elongate, bones reaccommodate, joints crack, and before you knew it, the supplicant[10] would be confessing to all that needed to be confessed, the instruments would be retired, the torture would cease. The body took more time to regain its original measurements, but time is the great healer and the supplicant would improve steadily, unless a bone had been accidentally broken or a tendon torn from its moorings, but what was this minor suffering of the flesh when compared to the anguish and torment of Jesus on the cross, who died for our sins, who suffered in order to alleviate humanity's suffering?

Zénobe knew nothing of the twisted justifications and the medieval reasonings of the Inquisitors. He thought that since he accepted Reason as a methodology for living his life that everybody else knew it existed and would accept it as real, even though they may not always honor its tenets or follow all its corollaries. He was wrong: the priests paid no heed to Reason, were unaware of its viability, were blind to its beauty, insentient to its allure. They blindly followed instructions set down in the 16th century, irrespective of the supplicant's guilt or innocence, and without considering if the alleged crimes were real or fictitious. They wended their way through their labyrinthine doctrines—thick, heavy folios bound in vellum that through the ages served as an immutable canon for uncompromising theologians—which freed them of any limitations set by a sense of humanity. They were able to work in a world devoid of mandates of human rights, where pity and compassion were not even imaginable, where their stern and unmovable God, through them, worked his divine retribution to smite the enemies of the church.

---

10   In French the word is *"suppliant"*, from the verb meaning to supplicate. The victim of divine punishment would supplicate earnestly for the torture to cease and for mercy from the torturers, although it was never an objective for the victim to die during the sessions; if it happened, it was by mistake. Frequently, however, the supplicant would beg to be given death. That was the moment in the investigation when the Inquisitors knew that their techniques were working and that a confession was imminent.

Something else that on that day saved Zénobe from the claws of the religious was the *chevalière* d'Éon. Realizing that he was so close to her birthplace, the young man, who looked upon her as his benefactress for having paid for his fencing lessons in Paris, thought he might as well go take a look. Tonnerre was an imposing nomenclature,[11] and he was curious of a place that had given rise to such a rare personage.

The ecclesiastics hunting for him had to divide their group into two: one going southeast to Dijon, where, it was recalled, Bosquet had first met Voltaire; the other group traveled west, in view of the account of the Christian farmer who had last seen the outlaw.

But Zénobe was now headed south, to Tonnerre. Through the unfathomable workings of fate, his path was not going to cross his seekers', at least not on this day. By the inscrutable intercession of the *chevalière* d'Éon, who had of late been in Paris trying different tactics in order to get onto one of Beaumarchais' boats to America, with or without the help of Benjamin Franklin, did Zénobe unknowingly receive an advantage that miraculously disrupted the objectives of the priests who had God on their side. D'Éon was no saint, but she beat Joan of Arc in this campaign, for the priests were to lose sight of their quarry for a few weeks, all because the boy wished to see the *chevalière*'s hometown. But God, it seems, works in mysterious ways, ways that are as mysterious as if He weren't there at all. Unaware that he had been saved from one danger, how could Zénobe have known that he would run into another one, just as perilous?

Zénobe expected to see in Tonnerre just another small village like Chaource. That much was true. However, his imagination could not have pictured the bizarreness of the place, and the enigmatic capriciousness that is Nature, with all her fantastic powers of creation. Crossing from Champagne into Bourgogne was barely noticeable, but the town of Tonnerre, when he got to it in the late afternoon, would prove to be unforgettable, and not just because it was the place that had bestowed the enigmatic and inscrutable *chevalière* d'Éon to the world.

---

11   *Tonnerre* means thunder.

June 3, 1778

Desperate Times

le 3 juin
Jacques-Henri Maurel
hôtel de Villette
quai des Théâtins
Paris

André de Corday
Corday residence
63 rue de Géole
next to the *Château* de Caen
Caen, Normandy

The winds of despair are come among us, master André, and they wreak havoc on all sides while we quake in their midst and hope that the destruction won't be great. The authorities come looking for master Zénobe here at the *hôtel* de Villette on a daily basis; *madame* Denis and the *marquis* de Villette are at each other's throats, one accusing the other of having murdered *monsieur* de Voltaire; the police lieutenant Lenoir and his henchmen have several times swarmed all over the house, even into your little room, my boy, looking for clandestine correspondence and black-market volumes, thank God, to no avail. Master Zénobe was a genius when he insisted that I hide some of his books in my– well, I better not write the place down in case this letter is opened on the way to you. Observe, by the way, how the envelope was sealed, or re-sealed. I use my ring to apply to the wax, I believe you remember the design on my ring, don't you, my angel?

I weep bitter tears when I think of master Zénobe all alone on the byways of France, being pursued by priestly brigands. Yet, I know that he is a smart boy, all right, and I believe that instinct will take over, just as instinct brought him to us in the first place. He had been in danger when he left Savoy, his master was looking for him and if caught he would have met the same fate as his father. What is it with these aristos who do not find it sufficient to punish somebody without punishing his whole family? I don't believe that master Zénobe had anything to do with his father poaching on the lord's lands. Why was he targeted as a miscreant, too? And why is death the penalty for poaching? When one's family is hungry, one does whatever possible to feed them! Life in feudal lands is impossible. Life in our lands is nigh well impossible as well! Look at us! We cannot live in peace, for every day, multiple times, the civil authorities come, the ecclesiastical authorities come, asking the very same questions, hounding us until we are but a wet rag on the floor, and still they ask, and still they prod. Poor *monsieur l'abbé* Alexandre Jean Mignot, *madame* Denis' brother, has been reprimanded severely, and is likely to lose his position at the abbey of Scellières, all for having dared to bury his uncle. The prior has already been dismissed. What a world this is that we are not allowed to bury our dead in peace! As if mourning were not enough, we have to fight for the right to let our friends lie in peace. What a strange institution this catholic church is, that it wants to punish us during our lifetime and continue to punish us after we're dead as well! But I better not continue writing badly about the church, for I am liable to be their next target.

Master Zénobe is now a target, my son, so whomever you pray for, or whomever you pray against, send your invocations for heavenly intercession towards master Zénobe, and against the church. If he left Scellières on the 1st, he should arrive in Ferney on the 5th or 6th. I know he has enough money, and I pray he has enough wits to elude the church, which has a long grasp and spies everywhere where there are the faithful willing to snitch in order to barter for their salvation. The idiots! Don't they know there is no salvation to be had? They sell out their brothers for no good reason, in order to abet an institution that has them by the throat. Fools, all of them! Would that Voltaire's plan be working soon, to sweep away the lies and the evil that come from these hypocrites! They don't even follow the rules they've set up for themselves! How many priests become fathers, how many ecclesiastics have libraries full of indexed books! How many sacerdotal clowns waste the money from their flocks on gambling and drinking! And yet, they will hound other men unto death! They will roast victims alive on the place de Grève while making the sign of the cross. Those smug, sanctimonious, false witnesses! And it's all for power, and money, as if that were to make them happy. They've had their heads up their arses for so long that they do not see the world, and they do not see the changes that are happening in the world. I hope that I am still alive when they get their comeuppance, and I want to see the expression on their faces when that happens. Please, deity of mystery, please let me live that long!

I don't dare send this letter the usual way. It is certain that it will be opened, and I won't live as long as I would want to. I'll send it care of the *marquis* de Thibouville's sister, Jeanne Lambert d'Herbigny, *marquise* de Fouquesolles, who is traveling to their estate in Herbigny, which you won't find on any map it's so small. The closest village is Victot-Pontfol. I know you can reach it from Caen in a couple of hours. She will send you a note once she's arrived. I regret having to make you work for this letter, but I really don't want to be a target. One in the family is sufficient, and we must be around to help master Zénobe whenever he needs us. I'll breathe easier as soon as he's with *monsieur* Wagnière in Ferney. You know, protestants have a long history of getting out of the way of catholics, so he'll be able to hide our friend so that even the Pope won't know where to look for him.

The *marquis* de Thibouville may travel to his estate in Herbigny as well, as soon as he puts some papers in order. He told me that he would rather wait for master Zénobe in Normandy than in Paris, since the priests are as thick as thieves here. I would hope that as soon as master Zénobe has finished transcribing Voltaire's manuscripts in Ferney, he will direct his footsteps your way. I am sure that he has been missing you tremendously, and won't want to be too long away from you. I, too, miss you greatly, and hope that your family and your work on the farm are keeping your mind occupied and your body healthy. Please give them my love, and for you, I send you a thousand kisses and hugs.

Signed,
Jacques-Henry[12]

---

12   [From the author.] It is useless to say that these are the christian names of *monsieur* Maurel, the *maître d'hôtel* at the *hôtel* de Villette in Paris. Maurel had departed from the christian church way before Voltaire and the other *philosophes* had any influence on him. Ever since he realized he was 'different', he knew that the churches of Christ, whether catholic or protestant, which taught hatred of homosexuals, were false. Did not Christ preach love of one's neighbor? Did not Christ teach tolerance of one's fellow man? Did not Christ instill in his followers an order not to be judgmental, not to throw the first stone? Moreover, Maurel was convinced that the Universal Clockmaker had not made an error when He created Maurel; he was natural, a creature of nature, therefore necessary to the Deity's way of creating the world and the society of men, and therefore not an aberration and definitely not evil. He accepted himself and felt comfortable in his skin. We should therefore not call these Maurel's christian names, for he was no longer a christian. Jacques-Henry are his given names, or his forenames.

June 3, 1778

Falling into Danger

A shining church stood high on a promontory that dwarfed the rest of the village. It was enormous, and was meant to signify to the visitor, while still a couple of leagues away, that here dwelled a proud Christian people, who sacrificed and tithed and had the temperance and the patience to build for themselves a towering edifice, filled with lavish accoutrements in gold and silver, all in the name of a god who apparently cared nothing for the poor, for widows, orphans or those who could not take care of themselves.

Zénobe spat as his horse approached Tonnerre. In corkscrew fashion he descended from the heights of the plateau that denoted the northern end of Burgundy, almost in the same manner that rainwater infiltrated through the layers of limestone and seeped unseen through dark underground recesses. At least one river, the Laigne, over twenty leagues away from Tonnerre, lost its waters to the porous rocks and disappeared abruptly from sight, reemerging at the very center of the town, helping to feed a miraculous karst spring that was at the origin of the creation of Tonnerre. This upside-down waterfall was the navel of the region, at the lowest elevation of the village, so it juxtaposed prettily with the mighty church whose grounds looked down on the source and from which one could see the flowing vortex. It flowed up, at an amazing volume, cold and blue and clear.[13] [14]

The afternoon was quiet, and Zénobe passed no one on the streets, save for a little boy who was playing with coins on the ledge of a window. Some of the coins had fallen on the dusty cobblestones of the street below and, as he passed, Zénobe got off his horse to retrieve them and threw them among the other coins. The boy just sat and stared, and Zénobe felt it odd that a child should be playing with money. Thinking of his own childhood, there never would have been enough coins in his father's house to play with, let alone use them in so frivolous a manner as to possibly lose them. When he was halfway down the street, he heard a male adult reprimand the boy, and the tinkling of change falling on the street as the window was quickly closed.

Continuing down, down the old streets, Zénobe eventually came up to the perfect circle of the Fosse Dionne, realizing he was facing a mystery of nature. Around one

---

13 [From the fact-checker.] Today we know that it averages 311 liters per second, ranging from 619 liters per second in January, to 87 liters per second in August. Zénobe's visit at the beginning of June, after a very wet spring, happened during a time when the spring was discharging water at around 200 liters per second, which without a doubt helped save his life.

14 [From the author.] *Bitte, Herr* Ralph, allow me to tell the story at my own pace!

end of the circle of water, a *lavoir* had been built, which diverted some of the water into large basins where laundry would be washed. A partial roof had been erected to protect the laundresses as they worked. This water was caught by a smaller channel and carried away from the main current. No use letting dirty water contaminate the pure flow of the Dionne pit.

But today there were no laundresses beating their linen or scrubbing their utensils. It was as if the world had ended and people had suddenly disappeared, taken by their lord in heaven as if to a repository of souls high in the sky. Zénobe was glad, because the water looked so limpid and clean that he yearned to bathe in it to remove the dust of travel. He looked at the houses around the Fosse Dionne, including one that looked like an inn, saw their windows shielded by curtains, and slowly dismounted. With measured movements, as if to give time to anyone to show up to tell him not to, he prepared to take a quick dip into the water. Out of modesty, he left his undergarments on in case anyone did show up. His palomino reached into the water to drink.

"Ah, my steed, it does look inviting, does it not?"

With both hands Zénobe reached in and brought water to his parched mouth.

"So fresh, so clear, not at all like the Seine that always flows brown and beige, and always smells foul."

He climbed onto the ledge of the Fosse and sat down, plunging his legs into the water. It was cold but refreshing. With one last look around, he slowly lowered himself until his whole body was immersed. His first impulse was to yell out in delight, but could only whisper to his horse, "It's so cold!"

Where he had gone in, close to the edge out of which tipped over the principal flow of water, he felt buoyant, as if the current wanted to spit him out as well. As his body got used to the temperature, he started using his arms and legs as if he were a big frog, to get close to the current and then, before he could be ejected from the pit, retreat at the last second. The force of nature was powerful and mysterious, and he felt that he and the current were dancing with each other, as he moved back and forth along the irresistible surge. He moved to one side of the pit, opposite the flow of water diverted into the *lavoir*. There, the water was calm, and he could detect no stream at all. He spent a few minutes floating and relaxing, away from the turbulence of the current. Would that he had stayed there for the rest of his bath, but unfortunately he swam to the side opposite the deluge's exit where he realized, too late, that there was another type of current, this one going into the pit. Without a sound, the flow of water quickly took him down, and his head made hardly a plop as he was entirely submerged into the well. His hands instinctively made for the well's edge and made contact. His fingers felt the rock wall sliding up while his ears sensed the increasing pressure as his body was pushed inexorably down. The realization that he had to extricate himself from this fatal current was instantaneous, and he brought his feet up to the rock and with as much force as he could muster he shoved off. His body stretched towards the light that he could now see above him, but the perception that his thrust had not had enough force took two or three seconds to emerge from his panic, for the circle of light kept getting smaller. All he had succeeded in doing was to distance himself from the wall, so he couldn't even use the stones to decrease his descent. His arms flailed, his legs kicked, but he could not break free of the current. He could see nothing now, just black all around him, with the small oculus above his head that seemed to mock him. Zénobe could not believe that he was experiencing the last seconds of his life, and he struggled maniacally as his lungs seemed to burn inside of him. What stupidity, what monumental stupidity, he thought, to have dared to trust Nature like this. Already he felt his arms flailing less, his legs coming to repose underneath him, and wondered if he opened his mouth and intentionally breathed in the water into his lungs, would it make his stupid death a little bit easier and faster? The water was black all around him and the whirl disoriented him completely. His chest felt as if it were caving in. His forehead felt the movement of something brushing past, and looking up he thought he saw something in the periphery against the dim light of the oculus—was it an eel?—and he turned to it and before he even realized what it was he had already caught hold of it. Then he felt a force opposite that of the water, sensing that the object his hands were gripping was being used to pull him up. It was a rope, a rope, and he started to aid in the movement by seizing it hand over hand, and the circle of light above him was growing, growing until it filled up his entire vision.

The forces at work propelled him out of the water and halfway onto the ledge of the well. He was no longer thinking, it was his body that demanded his full attention in getting air into his lungs, but he was sputtering because water had also gotten in. Then it was violent coughing that took over his abdomen as he began to weep over his near demise and subsequent survival. While he perused the particulars of his ordeal, he looked up with stinging eyes to see who it was who had saved his life. He saw several figures standing in front of him, but the one who focused his attention was the one holding the other end of the rope. It was the *chevalière* d'Éon, his dear *chevalière* d'Éon, dressed in her womanly finery, but looking a bit odd since there was no wig on her head. She was speaking to him, asking him if he was recovered, telling the others to help her remove the lad from the well, but her voice was not that of an aristocratic lady conversing elegantly in a *salon*, rather the stentorian bellows of a dragoon roaring out commands on a battlefield.

June 4, 1778

Letter to a Lover

In the care of Charles-Geneviève-Louis-Auguste-André-Timothée *sieur* d'Éon de Beaumont

le 4 juin
hôtel d'Uzès
Tonnerre

My cherished, my kind and gentle André,

Here I am in Tonnerre, the birthplace of our friend and sponsor, the beautiful and physically powerful *chevalière* d'Éon, enjoying the most wondrous hospitality in her ancestral family château. By an exceedingly fortuitous encounter, the *chevalière* d'Éon, in her stance of heroine extraordinaire, fished me out of a most dangerous situation that, had it not been for her, might have ended my days on earth. I had supposed that Nature would have been kind to me, in view of my current status as errant wayfarer and protector of *monsieur* de Voltaire's earthly legacy, but I neglected a sad fact: Nature is as deceptive and treacherous as any fraud that may come one's way. She will trick you, for the pleasure of it, and see you drown without the smallest bit of compassion or pangs of conscience. I know now that humans fall easily into fraud because Nature herself is duplicitous. It is She who has made us in Her own image. She will offer a tired and thirsty man an inviting vision of a safe and harmless oasis, yet hide in her depths a concealed current that will snatch him away to his doom. My innocence before Nature's cruelty is forever vanished; I shall no longer trust Her the way I once did.

I can only trust people like the *chevalière* d'Éon, and you, and *monsieur* Maurel: my friends, who with benevolence follow my every move and wish me safe passage. I believe in the *chevalière*'s upper body strength and feel invulnerable when she embraces me. The church of the Vatican herself can come to me and threaten and intimidate me with all the vile vituperation she can muster, while I feel safe in the protection of the *chevalière*. I shall be ready for the church when she comes calling, if she dares.

All the more reason to pity the *chevalière*'s interest in, and penchant for, reaching out to diverse church people. She says that it's the communal spirit of the church that she's after, not the rigid, unmovable structure that thinks nothing of individual human beings and attacks them when She feels that they are a threat to her. *Mademoiselle la chevalière* insists that she has this spiritual side, a gossamer, however tenuous link with the deity, who must exist, according to her beliefs, in view of the wonders of Nature. She and Rousseau both.

Let me tell you, I know this personally, Nature is certainly the creation of an almighty who cares not a whit for individual human beings. When I was young, a monster storm in Savoy caused a whole mountainside to collapse, taking with it the shacks of shepherds, poor farmers and their children and flocks. Nothing alive remained around the colossal wreck. Everybody had been dragged down and buried under tons of rock, and either they were crushed to death, or they died of suffocation. Pity those that didn't die right away, for they were entombed alive and had the time to think, while awaiting death, of all their sins that had brought this upon them and their children, and to select which particular sins it was that had brought down a mountain on their heads.

But the *chevalière* d'Éon has relationships with the mothers superior of several convents nearby, with some neighboring priests who share some of her rakish, sexual disorientations, and with a confessor whom she likes and on whom she piles up sins from her past, very much in the past, for she is constantly bringing up things she did when she was in battle. One would think that actions in battle would be excluded from the list of sins, being that war is always made out to be something that God wants. But no, d'Éon has a meticulous memory for sins: if he neglected one of his men in a long ago skirmish, if he disregarded, even for the tiniest moment, a sacrosanct rule of honor or virtue, he brings it out to his confessor, and he most scrupulously pays attention to his penance, always doubling it. He does, however, pray twice as fast as anybody I have ever witnessed. In a flash those rosary beads go through his fingers as he restlessly twitches his lips and as his head quivers in intense meditation. *Mademoiselle la chevalière* never does things in half measures. She confronts her battles, she embraces them, and she engulfs them. Her enemies, whom she honors and respects as much as her own soldiers, are just swept away in the deluge of her passions. I just wish she could sweep all the priests away from us.

I shall remain in Tonnerre a few days longer. I am still in mourning, and not an hour passes that the *chevalière* or I say something that reminds us of Voltaire. Then we weep together, embrace each other, and seek solace in one another's stories of that spectacular man. My dear André, how I miss you, but I miss my dear friend and patron with a violence that leaves me emptied of all energy, or, worse, that leaves me twisting with a fierce rage so that I want to take up arms against his enemies, against his detractors. The reports keep saying that Voltaire died in the torment of the unregenerate sinner who knows he is about to enter the gates of hell, that an expression of fear was frozen on his face as he approached the day of reckoning. But I was there! Voltaire died in peace, in philosophical serenity, in spite of his physical afflictions. You know, the doctor who did the autopsy discovered that it was cancer of the prostate that had eventually seeped the life away from Voltaire. It had spread to his bladder, and you remember how agonizing it was for him to pee. I think that Voltaire was very courageous, as valiant as the *chevalière* d'Éon in battle, for he fought his devils with fortitude and tenacity. All I ask is that when my turn comes I will be able to fight those same devils with the same type of alacrity.

The *chevalière* has heard of reports that these priest-devils are after me, that they have been after me ever since they discovered that they had been duped. I can't help but laugh at their stupidity. We led them to believe that we would be taking Voltaire to his grave in Ferney. By the time we whisked Voltaire away to Champagne, the priests caught on to our ruse and tried to stop the sepulture, but it was too late. Voltaire was safely entombed and out of their grubby, grasping hands. But now, I suppose, it's my turn to be hunted. You need not worry, my dear, my handsome, my beloved André. I won't let them get to me. I shall outrun them. I'll have you know that I bought a splendid steed, a Palomino, with the coat the color of light chestnut, and the mane and the tail a light cream. He shines even in the dark! He is an intelligent beast, and he seems to know where I want him to go just by the subtlest of movements. I have named him Gaignun, after the warhorse of the Saracen King of Spain, Marsile.

I have heard rumors that the *chevalière* d'Éon was raised as a boy because his father, Louis d'Éon de Beaumont, could get an inheritance from his wife's family only if he had a son. It is this same Louis d'Éon de Beaumont who in 1758 had a laundry built at the source of the Fosse Dionne, diverting just a little bit of the torrent to this civic marvel. There are rumors about this strange underground river. No one knows whence so much water flows, no one knows why the water is such an eerie blue, no one can explain why the outlet is in the shape of a perfect circle, and there have been throughout the years numerous sightings of a basilisk living near the outlet. Now, this is where I almost gave up my life, so I know. If a basilisk had grabbed hold of me, I would have felt the pressure of its bite on my foot or on my leg, but nothing of the kind occurred. It was a stealthy current that pulled me down from the surface. If it hadn't been for the *chevalière* coming around after having received the report of an outsider invading the town, I don't know where I'd be today. Stories say that those who have drowned in the Fosse Dionne are never seen again. Ah, the irony of it. "Fosse Dionne" comes from the ancient Celtic "Fons Divona" which means Divine, or Sacred, Source. Apparently, stemming from pre-christian days, there was a cult of a water nymph that was of course ruthlessly suppressed by the church. But the pagans did not quietly abandon their rites; even today, I hear, there are offerings of flowers to the water goddess. I am not sure how she and the basilisk are supposed to coexist. If you ask me, I think that this whole pit, or well, or whatever it is, is the only thing left of an ancient volcano. Everything else about it has eroded away, except for its vent that leads into a tunnel that penetrates deep into the earth. It is a conduit to the center of the earth, and I wish I were a fish so I could go investigate it. There are two conflicting theories about what's at the center of our earth: one, according to Buffon, posits that it is filled with fire and melted rock; but according to an older theory, our planet is hollow, filled with labyrinthine galleries and caves where, supposedly, men could build a second home. That is, of course, unless there are beings there already, in which case there would be a world war between the exterior people and the interior people. I think that there should be a third theory: our Earth is full of water, and perhaps basilisks and nymphs lived there together, along with millions of other types of alien beings of which we know nothing.

Now that the *chevalière*'s father is dead, *la Pucelle* de Tonnerre, as she likes to be called,[15] tells me that she is responsible for keeping her mother, her sister, and her brother-in-law *mister* O'Gorman, who is the one who keeps Benjamin Franklin in wine, in the gracious manner to which they have become accustomed. *Mademoiselle* writes to the King's ministers to beseech them to increase her pension, that her services to the Crown, her rank and even her wounds justify such a supplement. Silence is the result of her supplications, and it mortifies her. She, who still wants to go fight on the side of the Americans, who still finds herself useful and able to inspire a legion of volunteers who will accompany her to glorious battle, wants the world to know that she is a soldier and a patriot, and is willing to go to the grave so long as she resumes her intrepid career. How's that for loyalty to the Crown? You would think that she had learned her lesson, at numerous occasions in her life, when the Crown abandoned her in the middle of a venture, when the Crown cut her loose as things got rough, in Russia, in England. She should realize that the Crown views her as an asset, a dispensable one, one that it can use whenever it suits it, one that it can neglect or even divest of its usefulness. Sometimes I think that Louis XVI, who inherited the *chevalière* d'Éon from Louis XV, gives her money and jewels just to shut her up. She knows so many state secrets about the previous king that, were she to publish everything she knows, it would provoke England to go to war with France.

For the time being, the *chevalière* has her hands full, traveling to and fro from Paris to Burgundy, just taking care of her transactions. At the very least, her wines are excellent, and I have been in ecstasy visiting her vineyards and investigating her modern growing methods. She follows the directions given by the *Encyclopédie* to the letter. She is, indeed, a modern woman.

We have been having fencing bouts, *la chevalière* and I. She says that in Paris I progressed fast under the tutelage of *messieurs* de la Boëssière, father and son. According to her, I have a natural talent and

---

15   The Maid (or Virgin) of Tonnerre.

an innate courage. My feeling is that if one is to engage in the martial arts, one needs to present a ferocious aspect, a façade of villainy, against the adversary. Being aggressive, almost to the point of feigning mad recklessness and indifference to injury, only serves to overwhelm the adversary. I lunge and I lunge, and I press on with rapidity. It was easy to beat the fifteen-year-old scions of noble families in Paris. With *la chevalière*, it's a different story, for she seems to anticipate my every move, but when we're done, the point of her foil directly over my heart, she's terribly out of breath, her hand on her Croix de Saint-Louis pinned to her bosom, calling me her handsome hero. She beats me every time.

It is she who will take this letter to Paris, and *monsieur* Maurel will see to it that you eventually get it. I miss him very much, and I miss all our friends at the *hôtel* de Villette. I even miss our two *marquis*, yes, even Thibouville who, at the end, recognized our worth and came to respect us. I also miss my library, the one I was building for the *marquis* de Villette. It was my library, for I was ordering all the books that I ever wished to have. Villette was a good chap all along, save for his errant paws. They were constantly massaging my back, or my shoulders, or one of them on the back of my head and the other one on one of my biceps. Every once in a while, he would give me one of his bear hugs and I would feel his hands traveling down to my behind. But he was a loving rogue, and I do feel that he greatly appreciated our presence there. Oh, to be present there yet again, with you at my side, under *monsieur* Maurel's tutelage! Only next time, according to him, we should be staying at the *hôtel* de Villette as guests, not as servants. That will be a new twist, don't you think?

By the way, have you heard the news? The *chevalière* says that *madame* Denis has been entertaining a certain *monsieur* Duvivier at her new house on the rue Richelieu, even though the construction hasn't yet ceased. Can you imagine? That old biddy being able to attract a man? I don't believe for a second that it's her womanly charms that are creating this allure. Rather, it's Voltaire's fortune that is operating this comical seduction. Did you know that she's sold Ferney to the *marquis* de Villette? Without the slightest twinge of conscience, she sold off Voltaire's library, an incredible fortune in books with Voltaire's marginalia and all his unpublished manuscripts, and in the next moment she is divesting herself of the locus of the world's conscience. Voltaire's château in Ferney should become a shrine, a lay cathedral for the world's philosophers and scientists, the Holy See of Reason and Progress. Wagnière, I'm sure, has his hands full, between transcribing the manuscripts and getting ready for the exchange of property into the command of the *marquis* de Villette. I'm sure it'll be a debacle; the *marquis* de Villette has no head for organization or industry. He will alienate the clockmakers and distress the farmers. He will disrupt the household and interfere with the house and grounds that have for twenty years been run like a Swiss clock. I need to go to Ferney and help Wagnière before everything starts sliding down the slope of entropy. I shall be there before you know it. Next time I write, it will be Wagnière who will somehow think of a way to get the letter to you. Meantime, please write to me care of Wagnière at Ferney. I don't think there's any danger in that. I am dying to hear news from you, to find out how you are faring, to hear of the progress you and your family are making. Don't forget to tell me about your sister, Charlotte. Is she still a schoolgirl in love with Jean-Jacques Rousseau? Does she still defend his works? Does she still weep over his histrionic stories? I can't believe that that pseudo-philosopher nincompoop is still alive, while our dear friend and anchor is gone. The world is a cruel place, my beautiful André, but I'm glad that you are in it to bring me solace and peace.

I send you my love, my affection and my friendship,

Your loving and devoted Zénobe.

Flouting the Laws of God and Nature

Zénobe felt so comfortable and safe at the *hôtel* d'Uzès, the *chevalière* d'Éon's provincial residence, that he stayed on for four more nights. The grand house, while not as refined as the *hôtel* de Villette, was still opulent in its appointments, and great care had been taken to keep its residents in luxury. Zénobe let himself be pampered, enjoyed the attention he received from the serving staff, and concluded that the Sybarites had not been entirely wrong in their preferred mode of life. But besides the self-indulgence, Zénobe felt great pleasure doing things, or omitting to do things, that went against the teachings of the church.

On Friday, June 5th, Zénobe ate meat stew.[16] He relished it more than if he had had it on the previous day Thursday or on the following day Saturday. On Sunday, June 7th, he did not accompany d'Éon to church. He had not kept the Sabbath either, the day before, as he refused to take any repose. On the contrary, he quite militantly went out and worked in the garden, in spite of a light rain. Digging, uprooting, pruning, burying seeds in even rows, espaliering, raking, weeding. Even d'Éon's servants looked askance at such a blatant disregard of church law. But by Sunday, they were used to Zénobe's ways. He had been invisible when the Father Confessor arrived on Saturday to receive confession from those who wished to take Communion on the following day. On Thursday, June 4th, he had been indisposed when the *chevalière* d'Éon offered a prayer outside to St. Saturnine, patron saint of grains, who looks after farmers' crops. Zénobe did show up, however, as soon as the rite was over and bottles of wine had been opened. Crackers of wheat, rye and buckwheat were served, along with fresh cheeses sprinkled with fine herbs. All this took place by the kitchen garden, where the herbs lent their scent to a warm breeze that promised summer diversions and prodigious harvests. Zénobe made it known to all there that he thanked the farmers' knowledge and accomplishments, and that they were responsible for the successful harvests and

---

16   This, above all else, is the small detail that finally drove the author, in his youth, away from the Church. The injunction to stay away from meat on Fridays was one fine day rescinded, no explanations given. Only on the Fridays during Lent was the rule still in force. *Monsieur* Luna figured that if one law could be dropped, what about others? For some reason, American Catholics believe that it was Vatican II that revoked the law of abstaining from meat on Fridays. For us in Europe, it is still on the books, the Code of Canon Law in 1983 confirming it. The reader should know that in the past, people were imprisoned and tortured for consuming meat on Fridays.

the high yields of their fields, not some medieval saint of Germanic origin who was martyred in France (while defending her virginity!) and who probably never even existed.[17] The peasant farmers seemed pleased on hearing Zénobe's pronouncements, but dared not thank him out loud for fear of angering the saint. Who knew for sure, but the simple Christians remembered how jealous God could get, throwing tantrums and smiting the disobedient with alarming enthusiasm, and probably this resentful reaction trickled down to all the saints. In any case, they basked in Zénobe's opinion of their superior knowledge whose origins ensued from the *chevalière* d'Éon's copy of the *Encyclopédie*, which with her consent they consulted on a weekly basis. Zénobe called them "my Encyclopædic brothers" and embraced them, calling them the most essential citizens of their society. He said this, of course, out of earshot of the *chevalière*, for he did not know how accepting she was about the revolutionary winds that were blowing across the Atlantic. Truth be told, the *chevalière* wasn't much ready to treat her farmers as equals, even though they were men and she a mere woman. Still, Zénobe himself was overstepping the bounds of the Democratic ideals of the newly-independent colonials: equal were the landowners, the men with the means to participate in commerce, who were invested in the future, and in futures, and who had prospects of social advancement, pecuniary enhancement and political involvement. The landless, and women, had no seats at the table of Equality, to say nothing of the slaves, who were not even considered to be people. Slaves were worth less than the set of silverware at the table of Equality.

There was one peasant farmer whom Zénobe embraced with greater fervor. His name was Étienne Étamble, a bit thin but graceful in his movements, with the light of intelligence in his big green eyes, a tousled tangle of black hair on his beautifully-shaped head. Étienne had looked into Zénobe's eyes with an understanding that the two shared more than just a passing interest in different types of fertilizer and methods of tilling the soil. Étienne remained outside long after the others had gone in, teaching Zénobe about the latest methods that science was introducing into agriculture and animal husbandry. Étienne spoke reverentially to Zénobe, insisting on using the *vous* form and the title of *chevalier*, even after the pseudo-aristocrat divulged his true identity as a Savoyard farmworker. Étienne could not believe it, because Zénobe's demeanor was so refined, he was so evidently well-read, and his vocabulary was so learned. Zénobe could easily see in Étienne an inchoate elegance, a sweetness that could easily be transformed into sophistication. In an instant he realized what it was that the majordomo of the *hôtel* de Villette *monsieur* Maurel honed in on when searching for boys in the provinces. The desired qualities were natural intelligence, docility, empathy, poise and a modicum of courtesy. The rest Maurel could teach them.

In return for Étienne's tutorial on modern farm methods, Zénobe wanted to extend a hand to the farm boy and teach him about some of the things he had learned in Paris. Their conversation outside lasted until they were called in to supper, and Zénobe found it difficult to separate himself from his new friend who had to have his repast with his companions in one of the farmhouses. Zénobe was sitting at the *chevalière* d'Éon's table. Before they went their different ways, however, Zénobe suggested that they meet again after supper, in order to continue their agronomical conversation. During dinner, Zénobe extolled Étienne's qualifications to the mistress of the domain, and the *chevalière* d'Éon promised to keep an eye out for his tenant-farmer. Zénobe even suggested that d'Éon might send the young man to *monsieur* Maurel at the *hôtel*

---

17   Zénobe is most probably right: today this saint is considered to be legendary.

de Villette, in order to have the young rustic reach his potential under the tutelage of the best *maître d'hôtel* of Paris. After all, he had done it. Four months of a Parisian education, with visits to a fencing school and a library, had removed all traces of rusticity from the young Zénobe Bosquet, and he thought of himself now as a real gentleman, not a yokel in the guise of one.

"Ah, my generous boy! You would have Étienne follow in your footsteps? I shall certainly look into this possibility, but I would hate to lose him on the farm. You are quite right in identifying him as a superior worker, for his crops are always among the best, and he never shirks his duties. In the evening he's always coming round to consult the *Encyclopédie* for something or other. He is always coming up with new ideas. He is always there one hundred percent! The other day he built a magnificent trellis for some roses I brought back from England. Sturdy it is, pleasing to look at, with a graceful design and a strong foundation."

Zénobe smiled. That description would serve well to describe the lad himself.

He had a chance to admire the build and the design of the young farmer. After another promenade by the kitchen garden, this time accompanied by the *chevalière* d'Éon, where the conversation drifted to the stars and other heavenly bodies, Zénobe invited Étienne to his room when everybody had dispersed and gone to sleep. Zénobe discovered that Étienne had just turned twenty, his birthday having been on May 30th. That was the day Voltaire had died, and Zénobe could not help think that life went on, that those who remained must continue with the humanist ambitions to improve the world and the condition of men in it.

The Savoyard farmer and his Burgundy counterpart found it easy to compare their relative strengths and desires. Their mutual curiosity and attraction gave their impulses a sprightly energy that was tempered only by the serenity that all the farmers of the world seem to share. Let Nature take its course, one cannot rush a seedling to burgeon forth from the soil, one must accept with equanimity the favorable and the adverse from the world, one must admire the workings of Nature and recognize both her mysteries and her unfathomable wisdom that has nothing to do with the judgment of man. Étienne left before dawn so that the household staff would not find out he had spent the night in Zénobe's room.

Zénobe had made a new friend, and was loathe to leave him. And how would he be able to say good-bye to the *chevalière?* He was also wistfully attracted to the farm, which, in a way, made him feel closer to André on his own farm in Normandy. Going through some of the routines on the fields or in the barns, he would ask himself if André were going through the same activities. But he could not delay his departure any longer. He had to advance his steps to Ferney, where his sense of duty called him, where he had to help safeguard Voltaire's writings and keep them from falling into the wrong hands, or save them from immolation.

The Fates had handed him this destiny, to continue the fight that Voltaire had begun. He loved Voltaire, and would fight to the death to defend everything his hero had stood for. There was nobody else to take on this battle. It was his responsibility and his alone. He felt energized, primed, determined. His two foils were in readiness.

Waylaid

I t was early in the morning when Zénobe left the *hôtel* d'Uzès with the plan of reaching Dijon by late afternoon. The *chevalière* d'Éon gave him enough provisions to last several days, including as many bottles of wine as she thought Zénobe's Palomino could carry. She also offered him a hefty sack of gold coin, but Zénobe told her that between his salary as librarian and all the gifts he had received in Paris, he had enough money to last him for quite a while, and that she best hold on to as much money as possible for her excursion to America to fight the British. They hugged for a long time, she shedding tears for her hero, he thanking her again for having saved his life.

"We are friends of the heart," she said. "We love each other, appreciate each other, love to be in each other's company. I would so love to have you with me on the battlefield where we could together terrorize the enemy."

Zénobe responded that after he had seen to the safeguarding of Voltaire's manuscripts anything was possible. "It would be an honor to learn the art of war from you," he told her. After another embrace and more kisses on both cheeks, Zénobe took his leave.

The fervent priests by this time had dispersed widely in Burgundy, and a couple of sacerdotal phalanxes had already been sent to Savoy in the hopes of capturing the renegade apostate whose reputation of being the Devil's representative on Earth was being promulgated to the four corners of the realm. In Annecy, like spiders' webs radiating out around the lake all the way to Chambéry, they laid out interconnected groups of the faithful who would at a moment's notice turn in a foreigner who looked as if he didn't belong. As a result, all foreigners, none of them with a Palomino, none of them smelling of sulfur, some of them women—with children!—were turned in, and for a while, Savoy became anathema to migrants, including faithful pilgrims, traveling through its territory to get from Italy or Switzerland into France or Spain.[18] But the religious orders didn't care. They cared not a whit about disturbing hundreds of innocent travelers in order to catch that one who needed to be caught. The priests were in a frenzy, for if the heretic managed to escape to Ferney he would be out of their jurisdiction. He would then become the problem of the Genevan protestants, who deserved him, but the catholics didn't think the protestants would go far enough to punish the miscreant. They wanted to catch him first, in order to mete out the correct

18 [From the author] Please remember, kind reader, that Italy and Switzerland did not yet exist as countries, and that Annecy belonged to a separate king, who, being a catholic, allowed the French priests complete access to his territories. It would not be derelict on my part to say that the catholic church was pretty much autonomous and a rogue force in the lands where they were the dominant religion.

and proper punishment, which was death. As the priests themselves explained, in a run-on, breathless sentence that was typical of them, it would be death by fire, in a superhuman effort to save his soul by the purifying flames that would consume the body but liberate the spirit, and the spirit would be free to fly to its Creator and communicate with Him, and the Creator would decide the final punishment, to allow the spirit access to His presence forever in Heaven, or to be ejected eternally and delivered unto Satan under whose jurisdiction the soul would forever be ablaze in fire and brimstone in the sulfurous recesses of Hell.

In the meantime, here on earth, the weather was warm, the road was clear, the passersby free of either brigands or zealots. In the early afternoon, Zénobe stepped off the highway and went into a field of alfalfa, redolent of that fodder and humming with bees visiting its violet flowers. No one knew how to pack a better picnic than the *chevalière* d'Éon, who knew about supping on battlefields and drinking while on horseback. But here, alone in this field, Zénobe was at ease and unhurried. He had time to think of Voltaire, his hero, his mentor, and shed hot tears over him. A few of those tears were also for André, whom he missed terribly. While he mourned and reflected, and ate the *chevalière*'s fried egg and steak sandwiches,[19] without realizing it, Zénobe drank a whole bottle of Chablis, one from the *chevalière*'s own vineyards, and felt lulled into a tranquility that was enhanced by the perfume of the alfalfa and the lazy humming of the hymenoptera. A slight ripple of a breeze ran shadows across the sea of stems. With his tears drying on his cheeks, he fell asleep. How long he slept cannot be known, but in the far reaches of his slumber, he heard Gaignun, his horse, snort and nicker, and stamp his foot on the alfalfa on which he had been feasting. By the time Zénobe left Morpheus' embrace, it was too late. He saw a figure looming over him and instinctively he put up his arms in a posture of defense and assault. The figure threw its full weight bodily onto Zénobe's torso, impeding his movements. But before Zénobe could will his legs into motion, he heard a man's voice, deep and throaty, utter words that immediately disarmed him.

"No need to get all riled up! It's your farmer friend, Gil Blas, *monsieur*, from just outside of Troyes. Remember? You stayed at my family's farmhouse last week. You and I... You and I..."

Zénobe's fists unfurled and he brought Gil's face to his own and gave him a deep kiss.

"You and I... what?" he asked him when he came up for air.

"You and I..." repeated Gil breathlessly.

"Yes, you said, 'You and I'..."

"You and I... shared my bed, and we spoke of farming, and we made love until dawn."

"Do I remember this?" asked Zénobe in mock seriousness. "I seem to remember a farm boy helping me to get undressed in the evening. But do I remember this frolicking of which you speak? I thought perhaps it had been a dream!"

"Aye, *monsieur*, 'twas a dream. A beautiful dream, an enchanting dream, an unforgettable dream."

---

19 Sandwiches were the rage among the upper classes ever since Pierre-Jean Grosley's book on London had been published in 1770 in 3 volumes. Titled *Londres*, it ran a new expanded edition in 4 volumes in 1774. John Montagu, 4th Earl of Sandwich, is said to have invented this novel way of eating meat while occupied at playing cards, so his fingers would not get greasy. Of course, the *chevalier* d'Éon, having served in London as Minister Plenipotentiary, brought down with him many of the culinary oddities of the English, or at least, the cleverer ones.

Zénobe raised himself on the alfalfa, but still held on to Gil's face with both his hands.

"*Petit* Gil, whatever are you doing here?"

"I've been looking for you, ever since the day you left us, because a number of priests descended on our house like locusts asking for your whereabouts, and looking as if they were up to no good. Priests rarely bring good tidings or words of comfort. They're always a grasping bunch, who want something, or somebody, or want you to do something for them, or bring them something. They are demanding, and feel that you were placed on this earth to satisfy them in every way. Anyway, my family and I ignored them, gave them false leads, false information, our worst wine, and they left and never came back. Zénobe, why do they want you so badly?"

"Because I mocked them in Paris, because I misled them, because I made their archbishop, the high and mighty Monsignor Beaumont, look like a laughingstock, although he certainly doesn't need my help to look like one. I dared to slight their self-respect by stealing Voltaire's body from them and giving him a proper burial in Champagne. Beaumont wanted to fling Voltaire's body into the city dump, and I stole that pleasure from him. Voltaire's remains were treated with respect, with love, and with reverence. His body is now safe from the gang of looters that run the catholic church."

"But now they want you, dear friend. I found out that you stayed with the *chevalier* d'Éon in Tonnerre. The priests might also find this out. You need to get away from here as fast as possible."

"I'm on my way to Dijon, where I have friends…"

"Ah, no, you cannot go there. It's in a direct line to Ferney, and that's where they suspect that you are going."

"That's where they always suspected I was going. Voltaire was supposed to have been interred there, in his own crypt half in and half out of his own church."

"Half in and half out?"

"Yes, he didn't want to be completely in the church."

"Why, Voltaire was a wit, in this case an architectural wit."

"Yes, indeed," he said, laughing at Gil's quip. This farmer boy was not a bumpkin.

"We'll go through Beaune, instead of Dijon," said Gil. "It'll add a day of travel for us, but that's worth it. It's far enough south that they won't be looking for you."

"You say 'we', Gil. Does that mean…"

"It means that I'm coming with you. My parents gave me permission, and they figured that you were an important personage in view of the great amount of clerics that invaded our farm."

"But what about your vineyards, your grapes?"

"I won't be needed until the harvest, so I have some time to spare. My other chores will be divided up by the others, don't you worry about that. We believed that you needed help, and I can see by your carelessness," he said, pointing to the spot silhouetted by the crushed alfalfa where Zénobe had been fast asleep, "that we were right." Gesturing with his head towards Zénobe's Palomino he added, "Oh, and we're going to have to get rid of your horse."

"Get rid of Gaignun? Not for a million *livres*!" Zénobe answered.

"Gaignun?"

Zénobe smiled sheepishly. "Gaignun was Marsile's horse."

"Who's Marsile?"

"He was the Saracen king, in the *Song of Roland*."

"Saracen, what's that?"

"The muslim king, Charlemagne's enemy."

Gil's face lit up in recognition. "The heathen enemy!"

"Why, yes!" cried out Zénobe. "I'm not about to have a christian horse!"

They both burst out in laughter, embracing and caressing each other.

Gil stepped away and brought over his own horse. "Let me introduce my steed to Gaignun, warhorse of Marsile, the heathen king. But wait, my horse has no name! What shall we call him?"

"That's easy," answered Zénobe. "His name will be Aelroth. Aelroth was Marsile's nephew, just as Roland was Charlemagne's nephew. You see, there is a comforting parallelism in the catholic and muslim hierarchies."

"So, then, Aelroth, meet Gaignun."

Gil's brown stallion joined Zénobe's ghostly Palomino in chomping at the alfalfa. Their masters sank back down into their bed of alfalfa, not to eat it, but to engage in an activity that the horses were little interested in. All they knew was that when the humans got up again, they had perspiration on their foreheads, alfalfa all over their hair and clothing, and were breathing as if they had been galloping.

Traveling Companion

il Blas was a strapping young man, strong and lithe, with long chestnut-brown hair that ended in the middle of his back. It was a broad back, honed from many summers in the fields, muscled with the results of hard labor, but a beloved labor, useful to his farm, to his family, even to the village of Troyes where the wines from his family's vineyards enjoyed a reputation of quality and consistency. The Blas family was known for having modified the shape of the bottle destined for Champagne wine, making it squatter, with a thicker bottom into which the glassblower made an indentation with his thumb. The result was that none of their bottles had ever been known to explode. They were viewed by their neighbors as a God-fearing church-going family, even though they kept mostly to themselves, but the villagers bought their products and their wares without apprehension. They were well-liked and respected members of the community.

Had they known what Zénobe now knew, the villagers would have been horrified, would have shunned the entire family, turned their backs on them, refused to buy a single bunch of grapes from them, and without hesitation would have turned them over to the Holy Inquisition, with the hope of being able to take over their land. Gil's family were secret non-believers. They realized the danger of being found out, and in all aspects gave the semblance of being good catholics, but after they were all inside the house in the evening, the Blas lit no votives, offered no prayers, said no novenas. To them, having to go to church on Sundays and certain feast days, tithing ten percent of their profits, which of course they underreported, and having to bless themselves out in the open every once in a while, all of this was the extortion demanded by the church in order to continue living as farmers and to be left alone. But deep down they believed in none of it. Bereft they were of religious balderdash. All alone in the world without the succor and the consolation of God. Instead, they enjoyed life, to the fullest, free to inquire into the realms of science that brought them even more succor and consolation than prayer could ever bring. To Zénobe this was no surprise. Once you have the courage to deny the existence of God, the mind is unencumbered. Then the liberty of exploration, the freedom of study, the lack of inane obstacles, in all, the vocation of philosophy conveys such happiness to your mind, that your previous life spent repeating cycles of kneeling, sitting and standing behind pews is revealed as being empty and false. Reading a book considered sacred that reads false, and worse, nonsensical, was dispiriting. Once they broke with that, they found that the courage to be free brings hope that humanity will find solutions to many of its problems, as opposed to blind acceptance that life must be spent miserably in atoning for sins that aren't even yours, and fatalistically waiting for someone who might never even come. There's a lot to be said against a religion that looks forward to the end of the world.

Zénobe and Gil had marvelous conversations about all of this. Gil was not as learned as Zénobe, but he had had access to the *Encyclopédie* for over a year. It had been an expensive acquisition for his family, and a difficult one, since they had to smuggle the volumes piecemeal from Geneva. But it was a worthwhile investment. It paid for itself within months, as their farm's yields multiplied and the ease of knowing they were doing the right thing put an end to guessing and praying. Prayers were not needed, not even to pray for rain, for the meteorological information they garnered showed that rain, or the lack of it, had more to do with barometric pressure, prevailing winds and temperatures, than with any orders sent by God. God was taken out of the equation, and the result was the freedom procured by science.

Gil spent many hours of elation reading the articles of Diderot, d'Alembert, Condorcet, and all of the other *philosophes* who were making such progress into the provinces of knowledge based on direct observation and sound experimental science. The boundaries of many domains were being extended into areas unheard of until now. Now when he gazed into the heavens, the stars were more real, knowing that they were huge balls of fire, as big as the Sun, or bigger! They seemed tiny because they were so far away. The Moon looked brighter and more beautiful, knowing that it was pockmarked with thousands of meteor hits. The sky, the rivers, the trees, the bountiful creation of Nature, over which there was no god-creator; the cryptic functions of the human body, being scrutinized and analyzed and understood by a clinical eye; the perplexing province of the human mind, where precious details were being coaxed out into the light; all of this was an adventure to be enjoyed, a decipherment to be explicated, an act of Promethean courage, not for having stolen fire from the gods and then having used it to light the world, but of having demonstrated that the gods had never been there in the first place. It was man himself who procured fire from Nature, and was now wresting information from her, and both Zénobe and Gil said that they were happy to be living in such times when the revolution in science was making a difference in the way men lived. For hours as they rode, they discussed this, turning to smaller trails to wend their way to Beaune. They reached it during twilight, and quickly found a place to spend the night. Zénobe began to get anxious, for in twenty-four more hours, he would be speaking with Wagnière, Voltaire's secretary, in the philosopher's home-in-exile, Ferney.[20]

With the thought of Wagnière, a mounting alarm, tinged with dread, took hold of Zénobe. How much time would they have to find, organize and transcribe Voltaire's manuscripts? What about his correspondence? Catherine the Great of Russia had convinced Voltaire's niece, *madame* Denis—all it took was 30,000 rubles and a few presents, including diamonds, a fur coat, a portrait of the Empress, and an autographed letter inscribed to "the niece of a great man who loved me"—to surrender all the items

---

20 Not that the author needs any help in the exposition of his characters, but I feel that perhaps the reader ought to know that Gil Blas, an enlightened young farmer, is not entirely an anomaly or even an improbable personage, coming as he does from the area of Troyes. International commerce was frequent in this crossroads, the European center of popular fairs where storehouses procured food and equipment and emporia bought, sold and bartered supplies that came from many countries, including Germany, England, Spain, and Flanders, and in addition served to unify and consolidate weights and measures, so that a consistency was established in order to weigh, and sell, products as diverse as pearls, bread, spices and pharmaceuticals. Troy weight was in use until the French Revolution introduced the metric system into all of France.

in Voltaire's library in Ferney, every book, every note, every scrap of paper. The Empress promised that she would build an exact replica of Voltaire's château in Russia, with an identical library, and that Wagnière would travel with the contents of the library and arrange every item the way it had been in its original disposition. Zénobe knew that this excuse of honoring the philosopher was balderdash. Catherine wanted to regain the letters she had sent Voltaire through the years because they contained many confidences, many state secrets, that would have gotten her into trouble if other governments knew about them, in particular, those of Frederick the Great of Prussia and Maria Theresa of Austria, mother of Marie Antoinette, Queen of France. How many pleasantries had he told about those two in his letters to Catherine! How many impolitic comments had she made to him in return! International alliances were at stake, the equilibrium of power in Europe would become unstable, war could break out. In the past, war had broken out over more insignificant excuses. The fact that an Empress had had an epistolary dalliance with a highly public man meant that any confidential confessions she might have let slip out in her exuberant letters to him now threatened to blow up in her face. By buying Voltaire's library wholesale she would avert any possible catastrophic consequences. Diplomatic relations behind the scenes are convoluted and devious, and if aired in such a public manner as the publication of Voltaire's correspondence would be, the polite façade of protocol would certainly crack. Still, she also did want to honor her friend the philosopher, who throughout her reign had always given her such good advice, whose policies she had, up to a point, experimented with in her administration, and who had given her such wonderful recommendations in the writing of her own plays. She admired, respected, and loved the man, in her own way. The moment she learned that Voltaire had died, she felt in her heart "a movement of universal discouragement and great disdain for all the things in the world."[21] She contacted Voltaire's architect, Léonard Racle, in order to borrow his architectural plans of the château, and begin construction of an exact replica on the grounds of Tsarskoye Selo, her summer palace.

But in the meantime, Zénobe and Gil made their way to the original château of Ferney, where Voltaire's secretary, Jean-Louis Wagnière, would undoubtedly have already begun to copy the philosopher's unpublished manuscripts and to categorize and place into crates the thousands of books that his master had left behind.

---

21   The original statement was written in French: *"J'ai senti un mouvement de découragement universel et d'un très grand mépris pour toutes les choses de ce monde."*

Arrival into Chaos

By the time Zénobe and Gil arrived, safe and sound, at Voltaire's château in Ferney, it was too late at night to see the library. Wagnière and his wife, as surprised as they were, and already in their night apparel, welcomed the two boys as best they could, for the secretary had not received any word from Paris of master Bosquet's imminent arrival. Zénobe surmised that neither Maurel nor any of Voltaire's philosopher friends would have chanced one of their letters being opened by the religious zealots who would have combined all of their efforts to set a trap for the young traveler outside of Ferney. But Zénobe's friends needn't have worried. With Gil's expert strategy, the two had taken only minor roads to Ferney. Gil put a blanket on the palomino and did all the talking when they needed something, keeping Zénobe in the shadows, and they came into Ferney quietly in the evening without even many of the residents of the village having seen them. Besides, Zénobe had taken so long to get to Ferney that the priests were too widely in disarray. Many of them were no longer here but had gone back up to Dijon where they were aimless and distracted. Once Wagnière found out that the Inquisition was after Zénobe, he calmed the boys by pointing out that the inhabitants of Ferney had been living for so long under the lights of the Resident Philosopher, and that a big percentage of them were displaced protestants from Geneva (mostly the watchmakers), that he did not foresee anyone in town denouncing the boy to such a cruel institution. And even if someone did, since Ferney straddled the border, Zénobe could scurry into the Genevan side of the property and be safe.

Zénobe and Gil were given a cold supper of bread, cheese and fruit, and a room on the second story where they spent a comfortable night in the house where Voltaire had lived since 1758. In the morning, even before breakfast, they came down to inquire about visiting the library. *Madame* Wagnière, a pale blonde with deliberate movements and an excellent vocabulary, the result of being married to Voltaire's secretary, insisted on them eating first, and having some coffee, while they waited for her husband to arrive.

"He enjoys lingering in bed, why, I don't know. I'm not one to tarry, for as soon as my eyes open, I spring out of bed. There is always more work to be done than the day is long, a profusion of tasks and chores for everyone who lives in Ferney. You will soon be joining the rest and playing your part, but in the meantime, both of you need sustenance anyway, so tarry a while longer, enjoy your coffee. One lump or two? Moreover, he's the only one to have the keys to the library."

Wagnière came to breakfast three quarters of an hour later, seemingly in no hurry to get to the library. His wife had a copious breakfast waiting for him. Zénobe wondered why there was no look of panic, no zeal to get to Voltaire's books. It was either because

Wagnière was so used to being around Voltaire's books, or because, or because…he didn't know.

"*Monsieur* Wagnière. Have you been informed that the entirety of Voltaire's library, including his unpublished manuscripts, have been sold by Voltaire's niece, *madame* Denis, to the Empress of Russia, Catherine II?"

Wagnière looked at Zénobe with a frozen countenance and then visibly collapsed. "That woman!" he cried. "That despicable woman!"

Madame Wagnière shook her head in commiseration, saying, "*Oh, là, là, là, là!* That woman would win a prize in a contest to see who possesses more doltishness."

"That despicable woman!" repeated the ambushed secretary. "She only cares about the lucre! She wants to exchange books for frocks!"

Zénobe decided that it would be less cruel to let Wagnière have all the news at the same time. "She also wants you to accompany the library to its final resting place in Saint Petersburg."

The old secretary looked at Zénobe and stared at him.[22]

Madame Wagnière answered for her husband. "Let that old witch accompany the library to Saint Petersburg. Let *her* die of the cold and be lost in the snow!"

Zénobe smiled, and explained, "*Madame* Denis wants your husband to rearrange the library in the same disposition in which it is found now."

Wagnière finally reacted. Everyone in the room started, with *madame* Wagnière spilling coffee out of her cup. Voltaire's secretary, not given to mirth, let out peal after peal of laughter, throwing his hands to the heavens as if to beseech the testimony of God on the foolish antics of his creatures. Zénobe detected around Wagnière's eyes a look of lunacy, as if Sisyphus had finally decided to throw his boulder off the hill.

"*Monsieur* Wagnière… *monsieur* Wagnière? *Monsieur* Wagnière…" tried Zénobe several times to interrupt the secretary's maniacal exuberance. He turned to *madame* Wagnière for help, but she had placed a hand on her forehead, as if she had a raging headache.

Finally Wagnière calmed down, looked around the dining room as if he were surprised he was there, and pointing his thumb toward Paris he said, "*Madame* Denis is as stupid as her uncle was intelligent. She is so inane that I wonder how the patriarch of Ferney was able to stand her for so many years. She lost her looks and her figure long ago, and there haven't been relations between them for many, many years. Why couldn't he have guessed that this Jezebel would sell his library as soon as it was in her disposition to do so?"

The word 'relations' was said in a whisper, to lessen the effect of a subject that was distasteful to him.

"I wonder why Voltaire didn't let her go when she wanted to," he continued. "I would have given her thousands of *livres* just to have her go far, far away from me. But he didn't. He didn't because he loved her. In spite of her stupidity, her lost looks, her portliness, her inane conversation, he loved her. How that came to be, I don't know. I couldn't even begin to explain it, but Shakespeare could not have come up with a truer phrase than 'love is blind.' In this case, deaf as well. And this," Wagnière's voice rose

---

22   In 1778 Jean-Louis Wagnière was only 39 years old, but to 19-year-old Zénobe he probably looked older. Perhaps the twenty-two years that Wagnière had spent in the service of Voltaire aged him prematurely. Also, being a protestant, he was forever too serious and grim, and the wrinkles around his mouth made him look older.

in intensity as he gave the table a strike with his fist, "And this is how she repays him! By selling his books to the Russians!"

Zénobe decided not to tell Wagnière just yet that *madame* Denis had also decided to sell Ferney, village and château, to *monsieur le marquis* de Villette. That bit could wait for a day when Wagnière would be feeling better. In the meantime, he politely asked to go see the library, and Wagnière complied. With Gil beside him, they followed behind the secretary who looked like Sisyphus with the boulder returned to his back, hobbling slowly along the downstairs hallway. He took his time unlocking the door, and then threw both doors back, exposing Voltaire's great library.

It was Zénobe's turn to freeze and look aghast. The room was certainly large enough, but its spaciousness only served to reinforce his reaction of stunned disbelief. This was Voltaire's library? The library that erudite Europeans, and even some intrepid Americans, came to see, as part of their Grand Tour of the continent? Was this the modern seventh wonder? The collection that took Voltaire his long life to collect, and to write? This… this… was a library? Where Zénobe expected to see shelves with books arrayed standing up with the spines out, there were books one on top of the other, with the spines facing in all directions. From top to bottom there was disarray, chaos, as if the visitors had caught the books cavorting and dancing and then the music had suddenly stopped. There were uneven stacks of unbound papers interspersed between the dislocated books. As Zénobe's eyes swept across the room, he could not help emitting a sound of dismay, a deep disappointment that any bibliophile would have felt at seeing such a famous library in an upheaval. This was the library of an anarchist, who cared not a whit for the order of things. And Voltaire was not an anarchist, far from it. He may not always have been religiously meticulous about where he left his things in his bedroom at the *hôtel* de Villette, but at least there was method to his carelessness. Here, in the inner sanctum of philosophical research, the heart of Notre Dame de la Méthode, the cathedral where science met art and produced wisdom, there seems to have been a cannon ball, several of them, that had careered through the stacks and off the shelves.

"What has happened here? This…" whispered Zénobe. "This is Voltaire's library?"

Wagnière was immediately on the defensive. "Of course this is Voltaire's library! What you don't know and I need to tell you is that Panckoucke has already given me money to purchase Voltaire's manuscripts.[23] He has some of them in his possession already! As his secretary and librarian, I assumed this is what everyone would want, to have all of Voltaire's papers published in a fine edition to be purchased by subscribers only! I've been combing through the library uncovering and ordering Voltaire's texts in chronological order—"

"In chronological order? Why not in order of subject matter?" interrupted Zénobe.

"Because Panckoucke wants to include a portrayal of the development of Voltaire's thoughts, of the evolution of his philosophical endeavors. This has been seconded by

---

23   May the kind reader please remember that *monsieur* Charles Joseph Panckoucke was Voltaire's publisher in Paris. Unbeknownst to *madame* Denis, he had already been busy buying the unpublished manuscripts in order to prepare them for an historical posthumous publication of Voltaire's complete works. These purchases did not yet include the correspondence, which was high on the list of the items that Catherine was desperately seeking. We can only surmise that Wagnière had already begun to pull Voltaire's letters from his library to keep them separate. Furthermore, he would have been acting on the assumption that the decision to sell Voltaire's writings for eventual publication would have been one that everyone, including *madame* Denis, would have thought both sound and timely.

Beaumarchais, who has been lending money to Panckoucke in order to hasten the enterprise."

"Beaumarchais?" asked Zénobe incredulously. "The watchmaker harpist diplomat playwright who's been sending arms and uniforms to the American rebels? What is he doing in the middle of this endeavor?"

"Because there is much money to be made!" screeched the secretary. "*Madame* Denis will be filthy rich to the end of her days!"

At this point Wagnière turned away from the frightening chaotic collection of paper and books and looked directly into Zénobe's eyes, saying, "I'm only one librarian, and I have been given the Herculean task of removing from this library only the unpublished texts, Voltaire's unpublished texts, not those sent to him by the cartsful from writers who wished to receive a few words of encouragement from the greatest mind of Europe! All by myself have I been at this unprecedented task, this unremunerated labor, unappreciated by all, and poked and prodded by an impatient publisher and by a Mephistophelean writer, who come when they please and wish to remove manuscripts by the armful. I have to plead with them that before anything leaves this office, it has to be copied first. And believe me, I have been copying. My hand is ready to fall off..."

Indeed, the right hand that Wagnière presented to Zénobe and Gil's examination was permanently stained from thumb to third finger, and looked more like the claw of a wounded rapacious bird than a human hand. "See? The swelling won't go down, my wrist is locked, and the trembling of my phalanges lasts until the middle of the night. And still they come, to tell me what to do, to load more papers into crates, and whisk them to goodness knows where."

He led them into the middle of the room.

"But don't be concerned about the integrity of the library, master Zénobe. All his books are still here, none has left my safekeeping. It's just that looking for the manuscripts has left everything in shambles. With you here, my boy, perhaps together we'll be able to go a little faster. And if your friend here, master Gil, also shares in our secretarial duties, then it will certainly go faster. We need marathon transcribers who don't tire easily, who care about getting the transcripts right the first time, and we need to place the originals into their rightful places. Whether Panckoucke takes them, or Catherine of Russia takes them, we will have kept a copy of each and every written piece of paper produced by Voltaire, and his legacy will be safe. We shall also systematically ask his correspondents, at least those who are willing, to lend us his letters to them, so that we may transcribe those, too. Our work is massive; are you willing to undertake it?"

Zénobe was quick to answer. "Of course, *monsieur* Wagnière. That is why I am here. I am here to protect Voltaire's corpus, just like I protected his body all the way to Scellières."

"And I," said Gil, "am here to protect Zénobe, but I can also lend a hand to copy manuscripts." With the sweeping gesture of an overly-dramatic actor, the young man cried out, "Bring it forthwith! Where is the paper? Have I a quill? Can we clear a tabletop?"

There was no time like the present. They had had a sound sleep that night, a good breakfast, and felt the energy and the enthusiasm to begin. They each took a place around Voltaire's desk and table, and with Wagnière organizing the material and assigning the pieces, they began work that was just as intricate and meticulous as that of the watchmakers across the village. Only instead of tinkering with tiny cogs, springs and levers, the Voltairean secretaries dealt with verbs, adjectives, prepositions and punctuation, adding words, sentences and paragraphs to the known works of a great writer, and these works did not slip into oblivion, but rather, united with Voltaire's previously printed material, came to be published in a historic seventy-volume compendium which, if it did not cause the Revolution, did in fact hasten it.[24]

Let it be noted that Wagnière and his companions did not add, delete or change one word of what Voltaire had written. They felt that they were not worthy of editing the great man's work. If ever they came—but this was rare!—across a mistake in fact, they left it alone. If a word were smudged or difficult to read, the three of them conferred and came up with the best possibility. A few times, a piece of paper had been ripped off, taking a line or two into oblivion; the secretaries left ellipses in their stead. They were not about to compose for the great philosopher. The work that they passed on was authentic, unmitigated, unexpurgated Voltaire.

It also came to pass that Zénobe's sinistrality was not the only difference that set him apart from other people. After Gil had made the surprising discovery that his mate was writing with his left hand, he subsequently made another one. Wagnière had developed a system of demarcation of scrolls and stacks of letters by tying them up with different-colored string. Letters from aristocrats were tied up in blue string, letters from admirers in yellow, those from fellow writers were in green, those from business associates in red, etc., etc.

Gil saw that Zénobe confused the green, brown, mauve and gray strings, and had to lend a hand to denote the scrolls correctly. He only got the blue and the yellow piles right. After Gil had alerted Zénobe to his errors, Zénobe held up a handful of strings up to his eyes and started pulling some out.

"Here's the blue, here's the yellow, here's the white. Now, for the green, it's this one."

"No," said Gil, "that's a brown one."

"How about this one?"

"No, that's gray."

"This one?"

"Red."

"All right, this one!"

"Process of elimination."

"Well, there's not that much difference between these colors," complained Zénobe as he held out the handful of strings. "It's more a question of hues, isn't it?"

"My poor fellow," said Gil, sitting besides Zénobe, taking his face in his hands and kissing his cerulean blue eyes one at a time. "Seems all the color went to your eyes and none to your sight."

Wagnière discreetly went on writing while one of his co-secretaries continued kissing the other.

"Are you mocking me?" asked Zénobe.

"Oh, no!" asserted Gil. "On the contrary, I love you more because of your quaint idiosyncrasies."

---

24   The author is to the Kehl edition (1785-1789) of Voltaire's complete works alluding. The village of Kehl is just across the river Rhine in Germany, directly opposite Strasbourg, close enough to slip the clandestine books into France, but away from the hegemony of the meddlesome catholic priests. Beaumarchais installed presses in the old stronghold of Kehl, bought Baskerville type directly from John Baskerville's widow in England, bought three paper mills to produce enough high-quality paper, and published hundreds of beautiful leather-bound sets, one of which graces the library of the author, although I have not yet had the pleasure of seeing it for myself.

"My quaint... my quaint... I'll show you idiosyncrasies!" Zénobe began to tickle Gil. "I've never met such a sensitive creature as you! Look! You're ready to pee in your pants you're so ticklish!"

Wagnière couldn't help smiling at the antics of his two companions. He was happy, and relieved, to have them by his side.

"Well, then," decided Zénobe, "you had better code the letters, or I'll make a muddle of it!"[25]

"By your leave," said Gil, still laughing. "Strings are not your strong suit. Thank the world that letters are."

They continued working on the transcriptions into the afternoon, stopping only for a quick dinner in the late afternoon, and then into suppertime, and this established the pattern that they would hold for months. In time, Zénobe's left hand and Gil's right became as permanently inky as Wagnière's. They were happy about it. It was their shared emblem that they were committed to a sacred cause.

---

25   Had they had more time to look into this matter, Zénobe and Gil might have discovered achromatopsia, or color-blindness, a half-century before the British scientist Robert Dalton did. Dalton who, as a Quaker, would have preferred to wear a gray gown to the ceremony bestowing his college degree, instead chose a bright red one, to the surprise of all his friends and professors. He went on to distinguish the different deficiencies of color perception, and he would have classified Zénobe as being red-green color-blind, as opposed to the rarer blue-yellow or to the even rarer total daltonism.

Work Staves off Boredom, Vice and Need[26]

The weeks passed in happiness, exhaustion also, sometimes frustration at the pressure that came from outside forces, but the salient emotions that came out of Voltaire's library in Ferney for the rest of the summer and into the fall were those of satisfaction, pride and exhilaration. As the stock of copied Voltairean manuscripts grew, so did the secretaries' relief about saving these texts for the future. Catherine II would eventually gain possession of the original writings, of course, but France would never lose these texts from its borders.

When not working on the reproductions, Zénobe and Gil would take long walks on the estate. Gil especially was interested in the agricultural techniques employed by Voltaire's farmers, and he learned many facts about horticulture and a plethora of methods of cultivation and techniques in animal husbandry that he was impatient to introduce to his family's farm in Champagne. Of course, the terroir and climate of Savoy did not lend itself to good wines, but those that Ferney produced were fruity, piquant, and best enjoyed while young. Zénobe had turned into an avid œnophile himself, and enjoyed these moments of relaxation. They greatly appreciated the wines that Voltaire imported from Bordeaux, Beaujolais, Loire and Alsace, and since those lines of supply had not yet been interrupted, the two boys were able to educate their palates to an elevated degree.

Perhaps a word here about these two young friends might be found useful. To most readers, it is assumed, Zénobe's unfaithfulness to André is unpardonable. Had he not seen the need to travel to Savoy, Zénobe would most certainly have gone directly into André's arms in Normandy. Zénobe loved André ardently, and not an hour passed that he didn't think of him in some way. Cut off from him as he was, it was difficult to go through his activities every day and know nothing about André's life, health and thoughts, but it was too dangerous to hazard a correspondence with him. The priests would eventually find out.

Gil, on the other hand, was an amiable companion, whose protection and friendship Zénobe could never have rebuffed, but he wouldn't go as far as saying that he was in love with him. While true that they had sexual relations, Zénobe realized that, based

---

26 The original quote is from the last chapter of *Candide*: «*Le travail éloigne de nous trois grands maux : l'ennui, le vice, et le besoin.*»

on a strict definition of adultery, he and André as a couple first had to be married. Well, no priest would ever comply to such a union, scorning it as a travesty of religious law. Zénobe doubted that the established religions of the world would ever evolve enough to offer the sanctity of marriage to couples of the same sex. So, if there was no marriage, there could be no adultery. Deep down, however, Zénobe knew this to be false, and his reasoning was facile, for the argument was casuistic, based only upon words and their meanings. The emotions he felt for André showed that such reasoning was false. So was the rationalization that what André did not know could not hurt him. If he did know that Zénobe was being unfaithful, would he feel hurt? Zénobe's reasoning led him to the next question: if André did know that Zénobe was being unfaithful, *should* he feel hurt? The answer to that particular question was a resounding no. André should not feel hurt, because Zénobe was not taking anything away from him. His dalliance with Gil, while sweet and loving, was not profoundly emotional. It was physical, definitely, but it was just mutual arousal and gratification. Another question begged to be asked: To what moral purpose would self-sacrifice have guided Zénobe? What values would he have gained? Again, the answer was a resounding negative. He would have gained nothing by forgoing sex with Gil. Only religious fanatics forsook sex, renounced physical touch, extolled virginity and chastity, acclaimed neoplatonic virtues and recommended abstinence as both proof of self-control and as a mode of birth control. Abstemiousness, too, was considered saintly, so sacrificing eating, drinking and fornicating, three great physical pleasures, was praised to the heavens. Self-abnegation, denial of the senses, eschewing pleasure and renouncing the physical, this was religion. The religious avidly sought the contrary: lauding the spirit, chasing longingly after the soul, elevating the intangible, the transcendent, glorifying everything that could not be proven to exist, that was what was important to religion. What existed, was denied; the human body was viewed with derision for it was just a shell; what gave pleasure originating in that body was excised. To Zénobe, refusing to have sex with another person was tantamount to refusing to eat and drink with that person, just because one's spouse was not there. He was not going to deny the essence of his body in order to give importance to his soul, which might not even exist.

Zénobe's mind went further. What if André were suddenly present in Ferney? Would that mean that Zénobe would have to abandon Gil completely? The friendship for this other person was still there, the care and attention had not abated, so why should their physical relationship be discarded? What would André say to the three of them sharing their love and companionship? There, Zénobe's reasoning seemed to wilt, because of the fact that he would not want to share André with anybody else. His love for André was such that it was not communicable to others. Perhaps Zénobe could have allowed a third man to enter into his association with Gil, but his love for André, he wished to distance and segregate from everybody else.

So, in this manner, questions of morality were torn asunder from their moorings, and consequently were seen as the contrivance of arbitrary religion, for morality differed from country to country, and, indeed, from era to era in the same country. In the end, Zénobe thought it best to think of these moral issues as being contingent on his love for André. What was true and real, this love, gave everything else meaning, but he didn't feel the need to sacrifice the pleasure for which his physical self yearned just to prove his love for André. He wept more than once, not having Voltaire around with whom to discuss these matters of importance. Numerous times, he just plunged into his work so as not to be assailed by questions of guilt. Voltaire had shown how work staved off boredom, vice and need, but it also served to isolate remorse, melancholy and loneliness.

This last emotion let itself be felt to a remarkable degree when Gil finally had to go home. The vendange called, his family missed him terribly, and Gil had to tear himself away from Zénobe. But he said that the work the three secretaries had been doing was so far advanced—they could now see the end of the manuscripts amidst the riotous library—that a third secretary was now not that necessary. The remaining two could finish in a few weeks. Zénobe was nevertheless sad to see him go and realized the first night without Gil that he had been using him to attenuate the intensity of his feelings for André. With Gil now gone, Zénobe was free to go back to the agony of missing his one true love.

Gil left at the end of September.[27] It wasn't until the third or fourth day of October that Zénobe found a note that Gil had written and left hidden for him in his toiletry box. He was not shaving very often lately.

> *Cher ami* Zénobe,
>
> It has been my honor to have worked beside you on such a venerable task as safeguarding Voltaire's writings. It has given me a new direction in the battle against the infamy of the catholic church. It has been my good luck to have found you as a friend, and I cherish the forces of destiny that brought you to the door of my family's farm. Lastly, it has been my joy, to have known you and loved you, for you have given me such a magnificent gift, the possibility of happiness for people like us, free from guilt and prejudice, joined to the freedom to choose whom we may love. It is a splendid discovery to know that happiness is within our grasp, and I thank you for this revelation. I shall treasure my time together with you forever.
>
> I am today, and always, your companion, your lover, and your bodyguard, Gil.

---

27 Had Gil left for the vendange in Champagne in the year 2018, he would have had to leave at the end of August. Back in 1778, mid-September was the median start date. Science has calculated a ten-day variation in wine harvest dates for each 1° Celsius difference. Here is one more proof that the Earth has indeed been warming up.

Interstices Addendum

Fragments of letters of people who have nothing to do with this novel, yet shed some light on its context

In order to paint for the reader a portrait of the turmoil, the fracas that descended on Europe and indeed the world after the death of Voltaire, with competing voices vying to be heard, all of which represented viewpoints diametrically opposed to each other, herewith are presented snippets from real letters, some that remained in private correspondence, some that were published for all to read.

1. The letter of retraction that Voltaire's so-called confessor, the abbot Gaultier, brought for Voltaire to sign in the morning of the day he died, and which he never did sign, was published by *monsieur* Maximilien-Marie Élie Harel, priest, for all of Europe to read. Please remember, Voltaire did not write this, nor did he ever sign it. Why did Harel publish it, then? To throw confusion on the tranquil death of Voltaire, to sow trouble and foment chaos. This man of the cloth, in his insatiable pursuit of Voltaire, will eventually publish in 1781 a book which he entitles, *Voltaire, recueil des particularités curieuses de sa vie & de sa mort* (*Voltaire: a Collection of Curious Particularities of His Life & of His Death*), in which he assembles other priests' lies and adds quite a few of his own.

> I retract everything that I have been able to say, do or write against good morals, against the Christian religion into which I had the joy to be born, against the worshipable Person of Jesus Christ, whose Divinity I have been accused of attacking, & against His Church in which I desire to die, while doing reparation now in front of the universe that was scandalized by works which have appeared under my name for many years; which reparation is not at all the effect of the feebleness of my organs in my great age; but of the grace of Jesus Christ of which I was so indignant, Who opens my eyes to the horrible danger into which the delirium of my imagination has plunged me. I desire that this reparation be inserted into all the newspapers and gazettes of Europe, so that it be equal, as much as possible, to the scandals, which I should like to destroy at the price itself of the few days that remain to me of

life. Done in Paris, this 30th May, 1778, in the presence of *monsieur* le Curé de Saint-Sulpice & of *monsieur* l'Abbé Gaultier.[28]

2. Letter from *madame la marquise* du Deffand to her friend in England *monsieur* Horace Walpole, *le 31 mai, 1778*.

> Truly I was forgetting an important fact, that Voltaire has died; we don't know the hour nor the day. There are some who say it was yesterday, others the day before yesterday. The obscurity that lies on such an event comes from, according to what people are saying, the fact that no one knows what they will do with the body. The priest from Saint-Sulpice does not want to receive it. Will they send it to Ferney? He has been excommunicated by the bishop of the diocese where Ferney lies. He died of an excess of opium that he was taking to calm the pains of his strangury, and I would add, of an excess of glory, which badly shook his weak anatomy.

3. Epitaphs and poems begin to appear in different publications, despite the fact that King Louis XVI had forbidden any mention at all of Voltaire or Voltaire's death. Here is one that appeared in June of 1778, by a *monsieur* Le Brun.

> Oh, Parnassus! Shudder with pain & fright!
> Weep, Muses! Smash your immortal lyres!
> Thou, whose hundred voices & wings he exhausted,
> Say that Voltaire is dead, weep, & rest.

4. A wag suggested the following epitaph for Voltaire, who had been laid to rest in an old abbey in Scellières, Champagne.

> *Hic inter Monachos quiescit, qui nunquam contra monachos quievit.*
> Here among the monks rests he who never rested against the monks.

5. On June 2nd, *monsieur le chevalier* de Goudar publishes in his journal *L'Espion françois à Londres* the following letter, which he attributes to "a certain author":

> The old sinner is dead: he ended his days on the 30th of May, a remarkable day for Christianity, which rid itself of an Atheist who believed neither in God nor in the Devil, nor in the Saints.
> He existed no longer, even before ceasing to exist. His cadaver was so dry and so emaciated that the worms found nothing on which to gnaw, and his soul was so feeble and small that it evaporated before arriving in Hell. His witty works shared the same fate. His literary brush left nothing but colors after his death.

---

28   Had Voltaire signed this letter of retraction in front of the King and the Pope themselves, nobody would have believed that this badly-written missive, with its illogical, meandering, nonsensical sentences, came from him. Even while moribund, Voltaire's writing was expected to be brilliant.

6. Mozart happened to be in Paris when Voltaire died. A month later his own mother, who had accompanied him to the French capital where he desired to seek fame and fortune and found neither, died in turn. Mozart had to lie to his father, writing two letters after her death in which he announced to his father that his mother was sick, and then very sick, before finally delivering the tragic news that she had died. The report of Voltaire's death was apparently a lot easier to write:

> I must now give you a message that you perhaps already know, that namely the ungodly arch-villain Voltaire has croaked, so to speak, like a dog, like a brute. That is his reward!

7. *Docteur* Tronchin, Voltaire's protestant doctor, who was not present by his patient's bedside the day he died, nevertheless wrote a letter that poses as an eye-witness account to his friend *monsieur* de Viviers, a prelate whose prudence and virtues were too well known to doubt his veracity. Yet, the lie is continued in other accounts, in which Tronchin assisted the patient until his last sigh.

> Imagine if you will all the rage and all the fury of Orestes; you would have but a feeble image of those felt by Voltaire in his last illness. [...] It would be desirable for all our philosophers to have witnessed the remorse and the fury of the dying Voltaire.

Voltaire's secretary, Wagnière, in a letter to the doctor's relative, François Tronchin, a lawyer from the Republic of Geneva, attempts to set the record straight by stating: "Dr. Tronchin did not see Voltaire the day of his death." The lawyer agrees with Voltaire, writing him back that those words attributed to the doctor do not sound like him. "Besides", he continues, "people play great games by attributing the wildest citations to people who are no longer around."

8. Augustin Barruel, a Jesuit priest who always accused Voltaire of having dedicated his life to the destruction of the Christian Church, publishes parts of Dr. Tronchin's letter, and adds his own conjectures.

> [Voltaire's friends present beside his deathbed] will tell us that these terrors and frenetic transports of Voltaire were nothing but the effect of his organs weakened by pain; but this they do in vain, for Voltaire repented of his blasphemies, and of having fought against religion. [...] Voltaire feared a God whom he had outraged. It is the reality of his crimes and not of his fever that made him desperate.

9. The *Gazette de Cologne* in July of 1778 publishes twenty-seven anonymous articles dated from Paris, in which Tronchin's version of Voltaire's death is propagated.

> Moments before his death, M. de V... entered into awful agitations, crying with furor: "I am abandoned by God and by men." He was biting his arms, and bringing his hands into his chamber pot, and seizing what was in it, he ate it. Thus ended the life of the patriarch of the sect that believed to be honored by him.

10. In a later publication, *l'abbé* Barruel, makes another character appear by Voltaire's deathbed, the philosopher's friend the duke of Richelieu. The man of religion equivocates between writing a novel and writing the truth.

> All doors were closed to the priest whom Voltaire had called for. The demons henceforth were alone in gaining free access to him, and soon began the scenes of furor and rage, which continued until his final days. The marshal of Richelieu, witness to this spectacle, ran away saying, "In truth, this is too much, nobody would be able stand it."

11. Voltaire's true friends could see through the priests' wholesale attempts at disinformation. Frederick the Great of Prussia wrote to their mutual friend d'Alembert, on June 15, 1778.

> The most beautiful monument of Voltaire is the one that he erected himself: his works. They will subsist longer than the basilica of Saint Peter, the Louvre, and all those buildings that vanity consecrates to eternity. When French will no longer be spoken, Voltaire will still be translated into the language that will have succeeded it. What an irreparable loss for the arts, and perhaps centuries will pass without producing such a genius!

12. Catherine the Great of Russia was profoundly moved by the death of Voltaire, her philosopher-friend. Having professed for him an enthusiastic admiration, she would tell everyone that she was beholden to him, for all that she had learned from him, for all that she had become. She wrote to their mutual friend Grimm in October, 1778.

> I am his pupil; when younger, I loved to please him; with every act I committed, in order for it to please me, for it to be worthy of being told to him, and right away he was informed of it.

13. Letter from Lien Chi Altangi to Fum Hoam, first president of the ceremonial Academy at Peking, China.

> We have just received accounts here, that Voltaire the poet and philosopher of Europe is dead! He is now beyond the reach of the thousand enemies who, while living, degraded his writings, and branded his character. Scarce a page of his latter productions that does not betray the agonies of a heart bleeding under the scourge of unmerited reproach. Happy therefore at last in escaping from calumny, happy in leaving a world that was unworthy of him and his writings.
> Let others, my friend, bestrew the hearses of the great with panegyric; but such a loss as the world has now suffered affects me with stronger emotions. When a philosopher dies, I consider myself as losing a patron, an instructor, and a friend. I consider the world as losing one who might serve to console her amidst the desolations of war and ambition. Nature every day produces in abundance men capable of

filling all the requisite duties of authority; but she is niggard in the birth of an exalted mind, scarcely producing in a century a single genius to bless and enlighten a degenerate age.

14. Louis Mayeul Chaudon, in his introduction to his book entitled *Historical and Critical Memoirs of the Life and Writings of M. de Voltaire*, published first in French in Amsterdam, translated into English and published in Dublin, seems to view the philosopher's death with a just eye.

There seems to have been a kind of combat, between the priests and the philosophers, for the soul of M. de Voltaire. Every stratagem was used, by the former, to bring him to a recantation, and make him abjure those doctrines and writings, at his death, by which they had been so repeatedly attacked and ridiculed, during his life. The philosophers, on their part, wanted to outwit the priests, and have M. de Voltaire enjoy all the ceremonials they thought his due, rather, perhaps, as a citizen than a Christian, in the Church's despite. The artifices employed by both parties redound not much to the credit of either; and certainly contributed to embitter the last moments of M. de Voltaire. The philosophers ought to have had more philosophy, the Christians more Christianity; that is to say, more charity and less rancour.

15. A letter from *monsieur* Pierre François Muyart de Vouglans: *Motifs de ma foi en Jésus-Christ; Lettre à madame* de ***. *Monsieur* de Vouglans was a judicial magistrate who defended the Catholic Church as the rightful state religion and absolutism as the rightful political system. Voltaire called him the "lawyer from Barbaria."

You are much in alarm, *madame*, about the rapid progress that the Sect which we call the *Philosophy of our times* has made. You cannot hear without shuddering, you say, the horrible blasphemies that these apostles of incredulity do not cease to proffer against our Saintly Religion and its divine Author.

16. From Thomas Carlyle, in his essay on Goethe, 1778.

Voltaire was the cleverest of all past and present men; but a great man is something more, and this he surely was not.

17. From Ricardo Rey Coronado, ancestor of the author, writing from Spain in December, 1778 to his son recently established in Guatemala as an attorney in the offices of the viceroy. After the earthquakes of 1751 and 1775, which demolished the ancient capital, a new city was built some twenty-five miles farther away from the volcano that had caused the destruction. Construction was proceeding apace, and squabbles over land-grabbing were proliferating even faster, making it necessary to import lawyers from the mother country.

My son, you make me proud of your successes in New Spain, and your mother and I are ecstatic that you have located a prospective wife among the Spanish families who have rebuilt their houses and their lives in the new capital. The Luna family of which you speak is originally from Asturias, and at first glance stems from staid, catholic stock. However, I have seen that last name among others in an old manuscript citing the list of *conversos*, so we are even happier that you might be marrying into an originally jewish family. Observe them well, perhaps they have kept some of the old ways, but if you discover some proof that they were jewish, keep it to yourself: the Inquisition is rampant and fanatical in New Spain, as you know. The priests would do anything, even if it were just extortion demanded of a nice, catholic family with a skeleton in their closet, just for pecuniary gain. Steer clear of the priests, my son. Steer clear of the priests, especially, and expressly, when you think you need one. Don't give in to the temptation, for it will be your last. The tenacity of priests is like that of intestinal parasites: in order to get rid of them, the host is frequently sacrificed as well.

[…]

It is with trepidation that I announce to you the news that the French philosopher Voltaire has died. Some say that he died peacefully in his sleep, in spite of great pain occasioned by cancer of the prostate, which was the malady that finally killed him. Others say that he died in agony, afraid of going to hell, and cursing his philosopher friends of having flattered his writings, of having encouraged his denouncement of the church into which he was born and thereby having cut off his path to heaven. I have a tendency to believe the first version, for I have learned from Montaigne that philosophy offers sweet succor in the face of the fear of death, and that the priests can only offer a duality, heaven or hell, that leaves many questions unanswered and that smells heavily of that excrement that the clerics like to ladle into credulous minds. To say nothing of Limbo. Besides, priests plague the dying so that guilt might pry a few more coins from their skeletal hands.

But I am terrified lest we have lost the *primo uomo* of the Enlightenment, for it might create a vacuum that will temporarily leave the philosophers, if not exactly aimless, at least desultory in their mourning. Without a leader to keep them moving, they might find the church taking advantage and beginning to outflank them. The philosophers must not give up either their direction or their impetus; to do either will only improve the ecclesiastical challenge and badly sap their own strength. Already I see poets in Germany stirring against philosophy and giving way to a strange amalgam of the Romanesque, neoplatonism, and feudal ideas of love. This cannot bode well for our hard-fought scientific conquests. If Science and Reason are again eclipsed, we might as well join our ancestor, Francisco Vásquez de Coronado y Luján, in his futile search for the golden cities of Cibola!

Remain steady, my boy, for victory may be at hand. Voltaire's arrival in Paris unleashed a new component in our arsenal against the church: the rising visage of public opinion. Voltaire gave the common man the courage to think, quietly inside his own head, but then to communicate those thoughts to those around him. There is now a murmur of thoughts racing across Paris, across France, and even—can you believe it?—slipping across the Pyrenees into Spain. No nobleman can curtail it, for the *chevalier* de Rohan who had the young Voltaire beaten around the head for his insolence, would no longer dare to repeat his act, for there would be ten men running to the assistance of the victim. No priest can curtail it either, for religion's wares have become tarnished with the rust of ages. We are feeling our oats, and we are feeling worthy of the man who gave us the courage to stand up for fairness, for justice. He didn't see a revolution coming, but there is one coming for sure, for the old ways of the aristocracy, of theology, and of their united strength in absolutism, must finally give way.

In the meantime, keep a low profile, keep our encryption code a secret,[29] and, my dear boy, *écrasez l'Infâme!*

---

29   This encryption code was passed from father to son in the Luna Coronado family until the author was able to make use of it. Today, of course, it is no longer unsafe to publish such family matters.

Part 2

Expedition to Save a Library

Secret Convocations

T he sonorous, masculine voice filled the void without difficulty. It was a fine oratory instrument, honed by decades of sermons projected into the largest cathedrals, modulated by the acoustics of the most sumptuous halls. It amplified by dint of muscular diaphragm and reached out in all directions, ran down nave and transept, and echoed off the high vaults that were visible only barely through the smoke of a thousand candles. No mass had been offered; this was a convocation curtailed to the crucial business of the day. These were no ordinary times. These were times to test the mettle of each of those here gathered, to confirm their resolve, to organize their determination, for these were preparations for war. Their warrior-leader had spoken at length about their commitment and tenacity, about unbound energy, about truth being on their side, and in classic rhetorical form was now proceeding to his conclusion with a stentorian zeal whose emotive vibrations God in heaven would be able to hear.

"This so-called Age of Enlightenment that brings forth the light of knowledge can only end badly, for it is but an attack on civilization as we know it, and it brings forth doubt and conflict, confusion and upheaval, and above all, in the long run, suspicion. Suspicion of everybody: of those who are responsible for the coming of the new Science which, fortunately for us, is dead on arrival, but suspicion also for us, the clergy, those of us whose lives are dedicated to the well-being of souls and to the health of society, those of us who care about the clamor and the skepticism and the confusion that philosophers bring, troublesome creatures that they are, *they* care nothing for the well-being of the soul and the health of society. They broadcast their poison to all and sundry, and do not linger long enough to know that the seeds of suspicion have sprouted, against them as well, might I add. They themselves undermine the very ground on which they walk: what one man of science offers as truth, another one scoffs at and offers an alternate truth. Science is a monster, a Hydra with many heads, intractable and pervasive, and it brings with it the advance of impiety, with its never-ending but ever-changing tropes of a destabilizing philosophy that takes hold of a man's imagination in his youth, perverts his education, and forces the young man to disengage from the most sacred principles of morality and of religion that civilization has ever known, those proven by the centuries to be good and true, principles that have safeguarded the immutability of civilization, principles whose intentions have been tested by those very centuries, and which have succeeded persistently, namely, in saving men's souls and directing them to everlasting salvation. To those besotted with science, nothing else matters, nothing else is crucial; the soul falls by the wayside, as does the care of the soul. To those led astray by science, the soul might as well not even exist. Science can only corrode, while it purports to free humanity; all it does is penetrate young minds with its poisoned doctrines. No land is free from it, no class of society either, and we have seen how its convoluted precepts have touched, and tainted, even those upon the throne. In the case of Russia, the Empress consorts with all kinds of riffraff philosophers, corresponding with them, feeding and housing them as if they were her pets, but in her case we have the example, and the excuse, that she is a woman, and like all women—weak!—they are most easily led astray, since their religious convictions spring forth from Eve and are therefore pathetically deficient and easily diverted. In the case of Prussia, we have the example of a man who might as well be a woman, whose father before him kept regiments of tall, handsome soldiers, with whom to play at war and socialize for weeks at a time, with whom he bivouacked! With whom he held congress! Then contagion of this sort of diversion seems to have been passed on to the effeminate son, and that unnatural desire to be surrounded by strong, young men emasculated the Prince and left him open to hysteria and to science, made him available to all sorts of influence from those peddling philosophy and encyclopedias. When he in turn became King, he invited into his bosom a man whose name shall not be mentioned within these hallowed walls, the very Antichrist of philosophy,[30] harbored him for years, listened to his obfuscations, his incantations, his misleading cogitations, and became the diseased, inverted sovereign he is today.

"Thank the Lord that the King of France is different from the diffident and susceptible monarchs of Russia and Prussia! Praise God! Let's lift our spirits to God who keeps our French king strong and voluble against the new education that, under the appearance of the so-called *enlightenment* conducts children to the destruction of all religious and moral principles, as well as to the subversion of the proper social hierarchy. Let's offer our prayers to almighty God who keeps the heavens in running order and who has given us the earth as His gift, to keep His Royal Majesty firm and stern in his beliefs in the Holy Roman Catholic Church, and may he not equate mercy with indulgence or generosity with weakness, but let him always see the need of severity to uphold his Christian doctrines aloft, so that France will forever adhere to the dogmas of Rome and entreat the solicitude of our cherished pontiff; may they both reign for decades, like His Majesty's predecessors Louis XIV and Louis XV. May our loving Monarch inspire the entire nation with courage and fortitude, and sweep the enlightenment away, just like our Lord Jesus swept the money-changers away from the temple. The greed of philosophers and the sinfulness of science must be extricated from society like an ulcer from within its body. Religion, our religion, that of the Holy Roman Catholic Church, shall long reign, for it represents the truth, the only truth that matters, because science is only of the moment, and it harbors within it no succor for the soul, and will guide that soul away from God and all that is good, and lead it directly, ineluctably, towards perdition."

Christophe de Beaumont, Archbishop of Paris, Duke of Saint Cloud, Peer of France, Commander of the Royal Order of the Holy Ghost, Principal of the Sorbonne, etc., etc., brushed a wisp of hair that had escaped his miter during the spirited communication to his congregation of ecclesiastics. For this special assembly they were in the Cathedral of Notre-Dame, filling it to capacity. His Grace, the Most Reverend Archbishop, saw how successful he had been, for all were beseeching God in voluble prayer to keep their King safe and strong for the battle that was upon them. The vaults reverberated

---

30   It was, of course, Voltaire whom Frédéric II to his palace at Sans-Souci invited, for two years, 1750-1753.

in the crumbling old cathedral with their pleas to God. They were soldiers of God, and they felt within their souls that they had the wherewithal to uphold, and the power to defend, their faith. Their faith which was under attack from all sides, from the nobles, the merchants, the poor, from foreigners who arrived in Paris daily by the droves, and especially from the philosopher class, who appeared to do battle with glee, who cared not a whit for the salvation of the people, who fooled the people into believing inconsequential nonsense and left them naked and vulnerable, unable to fight off the incursions of the Evil One. The congregation of priests was energized, ready to do battle, willing to go forth and destroy Lucifer's minions, in order to extinguish the false light of science, in order to crush the followers of Voltaire, whoever they were, wherever they might be. The arm of the Church was long, and with the concerted effort of everybody in that cavernous nave, evil would be dispelled, and the followers of evil annihilated.

At that very moment, two of Lucifer's warriors were quietly at work, their long quills dancing in the air over their task. They labored in the very den of Lucifer, the crux of his earthly manifestation: the library of Voltaire in Ferney. Calm, methodical, the two soldiers of Satan wrote down the words of their general Voltaire, in order to save them from possible destruction. Voltaire's editor and bookseller, Panckoucke, was next in line to take over these diabolical words, these depraved texts, with the infernal task of publishing them, to disperse them widely throughout Christendom, indeed, throughout the world, so that the darkness of Lucifer, the fallen angel, he who lusted after the souls of men, would settle everywhere and help to destroy the benevolence of religion. In the meantime, Beaumarchais, the devilishly confident playwright and supporter of the American revolutionaries, was preparing his strategy to publish all of Voltaire's œuvre, bound in morocco leather and printed on heavy, high-quality paper, with gilt lettering on the spine. He would spare no expense, and might have to buy a paper mill or two to control the quality of the paper. The copyists and the editors toiled in unison to save the words of the sage, to propagate sedition throughout the world.

These followers of Voltaire, of course, held a completely disparate opinion of what they were after: they toiled in order to have the philosopher's words liberate men from their docile lives of captive indoctrination, in order to destroy the darkness of superstition, and to squelch the infamous double-headed dragon of government and cult.

Wagnière and Zénobe wrote as fast as they could. They knew that time was not on their side.

Meeting the Creator of Figaro, and His Publisher

Pierre-Augustin Caron de Beaumarchais, fop, watchmaker, musician, playwright, diplomat, arms dealer to the Americans, friend of Benjamin Franklin, confidant of the *chevalier* d'Éon, and now editor of the first posthumous edition of Voltaire's complete works, seconded by the philosopher's publisher, Charles Joseph Panckoucke, irrupted noisily into the tranquillity of Ferney. With ebullience and an oversized sense of humor, Beaumarchais could not stand silence to intrude into a conversation, and regaled his audience—the whole world was his audience, and he was forever onstage— with excerpts from his second Figaro comedy, *La Folle journée, ou le Mariage de Figaro*, which he was in the process of writing. He would recall funny adventures in the world of espionage and diplomacy, spilling secrets from the French Foreign Minister, the *comte* de Vergennes, or Lord Stormont, the British ambassador, or even the *conde* de Aranda, Spain's ambassador in Versailles, along with Aranda's political and private enemy, the Prime Minister of Spain, the *conde* de Floridablanca, changing from one language to the next as he alternated from the British retinue to the Spanish court to the French aristocrats. Not being an aristocrat himself, he appropriated the freedom to deride the upper classes with the aplomb of somebody who had made it into their milieu. Beaumarchais could tell them a million details about the French royal family for he had been music tutor to Louis XV's daughters, teaching them the harp, and learning from them the latest gossip. He himself would say that there is nothing like being in the middle of the vipers' nest to learn the choicest confidences of European aristocracy. Since he still kept in touch with the Royal Aunts, he was still among the first to know about the most recent clashes between the royal ladies' niece-in-law, Marie Antoinette, and her husband Louis XVI. The aunts had no sympathy for the Austrian queen, snubbed her whenever possible, and spread rumors about her, even, perhaps especially, when they knew them to be false. That they were indirectly disparaging their own nephew, His Royal Majesty the King of France, brought them no qualms.

Beaumarchais had entered Ferney with the deference and mourning he owed to Voltaire, his superior, and looked on with great sorrow at the old man's château and the possessions therein. He already knew that the *marquis* de Villette had bought the place, château, grounds and village, from Voltaire's niece *madame* Denis. He also knew that Villette would make a muck of Voltaire's skillful administration of the domain, including interference in the principal trade of Ferney, watchmaking. Time was up for his brethren the watchmakers.

But that evening at dinner, the irrepressible Beaumarchais let his humor escape. The story of how Beaumarchais was nearly killed as he raced into Paris with news of the American victory at Saratoga was met with hilarity, as he told them of his carriage reaching a new speed record and momentarily being released from its hold on gravity and taking to the air, his postillion unable to control it.

"When gravity finally returned, the carriage landed on one wheel and overturned in a shower of glass shards, one of which penetrated halfway into my right arm. The pain was almost as bad as having a play panned. Of course, the Paris newspapers reported the news of my accident, but nothing on Saratoga. All that hurrying for naught!"

After a moment of contemplation, he added, "All my life, my personal sacrifices, which have come at great cost to me, have served for no apparent purpose. Even my writing, whose purpose is principally to entertain, has brought me nothing but grief and condemnation. Her Majesty the Queen likes my work, but her husband has banned it from the court. Yet, he still relies on me to do the dirty work with the British, and insists that I carry on equipping the Continental Army with uniforms and arms while he pretends to look the other away. Ah, well, the aristocrats were the ones to invent hypocrisy, actually making it imposing and gallant and have it resemble a shining virtue!"

Zénobe could not help stepping in. "The clergy, *monsieur*, the clergy are also adept at hypocrisy!"

"Yes, of course, but theirs is a brand of hypocrisy that is much more pedestrian. The type of, well, chastity is a virtue, but only a temporary one. When you consider the high art that hypocrisy has become in the able bearing of a *madame* de Polignac, let's say, who gives her husband horns through *liaisons discrètes* only with lovers of the highest social echelons."

This last made Zénobe blush to his hairline out of a startled sense of propriety, and Beaumarchais made a mental note of it.

The playwright also knew how to make them shed tears, being the dramatist that he was, including Zénobe, when relating the story of the death of Jean-Jacques Rousseau who had died in July. Rousseau had returned from his usual morning walk and was at the breakfast table having a conversation with his wife, Thérèse. He was complaining about a headache, but suddenly fell into silence, and when Thérèse peered into his face, found that he was no longer of this earth. His friend, the *marquis* de Girardin, had his remains entombed on the Island of Poplars in the middle of a lake on his estate of Ermenonville, surrounded by the circles within circles that the philosopher so loved.

"He exasperated all of us," said Beaumarchais wistfully, "especially his closest friends, with his leave-no-stone-unturned memoirs, and now he enjoys universal bereavement, in an idyllic place, now that his pen is forever silent. People are happy that he can foment no more trouble!"

Then he turned his face dramatically to the heavens, as if that was where Rousseau had ascended, in the company of harp-playing seraphs, and said, "He did not compete directly with me, for he wrote no plays, nor I with him, for I wrote no philosophical pronouncements, but he did win me over with his ideas of the Primitive Man. Now, my Figaro is no naïve, and he's not an anti-social kind of lad, but his heart is pure, even though he schemes with every breath he takes, but that is only as a defense mechanism against the world, which at his every step schemes horribly against him. This purity of heart I took from Rousseau, for I truly believe, that in his heart, Rousseau was also pure."

Zénobe blushed again, this time out of guilt. He now regretted having yelled at Rousseau the day he came to his home looking for André and finding the *chevalière* d'Éon also present. But Rousseau's disrespectful remarks about the *chevalière*'s dubious sexuality had riled Zénobe. Who did Rousseau think he was that he should judge others, especially when he himself had been so harshly judged throughout his life? Yet Zénobe thought that now that the writer was dead, he deserved to be remembered for his texts, some of which were very interesting. Rousseau just never knew how to laugh, being a protestant, and his glumness took him into places too dark, too severe, where jealousies and narcissism, suspicion and mistrust, and never-ending delusions of persecution, disheartened him and made him unable to love humanity.

But Beaumarchais had kept talking, and Zénobe snapped back to attention because the humorist had now changed subjects and was speaking of Louis XVI's brothers and their wives. Both *le comte* de Provence and *le comte* d'Artois had married princesses of Savoy, and Beaumarchais was voicing his intentions, while he was in the region, of traveling to Turin where Victor Amédée III reigned over his far-flung lands. Preparations were underway to celebrate his fifth anniversary as monarch of Turin, Piedmont, Sardinia, Savoy and Aosta, "and I want to be there to congratulate him, and to tell him that his daughters Marie-Josèphe-Louise and Marie-Thérèse de Savoie are not the happiest princesses in the world. Along with Marie Antoinette of Austria they are known as the "foreign queens" and made fun of. They're your stepsisters…"

Here, Beaumarchais sought out Zénobe seated across from him at the dining room table. He was interested in this young man who, while in Paris, had been the object of a rumor that supposed him to be the bastard son of Victor Amédée III. "They're your stepsisters, after all, and perhaps you should help them to improve their positions at court."

Zénobe's face reddened once again, but this time it was no blush. He was astounded that Beaumarchais even gave credence to this rumor. What a social climber, thought the young man. He assumes that everyone is like him, that we all hold as our heart's desire to climb the rungs of the social hierarchy in order to reach the nobility.

"This Tyrant of Sardinia of whom you speak is not my father," Zénobe said, trying to put into his voice as much hostility as he could muster. "He's not even my king," he spat out. "His daughters are not my sisters. It was because of this family's vile despotism that my father was murdered in Savoy. I shall go visit my real sisters while those two whores join the whole pimping family in Turin."[31]

The company seated around the table were not horrified by Zénobe's outburst, being used to his animosity against the idiot aristos. Besides, they knew the story of how his father was made into an example for those who dared to wrangle against the feudal laws of the Sardinian king. Beaumarchais was not troubled, either, by the young man's vituperative comments against the gentry, for he had seen much, had suffered much under the mandates of the ruling class, and what he had not seen or suffered himself, he had written down in his plays. On the contrary, he seemed bemused by Zénobe's comments, but in a surge of generosity for the hot-tempered lad, he then answered with an overly doleful tone. "Not all of Figaro's pride and independence works in the real

---

31 The latest scion of this royal family is still at it: in 2006, Vittorio Emanuele was arrested in Italy under charges of having engaged prostitutes. In France, he had previously been tried on a murder charge, and everywhere he is known for his anti-semitism, commenting that the Mussolini regime was "not so terrible." More recently, he requested from the Italian government 210 million euros for the restitution of properties confiscated from his ancestors. It is doubtful he will even get an apology.

world, my young friend. Sometimes one does need friends in high places in order to succeed. Your mentor Voltaire should have taught you that. Also, *madame* de Polignac does not consort with commoners."

This last line, uttered in a dramatic stage-whisper, meant nothing to the company around the dining table. However, to Zénobe it meant volumes. The thought that the *duchesse* de Polignac was the authoress of the rumor that Zénobe was the scion of the King of Sardinia was breathtaking. If ever it had been found out that Polignac and he had been involved in a secret liaison, she would have been lauded for a brilliant dalliance with the son of a king, it being of no special consequence if he were a bastard son. Had it come to light that she had given herself to a servant at the *hôtel* de Villette—the truth was even worse—a peasant from Savoy, she would never have been able to live it down. In order to raise her status, perhaps due to her own pride, she had concocted this lie to protect herself, and which at the same time raised Zénobe's social prospects. He saw that Beaumarchais had been following his facial expressions, and that the playwright seemed pleased that his words had provoked such a cogitative reaction.

For Zénobe, the immediate reaction to the news that Beaumarchais had brought was to formulate his plans to visit his family in Annecy. With the royal family celebrating in Turin this would be the safest time to do so. He also promised himself to call on his old preceptor, Father Anselme, in whose hands he had received the nurturing and education which enabled Zénobe to become Voltaire's secretary, and in turn, Voltaire's protector, defender, and eventually, the philosopher's successor in revolution.

Villette Arrives to Oversee His Domain

O f course, the best of plans are rendered awry with the advent of a single, inopportune event. Zénobe would have to wait an entire fortnight before he was able to resume his objective.

Zénobe had been ready to leave for Annecy, secretively and under the stealth of night, when an overly excited, and a very boisterous, *marquis* de Villette punctured the peace and silence of Ferney, right in time for supper. The new owner of Ferney was come from Paris so full of aspirations and designs to enlighten the inhabitants of the château, as well as the townsfolk and the farmers, that things here would never be the same again. The aristocrat had projects, with accompanying designs and contracts, to render the proceedings of the domain more straightforward, less elaborate, and therefore more comprehensible to himself. Voltaire's way of doing things was too demanding, requiring much personal involvement and too much strategy, and absolutely ridiculous financial outlays and subventions to keep the watchmaking trade viable. No, the *marquis* was here to improve the system, to reeducate the workers, to modernize the operation. Not for him would be the subsidies with his own money that Voltaire used to exercise with his tenant craftsmen. With Villette now as the master, if Catherine the Great wanted to purchase more watches from Ferney, she could just as well forward the full costs in advance. With Villette, it was buy now, pay first. And the money would flow from the Empress to the watch people to the butcher and the baker, raining down to the farmers and the goatherds. Money always flows down, as his father the banker used to say. It never flows up. I will not interfere with economical progress, said Villette to himself.

Zénobe insulted all of the ancient gods of destiny for this encroachment from his previous master, and cursed in particular the trio of Christian gods for the master's new agenda. This time it entailed not just a library, but a whole country house with dozens of servants, and a whole town in the environs, home to a thousand workers and their families, to say nothing of the hundreds of farm laborers who kept everybody fed. Under Voltaire, the synchronous workings of the village had been smooth and self-winding, with just a few corrective movements every now and then. Zénobe cringed under the overbearing and self-serving instructions that began to rain on them from the very first evening.

Wagnière and Zénobe had just bid adieu to Beaumarchais and Panckoucke, the playwright departing with intricate resolutions and projects for the monumental publication of Voltaire's complete works. Beaumarchais would take on the responsibility of where, how, and when to go about it. It could not be in France, because of the onerous censorship to be suffered there, but it had to be close to France, for ease of transportation. He could not leave himself open to blackmail or to extortion, so Beaumarchais would have to control the place of publication as well as the tools, such as paper, type and ink. Once started, nobody would be able to interrupt, delay, or alter the enterprise. After Turin, Beaumarchais would travel to see where in Europe, close to France's borders, the Voltaireans would be able to set up shop. The secretaries were just weeks away from finishing their task of transcribing Voltaire's manuscripts, and Beaumarchais and Panckoucke had left Ferney full of optimism.

Had they known that Villette was coming, they would perhaps have left with some misgivings, or perhaps they would not have left at all.

"Have all the watchmakers prepare to hand over their books. I wish to inspect them within the next few days." This order was given as Villette was enjoying his first glass of *xérez*.

"Write up a list of manufacturers of springs and cogs and everything else that goes into our watches. Including gems and precious metals. From now on, I want all suppliers to be French, not Swiss, and—heaven forbid!—not German!" This was given after the main course.

And between his second and third cups of hot chocolate, he gave his next command. "I also want a list of those who have not yet paid up in full, especially Catherine of Russia. She has way too much money and does not need letters of credit. Her representative in Paris, the baron von Grimm,[32] can write to her and explain that the domain of Ferney is under new management. If she doesn't like it, she can buy her watches elsewhere."

But Villette had not arrived just with schemes and enterprising initiatives. In-between the other courses of his supper, he instructed that a packet of correspondence be given to his librarian Zénobe, letters from André and Thibouville in Normandy, by way of Paris, and from *monsieur* Maurel. Zénobe greedily took the packet and looked forward to reading the letters later on that night. Villette also announced the news, without qualm or tinge of chagrin (although it was confidentially addressed only to Zénobe and Wagnière) that his wife had had a miscarriage. He blamed the calamity on the miasma that had arisen from Voltaire's sickbed. But what made Zénobe queasy, and almost faint, and then made him weep copious tears, were the contents of an elaborately wrought Grecian-style urn, which the *marquis* placed, after dessert, in the middle of the dining room table.

"We shall place this prominently in Voltaire's bedroom," he announced.

"What is it?" asked Wagnière with trepidation.

"Why, it's Voltaire's heart!"

Zénobe looked up at the man who so cavalierly had transported so sacred a relic.

"It's… Voltaire's… it's Voltaire's heart?" he managed to stammer.

"Yes, indeed. And people will continue to visit Ferney from all corners of the globe, just like they used to. Only this time, it will be to visit Voltaire's heart. We will set it up

---

32   Friedrich Melchior, baron von Grimm, born in Regensburg, became a friend of the *philosophes* and helped propagate their ideas with his editorship of the *Correspondance littéraire* (1753-1790), addressed to the crowned heads of Europe. He aided in the purchase of Diderot's library by Catherine II of Russia in 1766 when the philosopher needed funds for his daughter's dowry. He introduced Diderot to Her Imperial Majesty when Diderot came to Saint Petersburg in 1773.

in his bedroom and make a shrine for him. People will love it! We'll rent rooms upstairs for the well-heeled. The rest can muck in with the villagers."

With a look to Zénobe, Wagnière took the vase in nimble fingers before the young man could do mischief with it.

"Yes, *monsieur le marquis*," he said quickly, inventing what to say as he spoke. "That is an excellent idea. People will continue to come and pay their respects to the great Voltaire, the venerable philosopher of Europe, the patriarch of Ferney, and there will be no need for foreigners to remove this hallowed site, the seat of Reason and of… of… of Enlightenment, from their list of places to visit on their tour of the Continent. They will, they will… Ferney will still be known as the very center of philosophy, a role that it has been playing for the past thirty years. And, and, and… And this heart, this revered and beloved heart, the heart belonging to our friend, will continue to symbolize his presence and influence, and prolong his influence, just as very soon the edition of his complete works will do the same."

Villette had heard nothing of this edition of the complete works of Voltaire. He began to ask Voltaire's secretary numerous questions about it.

In the interim, Zénobe had to leave the room. Tears strangled his constricted throat, his chest expanded with battling emotions, ready to explode in spasms, and his red fists with blanched knuckles were aching to find solace somewhere on the pink skin of the *marquis* de Villette's face.

Letters from Loved Ones

from the Corday residence
63 rue de Géole
à côté du Château de Caen
Caen, Normandy
the 3rd of September, 1778

My dearest Zénobe,

As I write you from Normandy I hear the rustling the wind makes as it rushes through the branches of the apple trees. The boughs are laden with fruit. Soon it will be harvest time and we shall all be very busy, my father and mother, and especially my sister Charlotte, who sorely needs to be distracted. She has been inconsolable since the death of Rousseau, and regrets enormously that she didn't make the attempt to go to Paris to meet him. I've told her numerous times that it would have been a wasted effort, that the great writer would not have stooped to greet a mere schoolgirl. I've told her about our visit, of course. Rousseau is her hero, just as Voltaire is yours. She's had me describe Rousseau's every gesture, his every utterance, his every sigh, numerous times. What was he wearing, what did he talk about, how did he treat us? I told her how he greeted us warmly, until the *chevalière* d'Éon barged in, and then how he threw us out. Charlotte is thoroughly scandalized by that part. She cannot conceive of any friend of mine talking back to such a celebrated philosopher, and thinks of you as a beastly, uncouth person. You must have been bred by wolves in a wilderness far from people. She doesn't know you, of course, the way I do, and she doesn't understand about *la chevalière*, and how you needed to come to her defense. Charlotte is far too young to understand who, or what, *la chevalière* is. Frankly, I have difficulties as well, for d'Éon is truly Nature's enigma, although I love her in spades, especially since she saved you from drowning.

I have been speaking about you to my parents, although not the parts that would scandalize them. They recognize your courage in going to Ferney to save Voltaire's library. They worry about a friend of mine doing things that would annoy the priests. It's folly, they say, to agitate the meddlesome priests, for they have ways of chastising the unruly. Remember what happened to the *chevalier* de la Barre, for «crimes» far less serious than yours.[33] Voltaire's *Dictionnaire philosophique* was found among his things. I think the priests planted it there. You travel with a dozen of Voltaire's banned books. You would travel with all of the volumes of the *Encyclopédie* if you could. I admire you for it. I am sorry not to be with you to share in the responsibility of protecting Voltaire's library, but I am truly remorseful about not being there to protect you. With one word you could have me by your side. I could be there in a week. I know that Wagnière is with you, but he doesn't know how to fence. You taught me well enough that I would be able to protect you. My only ambition in life is to make sure you are well and safe and far from danger. Away from you, I am powerless to do anything about it. I think of you all the time, and at night you are in my dreams. When shall we see each other again? Your trip to Saint Petersburg will take months, and you will be going through areas of Europe in control of those mad priests. Ah! Why can't they all reform and see that catholicism is as arbitrary a religion as could exist, full of invented and bewildering rules and rituals that make no sense. Why do men uncover their heads when entering a church, and women have to cover theirs? Why no meat on Friday, when the wealthy make the sacrifice by having lobster brought in at great cost from the coast? I better stop raging against the catholic beast before they come and get me. I need to be around to come to your protection. Just say the word, *mon cher ami*, and I'll be with you in a few days.

Until that happy day when I can once again hold you in my arms, I pray, cancel that, I hope that you'll be well, far from danger, and happy in your efforts to save Voltaire's library.

Your loving friend,
André

Zénobe shed tears over his friend's letter. He also felt a bit guilty in that until recently he had been sharing a bed with the young farmer Gil Blas, who had just as expediently also offered his services as his defender, then as a secretary. But Zénobe shrugged off the guilt as a useless emotion, for his main efforts and all of his energy were dedicated to the preservation of Voltaire's manuscripts, and to the organization and stowage of the philosopher's books, in readiness to transport them to Russia. He didn't feel it was even necessary to mention Gil's existence.

He wrote back to André:

Château de Ferney
October 25th, 1778

Dear André,

---

33   The *chevalier* de la Barre was the young man tortured, beheaded and burned in 1765 for not having doffed his hat during a religious procession.

Please don't think of coming to Ferney with the idea of defending me and helping me to protect Voltaire's library. There is absolutely no danger here. The priests do not dare enter the domain, for most of it is on the Genevan side, and the protestant clergy would not be pleased at all to know that the papists were invading their territory. It would be Saint Bartholomew all over again, except that in this case it would be the Reformers exterminating the catholics. Well do they deserve it! But for the time being, everything is calm and orderly, and the only thing being lacerated is ream upon ream of paper, as we toil day and night to copy Voltaire's manuscripts. The fingers of my left hand are permanently black.

I should say that the voyage to Saint Petersburg and back should last two or three months. We need to hurry, for the winter in Russia is as harsh as the protestants, and we won't want to linger in Saint Petersburg. As it is, during the last leg of our trip, we will most probably have to find berths on a ship to take us from Lübeck to Kronstadt. Going overland would be much too dangerous, even with the diplomatic passports that Wagnière is planning to get from Geneva.

Wagnière has asked me to tell you not to come to Ferney. He absolutely does not want to worry about another person. He says that we cannot know what will happen when we cross Prussian territory; Frederick might try to have us detained; he might try to wrest from our possession his own correspondence to Voltaire. Wagnière mysteriously insinuates with raised eyebrows that I would be in particular danger were Frederick to halt our progress. I'm not sure why Voltaire's secretary feels that he wouldn't be in particular danger as well.[34] [35] It was he who was asked by Catherine to accompany Voltaire's library to Saint Petersburg, not I.

In any case, we're almost done transcribing Voltaire's manuscripts, and once Villette leaves the premises, I should be able to take off for a few days to visit my sisters in Annecy. I will do it in the secret of night, for Savoy is crawling with tonsured creatures who would love to offer me up to their god as a sacrifice. They can't stand to live while they know that I'm still alive. They rage against my continued existence, and wonder why their god hasn't struck me with an avenging bolt of

---

34 [From the author] Here is incontrovertible proof that Zénobe and his fictional counterpart, Candide, share many characteristics, including both virtues and vices. Here we observe his *naïveté*, his ignorance of the hidden motives of connivers, and his innocence in matters sexual. Frederick would love to add Zénobe to his favorite battalion, made up of inordinately tall and handsome men. At 1m83 (6'0"), Zénobe would have fit the bill to perfection. In the same manner, Candide (at 5'5") is forced to join the Bulgar regiment and carted off to war. In addition, Frederick would no doubt designate Zénobe as a personal decoration in his bedchamber.

35 [From the fact-checker] No doubt this would have been true, save for the inconvenient fact that Frederick II had, shortly after he came to power, his father Frederick William's battalion of handsome giants disbanded. Not that the son didn't appreciate the aesthetics of such a fine regiment, but the upkeep was way too expensive, and the costs of buying the men from surrounding countries increasingly prohibitive. I do agree, however, with the presumption that young Zénobe would at the acquisitive hands of Frederick II his personal liberty risk.

lightning. I'll tell you why: their god exists only in fanciful texts, written originally by deranged men, collected subsequently by evil men, to instill fear in cowardly men. Everyone colludes to make of this bible the word of god, but no one bothers to say out loud that the bible groans under its flaws and incongruities, that it reeks of fabricated deceit whose main purpose is to lead men astray, for anyone with a sense of logic and proportion can sniff out the inconsistencies and the lies. People allow themselves to be deluded, for a false sense of comfort. They prefer to think of a pink-clouded heaven, with wingèd cherubim hovering around a bearded god wearing a mantle of gossamer light. How consoling, what beauty, what seraphic ecstasy! With bliss like that, who wants to think of death as final? Who wants to think that we shall never see our loved ones ever again? But no matter how hard people want to believe in an ethereal heaven and in a stern but loving god, this dream of theirs is an unmitigated putrefaction fabricated by the clergy. Voltaire said it best: "Religion was born when the first hypocrite met the first fool."[36] The proof: all that money collected by the church. The priests have certainly been successful in creating a business for which people will pay, even as the deceived idiots take food out of their children's mouths, but they pay out of fear and ignorance, and some from the extortion imposed by the church. Oh, what a pack of thieving wolves these priests are! But let me not waste another sheet of paper on them.

Our master, the *marquis* de Villette, has made a muddle of things in Ferney. He has changed the financial system, refuses to give credit to the aristos, including monarchs—especially monarchs, I think—and demands money up front before any article is dispatched. He also refuses to advance any money to the tradesmen themselves. Instead, he has set up a bank, and has made each worker open an account with him, and forces everyone to keep a minimum sum, which he calls "the basis" and from which the workers will be allowed to borrow, but with interest if they go below the sum. The watchmakers are up in arms, and some of them want to return to Geneva. But for some of them, it's been twenty or thirty years since they left Geneva. Of course, the Genevans don't want to take them back. They say that the workers who made their bets on Voltaire should now stay where they are and reap what they sowed. Geneva has gotten along very well without them. Ah, the protestants aren't any better at learning lessons of kindness and generosity. We're talking about their own brethren! But they feel that those who left to be with Voltaire were ingrates, and now they can very well eat their just desserts. Just desserts are bitter, indeed, and need lots of wine to wash them down.

The land laborers are still free, thank the gods, to do whatever they want. If Villette had changed one iota of their lot, he would have me to contend with. Just a few leagues away is Savoy, where the farmers still have no freedom. Their lot has not changed in centuries, and they are still forced to till exactly what their lords want them to till, and to cultivate a certain amount to fulfill the quota of their rent, since they don't own the land on which they labor. If it is a bad growing season, too bad, they must still fulfill the quota. The lord and his family get fed first, along with all the hungry clergy. The farmer's family always comes third, if at all. No one is allowed to leave, to marry as they wish, or to decide who is going to live where. If a farmer dies without leaving an heir to till the soil, the whole family is ousted from a place where generations of them have lived. They eke out an existence where the future is an eternal reflection of the past, where lives are wasted and the very will to live is shattered. The farmers of Savoy, like the serfs in all the remaining feudal lands of Europe, are a broken people, illiterate, starving, truly the wretched of the earth. Their only hope is to die and go to a better life, in heaven. One's heart goes out to them, and one doesn't want to kill their last and only hope. But I'd rather go to Savoy and rid the farmers of their true problem: the landowners and the bloody priests who don't allow the serfs to be educated or to improve their lot by better agricultural practices, who don't allow them the freedom to come and go as they please. The landowners don't realize that if their serfs were happier, healthier, better fed, the results would be better for everybody. Look at the Americans who are fighting for their freedom against their own tyrants. And they're being successful, too! It fills me with an eagerness to do the same for my people in Savoy. I am determined, one day, to teach Victor Amadeus a lesson, and his cruel overseer Lovera di Maria.[37] He's the one responsible for the death of my father, and for my father's sons all having had to take flight away from their homeland. My day of revenge will come soon enough.

But enough of these distasteful subjects. I am happy for the work we've done on Voltaire's manuscripts. Future generations will show their gratitude to Wagnière for having saved them from the maws of the Empress. Catherine would have us believe that she is an enlightened despot for corresponding with the *philosophes*, for having invited Diderot to live with her, for dabbling in the reading of fine literature and philosophical treaties, and in having herself surrounded by the products of high art and culture. But deep down, she is still a German who does not trust in what the *philosophes* have been saying for decades. Free the people; give them liberty and the chance to pursue their desires, and their happiness will help improve the condition of the rest of society. One cannot have a huge percentage of a population kept down in the mud for much longer. The winds of freedom are wafting in the air, and they will sweep across the Atlantic and throughout Europe and

---

37   Reminder to the reader: Victor Amadeus III was duke of Savoy and king of Sardinia. When the French Revolution breaks out, he will allow his two sons-in-law, the Counts of Artois and Provence and their wives Princesses Marie Adélaïde and Victoire, to live in his kingdom under his protection. In 1777, the king's chamberlain, Lovera di Maria, ordered the arrest of Zénobe's father and had him for having hunted game on the lord's domain tortured and executed. That the poor farmer needed to do this to feed his family fell on deaf aristocratic ears.

they will bring a whiff of a better life to all. No more subservience to tyrants. Catherine, or her heirs, will fall.

I shall write you before I leave for Saint Petersburg. In the next couple of months you will be extremely busy with the harvest, but I know that you will enjoy the work. I, too, would have liked to get back to the soil. I have not lost the pleasure one gets at reaping what one has sowed. Harvest, especially the vendange, is a happy time. I am glad that your father decided not to sell the farm. It is still useful, even though he is trying to make a living in the city. But farm work is honorable, necessary, and gratifying. One day you and I will live on a patch of land, contented as our hearts can be, to live from our labor, to enjoy the fruits of our sweat. Listen to me! I've become a Rousseauiste! Touting the benefits of country living! However, there will be a very substantial library in our farmhouse. Even Voltaire did not mention that little detail at the end of his *Candide*. Yes, the merry group realizes the importance of happiness as they cultivate their garden during the day, but my happiness lies in the books I would read at night.

> I send you my heart,
> Your loving Zénobe

> *le 5 septembre*
> Jacques-Henri Maurel
> *hôtel* de Villette
> quai des Théâtins
> Paris

Marie-Jean-Baptiste Zénobe de Bosquet
Ferney

The winds of despair are here, my son, and they threaten to tear the *hôtel* de Villette apart. The *marquis* leaves for Ferney tomorrow, and he leaves me with the entire responsibility of protecting house and home, plus the occupants inside, while outside the gale blows constant. Thank God the *marquis* de Thibouville left for his country estate in Calvados, and thank Goddess (I think you'll like this detail of mine on the deity) that *madame* Denis has moved to her new house on the rue de Richelieu. She spends so much time there with that Duvivier fellow, I don't know why they don't just get married. I suppose she needs to let a suitable time of mourning go by, but I don't know why she troubles herself: she is not even the widow of *monsieur* de Voltaire. She's his niece! Not too many people were aware of their special relationship. She can marry Duvivier at any time. But mark my words, Duvivier is only after her money. I feel it in my bones. When he looks at her, which he doesn't do very often at all, it's with a look of impatience, perhaps consternation, since she never shuts up. She's like one of those new-fangled automatons that can do one thing over and over again, like a monkey that removes its hat. Only she's a rotund old bat whose jaws constantly move up and down and a constant barrage of noise comes out of her mouth. That Duvivier certainly spends a lot of time at the new house. He completely took over the construction and the refurbishment, changing the disposition of several of the rooms. *Madame* Denis got to keep her precious salon, although who does she think will likely visit it? The lords and mavens of Paris won't be exactly lining up to enjoy her stewardship of a grand new salon. Duvivier got her to change a smaller *salle de séjour* into a billiards room. Imagine, a whole room dedicated to a stupid game that used to be played outside but that's now played on a huge table that's still covered by an artificial green lawn! He's no fool, that Duvivier, though he looks like one. He's having the table brought over from England, since it's not he who has to worry about the cost. I can make the bet that it's *madame* Denis' money that allows him to do this. Or rather, it's *monsieur* de Voltaire's money.

I still weep bitter tears for our dear, departed friend. This house will never again see the likes of him. Were the house to last a thousand years, it will be forever noted that *monsieur* de Voltaire lived here, and slept here, and took his last breath here. I am filled with such admiration for your courage and sacrifice, to have headed straight to Ferney to copy Voltaire's papers. What you do for the history of Letters and Literature is such a sacred task! A letter came here addressed to *monsieur* Wagnière, from Catherine II, Empress of Russia. I suppose that she thought that *monsieur* de Voltaire's secretary would still be here. *Monsieur* de Villette will be taking the letter with him, to hand over to *monsieur* Wagnière as soon as he gets to Ferney, although the *marquis* already opened it. He was miffed that the letter hadn't come addressed to him. In it, Catherine stipulates that *monsieur* Wagnière should accompany the library to Saint Petersburg, citing all the ruffians and thieves along the way who would be glad to have a piece of the philosopher's library. She makes it crystal clear that one of these thieves might be King Frederick II of Prussia! I do believe that *monsieur* Wagnière already knew that he would be traveling along with the library in order to protect it. There was an added bit of instruction, however, in Catherine's letter, in the form of a request that *monsieur* Wagnière stay in Saint Petersburg to lay out the library in the same design that it had while it was in Ferney. I daresay, I asked myself, won't he be needing furniture, desks and bookcases and secretaries, in order to accomplish such an enterprise? As soon as we knew of this, I took it upon myself to ask *monsieur* Racle, Ferney's architect, who happened to be in Paris at the request of *monsieur* de Villette, so as to simplify *monsieur* Wagnière's task. What was *monsieur* Racle doing in Paris, you ask? Well, don't ask! I'm sure it's for no good. I was told that it was to sketch out the disposition of the furniture in your library. I still call it your library because you were choosing all the books for it, and reading them! The *marquis* never has time to read any of them. Well, I believe that *monsieur* de Villette keeps secrets from his *maître d'hôtel* when he realizes that his plans are either ineffectual or downright incompetent. I'm sure that our master is hatching machinations to add, subtract or change walls at Ferney, transform rooms, or enlarge the wine cellar. I also know of another project about which I'm sure you will have learned by now: the building of a shrine in *monsieur* de Voltaire's old bedroom. He even will provide the shrine with a relic of our dear departed friend as if it were a carnival attraction: the heart of Voltaire! I am so distraught! But that's not all, the *marquis* also wants to enlarge the salon, so that by the time *madame* de Villette can go to Ferney, they will be ready to receive the droves of the famous and the titled who will flock to pay their respects to the memory of a great man.

By now you must have also heard of *madame* de Villette's great misfortune. She is better now, confined to her bedroom by doctor's orders, still the protestant *monsieur* Tronchin, and by *monsieur* de Villette's even stricter orders, confined to her bed. But she is awaiting with impatience her husband's departure, so that she can at least come downstairs and socialize a bit with her friends. She also wants to be able to sit in the garden, when it's nice out. I believe she thinks that *monsieur* de Voltaire's spirit is still in your little room in the servant's quarters. She weeps constantly, with sobs that seem to come from deep within her soul. I think it was her sadness that caused her to lose the infant growing inside of her. *Monsieur* de Villette, shamefully, made matters worse by talking about how he is destined to become *monsieur* de Voltaire's literary heir, and how he will continue to espouse great causes and protect the victims of infamy. Meanwhile, nobody is visiting him, let alone revealing the identities of those victims of infamy. I think that's why he purchased Ferney from *madame* Denis. His intentions are to keep *monsieur* de Voltaire's salon in Ferney vibrant, *au courant*, as the center of philosophy in Europe. I can hardly hope he will be successful in this endeavor, although it is difficult to tell an aristocrat that his dreams and ambitions are overwrought, especially when his whole person is overwrought. I just hope that I will be on hand when his aspirations eventually drop around his feet. All he wants is to be loved and admired, and without *monsieur* de Voltaire to buoy him up, he feels like a lost child, as we all do.

Please write. Knowing that you are well and happy in your task of saving *monsieur* de Voltaire's legacy will do wonders for my nerves. Between André in Normandy and you in Ferney, I feel like an orphaned father. Is that even possible? Well, you know what I mean. I would be so much happier were the two of you back at the *hôtel* de Villette, and under my protection. You especially, for I know you like to get into trouble. Try to be a little more circumspect, if only to alleviate my apprehension. Your health and happiness are absolutely necessary to mine.

Signed,
Jacques-Henry

Response to *monsieur* Maurel's letter:

I received your letter, along with those from André and *monsieur* de Thibouville, with great pleasure. Please do not worry about your two young boys, for you know that we are in good hands, André with his family, and I under the proper tutelage of a stern but generous protestant. Wagnière mothers me only second to the way you did. He refuses outright to let me go out for a walk without the proper accoutrements for the weather. He watches over me as I eat every last morsel on my plate. He massages my writing hand, my left, as I massage his right. He weeps with me, as we come across a tender sentence or a benevolent thought. We mourn the kindest man who ever lived.

We are just about to conclude copying the last letters of his huge correspondence. He wrote thousands of missives, about ten to twenty every day. Of course, we couldn't retrieve them all. I predict that there will be for centuries letters written by Voltaire that will continue to come to the surface, found in dusty attics or in the back of stuck drawers in forgotten escritoires.

I am very upset that Catherine wants Wagnière to organize Voltaire's library to the way it used to be in Ferney. That will add weeks, if not months, to our stay in Russia. Wagnière is also upset, for he doesn't want to leave his wife and children for that long. The poor man has still not assimilated the fact that *madame* Denis sold Ferney to the *marquis* de Villette! You know that she has rescinded Wagnière's salary? After all that talk that Wagnière was part of the family, and that she would never forget all that he did for her uncle. Well, trust me: she has forgotten. She has forgotten all save for her uncle's money. That, and the house on the rue de Richelieu he left her. No matter, *madame* Denis can choke on her money. Catherine is being very generous to Voltaire's secretary: he is to receive for the rest of his life a pension for his work in gathering up and organizing the library. It's not a measly sum: 1,500 pounds per annum. She says it's for his loyalty to the man who was his master and hers. I don't know about that; I haven't seen Catherine liberate anything but rubles.

I have written to André care of you. Please send it to Normandy as you see fit. Now that Thibouville is there, you don't have a convenient courier. I know that André can take care of himself, but do you see Thibouville's proximity as a threat to him? In spite of the *marquis'* apologies and protestations that he acted inappropriately with us, he is still an aristo, and accustomed to getting his way. Were he to engender new machinations upon André, it would be vexing indeed, and I would need to vindicate my honor, and André's, by unsheathing my foil and targeting the *marquis* at the very source of his transgressions. He may seem foolish to us, but the law will always be on his side. To think that letters of nobility and a *particule*[38] matter more than the character of a man makes my blood boil.

In the meantime, I plead with you to regain some semblance of calm and serenity. You need it for your own health. Don't let the exterior turmoil effect an imbalance in your body's humors. I realize of course that the *hôtel* de Villette is a difficult house to manage, but you are its heart and, for a lack of a better word, its soul. It is not the *marquis* de Villette. You speak kindly about him when you say you wish to be present to collect all the pieces the day he begins to fall apart—I know I would let the pieces lie as they fall—and he doesn't even seem to appreciate all that you do for him, but please take care of yourself first, and then the *marquis* second, for without you, the whole household would fall apart, and then where would the *marquis* be?

I send you my warmest affection and gratitude for all that you have done for me, and it is my greatest hope to be able to continue to make you proud,

Your dutiful son,
Zénobe[39]

[not dated]
Château de Thibouville
Normandie

Dear and beloved friend,

I sincerely hope that this letter finds you in good health and in excellent humor. André has told me about your work to transcribe Voltaire's manuscripts and correspondence before you have to expedite the whole thing to Russia, and I commend and congratulate you for this arduous task, as well as for your courage in having braved the elements, the pursuing priests and the sundry ruffians that roam France's highways, in order to get yourself to Ferney in one piece.

---

38   The *particule* is the preposition «de» that denotes the domain of landed gentry. The aristocrat is the possessor of the named territory, including any villages, farms and peasants who happen to lie within its jurisdiction.

39   The reader will have no doubt noticed that Zénobe wrote nothing to *monsieur* Maurel about his impending travel into Savoy to see his family. May we surmise from this omission that Zénobe thought the trip a dangerous one? Knowing that Maurel worried so about him, perhaps the young man didn't want the *maître d'hôtel* to fret about a short expedition of only a couple of days.

Along with this missive, I send you a packet of letters (over a hundred!) that Voltaire wrote to me through the years. It is my hope that the great man kept my responses to him and that those letters are at this moment in your possession and safekeeping. Please don't send these original letters to Catherine, for I wish to keep them with me. It is all I have now of Voltaire, and I enjoy taking them out and perusing them from time to time. After you have finished copying them, you may hand them over to Villette, who, after a quick excursion to Geneva, is planning to come right back to Paris. He will then forward them to me in Normandy, where I propose to sojourn for a while longer. I am happy here in my domain, where the quiet and tranquility soothe me and make me forget the frenzy of Paris, with its wild euphoria one day and its wretched anguish the next, to say nothing of the unruly crowds that every day besieged the house. I knew not where to run, where to hide, where to assuage my desolation. I thought that you perhaps would have given me consolation. But you had a different idea in your treatment of a silly sentimental fool. Please forgive a man who has lived, and who has had much experience, for the accusation that I am about to launch your way, but a lot of the despondency that fell on my head was your doing. Rest assured that I am cognizant of, and that I accept my share of culpability in the proceedings that transpired between us. I know that you felt wedged into a corner and could not tell anyone about the difficulties that you and André were in the midst of experiencing, not even to Maurel. I also know that any creature, when it feels trapped, will not hesitate to lash out. Yet I also feel that it is undeniable that you were gratuitously cruel to me, which wounded me to my very soul. Please don't judge me harshly: I know that in part it was my blackmail and coercion that compelled you to initiate a strategy of self-defense, and, as much as I hate to regard it as true, to retaliate with a modicum of revenge on your part. If I ever harmed you and André, I will forever be remorseful, for neither you nor André deserved such shameful treatment. I acknowledge my wrongful conduct towards the two of you, and apologize for it. In the same vein, perhaps you will see the advantage of recognizing your ill treatment of me. Not that I would ever demand an apology from you, since it was my harassment that induced you to mistreat me, but perhaps, in the midst of your resistance, aggravated by confusion or the consequences of your hostility, you went a bit too far in handing me my comeuppance. Many a time I cried myself back to sleep after you had barged into my bedroom in the middle of the night to make your demands on me. You were cold, intensely cold, insistent, and seemingly impenitent about your retaliation on someone whose only guilt consisted in harboring amorous feelings for you. Without once shirking my blame in all that transpired between us, I do venture to forgive you for all that you did; I had it coming. Yet, do you not think that it would alleviate your own sense of transgression were you to show some contrition about your own actions? Wrongdoing transcends all religions, and in the end it is up to the moral fiber of every individual to come to terms with his acts of immorality. The Golden Rule is at the basis of humanism, and I invoke it now for your sake, and for your own moral rectitude. It is my sincerest hope that you no longer harbor any hatred of me. I, on the contrary, feel only amity and solicitude for you, and pray that you will place your confidence and trust, as Voltaire did before you, in someone who may be in a position one day to assist you, and who may provide beneficial influence when the concerns of law and society might at one time or another place restrictions on you. Voltaire always knew the advantage of befriending well-placed individuals in society, and he never burned bridges. I am quite aware that you are his adherent in all ways and manners, so please accept this offer of aid, meant in love and friendship, from someone who enjoys a modicum of high social standing and prestige, for you never know when such wherewithal might be needed.

My château in Normandy is similarly at your disposal. Should you wish to come spend time with André, you might both want to stay here, far from the direct observation of his relatives, but close enough for visits. Thibouville is but two hours away from Caen, two and a half from the Corday farm. Additionally, you might enjoy the historical aspect of the château: it still harbors one of the best collections of treasures and wonders from Jerusalem, memorabilia brought back to France by my ancestor Robert de Thibouville, one of the original Knights Templar who followed King Richard Cœur de Lion, who you will remember was also the Duke of Normandy, on the Third Crusade. Moreover, since I know you were pleased with Voltaire's book on India, you might be curious to inspect the château's collection of Indian artifacts that were brought over by my uncle, Claude-Louis-Aimable Carrel de Mésonval, *chevalier* and *seigneur* de Thibouville, whose military career as an infantry lieutenant in the King's army ended in 1761 during the siege of Pondicherry, with a bullet that splintered his coccyx. He was able to bring over so many elephant tusks that most of the pianofortes and harpsichords in the château had their keys made of their ivory. There is also a splendid Buddha, over a foot tall, made of one whole piece of the greenest jade you ever saw, which goes so well with our set of blue Saint-Louis stemware. (The set of Saint-Louis at the *hôtel* de Villette was a wedding gift from me.) We shall certainly use them to drink champagne as we toast your success with Voltaire's manuscripts. Word has it that you are almost done, and I sincerely look forward to you coming to Normandy, perhaps before the year is out. Perhaps it is you personally who shall return Voltaire's letters to me. André awaits you with impatience, as do I,

> In everlasting friendship,
> Henri-Lambert d'Herbigny,
> *marquis* de Thibouville

Zénobe was more miffed than troubled by Thibouville's letter, including quite a modicum of anger against the nobleman. How dare he show any resentment at all about the way Zénobe had treated him? He had molested both him and André, and deserved to be treated in a rotten manner. Zénobe would do it all over again, without hesitating. Ah, but there was that point of honor in the heart of the aristocrat! The pride that inflates a whole social class, whether it's justified or not! Where had that bravura been, then, when Thibouville's regiment waited for him in Italy, and the *marquis'* bravery failed him in Lyon? It was *monsieur* Maurel who had confided this story to Zénobe. Returning to Paris from the brink of war, as nonchalantly as he could, certainly didn't place Thibouville on the exact same plane as his ancestor who bravely massacred Turks in the Holy Land or his uncle who gallantly received from an English rifle a bullet to the arse.

Still, Thibouville was right about one thing. Voltaire had always held aristocratic pride in high regard, lauding it and even stoking it when needed. It was like protecting an exotic flower from the cold winds of changing public opinion: the aristos, according to many in the lower hierarchies, could dry up and blow away, but Zénobe was smart enough to realize that the inevitable revolution had not yet come, and the world still belonged to the privileged classes. If Voltaire could be diplomatic with them, then so could Zénobe. This was his careful response to the *marquis* de Thibouville:

Château de Ferney
October 25th, 1778

My dearest *marquis,*
After having read Voltaire's letters addressed to you, I dare call you what he called you:
My dearest angel,
You need not trouble yourself any longer about the trials and tribulations that recently swept us away in their turbulent current. When strong emotions are felt by sensitive people, they cannot be blamed for reacting with forceful resolution. True, I initially felt subjugated by you, and my immediate response was to strike back. I didn't realize then what I know now: 1. Your actions were born of an emotion that should have honored me, not harassed me; yours was an emotion that should have flattered me, not shamed me; and 2. The ways of the high-born may oftentimes seem petulant or impatient to the rest of us, but I know now that patricians would have the rest of society rise to the occasion when they come calling. I'm afraid that I might have disappointed you in my unsympathetic reaction to your overly zealous attentions. I should have welcomed them as the persistent compliments of a generous heart, an appreciation that you thought highly of me, that you approved of me and the work I was doing for the *marquis* de Villette. It is indeed I who should be apologizing to you. Remember, all was forgiven when you suggested to *monsieur* Maurel that the next time André and I come to visit, it should be not as servants, but as equals. That to me, my dear *marquis,* was the best compliment you could have ever paid me.
Remain assured that I do plan on going to Normandy to pay André and you a visit. Thank you for your most generous invitation, and I agree that it would be more discreet if André and I were to stay at the

château de Thibouville, but I promise you that I don't need historic relics or exotic bric-a-brac to be enticed. It is entirely your person that I wish to visit, and only your person. I'd like to share your lifestyle while in your presence, and enjoy some of that peace and tranquility of which you speak. Zeus knows that I will need time in a bucolic idyll to counterbalance the hectic pace of transcribing thousands of pages, and to offset the fatigue and the aggravation of my impending trip to Saint Petersburg. You see, the Empress has sent instructions for Wagnière to accompany Voltaire's library to Russia. I, of course, shall accompany Wagnière to help protect the library. There are many robbers on the highways of Europe, and we could not leave to chance the transfer of such an invaluable consignment. I will be returning to France as soon as Her Imperial Majesty gives me the freedom to do so.

In the meantime, please receive all my iterations of profound attachment and my enthusiastic assurances of respect and admiration,

Zénobe Bosquet

Suffice it to say that a few weeks later when the *marquis* de Thibouville received this letter and read its contents, his countenance darkened and he flung the pages into the air in a gesture of petulance. The pages fluttered slowly to the floor of his library and, quickly coming to his senses, he ran around the room to pick them up. Unsatisfying as the letter was, it was still precious to him, and he still thought it important enough to grasp its untidy pages next to his heart.

"I don't want his enthusiastic assurances of respect and admiration!" he cried out to the empty room. After a gasp he cried out, "And he's traveling to Saint Petersburg!"

He rushed across the room to his globe. He turned it round and round until he found Russia. One of his hands quickly ran over his table until he found a pair of compasses which he brought up to the globe.

"Two hundred, four hundred, six hundred…" he chanted, until he got the final figure, "One thousand eight hundred miles."

When the monstrosity of the figure reached his brain, he yelled out, "One thousand eight hundred miles! One thousand eight hundred miles! In the name of Jupiter, what does that even mean?"

He ran to one of his bookcases and began to search for a particular volume. It turned out to be beyond his reach, and he grabbed for the ladder which he climbed with the dispatch of a much younger man.

"There you are, come down to me," he said to the book.

Once in his hand, he clambered down the stairs and proceeded to the nearest armchair and fell down on it.

"What can you tell me, dear book?" he asked as he moistened a finger with his tongue and turned to the title page. "*Mémoires historiques, politiques et militaires sur La*

Russie, depuis MDCCXXVII, jusqu'à MDCCXLIV, par le Général de Manstein, collationnés sur le manuscrit original corrigé par la main de Voltaire, publiés à Paris en 1771," he intoned.[40]

He plunged into the book and began to read it as if his life depended on it.

---

40   There is a fine irony invoked in the choice of this reading material. In 1751, in his room in Frederick II's palace of Sans-Souci, Voltaire was in the process of helping General Manstein to translate his Memoirs into French, when a poem penned by the Prussian king was sent to be by Voltaire corrected. The philosopher told Manstein, "My friend, let's leave your book for another day; here's the king who sends me his dirty laundry to be cleaned. I'll clean your laundry later." After the king heard of this insult, he retaliated when one of his subjects complained that there was jealousy in the court on account of the favored status and fortune in which Frederick viewed the French author, to which His Majesty responded, "Let it be: one squeezes the orange, then, after having imbibed the juice, one throws the rind away." Voltaire left Frederick's court soon after.

The Eve of All Saints' Day

A nd it came to pass that on the fortieth day of the first scribe, following the fortieth day of the second, which had followed the fortieth day of the third, that is to say, after one hundred and twenty days that all three scribes had been occupied with their sacred task, that the instruments of writing were laid to rest on the table, and the ink in the inkwell was not renewed. The main scribe said to the second, "There is but one more manuscript that remains to be transcribed."

The second scribe looked up. "Is that it, the one you are holding in your hands?"

"Yes, the one that was found stuffed behind one of the drawers in Voltaire's escritoire."

It was the farmer, Gil Blas, their fellow third scribe, who had recently left for the vendange, who had discovered it.

"May I see it?" asked Zénobe.

Wagnière handed the precious pages to his second scribe.

"This is in Voltaire's own hand," said he with admiration. "But wasn't this published during Voltaire's lifetime?"

Wagnière nodded. "Yes, in 1749. The first time he ever criticized the Bible directly. But he never avowed he was its father. It forever remained an orphan, and he always refused to have it included in every edition of his complete works. It was Rousseau who claimed publicly that it was Voltaire who had authored it. In retaliation, Voltaire let it be known that Rousseau had abandoned all five of his bastards. Voltaire, at least, only abandoned this one."

Zénobe had never read it. It was perhaps the only work of Voltaire's that he had never read. It wasn't a very long work, and it took him ten minutes to read it. Wagnière observed Zénobe's facial expressions as the young man's eyes swept across the pages, finding it amusing to see those eyes widen in surprise, his eyebrows rise in astonishment, the corners of his lips edge up and transform his whole face into a radiant smile of awe.

When he was finished, Zénobe put the pages down and let out his breath in admiration.

"Voltaire is the most courageous man who ever lived! He dared... he dared write what many thought, but would never say out loud. And he had this published!"

Wagnière thought of himself as courageous, too. "Well, he hid behind anonymity."

"But still, he launched this out into the open thirty years ago!" Zénobe laughed with incredulity. "No wonder the authorities wanted his hide!"

In answer to Wagnière's gesture to take back the manuscript, Zénobe said, "Allow me, please, dear Wagnière, to copy it out myself. It would be my honor to do so. I do it in the name of truth, for the love of truth."

And this is how it came to pass that the *Sermon of the Fifty* was included, for the first time, in the complete published works of Voltaire's writings, for which the scribes had assiduously been preparing. Voltaire could no longer be punished, but the scribes could, and all those who had a hand in the publication could, and yet, with bravery and audacity, they were compelled to do so, in the name of truth, for the love of truth.

Zénobe's hand did not tremble as he wrote out the following:

> Such crimes committed in the name of the Lord! Oh, my God, if you yourself came down to earth, if you commanded me to believe this tissue of murders, of thievery, assassinations and incest committed by your command and in your name, I would say to you, no, your holiness does not want me to acquiesce to such horrible things that are outrageous to you; you want to test me, no doubt.

As he wrote, Zénobe hoped that these words would finally dislodge the sanctity and the reverence in which the Bible was held. Such a violent, ghastly book, with mass murder and mayhem, and without one iota of compassion, could never have been written through the direction of God. The young scribe was filled with hope as he wrote the final words.

> May that great God—a God who certainly would not have inspired this book with all its contradictions, its madness and horrors—may that God, Creator of the universe, have pity on the sect of Christians who blaspheme against Him; may He bring them back to a holy and natural religion and spread His benedictions on the efforts we make to have Him worshiped.

Going Home

Zénobe's work was done. He put away his quills, gathered all the errant inkwells in the library, and placed them on Wagnière's desk. He decided that there was time to visit his family in Savoy before he and Wagnière were to set off for Saint Petersburg. The work that remained, placing the whole library in crates and sealing them, could be provided by other servants in the house.

The *marquis* de Villette also felt that his work was done. He was leaving the whole household and the entire village overwhelmed with his manifold instructions and detailed modifications for the improvement of stratagems and procedures. He was also leaving the inhabitants restless with impatience for his departure. He left early in the morning to set out for Geneva, there to meet with Panckoucke and provide, once again, his expertise and talent for administration, this time for the project of publishing the first posthumous edition of Voltaire's complete works. First, however, the publisher would need to take care of the business of the last remaining batch of unsold sets of the 1775 edition of the *Encyclopédie*. Three hundred sets had yet to find buyers, and Panckoucke's partner, Samuel de Tournes, did not want to begin the publication of Voltaire's œuvre with that surplus still in their basements. Villette had many bright ideas about how to move them. Voltaire's works had to be published immediately while the old man was still being mourned. The *Encyclopédie* was no longer new; it had been around for twenty-five years and, frankly, the novelty had expired. Voltaire's complete works would light the flame again for those bibliophiles who wished to own something illicit, to make their heart beat faster with the possession of the forbidden. To bite into the apple that the Serpent provided, and to send the church to hell; that is what buyers wanted! They wanted to wallow in the knowledge that the priests deemed felonious, and at the same time denigrate them for their sanctimonious ecclesiastical egotism. He could hardly wait to get to Geneva.

But first, Zénobe was to be his travel companion for the first few leagues. He was rather looking forward to that. They hadn't been alone since before Voltaire died, at the time when, unfortunately, the work on his library at the *hôtel* de Villette had come to a halt. He was curious to find out when Zénobe planned to come back to Paris to finish the task. Perhaps he could even convince him to accompany him to Geneva, if only for a few days. The *marquis* had brought no valet with him from Paris.

Apparently, the boy had plans to avoid conversation with his master. After saying that he was going to stay in Savoy for just one night or two and that Wagnière and he were nearly ready to leave for Saint Petersburg, he insisted on riding outside next to the coachman, citing that he did not want to bother the *marquis* in any way. Before the *marquis* could object, the boy was already on the box seat, holding the reins for the driver.

The detour wasn't much out of his way, and Villette did not mind helping his librarian out. He realized Maurel had been right all along: Zénobe was rather independent, and he couldn't be ordered around like other servants, like André, for instance. Still, his long-range plans to seduce the boy had not been abandoned. He longed to remove those gentlemanly garments that he knew were but a disguise, and be able to treat him as the servant he was. His imagination became quite occupied in the removal of clothing one piece at a time. He saved the white wig for last. Before long, the carriage had come to the bifurcation of the road leading south to Annecy.

"You really won't need anything to eat?" asked the *marquis* de Villette as the boy jumped off the coach.

"I'll be dining with my sisters in an hour," said Zénobe. "Thank you, just the same."

The boy had begun to saunter off, and seemed so happy and carefree. Villette called out after him, "*Adieu*, then, and have a safe trip to Saint Petersburg. You will communicate my salutations to the Empress, won't you?"

Zénobe turned around and was walking backwards. "Indeed, I will, *monsieur le marquis* de Villette. It shall be my absolute pleasure to do so."

And with a respectful salute next to his forehead, as if he were a military person, he was off.

Zénobe couldn't remember the last time he was this happy. Voltaire's writings had filled him with renewed vigor and joy. And hope. Even though his friend was no longer alive in the world, the world still hadn't lost the philosopher's writings. He, Wagnière and Gil had seen to it. Voltaire lived on, his voice still strong, and his influence would career into the next generation. His legacy was safe, and Zénobe felt so light and buoyant that he was practically running with joy. In what seemed like just minutes, he began to see the first houses of Annecy-le-Vieux. Before long, he was walking along the beloved streets of Annecy-le-Neuf, attracting the attention of residents and passers-by who thought they recognized him, but then quickly doubted their ability to identify this young man. He certainly looked like a Bosquet, but this person was wearing a gentleman's outfit, with red heels, a white wig and two foils, one on each side. The Bosquet they remembered was the son of a farmer. Moreover, a Bosquet male would not dare to return to Savoy after Bosquet *père* had been executed for crimes against the *seigneur*. Still, they followed this tall man with their eyes as he made his way to the rue Saint François and opened one of the huge portals of the Cathedral of Saint Peter.[41] He disappeared into the darkness inside, and the door shuddered to a close like the stone in front of Jesus' tomb.

When his eyes became accustomed to the darkness, Zénobe's feet followed a path they had followed thousands of times before, through the nave, to the left at the transept, up a circular staircase, to the private chambers of his friend and mentor Father Anselme.

---

41 During the Revolution, this street, which during the Middle Ages had been called the rue du Four for the public oven that was located there, was renamed the rue Jean-Jacques Rousseau, in view of the fact that Rousseau came to live there in 1728, when he was just 16 years old and met the love of his life, the *baronne* de Warens, 12 years his senior. Today, her mansion is divided between a music school and the municipal police station.

Zounds! But the Father was going to be surprised to see him! For all he knew, Zénobe was still in Dijon, working at the inn where he had found work after escaping from Savoy. How was he going to react to the news that he had been in Paris all this time, and that he had been in the employ of one of his favorite writers, one of *their* favorite writers. Father Anselme was a preacher in name only. His parents had sacrificed him, as the youngest of their sons, to the church, just as they had sent their eldest daughter to the convent. For such contributions to the church they had been guaranteed many indulgences for themselves and for the rest of their family. Reducing their stay in purgatory was such a boon. Besides, there wouldn't have been much money left to educate their last son. The church would educate him and edify him to their ends.

Little did the family know, as well as the priests to whom he was consigned, that their little Anselme had a mind of his own, and that he used the church for his own ends. He certainly made good use of their library, running through the tomes of the *Index Librorum Prohibitorum* like a fish through water. What a blessing, thought the young seminarian, and how convenient to have all these books in the same place! I don't have to budge one iota, or spend a single sou, to delight in the reading of these banned books. Afterwards, when he himself became the teacher, he would lend these secret books to his own students. Zénobe would never have received such an excellent education had it not been for the ministrations of his parish priest. He had a lot to thank him for, and, when he thought how at home he had been with the Parisian philosophers, how he had been able to hold his own during their discussions, how he had been able to follow their allusions, their inferences, even their intertextual puns, he realized what an outstanding education he had received at the hands of Father Anselme. He had been able just as easily to discuss weighty matters with the philosophers in Latin! Greek had not been Father Anselme's forte, but Zénobe hoped one day to continue his education, and perhaps learn English as well. English seemed like a language of the future, and he wanted to make sure he could speak with the American Insurgents.

With all this on his mind, Zénobe, once again, neglected to observe little details around him that could have provided more general information pertinent to his continued well-being. He missed trivial alterations that could have communicated to him that all at the Cathedral of Saint Peter was not as he had left it the year before.

First of all was that the gate at the base of the circular stairway was not only unlocked, but hanging wide open, and askew, the lock still dangling on the side opposite the hinges, its shackle untouched. How many times had Father Anselme instructed his young student to close the grating completely whenever he left his private rooms? Also, at the top of the stairs, before coming to the hallway that led to Father Anselme's chamber, he did not see a book lying in the shadows beneath the staircase's vaulted ceiling. Nor did he catch sight of some loose pages fluttering in the breeze between the bars of the wrought iron railings that looked over the church's back courtyard. Had he but glanced over this barrier, he would have seen a blackened circle of the sooty remains of hundreds of books that had recently been burned in a pyre. His nostrils caught the scent of smoke, but he attributed it to incense.

Lastly, there was a complete absence of children. Usually in this area, there were pupils of Father Anselme who congregated on the huge stone benches outside the rooms he used for lessons. Zénobe himself used to stretch out on the back of one of the benches, as if he were a cat, and use the decorative scroll at the top of the bench to prop up his head as he read his favorite tomes. As he passed the bench, he began to think that perhaps this day was Sunday, in which case the Father would be inside the church, attending to his sacerdotal duties, which he loathed. But he had just passed through the nave and had seen no activity. Zénobe was about to turn on his heel and head back downstairs, but he decided that he was so close to Father Anselme's bedchamber that he might as well scratch at the door.[42]

The man who opened the door looked pale and haggard, as if he hadn't slept for days and, though he looked directly into Zénobe's eyes, he seemed not to recognize him. Perhaps if he heard his voice.

"Father Anselme," said Zénobe. "Do you not remember me?"

Recognition lit up the priest's face, followed almost immediately by a great fear. He grabbed Zénobe by one arm and dragged him into the room, taking care to close the door noiselessly.

"My son, my son, whatever are you doing here?" he whispered. "Why didn't you... where had... you should have..." Closing his eyes to concentrate his thoughts, he said, "You shouldn't have come here. Don't you know they are looking for you? They arrived here three days ago. They've taken over completely. I myself am confined to my room. They found my books, Zénobe, they found my books!"

Father Anselme was holding Zénobe by both arms. "They found them, and they burned them all. They are all gone. And now they are looking for you, and they will do the same thing to you. You must go, you must go right this minute. I have no place to hide you here. You could go up to the bell towers and hide there, but how would I get you food and water up there? You must leave. And why are you dressed like this? And what is this?"

This last question referred to Zénobe's foil, a weapon that seemed to disquiet the priest. Then he saw the second foil, which astounded him.

"Father, I have so many things to tell you, I don't know where to begin. I have been with Voltaire in Paris for four months. I was there when he died, and I accompanied his body to Champagne. I've been in Ferney until today, helping his secretary to transcribe the unpublished manuscripts and correspondence. We're going to Russia, the Empress Catherine has purchased Voltaire's library—"

"Shh, someone's coming."

They both stopped to listen. Father Anselme was so unnerved that his hands on Zénobe's shoulders trembled. They heard nothing, but the priest pulled Zénobe farther into the room. Then he dragged a chair by the door and wedged it up to the door handle.

"They took my keys," he whispered. "If they come in, you'll hide under the mattress. There's no place to hide you in here, my son. Oh, why did you come?"

Father Anselme wrung his hands as he looked up at the ceiling, trying to find a hiding place behind a beam, but no such place presented itself.

"I will not hide under the mattress," answered Zénobe. "I am not afraid. I will confront these priests, just like I confronted them in Paris, and I shall pierce them through the heart if they dare attempt to harm me, or you."

"Do not worry about me. I shall come to no harm, although I will never again have access to children, and never again will I ever be allowed to teach. They shall demote me to deacon and have me light the candles. I don't care, but you, my son, they want to seize you and publicly expose you as an apostate and heretic. You will be tortured, and you will be executed, in a most horrible way. You will not be able to fight yourself

---

42 Reminder to the reader: scratching at the door was considered more discreet and polite than the startling knocking practiced by the lower classes, that is, when they had doors.

out of this, for they are legion. They are swarming all over the diocese. We've had to hide your sisters again, this time with people who have no knowledge of where they come from. They were told they are orphans, without a home."

Zénobe's face clouded over with anger, his fists clenching and unclenching.

"Please, my son," continued Father Anselme. "You must not confront these priests. They will take you. Please don't let your hatred overtake you. You must think, and you must be calm. You need to—"

This time they both heard footsteps outside and they froze. For an eternity they heard someone approaching, but then when the sound began to diminish, they both began to breathe again.

"Are they French priests?" asked Zénobe.

"French, Savoyard, Turingeois, Sardinian. They are come from the four corners of the Christian realm to look for you. They feel that they are close, and they found out you were in Ferney. They couldn't touch you there. If I had had a way... I had no way to send you a warning. They descended on us like a cloud of locusts; they control our every move; they have started to relocate everybody and bring in new people, from as far away as Chambéry. In three days, they have eaten and drunk through six months of our stored supplies. There is nothing in our cellars. They have marauded through them like rapacious looters. But it's you they want, and they will not stop until they find you. Oh, dear lord, I am so frightened for you. You must go back. Go back now. Be careful, please be careful."

Father Anselme embraced Zénobe and kissed him on both cheeks and on his forehead. Zénobe embraced him back, and said, "Before I go, I must tell you that I love you. You were my teacher, and you were an excellent teacher. You prepared me for Voltaire and his philosopher friends in Paris. I felt at home with them. You left nothing out, and I shall forever be grateful to you."

The priest had started to push Zénobe towards the door. By this time tears flowed from his eyes, and Zénobe began to weep as well. Never did a Socrates and a Plato embrace with such tenderness, with such conflicting emotions ranging from affection to terror. Neither one of them wanted to break the embrace, but Father Anselme had seen what those priests were capable of, and he pushed Zénobe gently away.

"We have no god to commend your soul to," he said to his young pupil. "But in the name of humanity, in the name of everything that is good and generous within the hearts of men, no matter how deeply concealed, I can commend you. Never lose hope that people's better nature may rise to the surface, never lose hope in that humanity. You must seek it out. It has nothing to do with a god."

With one final look into his teacher's face, Zénobe turned towards the door. Silently he opened it and walked out, going back down the corridor to the circular staircase, treading as lightly as he could. He could hear voices, but with the echoing effect for which the entrails of cathedrals are known, he could not ascertain from which direction they came. As he approached the last spiral of the staircase he halted, waiting for sounds, but after not hearing any, he bore down to the bottom. Peering in both directions, he ran out back into the transept, took a right at the nave, and, hiding behind the columns as much as he could, hurried to the front portal.

He silently held one of the heavy doors ajar and listened. There were excited voices, several of them, speaking about the presence of an unknown gentleman who had been walking on that very street, la rue Saint François. A man's voice was asking questions about the outward appearance of the gentleman. The responses came quickly. Yes, he was wearing a wig. Yes, his shoes had red heels. Some didn't remember if he had been wearing a foil, but others insisted that they had seen it, even two. Had the stranger gone into the cathedral? Yes, came several voices in unison. It sounded like they were feeling pleasure in acknowledging such a peculiar and dangerous occurrence in their village.

Zénobe backed away, but instead of going directly back up the nave, he turned aside to the left aisle where he would be ready to spring behind a saint's sarcophagus or an altar to the Virgin.

Suddenly he heard multiple footsteps leading down from the transept he had just vacated. He jumped into the side chapel that happened to be closest to him. It was right under the stained glass window dedicated to Saint François de Sales. There were two crypts there, and he wedged behind one of them. The area smelled musty and chalky.

A group of five priests walked past the side chapel and on to the front portal. There, Zénobe heard them open the door, and a conversation ensued between them and the people he had heard previously. Their words were indistinct, except for one which rang clear and strong all the way to Zénobe's ears.

"Bosquet."

They were on to him. He glided silently out into the aisle and, cutting across a row of pew chairs back to the nave, retraced his steps up towards the heart of the cathedral. He thanked the deities of destiny that the shafts of late-morning sun were on the other aisle, and hoped that the relative darkness here would conceal his presence. He knew not where to run, but his eyes caught sight of the gilded columns in front of the choir. He knew that the tabernacle would be close by with the Eucharist stored inside. Some mote of reason told him that perhaps if he took possession of it, he might be able to bargain for his freedom. Priests thought highly of the Eucharist, and had gone through great lengths to burn at the stake jews accused of desecrating the hosts. He couldn't remember if the ciborium would be covered with a veil or not, and whether or not the veil signified the presence or the absence of the hosts. He continued to run anyway and was able to slip behind one the of the huge columns holding up the chancel vault. No one had seen him.

Or so Zénobe thought. A priest who had just entered the nave from the transept thought he saw a flurry of shadow drop out of sight into the front altar. He intentionally did not shorten his stride and he certainly did not turn to go up the steps into the chancel—not by himself!—except to kneel quickly in front of it and make the sign of the cross. As he did so, he scanned the area and saw nothing untoward. But he was sure he had seen something furtive move into the shadows, and now that he thought of it, something had flashed with a glint of metal. He hurried to the voices at the front door, and making signs with his hands and expressions with his face, he communicated to the others that he had seen something, or someone, back inside. One of the people there, a tonsured priest wearing a purple cassock, held up his hands in a questioning gesture and mouthed the word *where*, giving him the expression of an owl.[43] The priest who had espied the moving shadow pointed vigorously to the chancel. The man in the purple cassock ordered the various villagers to stay at the front court, although they remained congregated around the open door to be able to peer inside. The group of ecclesiastics was given instructions to split up, some going up the two aisles, the others going up the nave. At the transept, the three groups converged around the chancel and slowly began to climb the stairs. From their vantage point, the priests coming

---

43   The French word for *where* is *où*, pronounced *oo*.

up the eastern part of the chancel saw the man first, and their feet froze on the step. The others continued for two or three steps more, wondering why their brethren had stopped, but in an instant, also catching sight of the strange man, they froze as well. The man was holding the ciborium high above his head.

The priest wearing the red cassock spoke with a trembling voice, as if he were an actor on the stage intoning threat and retribution. "Intentional desecration of the host is a sacrilege, a mortal sin, and punishable by excommunication. You cannot hold the Holy Ghost hostage!"

The gentleman, for it was indeed a gentleman, responded, "I would like nothing more than to be excommunicated from your degenerate organism."

The priests gasped in unison.

"Halt, before you do something irreparable," declaimed the Chaplain of His Holiness, for it was, indeed, a sacerdotal envoy come to Annecy to apprehend the evil apostate who had been eluding the Church for weeks. This was certainly the fugitive. They were convinced that they had their man, for who else would be threatening to defile the very symbol of Christ's presence on earth?

"The Eucharist abides in the Holy of Holies, and your presence here profanes the sanctity of the Holy Ghost and sullies the Bride of Jesus Christ. Give yourself up to the representatives of the Lord before you multiply your sins and aggravate your condition."

"And if I refuse?" came the impudent answer from the inveterate sinner.

"We are many, and you are only one."

As the priests slowly began to approach him from different directions, Zénobe looked up at the vaulted arch looming above him. The priests thought he was hoping to invoke God. They couldn't know that the man was wishing he were Samson so he could demolish the pillar behind which he had been hiding and bring down the Church to crush all these priests at the same time.

With a voice trembling with fury, he said to them, "I was under the impression that you follow the teachings of Jesus Christ, and that one of your principles is to do no violence upon any man."

"We are soldiers of Christ in the army of our Lord the Creator, and we have the authority of the Vicar of Christ and the approbation of our Lord God to take into custody any miscreant who flouts the tenets of our creed and outrages the articles of our faith. By your very presence here, in the Holy of Holies, you commit a litany of egregious transgressions, and the wickedness that has followed you into our Lord's Sanctuary must be stopped, even through violent means. Did not Jesus Himself forcefully expel the merchants and the money changers from the House of God, did he not justly beat them and drive them from the Temple of the Lord? We are Christian soldiers, and we are empowered to detain you, put you to the Question, and judge your violations. It will behoove you to put down the Eucharist and to allow yourself peacefully to be adjudicated."

Zénobe knew from extensive past experience that priests always had an answer for everything. He lofted the ciborium as high into the air as he could, and the golden chalice arced high over the priests' heads and began to fall many paces behind them. Again, they all gasped at once, and a few of them ran towards the falling sacred cup in an attempt to catch it. But the heavy ciborium fell with a clatter onto a pew chair; the cover bounced in one direction and the contents spread out in another in a wide dispersion of circular white hosts.

By the time the ciborium had landed, Zénobe had the tip of his foil leveled directly at the Chaplain's throat.

"You will allow me to leave, peacefully, or you will provide me with the pleasure of committing another sin, that of slicing open the throat of a representative of a most violent and enraged Jesus Christ. I will spill your blood with delight and relish the moment—"

Zénobe was unable to conclude his warning. Even though he never intended to follow through with his threat, he was nevertheless concentrating to instill as much savagery in his voice as he could. He never noticed when the priest who had picked up the ciborium hurled it in his direction. The cleric's accuracy was competent, the speed of the vessel commendable, and it hit Zénobe immediately above his right eye, gashing across his eyebrow and making him crumple to the floor, his foil clattering down right after him.

November 2, 1778

Dead to the World

When Zénobe regained consciousness, he did not know where he was. He could not tell if it was night or day, or for how long he had slept. He could not recall when he had fallen asleep. He was not in a bed; he was on a floor made of uneven paving stones. He seemed to be in an enclosed space that was very dark. As awareness slowly seeped across his mind, the first physical sensation he felt was an acute pain along his sides. Moving only his head, he realized that his head also must have been hurt. He was on the floor of what seemed to be a small cell, with a single tiny window high up one of the walls and a low wooden door on the opposite side. The only piece of furniture in the room was a small *prie-dieu*[44] facing a crucifix nailed to the wall.

When he tried to move, pain immobilized him immediately. He lifted an arm to his head and felt that one of his eyes was swollen shut. He couldn't remember what had happened to him or where he had been, but slowly it began to dawn on him that he was being held captive. Even though an incipient sense of panic began to make his heart beat faster, he willed his mind to be patient and wait for clarity. The last thing he remembered was having gone to see Father Anselme in Annecy, and the memory of being in his little cell brought back the image of fear on the priest's face. Father Anselme had been concerned about him getting caught, so he surmised that he must have been caught. He was a prisoner here, but the details of his apprehension were nowhere to be found.

Zénobe fell asleep. It wasn't until he woke up that he remembered the confrontation at the altar.

Why, the priests must have done this to me, he thought. Those bastards, they do use violence in the name of their god. The physical pain he felt ran from his ribs to his thighs. The clerics must have kicked him on both sides multiple times to have caused this much injury.

Zénobe had no idea how long he had been in this cell. He was extremely thirsty, so he assumed he had been unconscious for hours, perhaps days. He remembered Wagnière, and realized that there was no possibility of sending a message to Ferney, or even to Father Anselme. He didn't know where in the cathedral he was, for he had never seen a cell like this anywhere on the cathedral grounds. He realized he had not heard the bell toll the hours, so perhaps he was no longer on the cathedral grounds at all. Wagnière and Father Anselme might as well be on the other side of the earth, he thought.

---

44 A piece of furniture made for an individual to kneel in prayer, with a lectern on top to hold a Bible.

But when he heard distant voices he thought that perhaps he was no longer in Savoy. These people were speaking Piedmontese, and Zénobe remembered that Father Anselme had mentioned that there were Turingeois among the priests who had taken over the cathedral in Annecy. Was it possible that he was in Turin? Could Victor Amédée's mad priests have brought him to the very seat of the king's hegemony? Could he now be a prisoner of the king's lieutenant, general Antoine Marie Philippe Asinari, *marquis* de Saint-Marsan?[45] If so, he realized that the priests would do with him whatever they intended to do, for they would promptly be seconded by the king's representative. Zénobe was in great danger.

But there was nothing he could do. He was in too much pain even to be able to get up. He fell asleep, or fainted from the pain, several times, and each time dreamed that he was riding horses with André on an open field. It must have been in Normandy, for there were no mountains in the distance, only rolling hills.

Every time that he woke up, it was to pain, and to a frightening reality.

The priests finally had him. They must have already begun their torture, he just didn't remember it. Slowly he felt along his sides, wondering if he had broken ribs, and then brought his hands up to his open eye. He saw that he still had all his fingers and all his fingernails. When he felt along his closed eye, he could feel it was swollen grotesquely, and there was encrusted blood above it.

He began to weep. Oh, what have they done, he thought. What did they do to me? He had heard, of course, of the fate that befell prisoners of the church. Sometimes they disappeared, for years, some forever. Their families and friends never saw them again. They probably died in the dungeons, of neglect, starvation, savage indifference. Something lurked in the back of Zénobe's mind, however, that struck him with terror. The church wanted to make an example of him, ever since he had enraged the priests in Paris. These wanton monsters, as vengeful and wicked as the god of the Old Testament, as perfectly willing as their god to commit acts of brutality and retribution, wanted him, needed him, in order to be exhibited to the public, and for there to be a very visible penance for a sinner of his magnitude. The people would bring their children to the carnival, along with food and drink, and enjoy the spectacle of a trespasser who dared break their religious laws. Not only was he a heretic and an apostate, he was a blasphemer, a desecrator, and an aggressor of priests. His auto-da-fé would be the biggest, the most flamboyant and the best-attended in decades. He was a prize for the Inquisition, and they would flog him and puncture his armpits and groin in order to facilitate his being drawn and quartered. That's what had happened to both Ravaillac and Damiens who were mere regicides.[46] I'm more than that. I'm a Christ-killer, for I

---

45   It is evident that Zénobe Bosquet had more knowledge of the Savoyard King's lieutenant general than we do, and a better grasp and appreciation of the minister's collusion with the ecclesiastics. From our vantage point in the future, it is very difficult to ascertain the young man's allegations. It is historically factual, however, that the successor monarchs of Savoy, Turin and Sardinia were considered models of piety and morality, setting the example for their subjects, even as they waged war on their enemies and eliminated threats to their religion. It is easy to assume, as such, that Victor Amédée III's minister would emulate the precedents and the standards of comportment of his king.

46   François Ravaillac, a would-be priest who was turned down by the Church for his predisposition to "visions," in 1610 murdered Henry IV who was viewed by catholics as being too tolerant of the protestants. Robert François Damiens did not kill his king, Louis XV, just gave him a slight flesh wound in 1757. He nevertheless suffered the same fate as Ravaillac: both were drawn and quartered after having molten lead poured into their wounds. After hours of torture, both were burned, their ashes scattered to the wind.

deny the sanctity of that man as the son of god, for the simple reason that I deny god himself. To think, that I shall be tortured, dismembered and burned, all for things that don't exist, for figments of the demented minds of fanatics, for fallacies construed to deceive and dominate the weak-minded, the credulous, and the naïve. I shall serve as a warning to those who refuse to have faith in the imaginary and the illogical, so that those who use their mind in a rational way, who think for themselves, will be forced to conceal the independence of their minds for fear of ending up like me. It is coercion and violence that keep the edifice of religion upright, because the mortar they use is the thousands of lies that make no sense to a rational mind, and the faith that they extort from the gullible is nothing but a concocted deception meant to enslave them.

Zénobe's mind involuntarily kept going to the historic scenes of Ravaillac and Damiens' torture and execution. Rage and dread fought for his heart as his mind sought to bring calm and order to his frenzied state. But his efforts to bring all the composure and lucidity that the rational mind can bring were no match to the physical anguish he was feeling.

No wonder those who are tortured are quickly brought into submission, just as a beaten dog licks the hand of its torturer.

Sleep was the instrument that finally brought Zénobe to a state of calm. But it was a brooding and disturbing sleep that sank him lower into cavernous subterranean spaces where multitudes were restrained and kept in the dark.

November 2, 3 or 4, 1778

Inquisitional Stratagems

Since it is known that Zénobe never communicated with a single soul about his experiences during the time he was held captive by the Office of the Holy Inquisition, not even with André or *monsieur* Maurel, it is difficult to ascertain the sequence of events that occurred on the day, or days, the young man was incarcerated deep within the gloomy bowels of the Duomo di Torino, built on the foundations of the ancient Roman theater whose subterranean oubliettes doubled very well as torture chambers. It is nigh impossible for us to see through the haze of incense and the dust of ages, but, knowing the outcome of these events, which lasted from between one to three days, the condition in which Zénobe entered the premises, and the one in which he exited, and, more importantly, the letter that the sacerdotal torturer (Paulo is the only birth name we retain from him) wrote to his father, a retired cleric who had been released from his duties a decade earlier (after it was found out that he had fathered more than one child), it is feasible to weave a timeline of extrapolated proceedings. Details from the text of this letter, which hint at the statements made by the accused, were published in 1872 in a book of tribunals and persecutions committed by the Inquisition in Turin, a copy of which could be found at the Duomo. Most of the pages are still legible in spite of whole sections obscured by scorch marks from a fire that occurred well after the conflagration that damaged the Shroud of Turin. Most of the other copies of this book were lost due to the continuing conflict among warring Italian historiographers who took sides in the argument between the Duke of Savoy, Victor Amadeus, and the Church of Rome. It was the Duke of Savoy's contention that the Inquisition "arrogated an authority which amounted, as he said, to an usurpation of his own," and that "no sovereign in Europe would any longer suffer such abuse of power on the part of the Holy See."[47] It took delicate diplomacy between papal authorities and the king's ministers, and much pecuniary negotiation, all of which flowed northward from Rome to Turin, to restore the original balance of power. The influence of the Inquisition would not be diminished, the last victim of the Holy Office being a 6-year-old Jewish boy forcibly removed from his family in 1858, after a servant in the house had him secretly baptized and the child's soul thus became property of the Church. The boy was subsequently raised by the local inquisitor to be a priest.

---

47   Alexis Muston. *The Israel of the Alps.* London, 1875. Vol. 2, pp. 103-4.

Plausible Development of Events: Version of

The young priest, Father Clément, could barely hold on to the heavy set of pincers. In spite of the perpetual cold in the ancient cave-like subterranean passages of the cathedral—he could see his captive victim shivering—sweat made the metal in his hands slippery. Worse, when he put down the instrument of torture in order to put on a pair of thick leather gloves, he found the leather so stiff that they impeded the movement of his fingers. Instead of laying the pincers down gently, he inadvertently dropped them into the fire and then had to realign them so that only the ends were in the flames.

The cleric, dressed in the robes of the Benedictine order that stressed above all a narrow parochial ministry, as opposed to the international perspective of the Holy Office of the Inquisition, was still in wonderment over his superiors having presented him with this task. He had no previous experience in the torture chamber. He'd never even seen this chamber, nor suspected where it was, and could not lose his awe of its spaciousness both in breadth and height. He felt dwarfed under the vaulted ceiling, and marveled at the array of implements scattered about the room and attached to the walls. Much consideration and expense had been dedicated to the chamber's excavation and appointments. He had been in ignorance about this entire floor underneath the cellars, where it was so dark one had to bring fire down, even during the day. Down here, one could not even tell if it was day or night; it was always dark and it was always cold. All he knew was that he had surprised himself when he accepted his instructions so readily, unquestioningly, as always, agreeing to a strange new request, that of putting to the Question the young man who was kneeling in chains before him.

Whether or not Father Clément felt pity or sympathy for the captive cannot be known, but the letter to his father reveals a cleric who was overwhelmed by gratitude for his superiors who placed so much trust in him for so important a task. To his dismay, soon after his compliance with the representatives of the Holy See, he slowly began to recognize all the minutiae and the complications that the task entailed. The Question was not just an interrogation. It was an interrogation accompanied by a careful series of stratagems to facilitate responsiveness from the accused. The correct response, of course, was a complete and thorough confession of all sins and crimes, past and present, imputed to the accused. This was a solemn ritual, as he perceived it, and consequently he had dedicated numerous hours during the previous evenings to the careful study of the instructions that he was to follow during the procedure, but whoever had written them down had used a variation of Latin that lacked accuracy. The text, for instance, mentioned articulations, which he took to mean joints, and connectors, which he took to mean tendons, and—God help him—he still didn't know how these pincers, though they be red hot, could be used to sever sinew, unless he did an awful lot of thrusting and pulling. Why was there no directive to use a knife? The instructions seemed vague, and there were no images to help. In spite of the numerous devices and contraptions around the room, he had been instructed to make use just of the pincers, since *tenailles* were the only instrument mentioned in the text.[48] The text itself was buried deep within a tome of legal ecclesiastical arguments and decisions, as if bound up intentionally with innocuous religious arcana that had nothing to do with hurting people and making them confess.

He had received the book and his instructions from a prelate who purported to come from the Holy Office of the Supreme Sacred Congregation of the Roman and Universal Inquisition, but who offered no advice, and furthermore, who seemed to share his ignorance about the particulars of the actual torture. In spite of intense study of the text in question, the inexperienced inquisitor nevertheless brought the thick tome with him into the torture chamber and asked his assistant, an even younger clergyman who must have been chosen for his corpulence rather than for his knowledge, to prop the book open to the desired page. He thought he had memorized every detail, but just in case his memory needed refreshing, the text would be at hand.

Father Clément stole a few final furtive glances at the desired page, and approached his victim, called the supplicant, all the while beseeching God in silent prayer, asking for strength, fortitude and a miraculous on-the-spot grasp of anatomy.

Zénobe was on his knees, a chain from each wrist fastened to iron rings on the floor. His body shivered with the cold, his head hanging to his chest, his long black hair covering his face.

"What is the preparedness of the pincers, *Père* Ignace?" was the inquisitor's first utterance.

Father Ignace looked into the fire and said, "You've only just placed them in the fire! It'll take time to get them red-hot. They're not even a scalding pink."

Father Clément gave his helper a scolding look of impatience, as if to say that he was ruining the theatricality of the solemn event.

"Oh," Father Ignace. "The pincers are a bright red, *mon père.* They are a fiery orange, and the … the … the ends are glowing, glowing a golden yellow, *mon père.*

Father Clément turned his attention back to the supplicant. He took Zénobe's chin by the hand to raise up his head. When the supplicant's hair fell away from his face the ecclesiastic saw that the young man's captors had already beaten him about

---

48 *Tenailles,* or pincers, were the only instrument used to torture Damiens, the regicide who attempted to assassinate Louis XV. They were used mostly to lacerate at his tendons at his arms and loins, in order to facilitate his being quartered. Even so, the horses had a difficult job of it, and the pincers had to be used several times before the attempt at quartering was completely successful. Even after the quartering, Damiens was still alive, and his trunk was seen to be breathing as he was thrown into the fire along with his members.

  The reason why a knife was not allowed during the interrogation is that it would be too easy to accidentally kill the supplicant. The purpose of the Question was to induce a confession. The victim need- ed to be alive, conscious, and with enough energy left over to allow him to scream during the burning ceremony. The priests therefore considered this torture to be a delicate operation, and why it was in this particular instance given to an inexperienced cleric is questionable. It is perhaps reasonable to suggest that only an absolute novice would have agreed to undertake this deed, so late in the Eighteenth century.

the head for he had cuts and dried blood on his forehead and cheekbones and one of his eyes was swollen shut.

"Your name is Marie-Jean Joseph Zénobe de Bosquet?"

Zénobe could open only one eye to look at his interrogator, but he used it to stare directly into his eyes.

"No, it is not."

This response seemed to rattle the cleric, who quickly stepped back to the table and tapped his gloved finger on a piece of parchment next to his book of infliction of torment. Clearing his throat, he said, "It states here, on this document, that your name is Marie-Jean Joseph Zénobe de Bosquet. If your name isn't Marie-Jean Joseph Zénobe de Bosquet, then, what is it?"

"I am Marie-Jean Joseph Zénobe Bosquet, without the *particule*."

"The absence of the *particule* is of no particular importance," said the clergyman impatiently.

Zénobe managed a chuckle. "You must be a foreigner. There are Frenchmen who would give a limb for the *particule*."[49]

"You are then not a gentleman?"

"I am a gentleman, but I am no noble."

"Why were you impersonating one, then?"

"For no good reason, save for the panache it gave me."

"You know that impersonating an aristocrat is punishable by law."

"Is that why I've been arrested and await your pleasure?"

"Why, no, *monsieur*, you've been arrested for heresy, and I will derive no pleasure in putting you to the Question."

"Well, ask your Question, then, and let us get this over with."

Zénobe had noticed his persecutor's youth and lack of self-confidence. He also noticed the handles on the pair of pincers emerging from the fire on a stone slab.

"What are you intending to do with that instrument of torture?" Zénobe asked the priest-torturer.

"They're to be used on the sinews underneath your arms and loins," answered Father Clément.

"But you are required to interrogate me first, are you not?"

"Of course. But the instrument of torture is supposed to be in constant view, ready for use right away, if the supplicant prove to be recalcitrant."

"You will find me not in the least recalcitrant!" exclaimed Zénobe who had no intention of being tortured. "I will be pliable as a lamb, for I enjoy speaking about my heresy, I derive pride from it, revel in my attachment to it. I wish my heresy proclaimed throughout the land, that I am no christian. I wish for His Holiness the Pope to know about it personally so that he himself can prepare the documents to ex-communicate me forthwith."

Father Clément was astounded, and Father Ignace standing behind him by the fire made the sign of the cross three times.

"If that is the case, let me ask you the first question."

The priest took the sheet of parchment lying next to the recipe book of torture, peered into it for a few seconds while his lips moved silently to the writing he deciphered. Putting the sheet down he intoned with as much gravity as he could muster, "Are you,

---

49   The *particule* made one a noble, and rising to the aristocracy made many a bourgeois salivate.

or have you ever been, an adherent of the apostate philosopher Voltaire; do you, or have you ever, followed his heretical writings; do you, or have you ever, subscribed to the philosophical tenets therein described?"

"Well, then, that is not just one question, is it? There are really three questions in quick succession. But so as not to belabor this transformation of singularity into plurality, for which you ecclesiastics have always had a penchant, and not to waste your precious time, Father, I shall answer all three questions in unison. The answer to your three questions is yes, yes, and, why, absolutely yes."

The priest seemed relieved that a forthright answer, or answers, had come out so quickly. Then he looked worried, for now he knew not at what junction of the interview he should apply the tool of torture, or even if he had to.

Zénobe continued to speak, unbidden by anything the priest had said or done.

"Voltaire was my beloved teacher, just as Jesus Christ is presumed to be your beloved teacher. I assume that you would agree to this, that Jesus Christ is presumed to be your teacher, and that you love him."

The priest answered without hesitation. "Of course, Jesus Christ is my teacher. He is my only teacher! And I love him with all of my heart and soul."

"Then why," Zénobe asked, sweetness and tranquillity in his voice, "then why do you not follow his teachings?"

"Whatever do you mean? What makes you think that I do not follow Jesus Christ's teachings?" Father Clément looked to Father Ignace as if looking for a witness that he did, indeed, follow the teachings of the Messiah.

"Look into your heart," asked the supplicant. "What do you there see?"

"I see Jesus Christ in my heart, but, listen, you're not the one to ask questions. You wait for my questions, and then you answer my questions. You are not supposed to question me. Who are you to be questioning me?"

Once again, Father Clément shot a glance at his colleague, seeking support. But Father Ignace had his eyes on the pincers, now glowing to the correct temperature.

"I am only a humble observer who sees, and fears, that you're about to throw all of Christ's teachings into the mire. You say you hold Jesus Christ in your heart, but look at your hands. See with your very own eyes what you're about to do. Look at that very book you have placed on the table: you are about to torture a man whom you don't even know, burn his skin, sever his sinews, tear into his flesh. Tell me what is in this book, is it the Word of Christ?"

"How dare you, how dare you question me!" retorted Father Clément whose expression of hesitant discomfiture had become a red scowl, even as he did look down at his gloved hands. "I am doing my duty, and I am following the orders of my superiors! If you are judging me, then you are judging them!"

"But I am not judging them, for they are not the ones present in this dungeon today, they are not the ones wearing the gloves that will hold the scorching implement that you will use to dig into my flesh. You are the one who is turning a blind eye to the true teachings of Christ, not your superiors. If your superiors were to tell you to jump off a cliff, would you do so?"

"Stop it! Stop asking me questions! It is I who will henceforth ask the questions, not you!"

With an overcompensating sense of dignity Father Clément grabbed anew the piece of parchment, brought it to his eyes and asked gruffly, "Are you, or have you ever been, an adherent of the apostate philosopher Voltaire; do you, or have you ever, followed..."

His speech slowed and halted. He realized that he had already asked this bit. But he continued the inquisition with brave propriety.

"Have you been guilty of espousing heretical… heretical…" The priest again came to a moment of silence. Hesitating with disorientation, the priest seemed to fight off a desire to waver from the script. During this pause, the only sound came from the quivering of the flames. Without glancing at the page, he said to Zénobe, "What we do here is God's sacred mission, and we dedicate ourselves to His holy service."

"You may think you do, but I assure you, you do not. You do the opposite, for did not God, through his only begotten son Jesus Christ, teach you to be gentle and tolerant, even unto your enemies? Did he not instruct you to turn the other cheek when your enemy struck you? At what moment of his ministry did he teach his followers to torture, maim and execute the man who refused to believe in him? Tell me, where is it explained in the testimony to his actions and words, which you call a holy text, that an apostate should be murdered for not believing in his words? You yourself do not believe in his words, for you are willing to ignore them, and in ignoring them, to alter them, and commit the reverse of what Jesus taught."

Plausible Development of Events: Version B

The young priest's hands shook so much that he could barely hold on to the heavy iron pincers. Sweat made the metal in his hand slippery, but when he put on a thick leather glove in order to place the pincers into the fire he almost dropped them. The leather was too stiff and impeded the movement of his fingers.

While the ends of the pincers lay in the flames, the reverend father, Ignatius was his Christian name, who was hardly older than his victim, wondered why he had been chosen to torture this young man. He had no experience in the torture chamber. Worse, he had no particular predilection for torture. Still, he had agreed unquestioningly to carry on such an important task, and, indeed, felt much gratitude to his superiors for the trust placed on him. He had spent all night studying the sacred instructions from the texts given to him by the Holy Office of the Grand Inquisitor, but in case he needed to refresh his memory, he had brought the book down into the dungeon. The thick incunabulum, bound in lambskin, lay nearby open to a certain page, and he strode to it to give it a furtive glance, as if to gain courage from it. Zénobe, in spite of the heavy beating his captors had given him about the head, and with his eyes almost swollen shut, noticed the discomfiture and the lack of confidence in his torturer. His bloodshot eyes also ran to the tongs, beginning to glow orange in the fire.

"What is your intention with those pincers?" Zénobe asked.

The priest started when the captive addressed him with such aplomb. "They're to be used on the sinews underneath your arms and loins," he answered.

"Are you not required to ask me questions first?"

"Of course, but the instrument of torture is required to be visible to the accused at all times, ready for use at all times."

"Will it be necessary to use it?"

"Only if the accused prove to be recalcitrant, or reticent, or in any way reluctant to abide by the regulations of this procedure."

"Ah, commendable use of alliteration!" Zénobe chuckled.

The priest could not help but smile along with his victim. "Of what?"

"Your use of alliteration. The repetition of sounds: 'recalcitrant, reticent, reluctant, regulations.' Voltaire would have made good use of that."

With the name of Voltaire the priest's face grew dark.

Zénobe continued, "But I must confess that I won't be in the least recalcitrant, reticent or reluctant, and that I will follow all regulations. Respectfully. Resolutely."

"If that be the case, let me ask you the first question." The priest took a sheet of vellum lying next to the book of torture and peered into it for a few seconds while his lips moved silently to the writing he deciphered.

"Are you, Marie-Jean Joseph Zénobe Bosquet, or have you ever been, an adherent of the apostate Voltaire; do you, or have you ever, followed his heretical writings; do you, or have you ever, subscribed to the philosophical tenets therein described?"

"Well, then, that is not just one question, is it? There are really three questions in quick succession. I'm not surprised. You have a propensity for things that come in three in your religion. But so as not to waste your time, Father, I shall answer all three in unison. The truthful response to all three questions is a resounding yes."

The priest seemed relieved that a forthright answer had come out so quickly, and so pacifically. Then he wrinkled his brow, for now he knew not at what juncture of the interrogation he should apply the pincers, or even if he had to. His superiors had all assumed that the accused would prevaricate, or refuse to speak at all. He himself had expected the supplicant to remain mute.

But Zénobe continued to speak, unbidden by anything the priest had said or done. "Voltaire was my teacher, just as Jesus Christ is supposed to be your teacher."

This brought a gasp from the priest. Now he understood why this prisoner was here, in the dungeon, ready to receive penance. Equating Voltaire with Je—

"I assume that Jesus Christ is your teacher, is he not?"

The priest spluttered, "Of course, Jesus Christ is my teacher. He is my only teacher!"

"Then, why," Zénobe asked, sweetness and tranquillity in his voice, "then why do you not follow his teachings?"

"How dare you question my faith! You are the accused here, not I. I follow, and have ever followed, the teachings of our Lord Jesus Christ, our Savior, the Son of God!"

Zénobe waited a few seconds before answering, in order to enhance the drama of his response.

"Looking at those red-hot pincers shows me otherwise."

The priest followed Zénobe's gaze towards the fire. The flames were mesmerizing, and the metal embedded in them was a golden red.

"Tell me, Father. Can you envision Jesus using such an instrument?"

The priest was silent.

"Can you see any of his disciples applying such an instrument to the sinews of their enemies?"

The priest looked at Zénobe, anger dissipating from the wrinkles of his face and dissolving into an awareness of truth.

"Would Peter have used them? How about Andrew, his brother? Can you see James, or John, Philip, perhaps, can you see any one of them approach an enemy bearing such an instrument? What do you say of Matthew, or Thomas the doubter, or either of the two Judases, including Judas Iscariot? Peter denied Jesus, thrice! Just as you are denying Jesus now. Judas Iscariot betrayed Jesus, just as you are doing now, for you are willfully betraying his teachings. Don't you see, as soon as you begin to torture me, nay, as soon as you began to threaten me, you diverged from the teachings of Christ. But even Judas Iscariot the betrayer, would he have used these pincers to torture a man?"

Father Ignace could find no words to answer Zénobe. He seemed frozen in place between the fire and his captive.

"And could you please tell me, loving Father, if His Holiness the Pope, whom you call Pio VI, pious, for he is devout and righteous, could he ever grasp those pincers and use them to tear out the flesh of any man?"

With hands clasping the leather glove hard to his chest, the priest answered, "No, I cannot. I cannot see these things. But my superiors have given me instructions, they put their trust in me, to put you to the Question, and as a simple parish priest, I feel it is my duty to obey. I have sworn obedience to the ecclesiastic hierarchy. My salvation would be at stake if I were to neglect my duty."

Zénobe looked straight into the priest's eyes. He could see an incipient sheen of tears making his inquisitor's eyes gleam.

"The ecclesiastical hierarchy extends to the Pope, who is merely the Vicar of Christ, and from him the authority goes directly to Jesus. Jesus has the final word on what your duty is supposed to be. Why do your superiors expect you to commit an action that goes against the teachings of the final authority on this and all other matters? They intend for you to commit an atrocity which they themselves are loath to do. They suppose you will suspend your conscience in order to follow orders. Do you not know, your conscience is your own, it is independent of all things and belongs only to you, and it is sacrosanct? Do you not know, when you seek the solace and tranquility of prayer, that your conscience is but an emanation of all that is good, all that is just, all that is compassionate? Nobody should dare to interfere with your own conscience. You know what is right, and what is wrong. Jesus is your source of what is moral, and what is not. Act as Jesus would have acted, follow your heart, which is the seat of the conscience. Everything else can be cast aside, including the consequences of your refusal to follow orders. Did not Jesus disregard the consequences of his own actions, knowing full well that it would lead to his torment and to his death? Did not Jesus teach only what was good and just? Did he not teach you to clear your heart of what is wicked and sinful?"

The priest had by this time put his glove down and he slowly approached Zénobe. A tear escaped to run down his face. The horror of the atrocity he had been ready to commit was clearly written on his expression. He took one of the young man's shackled hands in both of his own and said in a whisper, "I know all of this, my brother, but what is being questioned here is why you don't accept Jesus as your moral authority. If only you were to do that, my superiors would be joyous, their cup would runneth over, as would mine. They would be willing to forgive your past transgressions if they were to know that you were a true follower of Christ."

The priest's gesture went right into the captive's heart. It was Zénobe's turn to shed a tear. "I understand you, Father, and implore you to try to understand what I am about to tell you. I have no doubt that Jesus Christ was a good man, and that all his life, leading to his ultimate sacrifice, everything he stood for, everything that he taught mankind, was for the good of humanity. I accept Jesus as a benevolent teacher, as a truly unique and superior being, whose sole intentions were for the betterment of humanity everywhere. However, his intentions were appropriated by others, men who were not at all superior, and who gave in to personal ambition and the corruption of power. Jesus's message was commandeered by others and twisted in such ways that the original meaning was lost. The Office of the Holy Inquisition is such a distortion. How could such a bloody and vindictive hegemony have come into being? How could such an organization brutally enforce its tenets, annihilate whole populations, massacre entire villages, persecute unbelievers? Is this how they attempt to persuade them to come into the fold of Christianity, with the sword hovering above their heads? Is this how Jesus attempted to persuade the crowds in Galilee? It seems to me that he sought to prevail upon the unbelievers with love, kindness, charity, and tolerance. Today as I observe your institution, I see none of that. I see the contrary: acrimony, reprisals, ambition, the acquisition of wealth, injustice, total corruption. Jesus's original message has been lost, seized, altered and diverted, for the sake of power, so that this power will continue, unabated, forever. I have sad news for your superiors: they will fail, as all religions do that allow evil to come unto their altars. They cannot rule over the conscience of individuals, those who know the difference between right and wrong. What the catholic church is doing here, with us, now, is wrong. We both know it. They know it, though they are unwilling to let go of the power that corrupts them. They also know, if it take a thousand years, that their religion will fail, weighed down as it is with countless persecutions, prolonged hatred, and everlasting oppression."

Both torturer and victim were weeping now.

"I cannot let you go," the priest finally said.

"I know, Father. But when your superiors realize that you have not acquitted yourself of your obligations, they will send another in your stead, some other clergyman who might not have a conscience, who is without pity or compassion, someone who might even enjoy the torturing of others. He will without qualms take those pincers and rip out my flesh, and you will have your share of responsibility in his heinous act. You must do what Jesus would have done, and if you cannot confront your superiors and confess to them that you were the one to free me, then you must allow someone else to free me. Please send word to *monsieur* Wagnière, Voltaire's secretary in Ferney, and have him come immediately to collect me. He is a protestant, so he doesn't fall under your jurisdiction. Surely you could allow a protestant to save a miscreant catholic who cannot come back into the fold. I've given you my reasons why I refuse to adhere to catholic tenets: it has nothing to do with Jesus, and I have never meant any disrespect to Jesus. It is the institution that purports to follow his teachings that is my enemy, made up of mortals who have corrupted what Jesus taught us. He taught us to be merciful, compassionate, tolerant. The class of priests, of which you are a part, show us cruelty and repression, and demand from us blind loyalty. Please, Father, for the sake of even one victim, you must do as Jesus would have done."

The priest had done weeping. With a dry eye he looked Zénobe up and down, his contemplation of the penitent lingering on the blood stains on his ripped shirt, on the cuts and bruises on his face, on the dried blood matting his hair. He slowly backed away from Zénobe, then turned around to face the fire. He took a wooden cask from the floor and poured its contents onto the flames. It was water, and the fire hissed and popped as it died.

Just before this book went into publication, the following handwritten text was discovered in the papers of the Revolutionary Jacques Pierre Brissot de Warville, whom Zénobe will accompany to America in 1788, and with whom he will return to France the following year and help to foment the Revolution. There are no notations on the text, and it is not written in Brissot's handwriting. The handwriting is, however, similar to that found in the letters Zénobe wrote to André, to *monsieur* Maurel and to the *marquis* de Thibouville. One can surmise that the Z refers to Zénobe himself, and the E to *ecclésiastique*. The note may have nothing to do with the interrogation in Turin, but it may shed some light as to a possible exchange between the priest and his victim.

Z: I believe in virtue.

E: But you don't believe in God!

Z: What does one thing have to do with the other?

E: It is God who is the harbinger of virtue. Without God, there is no virtue!

Z: How do you come about that glorious deduction? Atheists may be virtuous! The most virtuous people in history have been atheists.

E: Impossible! They are without the Word of God, and it is the Word of God that grants us the conscience to be virtuous.

Z: We atheists seek our code of ethics elsewhere, since we are convinced there is no god. It is called the Golden Rule: I do unto others as I would have others do unto me; I don't do unto others as I would not have others do unto me.

E: But that is Jesus Christ who granted us such godly words!

Z: Verify your history, sir. The Golden Rule came to us from Confucius, from ancient Greece, from ancient Egypt. Belief in a god is irrelevant to this maxim.

E: It's a commandment directly come from God.

Z: It is a basic rule of virtue that has nothing to do with a fictitious supreme being.

E: Blasphemy!

Z: You attack me with senseless and illogical words when you've run out of logical things to say.

E: Impiety!

Z: You call me names when your power of reasoning runs out.

E: Apostate!

Z: Of course I'm an apostate. I'm an atheist, for the love of god! And those words you use against me are illogical, for there is no supreme being in whom to believe. I cannot insult a spirit that is not real. It's as if I were insolent towards an elf, or a fairy, or, if you prefer, a ghost. None of those exist, either. We are alone, all alone in this world, and that is a frightening prospect to most people. We suffer a thousand agonies to think that we eventually will end up at the end of our existence, that this world and our existence in it are all there is, and there's never to be anything more. We will be forever unconscious, never to awake again. It is so enticing to believe in a soul, and that this soul will somehow continue in some sort of peaceful afterlife. But just as we do not remember our existence before our birth, we will not be aware of anything to come after our death. This is why it is so imperative that we live well in this life because this is the only life we'll ever have. This is why it is so imperative that we not kill each other as easily as we kill flies. We are wasting our life when we give credence to and hold hopes for a life afterwards that will somehow make up for the hell we've made of this one. We should be kind to one another, and live our lives to the fullest, and savor this life, which is our only life.

E: We shall have life everlasting. It has been promised us by our Lord Saviour Jesus Christ who for our sins was crucified and died—

Z: And yet, you don't even follow Christ's teachings! Love for one's neighbor, what's that? You turn it into a fictitious notion. You show no more love for your neighbors than any of the other religions do. You'd rather kill an apostate rather than see him go on living, quite successfully, and perhaps happily, without god. You rage against anyone who is happy without god, you foam at the mouth to see the likes of me fulfilled in life, untroubled by religion, unburdened by dogma. It must be the tithes that you want from me and that are not forthcoming. It must be the control and influence you want to have over me and that I disregard. It must be your lust for authoritarianism and your need to subject everybody to your manipulation and from which I make myself independent. The problem lies with you, for you cannot abide to see me go in peace. I, however, bid you adieu and hope you go in peace. Go and continue to build your edifice which is based on legends and myths, that is your affair. Go and make a god out of a man who after death rose again, and I sincerely believe that you should be allowed to do so as well. But do all this, and more, should you wish it, without me. You don't need me to continue to build your house of cards founded on willful fallacies and imagined longings. Go, go in peace, for you will never be able to fool me. I just implore you to leave me alone. Think what you will, but I beg you to leave me alone. I wish my life to be free of you.

Bolt to Freedom

The next verifiable situation in which Zénobe is observed occurs as he flees from the Cathedral of Turin as fast as his damaged legs could carry him. It was under the cover of night, during a violent hailstorm, with lightning and thunder tearing the sky asunder, that Father Clément, or Father Ignatius (there is disagreement as to the name of the priest, although his birth name seems to have been Paulo) released the captive. All of Zénobe's belongings had been returned to him, save for his money, which one of the Annecy priests must have taken, and the only Voltaire book Zénobe had been carrying, *Histoire de Jenni, ou Le Sage et l'athée*, published only in 1776 and which, fortunately, bore a pseudonym, M. Sherloc. The manic ministers had probably not yet made the connection with Voltaire, but they confiscated the book nevertheless.

It was Father Clément himself who gave him instructions on how to find the ecclesiastical stables, in order to steal a horse.

Zénobe dashed away from the capital city of the realm of Victor Amadeus III with so much haste, and anger, that he stopped neither for food nor for repose. How he wished he had Gaignun with him. His Palomino was young and in good health, would have been able to see very well by the flashes of lightning, and would have needed only a half hour here and there to rest. The best horse he could find in the cathedral's stables was a plodding dispirited thing, a far cry from his Palomino. Gaignun was a pale phantom horse, wild and ethereal, an equine spirit who, as he galloped, barely touched the earth and made hardly a sound. The priestly horse he ended up with might as well have been an ass, it was so sluggish and sullen. It was going to take a while to get to Geneva.

Geneva was his destination. It was on the way, and it was run by protestants. He expected them to be uninterested in a commoner disguised as a French aristocrat fleeing the catholics. But perhaps they would not find out that he was a commoner, or that he was fleeing the catholics. He was under the impression that he could be a convincing French aristocrat. It was easy enough to imitate the rapidity of speech and the nasal quality in the voice of the Parisian noblesse. He had lived in intimate proximity with two of France's wealthiest *marquis*, and he could impersonate them down to their last haughty and condescending gesture. All he needed was to dry out, and to get a better horse. No one would believe an aristo would be shivering from the cold and riding such a nag.

But before he was even out of Turin, a bolt of lightning struck a building as he was riding past. He thought he could smell the energy of the discharge, and he certainly had felt a tingling on his skin. Anyone else would have thought that God was trying to fulminate him, to make him run back in terror to the church. Zénobe knew better: there were more hazards inside the church than out here, dodging thunderbolts and being pelted by hundreds of little hailstones that were hard and cold. He was drenched, but slowly his anger at having been imprisoned gave way to joy, and, to some extent, pride. He had managed to evade mortal danger, and he had done so with words. His argument was what made the priest release him. He had used no force, no act of belligerence. He had used the truth, and the truth had made him free. He felt gratitude for Father Anselme who had educated him thoroughly about the bible, and John 8:32 had always struck him as genuinely honest. Lying did make one a slave to sin, and the truth was always the better path, in every situation. Why didn't these idiots even accept what their own man had taught them? Never did any followers repudiate their leader as often and as thoroughly as these hypocritical Judases, kissing him and in the very act denouncing him! Jesus Christ knew he was going to fail, shortrun and longrun, surrounded by disciples who lacked both conviction and courage, and who, in the centuries to come, would be succeeded by charlatans, hypocrites and malefactors who found they could hide, and be protected, in the shadows of the temples erected in Christ's name. The Lord Son of God knew that his works would be futile, yet he went through with his efforts nevertheless. Ergo, God was complicit in the savage litany of numberless crimes committed during the long centuries to come, dedicated all to His Son's name, under His Son's ascendancy and bearing His Son's imprimatur, or—or—the Bible had it wrong. Jesus knew nothing of what was to come, for he was just a man, a son of Adam and just as blind to the repercussions of his acts, but more importantly, blind to the malignant and injurious crusades that for aeons his followers would manage to contrive.

With these merry thoughts, Zénobe continued to guide his horse through the mud of fields and woods. He was wise enough now to stay off the main roads and keep a low profile, sidestepping villages and steering clear of any place where he heard human voices. The next day, with the rain still falling, on a farm near Aosta, he sold one of his foils, André's, in order to buy food. In spite of his hunger and the pain of his injuries, he still could marvel at the speech of the inhabitants: it was magical language that he could understand, since it was half Piedmontese and half French.

The road to Chamonix was difficult for his nag, for the land rose and the poor steed slowed to a crawl. In his mind Zénobe drew triangles with vectors of forces, but he couldn't explain to himself the exact physics of a steep incline. It seemed the force of gravity increased as they ascended into the mountains. He promised himself to read Voltaire's book on Newton, and Newton's own *Principia Mathematica*, as soon as he returned to Ferney. Looking around him, and up at Mont Blanc, he was moved to tears at the beauty of nature. To think that he might not have been alive for much longer. Even with rain clouds that merged with the mountainsides, the panorama was magnificent. No wonder Rousseau had placed such importance on this part of the world. The thought of the Genevan philosopher reminded him that *madame* Rousseau had returned to Geneva after her husband's death. Perhaps he would be able to pay her a visit. She had been kind to him in Paris, and he wanted to offer her his condolences.

Zénobe's fear of being apprehended did not diminish as he traveled west. He would be in Victor Amédée's lands until he crossed the border into Geneva. He did not know if the Savoyards had been alerted by the Turingeois, or if anybody was following him, but he did know that the French were. The despot of Savoy took exception to French priests crossing into his lands, even though catholics from different countries had a way of dispensing with regional xenophobia and joining forces for a higher good. At any moment he might be caught in the middle between clerical phalanxes coming at him from two directions, and here there was but one road leading out of the Alps. He would not feel out of danger until he had crossed into Geneva, hoping that the protestants there would truly not be interested in him, and that they would not release him to the papists.

He was right. They let him through at the custom's gate and nobody gave him a glance, in spite of his bruised face and swollen eye. He had released his nag from bondage before walking the last league into Geneva, hoping that nobody would be interested in an old debilitated beast. He wanted her to be left free to roam for the rest of her life in the beautiful terrain around Lake Geneva. It was a fine fate granted to an ecclesiastical horse.

In the Land of the Protestants

Z énobe knew that all was not well in the world of the protestants, either. The original lutherans hated the calvinists, arminianism was viewed with suspicion by both, all three abhorred the anabaptists, who despised the mennonites, who loathed the pietists, and they all derided the anglicans for being too much like the catholics, including the methodists, who split off from them. The baptists, whether or not they had existed continuously since the time of Christ, also could not get along with their protestant brethren. The quakers, poor dears, were viewed with distrust and alarm. Splinters, fragments, shards, fracturing and splitting, branching off and diverging into antagonistic fractious divisions, Zénobe thought, like a worm disintegrating into disparate segments, all without a head, forging ahead in ambivalent directions, meandering irresolutely for the most arbitrary, capricious and fantastical reasons: fatalism, good works, deistic cannibalism, divorce, marriage, virginity, chastity, circumcision, when to baptize, when not to, absolution, condemnation, conception (immaculate or otherwise), confession, communion, all of these were confounding concoctions. Such silliness would be ridiculous were it not for the fact that the protestants massacred each other as well. Zénobe realized that religious diversification was the proper of man, because dissension, intolerance and the unquenchable desire for novelty were an innate part of man's fundamental constitution. How many men, women and children were burned alive for their refusal to identify the presence of Christ in an insubstantial wafer? How many intangible beings must be created before humans realize that their beliefs are all absurd figments of their febrile imagination, and that it is religion that is the illness that causes this fever, these hallucinations, these delirious imaginations that their sick minds project onto the real world?

However, Zénobe remembered well Voltaire's lesson: "If there were in England but one religion, its despotism would be fearful; if there were but two, they would cut each other's throats; but there are thirty of them, and they live in peace and happy."[50] He also remembered another quote of his: "Every sensible man, every honorable man,

---

50   «*S'il n'y avait en Angleterre qu'une religion, son despotisme serait à craindre; s'il n'y en avait que deux, elles se couperaient la gorge; mais il y en a trente, et elles vivent en paix et heureuses.*» (From the chapter on Quakers in Voltaire's *Lettres philosophiques*, published in 1734.)

must hold the Christian sect in horror."[51] With a chuckle, another one came to him: "When it is a question of money, everybody is of the same religion."[52] Voltaire was still with him, and through him would have another life, and Zénobe would make sure that even after he was gone, Voltaire would keep going. He needed to go back to Ferney and help Wagnière take Voltaire's library to Saint Petersburg. Wagnière would be very worried about him now.

But since he had to traipse through Geneva anyway, he might as well go say a quick *bonjour* to Jean-Jacques's widow. "Widow" was saying much, since they never, legally, married. At least that was one thing he could respect about Rousseau, and the same with Benjamin Franklin. Neither cared enough for society's arbitrary rules to worry themselves about the so-called sanctity of marriage, and all the statutes and bylaws that marriage entailed. Being a philosopher meant being able to flout societal propriety. He and André, for instance, would never be able to marry. But who wanted to marry in the first place? He harbored such hostility against a society that would rather see him dead, that all of those sacred cows which had become the pillars of society were disgusting to him. All he wanted was to smash the pillars down and bring society to its knees, cut off its heads, and fashion it anew to the ideals of the Utopia of Reason, where everything had a purpose free of superstition, free of blind conformity to tradition. Exemptions would be made, of course, from the standpoint of fairness and individual rights, for the gullible who insisted on following their religious prerogatives, so long as they did not attempt to shackle anybody else. Zénobe was acutely aware, as had been his teacher Voltaire, that just because you offered enlightenment to the masses, it did not mean that everybody would welcome it. Some people preferred to be shackled. And, according to Voltaire, those who willingly gave themselves an oppressor, deserved their chains.

Even Jean-Jacques Rousseau had remained unfettered throughout his entire life. Having given his allegiance to the protestants, then to the catholics, then to the protestants again, he saw to it that in the end he gave his allegiance to no one and remained free to follow his own counsel at every turn in his life. Surely, the man would be remembered for that, Zénobe thought. We criticize him for having abandoned all five of his children, but no doubt he was thinking of finding happier circumstances for them. A rolling stone would have found it difficult to be followed by five, no six, if you count their mother, smaller stones rolling along beside it. How would the children have felt, to be uprooted every time their father became enervated by the charity of friends and absconded to a new place? And how would he have fed them? Most of the time, Rousseau had no money, even when his books became best sellers, for money lacked meaning to him, and he valued it like he valued dirt: necessary to grow things, but dirty nonetheless.

If only he had not been so intolerant of the *chevalière* d'Éon's sex, so holier-than-thou, Zénobe sighed to himself while walking the streets of Geneva. He could have been my friend as well.

Finding where *madame* Rousseau lived was easy since she was now the resident celebrity. Even Genevans had become more nostalgic and accepting of the *philosophe* since he had died, forgetting how angry he had made them feel. Rousseau's best quality was

---

51 *«Je conclus que tout homme sensé, tout homme de bien, doit avoir la secte chrétienne en horreur.»* (From *Examen important de Milord Bolingbroke, ou le tombeau du fanatisme*, published in 1736.)

52 *«Quand il s'agit d'argent, tout le monde est de la même religion.»* (From a letter to *madame* d'Épinal, December 26, 1760.)

his fierce and total independence; it eventually made everyone who ever tried to help him feel that he was infringing on it. But now, the man was dead, and all was forgiven. *Madame* Rousseau was back for a temporary visit, and the townsfolk welcomed her in their midst.

At every junction where Zénobe needed instructions, the people he asked interrupted their activities and gave him their unreserved attention. These people are so different, thought Zénobe, for Parisians have a tendency to ignore passersby, if not intentionally jostle them as they go past.

With the help of the friendly and accommodating protestants, Zénobe was directed to the rue de la Fusterie. There, he scratched on the front door, and *madame* Rousseau herself opened it.

She recognized him immediately (who could ever forget those brilliant blue eyes?), even though the upper half of his face had seen some recent realignment. His left eye was still swollen, although his pupil now peered out a little bit.

Without a word she drew him inside by the lapels.

"How do men get into so much trouble?" she asked, not expecting an answer, of course.

Zénobe gave her one anyway. "Because other people believe that it is within their rights to attack us."

"If you're anything like Jean-Jacques, you gave 'em plenty of cause to attack you."

She directed him into her small kitchen and pointed to a stool. Zénobe obediently sat down. Out of a drawer in an ancient buffet she brought out a flat basket containing an assorted motley collection of bandages of different colors and lengths. There was a round canister with a mysterious brown powder in it, from which she ladled two heaping spoonsful into a bowl, and, applying some water to it, began to mix it violently. But with what care and tenderness did she apply the resulting poultice to the lacerations on Zénobe's head and forehead! The only thing she said was, "Close your eye a bit. This won't sting."

Zénobe let the last remaining quantities of torment, offense and hurt drain from his body and heart, as he gave himself over to the succor offered to him by *madame* Rousseau. The evil festering in Turin could not reach him here, and he felt that he was melting in the soothing care and attention of the world's most famous widow. There, in a world unto themselves, as is often the case between patient and caregiver, they exchanged two of the most important gifts of humanity, compassion and gratitude, he who had never had a mother, and she, who had not been able to keep any of her five children.

After the poultice had been applied and the bandages secured around Zénobe's head, *madame* Rousseau said, "You remind me of Jean-Jacques. He was always getting into trouble. Once, in Môtiers, the whole village came to our house and started throwing rocks through the windows."[53]

She laughed with the nostalgia of the thought.

---

53   This famous lapidation of Rousseau's house occurred on the night of the 6th to 7th of September, 1765. All the windows were broken, and so many stones accumulated inside that an intendant who witnessed the scene the following day cried out, "My God, it's a quarry!" It would have been of interest to know if Zénobe was aware that the attack had been instigated by the village pastor, Frédéric-Guillaume de Montmollin, who, in spite of his initial joy at welcoming a celebrity into his congregation, grew to dislike, and then condemn, Rousseau's abominations, i.e., his beloved freedom of conscience that left him impervious to the dogmatic theology of the protestants.

"How scared we were!" she said as she combed with her fingers what hair of Zénobe's remain uncovered by bandages. "Jean-Jacques had just traversed the hallway into the bedroom when a boulder came crashing in, missing him by just inches."

Her eyes looked faraway into another life, a previous life of hers that didn't seem to have been hers at all.

"It was one of the few times that Jean-Jacques hugged me for dear life, and that hug was worth all the rocks being pelted into the house by the raging mob."

She laughed. "Only Jean-Jacques could get an entire village that mad at him. We had to leave the very next morning. Of course, Jean-Jacques wouldn't pay for the broken windows, said it wasn't his fault. I doubt that landlord will ever take us back!"

That is one of the heartaches of life, catching oneself in the thought that someone is still alive. Of course, that landlord could never take them back, for Jean-Jacques was dead.

Zénobe saw as the thought became visible through her eyes, and tears ran down his one unbandaged eye. In his sitting position he embraced *madame* Rousseau, who embraced him back, and while they both mourned their dead, they exchanged two other gifts of humanity, condolence and solace.

Madame Rousseau prepared a meal for the two of them, and they chatted like long lost friends. It never occurred to her to ask him how he had received his wounds, and Zénobe didn't volunteer the information. He did, however, tell her of his impending trip to Russia, to convey Voltaire's library to Catherine, which she thought amusing.

"In the snow, through Prussia and Russia? My, you do invite trouble, don't you? Just like my Jean-Jacques. He never bothered to follow the consequences of his actions, so avid was he to do in the present what he felt he had to do."

She washed her hands in a bowl of water. "Jean-Jacques never accumulated a library," she informed him. "We were never long enough in any one place for him to be able to do so. Books are such heavy things! Whenever the publishers gave him a pile of his own books, he gave them away, to friends, to enemies, to whomever needed them the most, is what he said."

"Since I am here in Geneva," Zénobe told *madame* Rousseau, "I might as well visit Panckoucke's bookstore."

"Oh, you will revel in it, I am sure! Here, he is allowed to sell anything he wishes, not like in Paris where most of the books are forbidden. In Geneva you will see all of Jean-Jacques' books, and all of Voltaire's, and the rest of the bunch. The *Encyclopédie* is there, in full view, with all the volumes of plates, and a disturbing collection of books of odious stories."

Zénobe was too curious to refrain from asking, "Odious stories?"

Madame Rousseau widened her eyes and spoke in a whisper. "Yes, stories of bedlam, where people show everything, you know, of themselves, to everybody, without any shame or modesty, and go lurking from boudoir to boudoir, or even in public places. Very disturbing, and one of the female characters is even called by my name!"

Zénobe surmised the book must be *Thérèse philosophe*, a hedonistic novel of licentiousness and libertinage.[54] He had never read it, never having been able to get his hands on a copy.

"Well, thank you for the warning," Zénobe said to *madame* Rousseau. "I shall stay away from such books. I had no idea of the danger."

---

54 A huge bestseller, from its first edition in 1748, to the end of the 18th century and beyond.

It was a little white lie he told, of course. Zénobe realized that in spite of his undying love of the truth, at times like these it was important to avoid vexing an old prude who could be pardoned for holding an old-fashioned prim and censorious opinion.

All she had done, however, was to whet his appetite even more for his visit to Panckoucke's bookstore. As luck would have it, it was only a few blocks away, on the rue du Lac. He walked to the door of *madame* Rousseau's house with more buoyancy to his step than when he had come in. After heartfelt thanks, he hugged her again, and finally said to her what he had come to say.

"I also want to communicate to you my sorrow and my remorse about having become upset at your husband. It was on the spur of the emotional moment, and I was so caught up in the defense of my friend, *la chevalière* d'Éon, that I was unable to—"

"Shush," answered *madame* Rousseau. "You needn't explain. Jean-Jacques was so used to these outbursts from his interlocutors that it didn't make any impression on him. He was so used to being yelled at, and, to tell you the truth, he viewed these attacks as proof that he was universally rejected and loathed. You see, Jean-Jacques always had to stand all alone. The man who insists he is always right is surprised when others think him wrong. But he doesn't learn. He still thinks he is always right. He will never accept that he is the one to vex others."

"Still, he was a great man, a great philosopher, and he deserved my utmost respect and admiration, which I still feel for him."

"Thank you, my son. Now that he is gone, that he will write no more, he has entered into the realm of the legacy of the future. Multitudes will judge him, and some will love him, others will not. Yet I know that my Jean-Jacques has a secure place in that legacy, as does your *monsieur* de Voltaire. They belong to the ages now, away from our protection, and we must be happy for them, for they lived the way they wanted, and they wrote what came from their hearts. Who could ask for more?"

Zénobe turned slowly away, in admiration of *madame* Rousseau's sagacity and comprehension. She might have begun life as a washerwoman, but she had become, by dint of proximity to a great and complex mind, a philosopher in her own right.

After a left turn, a right, and another left, Zénobe was standing in front of the vitrines of Panckoucke's Genevan bookstore. There, in full view under the late afternoon sun, were copies of books that would have driven the French censors wild with rage. There was a whole collection by Jean-Jacques Rousseau, including his *Émile*, a treatise on education, that enraged even the protestants of Geneva. Yet here it was, thick and luscious, half open in an alluring pose, with part of its soft leather binding showing. Next to it, *Letters from the Mountain* and *The Social Contract* proved to be stunning companions, in blue leather binding, a color which he had never seen for books. To the left he espied Diderot's *Rameau's Nephew* and his *Supplement to the Voyage of Bougainville*, both bound in leather the color of cream. Bright red was the color chosen for Helvétius's *De l'Esprit, or Essays on the Mind*, and beige the color of d'Holbach's *The System of Nature*, which, here, displayed his true name, as opposed to a pseudonym. Zénobe rushed to the next vitrine, where he found his beloved friend and mentor, arrayed in double rows of tawny leather, his plays mixed with tales and philosophical treatises, some open, some standing, some stacked. An illustrated over-sized *Candide* was front and center, open to a beautiful illustration depicting the scene in Lisbon where the young hero is being given a thorough spanking in time to dirge music while in the background his beloved teacher Pangloss is being burned alive at the stake. It was placed in the middle of diagonally-positioned volumes arranged to the sides. Zénobe was overwhelmed with emotion, and he tore his eyes away from the books and looked all around him. People were walking by on the sidewalk with great tranquillity and composure, speaking about everyday things as they passed by, glancing at the books through the glass and thinking it the most natural thing in the world. What a most wonderful society, thought Zénobe. This is ordinary and commonplace to them. The police are not breaking down the doors and arresting everybody inside, booksellers and buyers alike. And we are but a few leagues away from France! Is this, then, the progress that the Enlightenment brings to society?

Zénobe calmed himself down, and opened the front door. The bazaar that greeted him took his breath away and brought tears to his eyes. Everywhere he looked were treasures and adventures, all calling out to him at once. He did not know where to turn. Where would he begin? But then, a discouraging thought fell on his fervor with the weight of reality. All his money had been stolen in Annecy. How was he going to pay for any of these books?

An ebullient voice startled him. A short, rotund man was walking towards him. It was Panckoucke himself, with a walking stick to accompany his portly gait.

"I have seen better-looking things than you that my cat dragged in from goodness-knows-where! My boy! What happened to you? Did you fall off a roof? Were you knocked down by a cabriolet? Have you had a fight with the *chevalier* de Rohan?[55] I suppose you must still be fighting off Voltaire's enemies?"

He was laughing, and Zénobe joined him. "Indeed, *monsieur*, I am still fighting *l'Infâme*, still trying to extirpate it from one end of the realm to the other!"

"Well, you will not find it here, at least. Here we have dealt with it the way Voltaire would have wanted us to. With books!"

Monsieur Panckoucke gestured with his arms around the shop. "With books, not weapons, with ink and paper, not with gunshot or muskets. One has to fight the barbarian with enlightened principles, one reader at a time. Do you not think so, my boy?"

Zénobe smiled his approval.

"Why are you not in Ferney? I hear that Wagnière is poised and ready to leave for Saint Petersburg. You're still prepared to accompany him, yes?"

"Yes, indeed, but I went to Annecy with the thought of spending a few days with members of my family but, as you can see, I had skirmishes I had not anticipated."

"Well, do not worry. I doubt Wagnière would leave without you. He is too much of a chicken to attempt the trip by himself. Your patron, *monsieur le marquis* de Villette, was here, and he left just a couple of days ago."

---

55 Guy Auguste de Rohan-Chabot, the aristocrat who ordered his valets to attack the young Voltaire and who had him presented with his first sojourn at the Bastille. His name will forever be synonymous with that of bully and coward.

Panckoucke lowered his voice to a whisper before continuing. "He pestered us and he plagued us, he was a devil sent from hell, and Beaumarchais sent him back to the devil! I had to swallow my gall, for I have no noble *particule* in front of my family name (although I swear on the graves of my ancestors that I will, eventually, get one!), so I had to take his abuse. He gives commands, he is a general, he is feisty but he is an orchestra conductor without a score, and he only succeeds in bringing much disarray to us soldiers on the battlefield! He wants things done immediately, without possessing one shred of comprehension about how the publication business works. And, and!—"

Here Panckoucke raised a finger to denote the worst of all of the *marquis* de Villette's evils. "And he does not offer one shred of pecuniary subsidy! He wants to direct, but thinks we are a charity! No, no, Beaumarchais sent him to the devil, and it was the correct thing to do, mind you. Right before Beaumarchais left to go find the place where we shall be publishing the complete works of Voltaire, I think in one of the German states, the playwright sent the dilettante to the devil!"

The publisher laughed so heartily that Zénobe had to join him.

After a moment, Panckoucke asked him, "But tell me, lad. What are you doing here?"

"I was on my way through, and I had to come and take a look at your bookshop for myself. *Madame* Rousseau spoke highly of it, and I am come to pay my respects. I may not have the *marquis* de Villette's resources, but I certainly have the energy and the enthusiasm to help you and *monsieur* de Beaumarchais in your endeavors."

"Indeed you shall, my boy, indeed you shall. I will not stop you! We will certainly need your help, especially since you were the one transcribing many of the manuscripts. Ney, ney, I should have thought of this myself! After you return from Saint Petersburg, I certainly will be the one to count on your help. Return all the quicker, I say, for by then you will be sorely needed, I am sure."

"I would be honored, and proud, to help you," answered Zénobe. "It is my promise to Voltaire to have all of him published everywhere and for all the ages to come. In the meanwhile, I would not mind at all if at the present moment I were to acquire some of your beautiful volumes and take them to Ferney, under cover of darkness, of course. I do not wish to be pummeled a second time by *l'Infâme*."

"Yes, of course, anything you want!"

"But..." Zénobe almost lost his courage. "But all my money was taken by *l'Infâme* in Savoy, and I'm come here directly from Turin—"

"Oy, oy, oy, my poor lad. That's all you have to say. You were seized by Victor-Amédée's henchmen, and you lived to tell the tale! I am so sorry and I bleed for you! Wagnière will be thrown into a fit of melancholy!"

"No, no, please, I do not want Wagnière to know. I would rather not have any one know of this. It was all my fault. I was the one remiss in anticipating this attack, but, like you said, I lived to tell the tale."

"Oh!" said Panckoucke. "You are so brave, my lad! So brave! And you do not want to burden Wagnière with this terrible, savage assault. I understand. No one will hear about this from my lips. I never learned about it. But, tell me, son, to turn to another subject, have you ever heard of credit?"

"Credit?" Zénobe looked puzzled. "As in reputation? To have credit with someone is when that person has confidence in you, in your integrity."

"Ah, yes, that's indeed what credit is! But now there is a new way to use this word. It is called financial credit."

"Credit of money?"

"Well, it works as an extension of the *monts-de-piété*,[56] only that the borrower need not pawn any object. What stands for the guaranty of your loan is your personal integrity, your credit worthiness, so to speak, backed by your financial circumstances, and, in your case, I know that *monsieur* Wagnière would keenly vouch for you. What I am trying to say is, I know you, and I know your background, so the end result is that you have much credit here at Panckoucke's bookstore!"

Panckoucke gestured to Zénobe as if to say, get underway! With a huge smile, the young bibliophile turned to the books stacked high on tables and double-deep in bookcases, like a child in a confectionery shop, leaving no bonbon unturned. Thus began the famous Bosquet Library destined to provide much fodder in the development of revolutionary ideas and in the formation of revolutionary minds. It will be a legendary much-used library, organized to emulate both the d'Argenson Arsenal Library, of which Zénobe had personally made use, and Benjamin Franklin's concept of a free public library.[57]

---

56 The *monts-de-piéte* were a sort of charitable pawnbroker's set up to go around the prohibition of money lending. Donations were provided by the wealthy, but low interest rates also helped to finance operations.

57 Through the vagaries of fate, the accidents of bequests, and the astonishing fickleness of serendipity, the prominent remnants of the Bosquet Library have ended up in the possession of the author, and reside in the incongruous site of Miami, Florida.

Interstices Addendum

The centuries leading up to 1778

Fragments of ancient kingdoms and their dispersed monarchs

For the next ten chapters Voltaire's secretaries will be traveling through that miscellany of lands that the Holy Roman Empire had become. The author, therefore, seconded by the fact-checker, decided to insert this addendum for the benefit of the reader. By 1778, the Empire had become a tattered rag, frayed at the ends, threadbare in the middle, moth-eaten by a thousand craven dukes, marquis and barons, the work of generations of a miscellany of diverse Princes reigning over a patchwork of differing governments. Each caught up in his own petty affairs, each bickering and warring with his neighbors, none having a vision of grand unification, even among the German-speaking peoples. That is, until the arrival of Frederick the Great, and even he accomplished much of what he did by bellicosity and ruthlessness.

Fragments of kingdoms, principalities, duchies, and palatinates were all that was left of an Empire that, at the heart of Europe, had once held the reins of history. Then again, perhaps it was folly to have desired an Empire unified by a single religion; the experiment was sure to fail with the fracturing of religious denominations and the creation of alternative cults. Now, the tapestry lay in patches, its ancient power and glory covered by the dust of a thousand squabbles of monarchs too weak, or too stupid, to repair the confederation. The uneven and politically impotent remnants of the Holy Roman Empire, with its myriad of different laws, with its irregular borders and frequent no-man's-lands, posed a threat to those who traveled across it. Highway robbery was rampant, since many were led to despair from the lack of work, the lack of food. Young travelers were frequently accosted, kidnapped and forcibly conscripted into armies, shot or hanged if they attempted to desert. Even in cities there was danger, especially for foreigners come within the walls who were not trusted, who were thought of as spies.

This land of hostilities and hazards and constant threats was what awaited Wagnière and Zénobe. Even with the proper visas, missives of safe conduct, and letters of introduction, there were too many outlaws and scoundrels out there who had nothing but disdain for the rules of civilization. If these ruffians thought for a minute that two secretaries ambling in the wilds of the decadent Holy Roman Empire held in their possession anything of value, they would help themselves to it and liquidate the witnesses.

The only thing in the two secretaries' favor was their cargo. They carried books, Voltaire's books to be sure, a commodity that to them was invaluable, a treasure with a worth greater than gold. But to others, thankfully, especially to ignorant thugs, books held no value. Wagnière and Zénobe were counting on this ignorance to see them safely through those perilous lands.

Still, as they prepared to leave the relative safety of Ferney and the Swiss cantons of Geneva and Basel, they peered into the horizon with foreboding. With many leagues to go, at least two weeks' worth if they were not waylaid, what were the chances that misfortune, either by man or nature, would overtake them? Wagnière had his protestant God in Whom he placed his trust; Zénobe had his foil ever at his side, and the courage he derived from his desire to see his beloved André again.

Part 3

Safeguarding a Legacy

November 10, 1778

Off to Russia

The price that Catherine the Great herself had placed on Voltaire's library was 135,000 *livres*. In addition to this princely sum, Her Imperial Majesty added jewels, exotic fur coats (made for Russian winters), and a portrait of herself surrounded by a hundred diamonds. All of this went directly to Paris, into the avid hands of *madame* Denis, who had not thought of her uncle's library since she had decided to sell it back in June. None of this trickled into Ferney, where her uncle's faithful secretary, in the philosopher's service for twenty-four years, worked doggedly like a beast of burden making sure the 7,500 volumes were well packed into twelve wooden crates, along with numerous letters, personal papers, and, more importantly, unpublished manuscripts written in Voltaire's hand. A more precious cargo there had never been, and the long trip to Saint Petersburg loomed ominously ahead, leagues and leagues of difficult—and dangerous—terrain. Highwaymen awaited travelers at every turn, especially in the interstices between principalities whose princes cared more for the state of their hunting lodges and their mistresses, in that order, than for making sure that their roads were free of bandits. In addition, the states in the south would be interested in intercepting protestant interlopers, and the states in the north would be interested in arresting catholic trespassers. Both parts, north and south, would definitely want to confiscate contraband that disparaged both religions, and other faiths as well. For instance, many of Voltaire's enemies loved to point out that the celebrated philosopher, who was known for his manic references to tolerance, was an anti-semite himself. Wagnière and Zénobe knew, in a way, that this was true, for Voltaire was a comprehensive anti-religion antagonist, fair and equitable across the world's gamut of multitudinous faiths. But it was unfair to single him out for just one of those religions. Which is not to say that Voltaire's detractors weren't anti-semites themselves.

The expedition was all planned out, special passports had been received from the Republic of Geneva (for two protestants; Wagnière didn't think he was lying about calling his assistant a protestant, since Zénobe protested against religion constantly), and the library was in readiness. However, Wagnière's helper was nowhere to be seen. As the days went by, there was no sign of Zénobe, no letters had arrived, no news was forthcoming. Wagnière had already sealed the crates, finalized the dockets and copied them out in triplicate, and he looked up at the sky every day with unease in the knowledge that every day that passed meant another day trudging through the frozen tundra of a Russian winter landscape. He had knowledge directly from Diderot, who had spent five months with the Russian empress from the beginning of October, 1773 to the beginning of March, 1774, that the Russian winter was a terrible adversary. Wagnière wished to be in Saint Petersburg before year's end. January would be terrifying if caught out on the open road, to say nothing of February. Diderot said that when urinating on the snow, his piss would freeze before hitting the ground. This sent chills up Wagnière's penis, and he rushed inside to sit by the fire. He was running out of time and patience.

Zénobe finally came back, traipsing in early one morning in a tiny one-horse cabriolet, with his head all bandaged up. There were no passengers inside the vehicle, only books. He had come into the village of Ferney through the Swiss side, to avoid the French customs officials, he said. He was carrying hundreds of contraband books, including a full set of the *Encyclopédie*. Wagnière could not help but laugh.

"Ah, I see you are preparing reading material for when we come back from Russia," he told Zénobe. Looking at the young man's bandaged head, Wagnière added, "You've had to defend it from marauders already, from the looks of it."

"No, the road from Panckoucke's library to Ferney was free from marauders. These battle scars I picked up in my own country. Savoy is very unforgiving to people who think differently. I shall let them stew in their own fear and ignorance for now. When I come back, I will make sure a lot of these books slip inside their borders and into the hands of as many readers as can be managed. This will be my lot in life, to liberate the people from the dark malevolence that blankets the whole country!"

"Well, come in for a cup of tea before you consign yourself to such a crusade. We must first go to Saint Petersburg before we turn to any other projects."

As they went in, Zénobe instructed a couple of the house valets to place the volumes he had brought with him from Geneva into the shelves recently vacated by Voltaire's books. At least, he thought, the room would begin to look like a library again.

Waiting for Zénobe were letters from all the men in his life: André, *monsieur* Maurel, *monsieur le marquis* de Thibouville, and Gil Blas. He quickly read those and answered them in the afternoon, without wanting to alarm anybody about his misadventure with the catholics in Turin. In addition, there was another letter addressed to him from Voltaire's friend and fellow philosopher, *monsieur* Denis Diderot, a voluminous missive containing much information, counsel and warnings, mostly about the empress Catherine, which could not be answered in a few hours. He decided to take the letter with him and to answer it piecemeal as Wagnière and he journeyed towards Russia. A second voluminous envelope contained a manuscript that the French writer wished to be conveyed to his German homologue, Johann Wolfgang Goethe.[58] Both Zénobe and Wagnière had already read the manuscript when they were in Paris, but neither one of them was able to identify the fine irony that their own situation so closely mirrored

---

58   As Goethe was of 1778 still not ennobled by the Duke of Saxe-Weimar-Eisenach, the «von» cannot as yet be before his name placed. He will von Goethe only in 1782 become.

Diderot's novel, *Jacques le fataliste*.[59] Back in Paris, Diderot certainly recognized the similarity between history and fiction, and began to contemplate a new book on the adventures of two librarians as they traipse through the difficult and dangerous roads of the Holy Roman Empire. There would be nothing holy in this story: it would be filled with burly highwaymen and Teutonic brigands who would try to rob them, or to hold their precious cargo for ransom. There would be army deserters who would steal their horses, or accost them in black forests; marauders, including official toll keepers, who might appropriate their money, or even hold the secretaries themselves for ransom. Catherine would certainly be able to pay, or perhaps she would prefer to punish the miscreants. Would the two librarians be caught in the middle? Would they survive the assault of Catherine's hussars? Diderot smiled in anticipatory glee as he pondered the excitement and the verve of his fiction while at the same time savoring the picaresque aspect of the librarians' exploits. That all would end well in the story was a given: even Diderot did not dare tempt destiny and prompt the Fates, those awful weird sisters, to punish the real librarians in life for what the writer was creating on the page.[60]

59   In case the reader has not yet *Jacques le fataliste et son maître* (*Jacques the Fatalist and His Master*) read, we provide here a quick synopsis: Jacques and his master travel the countryside while telling each other stories. These stories, of course, illustrate the concerns of Diderot, the *philosophe*, including themes of anti-clericalism, moral relativism, materialism, sexual morality, social criticism, etc. Diderot also plays with the definition, limits and possibilities of fiction as a literary genre, throwing the novel inside out to show its inner workings. The fatalism of the hero is aligned with the power of the omniscient author who is both tyrannical and infuriating in his autocratic domination of the plot, which makes the reader think of God as control-freak.

60   This novel, which Diderot entitled *Le Rêve des bibliothéquaires de Voltaire* (*The Dream of Voltaire's Librarians*), circulated, as many of Diderot's stories did, as a manuscript before the writer's death in 1784. These unpublished works were considered too dangerous to release to the public during the author's lifetime. However, unlike *Jacques le fataliste* (published first in a translation in German by Goethe in 1785, then retranslated into French in 1796), or *Le neveu de Rameau*, whose manuscript was discovered in a dusty bookseller's stacks in 1890, the manuscript of the story of Voltaire's two librarians simply vanished. Perhaps one day it will also from out of a dark trunk in an underground wine cellar, or behind a secret vault in an Eighteenth-century town house reappear. I for one would X-ray the walls of Diderot's last home on the rue de Richelieu. This manuscript, when found, will be worth a fortune.

Visits to Historical Places

Monsieur Wagnière and Zénobe turned out to be wonderful travel companions. They had shared secretarial duties, they had loved their master more than themselves, they had been born in the same part of the world, Zénobe in Annecy in the country of Savoy, Wagnière in the Swiss canton of Vaud whose capital is Lausanne. Zénobe had recently found out that he could not go back home, under peril of incarceration, torture and death. Traveling through Wagnière's homeland, he realized that there were places in the world where he could travel unmolested, unafraid to show his face on the roads, or to enter into inns for a hot meal and a bath. People didn't even seem to care what religion he was, or even if he had one. They didn't stare to see how many times he crossed himself, or listen to him say, "May it please the Lord." True, he didn't have the courage to test their tolerance by claiming he was an atheist. How could he work that into a natural conversation in the first place?

"What would you like to eat, *monsieur*?"
"Oh, anything, really, even though I know it's Friday. I'm not limited. I'm an atheist!"

"Will *monsieur* be joining us for breakfast on the morrow?"
"Why, yes. I never go to church. I'm an atheist!"

"From what parish dost thou hail?"
"Parish? Why, I've no idea. I'm an atheist!"

"Bless you, kind sir, may God keep you well!"
"No need to tell me that, *madame*. I'm an atheist!"

At each imagined conversation, Zénobe saw the other person cringe, cross himself three times if he were a papist, or not, in case he was a protestant. But both protestants and catholics would be troubled to be in the presence of an avowed atheist.

Atheists certainly had a bad name. Since they were godless, they were supposed to be without a sense of morality as well. They were considered to be wicked, selfishly looking to satisfy their sinful cravings, using and abusing christians for their own ends, making them commit sins with no worry as to the state of their souls. Since many atheists did not believe in the existence of the soul, they therefore took no time or care for the spiritual maintenance of that soul. There was no need for prayer, nor meditation, nor moments of contemplative invocation of heavenly support. To others they were libertines, liars, cheats, monsters of nature. As atheists, they were known to roam the world seeking to demolish Christian values, trying to undermine Christian institutions, reaping the souls of the faithful to present to Satan.

When people spoke about atheists and Satan in the same breath, he would grow weary. "But we don't believe in Satan, either," was what he wished to say. But the religious wouldn't listen. They had already made up their minds. It's as if they wanted a simplistic answer to the question as to why evil existed in the world. The personification of evil was necessary to their world view, for their religion did not want them to know that evil came from within them, that evil lurked inside them ready to come out at an instant's notice. The religious didn't even realize that their own hatred of atheists and other infidels was a form of evil. They felt more comfortable transferring the cause of evil to the Lord of Evil who caused mayhem and death to be visited upon the world. Blind to the evil residing within them, they acknowledged solely that which made them victims. Hating atheists, bashing them and torturing them and burning them alive in their city squares, well, that was a virtuous thing to do. Even for the good of the atheist, they concluded in their religiously addled universe, for his soul would be purged and sent to the Lord of Good who would be the final arbiter.

Zénobe preferred to keep his mouth shut, as they traveled from town to town. Why stir up a hornet's nest everywhere they went? It was better to keep a low profile, and keep his wits about him. Yet he never crossed himself, and he never blessed anyone.

He suspected Wagnière of believing in God. In spite of his lifelong proximity to philosophers and professional nonbelievers, Wagnière never recanted his protestant faith, never spoke against the papists, and neither supported nor condemned Voltaire's rants against religion. But he never defended the religious, either. He, too, kept mum, even with Zénobe. In no other subject was their conversation limited, but as they ambled along the byways of the Swiss cantons and of the Holy Roman Empire, they didn't know whether the next village was going to be catholic or protestant, rabidly papist or unrelenting lutheran. Zénobe realized that silence was golden. Keep it to yourself; never give reason to have others hate you without even knowing you. That was a wise decision, he thought.

Having arrived in Basel, the last Swiss city before they ventured into the fractured lands of the Holy Roman Empire, Zénobe was tickled to know that three different countries come together here: Alsace, the canton of Basel, and the Margraviate of Baden. From Basel, he placed his foot in Baden, then he made a left, and placed his other foot in Alsace.

"Look, *monsieur mein Herr* Wagnière! I'm now in Alsace. But now I'm in Basel. Now I'm in Baden."

Monsieur Wagnière looked over to him like an adult at a child, but he couldn't help smiling.

"Look, *Herr* Wagnière! Now, now, my head is in Basel, my right arm and right leg are in Alsace, and my left arm and left leg are in Baden! I can be in three places at the same time!"

If only the lad had left it at that, thought Wagnière. But Zénobe's indiscretion knew no bounds, and his next statement made Wagnière's eyes sweep the passersby for an adverse reaction.

"I'm ubiquitous, like God!"

Zénobe stood up and began to step from one country to the next. His steps began to quicken and he broke into a saunter, running in circles, faster and faster, laughing and crying out, "Now I'm in Basel, now I'm in Alsace, now I'm in Baden. Basel, Alsace, Baden … Basel, Alsace, Baden …"

Wagnière couldn't help but laugh at Zénobe's antics, although to himself he allowed astonishment that catholic children were never taught the conventions of a sober comportment. Suddenly, however, he realized that this was no laughing matter. He thought about the Alsatians, who still hadn't overcome their rancor over their forced annexation into France. Not that they felt a need to remain a part of the Holy Roman Empire, either. Rather, they felt that they deserved to be independent, a free state all by themselves, living on the border between two warring peoples and wanting to be left alone. For its part, the Margraviate of Baden had for centuries seen conflict between rival factions of the same family, one lutheran, the other catholic. Only recently had the reunification of Baden taken place when, in 1771, the last of the catholics died out. Basel itself had to rebuff political and economic pressures from both Alsace and Baden, retreating to a xenophobic confederation of cantons established after the Thirty Years' War. While Zénobe ran around in circles, Wagnière was picturing the constant conflicts, the antagonism and warfare that had taken place on the very ground where his young colleague was crying out, "Basel, Alsace, Baden!" Wagnière wondered how many people had been killed within the circle beneath Zénobe's feet.

The customs officials stood by unamused, their protestant dignity restraining any possible reaction to the antics of a foreigner. They could not arrest a man for being an idiot. Wagnière noticed the discomfiture of his fellow protestants, and stepped in to retrieve Zénobe by the hand.

"What is it?" asked Zénobe, who felt a bit dizzy.

"Nothing at all," answered Wagnière. "We just need to go on our way. I'm a bit tired, and I have no idea where the inn is."

"That's easy. Allow me." He turned to one of the customs officials and asked, "*Wo ist, wo sind, die Drei Könige?*"

"*Les Trois Rois? Suivez le fleuve!*" ["The Three Kings? Follow the river!"]

"*Merci, mein Herr.*" And to Wagnière he said, "They must all be polyglots here."

"They have to. Through the centuries they have had to understand all their enemies. Their conquerors, especially."

Zénobe thought about this statement all the way to their inn.

The next stop was at the fortress and small village of Kehl. An old and unused part of the military fortifications of the city of Strasbourg, the fort[61] struck Beaumarchais as the ideal place to publish Voltaire's complete works: the French censors had no jurisdiction here, and it was just across the Rhine from France. Eight years before, Marie Antoinette had been officially handed over to the French by the Austrians on an island in the middle of the river. It was going to be more difficult to bring Voltaire's volumes over.

But no printing was as yet going on. Beaumarchais had just bought, and brought across the English Channel, John Baskerville's font for which he paid his widow £3,700. However, Beaumarchais was not on the premises because he was now on the hunt for paper mills to purchase. Wagnière and Zénobe spent only two days freezing in the echoing hallways of the fort, speaking with the few workers that the playwright had already hired: they knew nothing of the business for which their employer was making haphazard arrangements.

Nothing of great import occurred to Zénobe and Wagnière during their stay in Kehl or soon after they had left it. True, French was nowhere spoken now, and Zénobe's linguistic talents were put to a test. Wagnière's German was passable, and as they wended their way across the countryside, they would practice their guttural sounds and noun declensions. For some odd reason, English was dislodged in Zénobe's brain at the same time he memorized German vocabulary, so his English improved as well.

Sometimes it was Wagnière who held the reins, sometimes it was Zénobe. The roads were passable, a bit muddy at times, and a cold wind swept down from the north seemingly without interruption. Fortunately, every twenty leagues or so they came to a village, which afforded them warmth as they ate, and a bed every evening. Only once or twice were they forced to sleep in their diligence. But the vehicle was roomy, and they were able to spread themselves out over the crates of Voltaire's library.

Worms was directly on the way from Kehl to Frankfurt so it was effortless to plan a stay of three nights in order to do some research. To Wagnière's amusement, Zénobe wished to visit the places of historical importance that had to do with the famous Diet of Worms, an imperial assembly of the Holy Roman Empire that met in 1521 and in which Martin Luther was declared a heretic. In the end, though, they only spent two nights, because it was impossible to ascertain where the actual assembly took place.

Zénobe was disappointed. He would have wanted to sit inside the building where Luther spoke to the Archbishop of Trier and told the council that he could not reject the books in his possession because they attacked the abuses of the catholic church, nor could he recant the 95 theses he had written against the church, for then he would be doing nothing but strengthening tyranny. Zénobe's favorite part of Luther's testimony was when he told the catholics there that he did not trust either the pope or the council, for "they are known to err often and contradict themselves."

The inhabitants, when asked where the Diet had taken place, would point indifferently to the old St. Peter's Cathedral, or to St. Paul's Church, or sometimes even to the Reformation Memorial Church of the Holy Trinity, which was the city's largest protestant Church and so logically could not have existed during the 1521 Diet of Worms! Zénobe and Wagnière left town just as quickly as Luther had exited it: afraid of reprisals, he had escaped before the catholics could get a hold of him. Zénobe knew how he must have felt.

---

61   Today nothing but a few odds and ends remain of the original fort which had been built in 1683 by the French military architect Sébastien Le Prestre de Vauban. The fort was destroyed in 1815 after the Napoleonic defeat. A restaurant, La Villa Schmidt, offering French cuisine with an Italian influence, was over the south battery of the fortress built. The Garden of the Two Riverbanks graces the remaining terrain.

Last week of November, 1778

Books in Danger

onsieur Wagnière did most of the driving, while Zénobe did most of the reading. The young man had an uncanny ability to modulate his voice and to design different tones and pitches for the different characters so that one knew instantly who was speaking. He also had a talent for dramatic narrative, infusing emotions into his speech as the story unfolded, and he was accurate most of the time, even though it might be his first time reading a certain book. He thoroughly entertained them, and frequently hours passed when they didn't even register how many leagues they had traversed.

They had brought some of their own books, which they loved to share with each other. There were very few philosophy books, to be sure. Those are best read by one's self, in silence, haltingly, meditating after every few paragraphs. For the long, boring days spent traveling on the roads towards the north and east, the librarians had chosen books of poetry and novels. Poetry fed the imagination in ephemeral, trenchant moments, with a pause after each piece to appreciate the import of the meaning. Mornings were usually reserved for poetry, when the world was fresh and their minds uncluttered, although *l'heure bleue*, the hour right before sunset, was especially alluring for poetry as well. For the rest of the day, however, novels proved to be the most appetizing for they infused a rambling sense of adventure and romance to their otherwise drab monotonous journey. Wagnière had brought a novel that Zénobe had never read, *Pharsamond*, and it proved to be quite buoyant to their humor.[62] [63] He had also brought some English novels, which they read with an open dictionary by their side in order to improve their vocabulary. These included *Joseph Andrews*, *Tom Jones*, *Moll Flanders*, and *Peregrine Pickle*. Zénobe had brought the entire adventures of *Gil Blas* (three volumes) because they reminded him of his friend of the same name in Champagne. Interspersed throughout the long voyage, whenever they didn't have a book in hand, he also recited chapters from *Candide*, which he had memorized. Zénobe also had the manuscript copy, in Diderot's own hand, of

---

62 A word about the novels mentioned in this chapter: *Pharsamond, ou le don Quichotte françois* (inexplicably translated into English as *Pharsamond, or the New Knight-Errant*) by Pierre Carlet de Chamblain de Marivaux; *Joseph Andrews* and *Tom Jones* by Henry Fielding; *Moll Flanders* by Daniel Defoe, and *Peregrine Pickle* by Tobias Smollet, are all examples of the European picaresque novel. The two novels written by Voltaire and Diderot, *Candide* and *Jacques le fataliste*, also belong to this genre, as does *L'Histoire de Gil Blas de Santillane* by Alain-René Lesage. Please keep in mind that Wagnière and Zénobe are themselves a picaresque interlude in their lives experiencing.

63 [From the author] I sincerely appreciate your efforts to facilitate for the reader the historical aspects of this novel, *Herr* Ralph, but some things are best left for the reader to figure out for herself.

Jacques le fataliste that needed to be delivered to the philosopher's friend and fellow novelist *Herr* Goethe in Frankfurt. Since they had to pass right through Frankfurt before they turned north-west towards Minden, it was but a delay of a few hours to visit the German writer. It turned out to be a very pleasant way to pass the afternoon. They met *Herr* Goethe in his ancestral home, flush with the success of his novel which had catapulted him to fame (*Die Leiden des jungen Werthers*),[64] but they spoke mainly about plants and flowers. Zénobe thought he was with a younger Rousseau. In exchange for Diderot's manuscript, for which Goethe thanked him profusely,[65] Zénobe walked away with a copy of *The Sorrows of Young Werther*, which became the next novel the two secretaries shared on the road. Frankly, it shocked them, and not necessarily with pleasure. Besides the obvious similarities between the German novel and Rousseau's novel, *Julie, ou la Nouvelle Héloïse* of 1761, which both Zénobe and Wagnière recognized, they thought the plot wantonly cloying, yet the exegesis of the human emotion described in the story was excruciatingly well delineated. The ending, of course, was disturbing, as it was to most people at the time. Zénobe and Wagnière debated for longer than it took to read the novel whether or not the young Werther, the hero of the novel, if he indeed can be called a hero, was justified or not, in his final act.[66] [67] The immediate consequence of having read it was that it provoked Zénobe into writing a long letter to André, anonymously, of course, in case it fell into the wrong hands.[68]

Zénobe had wanted to go into Westphalia in order to see the town where both the *chevalière* d'Éon and the *marquis* de Villette had fought during the Seven Years' War, and Wagnière was keen to avoid Hanover since it belonged to the British kings. A slight detour to the west would not result in much time lost. If they were detained by the Hanoverians, they might lose weeks before it was determined that Wagnière was Swiss and Zénobe was a Savoyard.

In hindsight, Minden was a disappointment, for not too many people even remembered that there had been an important battle there, and those few that did begrudged

---

64   *The Sorrows of Young Werther,* first published in 1774.

65   Goethe translated Diderot's novel and had it published in Germany in 1785. The original French version was not published in France until 1796.

66   In case the reader has not yet *The Sorrows of the Young Werther* read, the hero's final desperate act is to ki—

67   [From the author] *Nein, mein Herr Doktor* Ralph, *nein, nein, nein!* I am in charge here, and in a desperate act of autonomous volition I shall allow the kind reader to discover the world at her/his pace. It is my hope that the reader take the incentive here and read Goethe's great historical novel on her/his own.

68   [From the author] It is incredibly sad when certain letters of historical import become lost. In spite of searching everywhere for this letter, among the Corday papers, in André's affairs that ended up with Zénobe's library, no trace of it has ever been found. It would have been insightful to learn how Goethe influenced Zénobe, other than just surmising that *The Sorrows of Young Werther* dislodged much sentiment and nostalgia in Zénobe's heart.

very few details of no consequence. It wasn't even clear where the battle took place, and only twenty years separated the event from the present moment.[69] Many people whom Zénobe tried to interrogate simply walked away. A little boy was more amenable, but even he wondered why the enemies hadn't fought their battle at Hanover, since that was the prize that France wished to conquer.

Zénobe was astounded about the futility of war. People died in the battle of Minden,[70] and there was no one here to care about them, to even remember them. No tributes were to be found, no commemorative plaque, no statue. But when he came across a book that listed the combatants, he realized that many of them were not even from here. Had any of the participants been from Minden? There was a Fitzjames, a Nicolay, a Beaupréau and a von Sachsen, and those were all from the French side. On the German side were names to be expected: Holstein, Wangenheim and Imhoff. Who were those people, and why had they fought? They had fought because their kings, Louis XV and George III had ordered them to fight. Zénobe wondered if the many who died were aware of what they had given up their lives for. For Minden? The town wasn't worth it, he thought, as he looked around him.

He remembered the *chevalière* d'Éon's bravery and exploits during the battle. She had been proud to fight for honor, whatever that was. He assumed that honor was one of those other ineffable qualities that the aristocrats inherited, along with the documentation proving their nobility. Duels were a quotidian affair among the upper classes: they had their honor to uphold, their escutcheon to defend, their ancestors to revere. When one was born a peasant, honor was not one of the things granted at birth. To Zénobe, honor was a foreign commodity which had no meaning, no value. Had he been present at the Battle of Minden, for what would he have fought? Would he have even agreed to sacrifice his life for something as inane as honor?

He could see that honor and patriotism were closely intertwined. A French aristocrap[71] was keen on his honor, and also his origin. Even that extremely non-military *marquis* de Thibouville was proud of his French titles, one of which went back to Charlemagne. Titles improved with age, Zénobe supposed. They gave legitimacy to the family's standing in society. Many of the old-time aristocrats felt contempt for a brand new title of nobility such as the one that the *marquis* de Villette possessed. But he had money, so that shut up a lot of mouths. What a world, Zénobe thought. These titles, these dry old documents, ultimately this whole system of nobility are worth as much as the Church's market of indulgences. Those ecclesiastical hoaxers had devised a worthless commodity, but managed to convince the people that not only were indulgences necessary, they were desirable, too. The secret lay in having more power, more

---

69   Nineteen years, to be exact. The reason why many residents didn't remember where the military conflict took place on August 1, 1759, was that the combat occurred right outside the city gates. Westphalians still resented having been under Swedish occupation, and they could not garner much interest in a battle being fought between an Englishman, Ferdinand, duke of Brunswick (and brother-in-law to Frederick the Great), and a Frenchman, the *marquis* de Contades.

70   The Anglo-German alliance lost 3,000 men; the French lost 7,000. While not exactly a rout, it did end France's threat to Hanover. One of those Frenchmen killed on the battlefield was Michel Louis Christophe Roch Gilbert Paulette du Motier, *marquis* de La Fayette, whose infant son will one day join the Americans in fighting the British on another continent.

71   This is not a typographical error, but rather a translation of the neologism, «aristocrotte», that André and Zénobe came up with to insult the nobles.

influence, and more brutality than the victims. Anyone can be persuasive who has the power to kill you.

But Zénobe's disappointment in the battle of Minden was not the only consequence of their quick detour. There was another ramification that fate was preparing for them, one that would prove to be a bit more of a hindrance.

Minden had been a part of Prussia since 1648, and was therefore under the jurisdiction of Frederick the Great. Nothing of interest occurred in his lands that he didn't find out about. Word reached him at the battlefield in Bavaria, where he was busy fighting the Austrians, that Voltaire's secretaries were ambling their way towards Lübeck, but seemed to be taking in some recent history. Frederick didn't waste any time sending escorts to intercept them. He knew they were on their way to Saint Petersburg, and he knew what they were carrying. Perhaps he could have a bit of fun before Catherine could lay claim to her investments.[72] [73]

The very day after they left Minden, the two voyagers fell into their first misadventure. Most roads in the Holy Roman Empire were sporadically policed, and ruffians of all sorts, German marauders, Romany gypsies, Austrian deserters, French outlaws (of which Zénobe was an egregious example), and defrocked priests of all nationalities, all of them circulated on the byways needing to conjure up daily the necessities of life. Travelers were a convenient method of harvesting the essentials since they usually carried food and drink with them, and most had money and valuables that could be pried from them, if the outlaws were shrewd enough in finding out their secret hiding places.

The raiders who accosted Wagnière and Zénobe one cold but sunny afternoon were army deserters running away from their regiment. Even though there was no war going on at that very moment at that very place, it was still an offense punishable by death to abscond from one's military service. Four horsemen appeared suddenly, and silently, from both sides of the road which cut through a forest. Zénobe was deep into an adventure of *Gil Blas,* and Wagnière was looking inwardly at the images painted in his mind by the reading, when they both realized, after a few minutes, that they were being squired.

They looked to their two flanks and their hearts sank. The four horsemen were armed with all the accoutrements with which they possibly could have absconded. Wagnière did not reduce the speed of their diligence, but did not dare provoke the

---

72 [From the author] Before we leave Minden, I would like to offer my condolences to *Herr* Dr. Ralph. One of his ancestors, *monsieur le docteur* Ralph, was found sprawled on a Minden street in 1759, overcome by an apparent heart attack. In his pockets were found additions to his translation of Voltaire's *Candide* into German. It seems that Goethe was not the only translator of dangerous French works.

73 [From the fact-checker] I thank the author for his solicitude concerning my ancestor. It is a false rumor, however, that he died on the streets of a heart attack. Family lore has it that he died of a cold gone bad at home in bed.

interlopers by speeding up, either. Zénobe looked down at his foil, then back up at the muskets, axes, knives and sundry bayonets hanging from the strangers' horses and about their persons like gleaming Carnival decorations.

Not knowing what to say or do, Zénobe simply looked up at the sun, scrunched up his face as if enjoying the feeble rays, and called out, "*Guten Tag, mitreisende!* (Good morning, fellow travelers), before his useful German sputtered out. What could he say to them. "I hope you are well?" "How can we be of service?" "Please don't kill us?"

In response, one of the horsemen, apparently their leader, rode up ahead and positioned himself directly in their way. Wagnière's horses automatically came to a stop without having to be reined in.

"Now what?" said Zénobe under his breath to Wagnière.

"Now we see what they want," answered Wagnière.

"For sure they'll want money," observed Zénobe.

"Well, thank God we don't have much."

"Thank God? They might become a bit angry at that."

"Well, these are not the types to want to steal books, that's for sure."

"They'll know Voltaire's books are valuable."

"Well, they won't find out that these are Voltaire's books, will they?"

"I hope they won't break the crates open," said Zénobe with exasperation in his voice, before abruptly deciding to climb down from the diligence.

"We are on a long slog through Europe," he said in French, hoping the cavalryman would understand. "It is a pleasure to meet fellow travelers on the road. Whom do I have the pleasure of addressing?"

He didn't approach the man or, worse, extend his hand. He would prefer no physical contact at all with this man who was smiling at them.

From all indications that they had been reading in their books, Zénobe surmised that he and Wagnière were in deep trouble, and that any little gesture or word from their part could rile up the hussars surrounding them.

After a few moments, and still without losing his smile, the leader announced in execrable French, "We are the toll administrators. You have to pay your toll."

"Ah," said Zénobe, also with a smile. "We were not aware of any toll on this road, but since you are telling us otherwise, please let us know how much we owe the lord of this land to maintain and preserve this road. We had been in admiration of it, hadn't we, remarking with my friend here that there are hardly any potholes in it at all! Those that our wheels do happen to find are small and not very deep!"

With a backward glance to Wagnière, he saw his friend nod his head in agreement. He noticed that Wagnière was looking a little white.

"By the way," continued Zénobe, "who is the lord in whose lands we now traverse?"

The hussar answered pleasantly, "These lands... these lands to the lord of Bassum belong."

Wagnière's ears pricked up at this. "Oh, how is the dear old Duke of Brunswick-Lüneburg? How is his feud going with the Americans?"

The hussar looked at his friends, then responded, "Fine, fine. He is doing very well, indeed. Nothing stops the dear old Duke of Brunswick, ah, Brunswick-Lünenbourg. He keeps with fortitude and perseverance with the Americans feuding. He won't stop, never, until he gets what he wants. We admire him so."

"I am so relieved to hear this. His many responsibilities, and his many lands, leave him no time for such trivial tasks as toll taking. We are delighted that gentlemen such as yourselves have been granted this honor."

Zénobe looked up at his friend as if the man had taken leave of his senses. What confounding conversation was this? And he had never heard of the Duke of Brunswick-Lüneburg. Not Lünenbourg, as the toll-taker had said. The Duke of Brunswick-Wolfenbüttel, yes, for that duke had visited Voltaire in Ferney after the Seven Years' War with his bride in tow, the sister of King George III. Brunswick-Wolfenbüttel liked to think of himself as an enlightened prince, and won praise from Voltaire's followers.

"We do as an honor view it, and try ourselves well in our duties as highway guardians to acquit."

"Very well, then," said Wagnière. "We, too, take our responsibilities seriously, and as users of this splendid path we accept our part in the maintenance and protection of such. What amount are we to disburse to the toll keepers?"

"Well," said the hussar. "That depends on how much merchandise you carry. We charge a percentage of what is in your coach. I trust you are not diamonds and emeralds conveying," he finished with a laugh.

The other horsemen dismounted and began to walk towards the diligence.

"*Messieurs*," said Zénobe. "If you please, a search won't be necessary, for we merely carry books. We are librarians, and our purpose is to set up libraries in the style of Benjamin Franklin's lending libraries of the United Colonies. We found libraries across the land, and what we have here," he said, pointing to the back of the diligence, "is the library ordered by the Duke of Brunswick-Lüneburg which we are to deliver to his court."

"His court in Bassum?" asked the leader.

"No," answered Wagnière, "his court in Brunswick."

"Of course," said the horseman, laughing, as if he had forgotten that simple fact. "I understand the nature of your business, but I still must insist on taking a look. It won't take a moment, I assure you."

The irony was that the contents of their coach were worth more than diamonds and emeralds, more than any treasure, more than the goods and chattel of any other migrant tradesman or itinerant mercenary. The two Keepers of the Library needed to comply with these horsemen, and smilingly allowed them to do so. Zénobe himself opened the few wooden boxes that were their personal belongings, in order to allow for easy inspection. He hoped that they would be satisfied to rummage through those, and leave Catherine's boxes sealed under their string and wax.

These thieves, for that is what they were, went through the open boxes avidly digging for treasure, but finding only papers, books and manuscripts. They muttered as they turned the bound manuscripts over in their hands, sometimes stopping to open one or two of them. Much to their disappointment, they found inside only pages and pages of lines of mere words. At intervals, the suspicions that they had of their fellow travelers made them hold a book up to their noses and sniff deep into their lungs, thinking that perhaps there was more to this item than paper and ink. This strange conduct surprised Zénobe. What were these idiots thinking? Could they possibly think that a book was like a hunk of cheese, to be sniffed for freshness? Were they trying to smell out gunpowder or any other substance that could be used to cause them harm? Was the sense of smell a good analyzer of the relative danger of books? No, concluded Zénobe, these people were too stupid to realize the worth of the booty the wagon held. Lacking brains, they put all their faith into guns and knives, making sure that might made right, and that they ruled over that area of road like a rooster rules over its dung heap. From there, they attacked others and lived like social parasites, without conscience and without honor. Honor? Zénobe's inner voice was surprised at his thought, but he had to put it aside in view of his possessions being pawed over by these marauders.

They took all of their food and drink, personal grooming items, and all the money they were able to find, but they believed that the crates held only books, and books were not on their agenda. Still, their leader asked Wagnière for a book, saying he had never had one. He received in return as a prize a copy of the *Henriade*, Voltaire's paean to Henry II. There were a few of those to spare, and furthermore, Wagnière didn't think that it would alert the vandal—if he could, after all, read—to the dangers involved with certain of Voltaire's other books. In those books Voltaire spoke about bringing down the tyranny of throne and altar, and if these nomads felt their god, their lord or their person were being insulted, they might murder the Keepers of the Library, and then in the middle of the road, they would kindle a huge bonfire of books. These people might defend savagely their right to be idiots, and both Wagnière and Zénobe needed to respect the might behind the right.

The man who confiscated the book took away his booty with a boastful stride, holding it up so the others in his travel party could see it, and then took a whiff of the leather binding, with apparent satisfaction.

"It's a book written by Voltaire, nitwits!" he cried out to his friends. "A book written by a philofficer!"

And with that they were off. The sigh of relief coming simultaneously from Wagnière and Zénobe was a mighty one. They had lost a few toiletries and all their food, but not their wits, and certainly not their lives. The treasure they defended was also intact.

As they continued on their way, not to Bassum but directly to Lüneburg, Wagnière and Zénobe had plenty of time to reflect on the sweeping march of civilization. They spoke to each other of the painfully slow progress that culture made, at frangible intermittent times, but remarked at length of the extended periods of regress when decadence prevailed, during wars of conquest, the clash of religions, social unrest, the fall of governments, when prolonged agitation interrupted the beneficent influence of morals and the social institutions that supported those morals.

Zénobe also had time to interrogate Wagnière on his strange conversation dealing with the Duke of Brunswick-Lüneburg.

"There hasn't been a Duke of Brunswick-Lüneburg in generations! I just said that to test the bandit's knowledge. He certainly wasn't from around here, or he would have known that the current Duke of Brunswick-Lüneburg is none other than George III himself! It is he who holds these lands now, and as Frenchmen, we need to get out of them as fast as possible. We shan't be stopping in any towns for the next few days. We must get our food from farmers, and we won't get combs and soap until we get to Prussian lands, and then heaven help us if Frederick is on to us. The last thing we need is to get picked up by Frederick!"

By that time the sun had set and they got off the road and hid as best as they could in the forest. Luckily, Zénobe had tucked away by their carriage seat some chocolate and a bottle of Liebfrauenmilch which they had picked up outside Worms, and that was their dinner for that night.

Librarians in Danger

rederick William I, Frederick the Great's father, during most of his reign kept an expensive regiment of giant soldiers. Whenever the old man caught sight of a soldier in one of his regular regiments who measured six feet or more, the soldier was automatically transferred to the special unit. Coddled and housed close to the royal palace, the brigade of favorites was close by whenever Frederick William needed them. Prone to periods of depression, the king would have his special troops march through the palace, sometimes even through the king's bedchamber, in order to cheer him up. That they left a trail of mud, scuff marks and streaks on the parquet floor concerned him not at all.

When his collection of tall men became an obsession, the king would have his minions search far and wide in the countryside, but sometimes in another country's countryside. Many young farmers were bought in this way, and town merchants, too. Anybody who could be purchased for a bribe or even a promise of affluence in the capital Berlin, was rounded up and smuggled into the special regiment. The time came when tall men became so scarce in Prussia and in the neighboring countries of its allies, that Frederick William began to kidnap tall men from enemy countries. This made his enemies roil even more, and made war with them all the more inevitable. But war he waged, although he kept his royal battalion of giant soldiers safe from combat. They were fed better than any burgher, dressed better than any aristocrat, and groomed for pomp and aplomb. Daily they practiced their marches, displaying a pageantry of precise movements and manly struts, all to the beat of a hundred drums. Sometimes the king had his son, prince William, run them through their paces, and he would be criticized if the men didn't lift their legs high enough or failed to march in complete synchronicity. Many thought that this is how the future Frederick the Great learned his love of men, from being around so many perfect specimens: tall, muscular men, with angular faces, tight abdomens, hemispherical buttocks, and ramrod postures.

But Frederick himself knew that this was not the case. His love of men came from before the special regiment, before he was even verbal. As a small boy he was always more interested in looking at men than at women. He remembered the excitement he felt when a man would pick him up and carry him. If a woman picked him up, he would squirm and become so heavy that he wouldn't remain in her arms for very long. He loved men before he could even remember his first sensations of being in this world, which were mostly fright to the point of terror, pain to the point of torture, and solitude to the point of utter isolation. His mum, his favorite sister, his friends, all of whom needed great courage to even come to his succor, were nevertheless ineffective in bringing him aid. His father, the king, was a brute, a force of cruel nature who liked to mete out pain and humiliation upon others, including his own family. None could contend with him, none could use reasoning or emotion to lessen the king's frequent bouts of dreadful humor. On the contrary, the royal family learned early that to attempt to bring compassion and pity into the king's heart meant only that his rage would swell to an even higher pitch. Frederick William I was a miserable, vicious man whose malevolence increased exponentially by the unattenuated power granted to a king. How many of Frederick's friends were assassinated for having attempted to help him. Hans Hermann von Katte, with whom he had had a secret intimate friendship, was beheaded right under the window of the prison where Frederick William had cast him. To see his beloved Katte die such an ignominious death right below him as he was forced to watch was one of the inhuman things he had to endure. His father was a monster, a tyrant, despised by his people, disrespected by his generals who were afraid of his violent temper. And yet Frederick William singlehandedly built one of the largest armies in Europe, the proto-Teutonic force with which the rest of the world would have to contend for centuries.

When Frederick himself became king, he vowed to establish a reign that was more in tune with the philosophical times. Frederick had always been involved in the life of the mind, having been an avid reader since childhood. Indeed, books were his only source of comfort and serenity. Often ordered to stay in his room for days, the isolation taught him to live inside his mind, to use his imagination and learn to liberate his body through daydreams and spending endless hours in entertaining thought. When he was allowed to read, he read quickly and voraciously, from the poets and playwrights, to the novelists and historians, and his autodidactism led him eventually to Voltaire.

Frederick was always torn in two by his friend Voltaire. The love and admiration Frederick felt for him were frequently obliterated by the exasperation that the old philosopher produced in the Prussian king. Voltaire was too independent, too impulsive and too mercurial to be ruled over. There was also the sentiment that he was always right that lead Voltaire frequently to clash with the king. Still, Frederick would have loved to have had a father like Voltaire, one who thought, and who held that thought to a high standard. His real father the king would react spontaneously with only one emotion: rage. He was constantly in a rage because others did not live up to his expectations, including and especially his son. Voltaire treated Frederick with respect, most of the time, and praised him as a teacher praises a student. After the old philosopher died, Frederick went into mourning but was not able to grieve quietly for any length of time because the Austrians decided that the time was ripe to take over Bavaria.

Frederick the Great had had in effect two fathers: the military man and the philosopher. In the War of the Bavarian Succession, it was the education he had received from his military father who gave his son the instructions he needed to wage belligerence on those too uppity to know their own place. But when Frederick heard that Voltaire's librarians were on the road to Saint Petersburg with the old man's library in their possession, well, his joy knew no bounds and he immediately sent his best hussars to invite them to his palace in Potsdam.

Wagnière and Zénobe were ambling somewhere in the farmland around Lüneburg when the Prussian guard caught up with them. This time there was even less resistance than there had been when they were accosted by the marauders. The librarians were instantaneously overwhelmed. Ten colorful soldiers on steeds came thundering at a gallop and quickly overtook their vehicle. However, their mien was so much more deferential and distinguished than that of their previous aggressors. Their officer bowed low to the librarians and in a loud baritone bade them felicitous salutations from the King of Prussia and informed them that Frederick the Great would delight in their company at Sans Souci. The soldiers's martial stance and their tight formation around their vehicle made it quite clear that this was an invitation that could not be politely refused.

This is why, instead of going north to Lübeck to await the arrival of Catherine's packet boat from Russia, Wagnière and Zénobe wound up taking a side trip due east to Berlin, where their host, one of the most powerful monarchs of all Europe, awaited the pleasure of their company with regal impatience.

First week of December, 1778

At Sans Souci
with the King

Frederick the Great named his summer palace «Sans Souci» with the intention of residing in it far from the pomp and responsibility of quotidian command and administration, where he could live "without a care" and exist with "no concerns." However, care and concern were writ large on the expressions of both Wagnière and Zénobe as their carriage ground to a halt on the gravel at the south side of the palace. Layers of foreboding over trepidation and anxiety were the recognizable facial expressions as they exchanged glances. Their sight was directed out and up along an enormous set of stairs comprised of six staircases lined up in a long row that lead up to the faraway palace.

"You have got to be kidding!" announced Zénobe. "You think he would have spared us this last exertion!" Turning to the postillion, he asked, "Is there no back entrance to this thing?"

"All guests are required to climb the Grand Staircase. There are only 132 steps."

"Yes, indeed. And from the looks of them, sixty-six are covered in ice."

"It is winter, *monsieur.*"

"So there are no other entrances that could afford a bit more convenience?"

The postillion remained silent.

"Ah, so there are. Would you be so kind as to take us up closer to the palace? My friend here is no longer a spry young man, and he has trouble with his knees."

"Much trouble, much trouble," agreed Wagnière as he appraised the long sweep of stairs.

The postillion seemed to go through a moment of indecision.

"Besides," added Zénobe. "We're not really guests, are we? We are more like captives. We are not here of our own volition. Voltaire's friends in Paris will not be happy when they hear about this, especially *Herr* Grimm, and neither will the Great Catherine of all the Russias."

This reasoning seemed to convince the postillion into slowly directing the horses around to the east side, where he followed an avenue that would take them through the park and up the hill. As they traversed this new terrain, Zénobe recognized that there was only one type of plant arranged on the terraces flanking the hill: they were grape vines! He marveled at the aesthetic patterns that the leafless vines drew on the hillside, and would have loved to compare them with those he saw in Champagne, when they were in their full, summer-green leaf.

At last they came upon a small entrance door. The postillion told Wagnière and Zénobe to wait by the carriage, then he walked to the door, opened it and disappeared inside. Seconds later he came out with the doorman, and both flanked the captive visitors as they walked into Frederick the Great's Palace of Sans Souci.

Zénobe's jaw dropped as soon as he beheld the rococo incrustations upon the walls and ceilings, the intricate carvings dripping in gold leaf, the ornate chandeliers made to look like growing plants, with more gold vines crawling up doorways. The hallways felt like corridors inside an obscure mysterious forest glowing incandescently with golden boughs. Wagnière, too, was impressed, but he had once been to Versailles, so his threshold for amazement was much higher than that of the boy from Savoy.

At the entrance to another hallway, the postillion and the doorman stayed behind while a pair of valets took over. They were dressed in livery that looked like full military regalia. Perhaps they were soldiers, Zénobe thought. He studied their ornamentation and elaborate clothing in case he would ever need to impersonate them. Their insignia alone seemed very expensive. Their epaulettes were made of gold thread.

As their steps echoed up and down the hallway, other valets appeared in doorways here and there as they scurried on their way to other tasks. Lesser servants turned up, dusting and fussing over candelabra and sconces, but they too wore blue-and-gold finery. Zénobe noticed that all the domestics were men. He had yet to see a single woman.

In a few minutes, they arrived at a huge portal, flanked by two heavy wooden doors that were charged with heraldic bearings and ancient family shields festooned with wreaths of gilded laurel. The opulence and weight of all this embellishment was starting to oppress Zénobe. He needed air.

There was more air in the salon, since there was more open space, but no less opulence. On the contrary, the decoration seemed to reach a zenith of resplendent restlessness, of overwrought agitation, and there seemed to be movement everywhere, crawling up the walls, dripping down the lusters, while simultaneously a galaxy of lights sparkled redundantly and persistently across huge framed mirrors.

Zénobe had to laugh. This is what aristos did with their money, and kings with their people's money. They surrounded themselves with a whimsical world of empty effervescence, a shimmering fantasy of illusions, a dream of Puck's forest become a nightmare of flash and gleam, and everywhere costly structures to decry the expense which snatches away the bread from an infant's mouth and removes the roof over a family's heads.

The valets were gone, and quickly Zénobe told Wagnière that he was going to hide behind a thick column until he saw that they would not be in any danger. The valets had not confiscated his foil, and he would be able to use it, even against the king, if the welcome was not to their liking. Wagnière walked by himself into the middle of the room.

After a few minutes, steps heralded the arrival of a single person. It was Frederick the Great, king of Prussia.

"My dear secretary, *monsieur* Wagnière," he intoned with a general's voice, "friend and confidant of the great philosopher Voltaire! How happy I am to see you again. How do you do? I trust your voyage was comfortable?"

"Our conveyance is big and comfortable, Your Highness," returned Wagnière as he bowed low, "but unfortunately the postillion you instructed to fetch us, I mean, to drive us, was in too much of a hurry and none too subtle. The crates behind us were constantly rearranging themselves in such a clatter, according to the rules of physics established by Newton, I daresay, that I thought for sure they were being dismantled by opposing centrifugal and gravitational forces."

"But they arrived unbroken?"

"Yes, although we ourselves arrived a bit bruised."

"Well, I'm afraid that was my fault. I ordered the postillion to make haste for I was impatient to meet you. I'm afraid you have caught me in the middle of a war, and I cannot loiter, I'm afraid. Battle calls, skirmishes must be attended to, and the enemy won't wait too long."

"I wish you well in your war, Your Highness. I am certain you will acquit yourself of this one as well as you have settled all your previous wars. Praises abound from many quarters—"

"You sounded just like Voltaire, right then! You are indeed an adherent to his method. As his secretary you certainly do him proud."

Wagnière bowed a little and thanked the Prussian monarch, although he thought him fresh to allude to Voltaire's irrepressible sycophancy when in the presence of a leader whom the philosopher deemed enlightened. Wagnière had only thought it polite to wish him well in his bellicose affairs.

"Secretaries, Your Highness, for there are two of us."

"Why, of course, I myself employ three or four secretaries; one solely for poetry. Where is your colleague, then?"

"He's seeing to it that the seals remain unbroken on the crates. Her Royal Highness the Empress Catherine is expecting them in Saint Petersburg with seals unbroken."

"Oh, what a shame. I was hoping to rummage through some of them, especially those that contain my own correspondence with Voltaire."

Frederick beckoned to Wagnière and said, "Please sit. You must be weary after having traversed the sundry lands and territories of this loosely knit region of what should be one kingdom."

Wagnière sank into an armchair the likes of which he had never seen. Heavy gold brocade with raised patterns of gold-thread fleur-de-lys enveloped him in a cool embrace. Frederick took a seat right next to him and promptly folded one leg over the other.

"I do have the manifest that Your Majesty is welcome to inspect should he be so inclined. It details the contents of all the crates."

"Stupendous!" exclaimed the King. "Furnish it to one of my secretaries at your earliest convenience so that I may peruse it. Not that I envy Catherine's proprietorship of Voltaire's library. She is welcome to it. However I am a bit curious as to why she was in such a hurry to acquire it, and why she paid such a handsome sum for it.

"I was not privy to Her Royal Highness' correspondence with *madame* Denis, since I was in Ferney and *monsieur* Voltaire's niece was in Paris."

"So I heard! So I heard! Purchasing and outfitting a new house on the rue de Richelieu, across the street from *monsieur* de Choiseul's mansion. I can certainly see how a former Foreign Minister of France might have the wherewithal to reside in such an opulent neighborhood. But Voltaire's niece? He was always crying that he was halfway into the poorhouse. I've never met such an acquisitive philosopher. He hatched more pecuniary schemes than he had friends in high places, so each friend had to oversee multiple schemes. Yet who could blame him? He did like his little luxuries, didn't he? He was like a child in a confectionery store."

Wagnière wasn't sure if Frederick were criticizing or praising his former master, but just at that moment the monarch's eyes had a sheen and he seemed ready to weep. Just in case, Wagnière decided to answer in a sober manner. "Philosophers may range from penurious stoicism to epicurean materialism, but *monsieur* de Voltaire always made his money the legal way."

"Not when contravening a direct order from the king. There you and I hold opinions diametrically opposed to each other, dear Wagnière. Voltaire never allowed legality to be a barrier to trying to make a thaler."

King Frederick's big blue eyes were just beginning to spit fire, but they were distracted by a new person approaching, a tall young man with a soldier's bearing. "But this must be your fellow secretary," he observed.

Zénobe had come out from his hiding place behind the pillar when he realized that he and Wagnière were in no imminent physical danger, and when his appearance would interrupt a conversation that might be in danger of leading to kingly recriminations and fulminations. Frederick had once almost ordered Voltaire out of his realm after the hapless philosopher had been caught in shady financial dealings with a Jewish jeweler who had earned the king's disfavor. For a favored guest of the king, this was a dishonorable enterprise, one which had nothing to do with what Voltaire was doing in Frederick's court in the first place: he was one of Europe's foremost thinkers and writers whom the king had gathered around him. The likes of Voltaire and Maupertuis, Algarotti and La Mettrie,[74] added a touch of class and intellectuality to the Prussian court. For a king who wanted to be known as an enlightened monarch, the proximity of philosophers and men of science was as important as his treasury being well stocked. The Royal mind needed to be stoked, his French poetry needed to be corrected, and above all, the Royal person needed to be flattered.

Zénobe was not one to eschew the game of flattering despots in order to get what he wanted. What he wanted was to be allowed to continue on his voyage to Russia. Voltaire's last secretary dropped to one knee and bowed low before Voltaire's old friend, the King of Prussia. The young man even managed to place his right hand over his heart, to encourage the thought that he was sincere and principled. Following protocol, he said not a word.

Frederick stood up and took a step forward. "But you seem surprisingly young to have been one of Voltaire's secretaries!"

"I turned twenty this past 15th of October, Your Highness."

"That is young. I assume your intellect must have passed muster with the old man. You are a Libra, then. You search for balance in the world, and you are interested in the pursuit of justice, truth, and beauty, and where you do not see perfection, you revolt. You come from an air sign, therefore you are a deep-thinker, sociable, an intellectual who loves to communicate. You love social gatherings, and your preferred theme of conversation is based on good books, good philosophical books. But your faults are just as numerous: you flit from one idea to the next; you are not extremely loyal, even to loved ones, and you lack perseverance and stamina."

As he said this, Frederick walked around the kneeling Zénobe in a full circle. At the end of it, he proffered his hand to the young man, who took it, and the King raised

---

74   Pierre Louis Moreau de Maupertuis was a French mathematician; Count Francesco Algarotti, a Venetian poet and philosopher; Julien Offray de La Mettrie, a fellow philosopher who had died "while in office" as court physician.

him to a standing position. Holding him by the hand, Frederick twirled the young man completely around, the royal eyes brightening with amusement, the eyebrows halfway up his forehead. Zénobe's clothes looked a bit bedraggled and his hair disheveled from the last leg of his trip, and he didn't feel in the least bit energetic, but he recognized sexual interest when he saw it. Surprised as he was by this discovery in the august person of the Prussian monarch, his innate dislike of kings, and the half-smile playing around Frederick's lips, gave him the temerity to speak without first having been spoken to. He did not, however, meet the king's gaze as he spoke, but kept a discreet and demure gaze at the king's feet, which were remarkably small.

"Your Majesty is therefore a partisan of astrology?"

"Why, yes. It has always been a branch of traditional science. Even Newton was not adverse to it. You do not believe that the movement of the stars in the firmament have a direct effect on our lives?"

"Absolutely, ah, yes, especially our resident star, the Sun. Without it, ours would be nothing but a cold, lifeless planet, wandering without mooring through the eternal silence of space. Without that particular star, we'd all be dead, Your Highness."

"I am beginning to realize why Voltaire chose you for his last secretary. You are outspoken, bordering dangerously on irreverence, and you manage to steer the conversation in a different direction. We shall recall our topic of conversation on astrology at a later date. For now, however, know that Voltaire loved Newton, practically worshiped the ground he walked on, if it could ever be said that Voltaire was capable of worshiping anything."

Wagnière, who had also stood up when the king did so, laughed politely at Frederick's quip. Zénobe, however, remained silent and with his gaze still held aloof.

"But I often wondered," the King continued, "how many of Voltaire's translations of Newton into French were from his own pen, and how many were from his concubine *madame* de Châtelet?"

Frederick was being as spiteful, as churlish and as envious of Voltaire as he had ever been. It was as if the intervening decades had not changed a thing. And wasn't Frederick, along with all of Europe, still mourning the philosopher's death? Of all the most important people the king had ever met, of all the exceptionally talented individuals, from mathematicians to musicians to military geniuses, it was Voltaire, and only Voltaire, who had never raised Frederick's sexual penchant, had never alluded to it, never referred to it, and truly accepted him in all his regal totality. Voltaire had been his friend. Of course, they quibbled, as all friends do. But Frederick always knew that he was loved by his court sage. Why was the king being surly now? Perhaps it was the fault of the uppity Zénobe whose fingertips the king still squeezed that elicited this royal comportment?

Frederick had expected no answer to his provocative statements. He received one, however.

Zénobe's fingertips squeezed back before the king released them.

"Voltaire worshiped science, and men of science, and even women of science. *Madame* de Châtelet had an exceptional mind, and one that calculated very easily through the mathematics of science. Voltaire was able to translate Newton by himself, of that I am sure. But *madame* de Châtelet, his lover, was a boon to his understanding of the mathematics. Voltaire preferred poetry to calculations, which was a boon to Your Majesty, for he took an interest in you as a pupil, and under his tutelage, Your Majesty's talents flourished and your publications impressed the world over. Even Catherine was inspired by you to try her own hand at writing. So you see, we are thankful to Voltaire for his interest in both science and literature."

Frederick was appeased. An idea came to him.

"Perhaps while you are at Sans Souci, you will do me the service of looking over my eulogy of Voltaire, which I am writing in French."

Zénobe's eyes darted to the king's in order to discern the emotion behind his statement. He read sincerity and concern.

"It will be my pleasure, Your Majesty. It will be my pleasure indeed."

Wagnière, who had learned much in his lifetime, especially when working for Voltaire, looked from the countenance of the king to that of Zénobe, and, observing that they happened to be holding hands again, he breathed a long sigh. He muttered to himself, "We'll be here for weeks and miss the boat to Saint Petersburg!"

First week of December, 1778

The Intimate Guest of the King

Frederick ran Prussia the way his tyrannical father did, but conducted himself in such a way that his subjects did not despise him. That some of them loved him was proven by a nickname that was just beginning to make the rounds, «*der alte Fritz*» (the old Fritz), only without the «*lieber*» (dear), because the Teutons were not known to be tender and affectionate.[75] [76]

The great Prussian king wrote poetry, composed music, played the flute, became a Freemason, surrounded himself with French culture, corresponded with Europe's best artists and thinkers, and, indeed, invited many of them to come live with him at Sans Souci. In short, he was deeply engaged in the agenda that Voltaire propounded, so that when Zénobe was invited to stay on at the palace, Voltaire's youngest secretary found it difficult to refuse. A king's request, however politely asked, carries as much weight as a lesser person's command. Moreover, Zénobe was curious about this monarch who fashioned himself, or at least purported to fashion himself, on modes of Cartesian structure and administration.

Finally, there was another reason why Zénobe wished to linger a while longer in the court of Frederick the Great. It was not an everyday occurrence to be in the presence of a sovereign of an important country, especially a sovereign who clearly desired his presence and whose preference for him was made abundantly evident. Zénobe's previous experiences in this domain, namely the queen's favorite, *madame* de Polignac, and his fellow resident at the *hôtel* the Villette, the *marquis* de Thibouville, both had taught

---

75 *Teuton and Teutonic* are terms that refer to the barbarians from Jutland who one hundred years before Christ fought the Romans in what is now France, and therefore serve no purpose in this context, save perhaps to indicate the author's bias against the German people. The late 18th Century announces the Romantic movement, and German authors and artists were active participants and proponents of it. Romantic means being tender and affectionate.

76 *Herr* Ralph, *lieber Herr* Ralph, please don't get yourself into such a state of agitation by the usage of my vocabulary. I insist on keeping the noun «Teutons» here in order to relay the message that Frederick the Great was a despot, notwithstanding his own royal assessment that he was an "enlightened" monarch in the guise of Voltairean ideals. He could still order Zénobe executed with a gesture of his finger, with no one and nothing to stop him, and I wish the reader to realize that Zénobe is treading on dangerous ground, especially when the boy treats Frederick as if the king were an enlightened monarch. My surmise is that he was not; and neither was Catherine II of Russia, by the way.

him the advantages and the pitfalls of trysts with the nobles. In this respect, having the king's attention was a sort of flattery beyond the limits of Zénobe's imagination. He felt enhanced, in status and reputation. From Voltaire's confidant to Frederick's favorite was a step too gratifying to be spurned, thought the young man. What was the harm in staying a few days longer?

Wagnière observed with intense scrutiny the daily interrelation between the two men. With his additional years and experience, especially with his knowledge of how monarchs had behaved with Voltaire, Wagnière was aware of the harm that could come to Zénobe. The older secretary even told the younger one the story of Erhard Ursinus, the King's Secretary of Finances. This renown expert in economics had in 1767 received instructions directly from the king to do research on, and to come up with possible solutions to, the monetary downturn experienced by Prussia after the Seven Years' War. While manufacturers, merchants and financiers had made handsome profits during the war, the rest of the population remained tenaciously in the doldrums of reduced economic activity. Ursinus acquitted himself admirably of his task, delving into all corners of economic activity in the realm. The result was a heavy leather-bound report of every venture, every enterprise and every scheme that was either making money or losing money in Prussia. Ursinus extolled certain projects, others he criticized as being ineffective, and some as being downright detrimental to the economy. Did the economist know that some of the ventures he disparaged were projects that Frederick had been pushing? Subsidizing beekeeping, the cultivation of mulberries for the silk industry, the growing of certain crops like sugar beets and the fabrication of velvet were, according to the report, useless in the effort to improve the economic situation. Indeed, the silk and velvet being produced in Prussia were inferior and more expensive than those imported from other countries. The economic situation in Prussia was depicted as interventionist, restrictive, controlling and tending towards monopoly. This candidness resulted in royal disfavor; Ursinus was reprimanded for his audacity, charges of malice and corruption were concocted, and the appropriate punishment was duly meted out on the hapless messenger: one year of hard labor at the Spandau Citadel.

Zénobe heard this story with polite interest, and promised Wagnière that he would tread carefully. Then he left for his afternoon audience with the king.

The first thing he asked Frederick, after they had exchanged formal greetings, was if it was true that *Herr* Ursinus had been convicted to one year's imprisonment at hard labor for having given His Majesty bad marks on his economic incentives.

"Who has been telling you these tales?" the king wanted to know.

"Reports, reports heard around the palace. I don't recall who divulged that particular piece of information. But is it true?"

"You are even more impertinent than Voltaire ever was! You, yes you! Don't look so innocent. You don't even have the old man's fame and status for protection. But you do have beauty. That you do have. It has always been my misfortune to be charmed by a well-turned nape, a graceful stance, a confident mien. Your eyes are perhaps a bit too otherworldly for my taste; I usually prefer a more earthy expression, and I find horses' brown eyes a perfect color for men as well."

"But you have beautiful blue eyes, Your Highness, if I may be allowed to be bold enough to compliment your person," Zénobe said with a bow.

"Usually the request to be allowed to be bold comes first, young man, before you compliment the king's person. But you have my permission."

After having gestured to Zénobe to sit beside him on a small settee, Frederick continued, "Blue eyes the color of the sky: too ethereal. Green and brown are the colors of the earth, of Nature herself who grows rampant and wild, but also of agriculture that we establish within her bosom. Those are the colors that eyes should be. I look at you and I marvel that you can even see out of those eyes. You almost look blind, your eyes are so limpid."

"I assure you, Your Majesty, that I can see very well with these eyes. I can see every expression you make, from the elegant way you hold your head, to the twinkle in your own eyes when you speak of something you love. I gather you love nature and agriculture."

"By God I do," was the king's exuberant reply. "Those are the backbone of a country, that and its people. And what feeds and clothes the people? Nature and agriculture. A kingdom's wealth is measured on the number of its subjects, and the number of its subjects springs from the ground. That nincompoop Ursinus failed to realize this, belittling our favored undertakings. He wanted to take the country in the direction of banking, of speculating, of markets where pieces of paper would be valued more than the silver in the realm's coins. I countered by increasing the content of silver in our coins. That has value, and where does silver come from?"

"From the ground?"

"That is correct. It comes from the ground. It exists; it has value; none can contradict it."

"Paper money has no value?"

"None but what foolish men imprint on it, and then expect others to accept their arbitrary determinations. A further folly: with this bizarre money one is supposed to buy what are called stocks, which are but a valueless representation of the intrinsic worth of a business enterprise. The Church offered a better deal when it was trafficking in indulgences. At least that had an ultimate practicality: getting one's soul into heaven!"

Frederick chuckled at man's fallacies and defects. Such wild imaginings in certain people made him believe that God, or Providence, or Destiny, whatever you wished to call it, had placed him on the throne of the Prussians for a reason. These social experiments being devised in Holland and in France were all the rage, and perhaps they worked well with the Dutch and with the French temperaments. But for Prussians, the newfangled trends would not work. His people were too grounded, too incredulous, too intelligent to agree to accept value where there was none.

"We shall continue to push for agricultural improvements, to modernize farms with new varieties of old favorites, with new crops that come from other lands and that can be grown here, even with innovations in animal husbandry that will increase our flocks of poultry and therefore increase the proportion of eggs. Eggs are what fortunes consist of, not pieces of paper!"

Zénobe smiled at the king and said, "I do like a good omelette for breakfast. In my family's farm…"

"Ah, you come from landed nobility!"

Zénobe realized he had said too much but could not retract it now. He continued with his story, feeling ashamed that he could not rectify the big lie at the center of it. How could he reveal to the King of Prussia that he came from a line of peasants who tilled the soil they did not own?

"We don't have much, but we do enjoy what we have. Our chickens were our pride and joy, for we had many that were unusually shaped. Some had bonnets on their heads, some had feathers that looked like hair, and others looked as if they were walking around with boots on."

Frederick scrunched up his nose. "Chickens with boots on, what a wondrous—and insane—image it conjures up in my mind. Perhaps you could speak with the Secretary of Agriculture while you are here. Apparently he could learn a few things from your family's expertise."

"It would be my honor, Your Highness," said Zénobe as he bowed from the waist.

Supper that evening consisted of chicken, simple roast chicken, served with potatoes *au gratin* and cabbage. As a surprise, Frederick had sent instructions to his chef to make *îles flottantes*, floating islands: soft silky meringue floating on *crème anglaise*. Frederick explained that the conversation he had had with Zénobe earlier that day had made him yearn for something made with eggs.

"You see, the meringue is of course made of egg whites, whipped into a frenzy, and the *crème anglaise* is made of egg yolks, vanilla and scalded milk. The egg is separated only to be recombined in this delicious fashion."

Zénobe declared that it was delicious and that on the morrow he would go out and visit the hen houses.

"Oh, that is a marvelous idea," replied the king. "I shall also go and look over the farms. I've been wanting to add a pheasant house."

Wagnière studied his two dining companions. He wondered when His Majesty needed to go back to his war in Bavaria. He wondered what Zénobe was after. This story of fowl was just a façade, he was sure, but could not define with much precision what the façade was hiding. He hoped the chickens the next day would be enough to occupy the attention of Frederick the Great and his new friend.

What Did They Talk About?

Zénobe spent a week with Frederick the Great of Prussia without having the minutest inkling about what sort of protocol to follow when associating with a king. He did have experience dealing with aristos, but the highest ranks to which they rose were marquis and dukes. Besides, he felt no real respect for social classifications, and the only person for whom he did feel respect had been Voltaire who had treated him, Zénobe, as a protégé, a friend and an equal. Zénobe was on new terrain when dealing with Frederick, but felt it was his moral duty to refrain from sycophancy. This king, who had written his first letter to Voltaire in 1736 while still the young Crown Prince of Prussia, at 24 years old to Voltaire's 42, deserved better than that. Also, Benjamin Franklin had inoculated Zénobe with the new democratic ideas exported from across the Atlantic, in which lineage and family ties counted for nothing, and Zénobe wished not to demean himself by letting caste and birthright be barriers to forthright conversation with the king. Their conversation was therefore free, intimate and mostly honest, broaching all sorts of themes and eschewing none. Zénobe never did admit to being a mere peon.

Courtesy was Zénobe's sole protection when dealing with matters that went against monarchical opinions. He relied on Frederick's fairness not to be placed in chains in the dankest cell of a Prussian dungeon. He had found out that even recently Frederick had hauled a whole cabinet-full of magistrates to jail when their legal decision had not been to the king's liking. Zénobe also retained in the back of his memory the time when the King of Prussia had kept Voltaire under house arrest. Metaphor guided Zénobe through this time of quandary. His family had kept bees on their farm and he had learned his lesson while still a young boy: don't tease the bees.

In a world where good conversation was prized and quick wit extolled, Zénobe did exceedingly well. It was his knowledge and resourcefulness, especially in one so young, that captivated Frederick and prompted him to prolong the secretaries' stay in Potsdam. The war could wait. He had seen so many wars, including those for which he had been responsible, that this one could certainly wait. It was a minor conflict, for only Bavaria was at stake. All that needed to be done was to deter and intimidate the aggressive Austrians. Time, and his generals, would take care of the rest. For a few days at least, he could command the presence of a young man who produced in him such nostalgia for all the past young men who had ever brought him pleasure, and his strongest dragoons could not have dragged him back to the battlefield before he had had his fill of Zénobe. The War of the Bavarian Succession could wait.

So what did they talk about? They spent a total of seven days together, four or five hours alone in the afternoons, then the two or three hours of supper, with Wagnière present, followed by postprandial liquors, cigars and colloquies. They spoke of everything. While the historical records include many of the themes of their conversations, there is a limit to what they provide: besides Wagnière's entries in the journal of their travels, there are letters from Zénobe to André and *monsieur* Maurel back in France. Frederick himself kept an unusual silence about this week in his life, writing not a word of it in his own journal, perhaps resentful of his complicated duties and responsibilities which allowed only a few days with Voltaire's disciple. Some joys had to be hidden, to be kept jealously away from the rest of life, to avoid them being disrupted or spoiled. Frederick of all kings knew best that a sovereign was never in complete command of his own life. Strict controls belonged to the exterior world; destiny had an ascendancy over all beings, including kings. All he could do was attempt to thwart the fates as he did his enemies: put up impediments to slow encroaching time, and increase the pressure on the forces he could command.

Interestingly, there was another journal being written at this time that eventually revealed some of the themes that engaged Frederick and Zénobe. Frederick's latest chamberlain, Girolamo Lucchesini,[77] himself also of Italian extraction like Zénobe, jealously kept watch over their intercourse. Wishing to keep himself nearby, in case Frederick sent for him, he spent the afternoons reading and drinking tea in adjoining rooms. Every once in a while he would pace, and some of his trajectories would take him close to the door dividing his room from that where His Majesty and his visitor were conversing. While he never stooped to peek through the keyhole—such an endeavor being beneath his dignity!—he nevertheless was able to catch a word or a phrase that elicited from him enough interest to include in his journal entries later on in the evening and that fortunately also served to ease his mind. He never eavesdropped on any untoward expressions, on any sighs or gasps or other inarticulate sounds that would have betrayed an end to the interlocutors' conversation and a slide into a different kind of activity, an intercourse of increasing intimacy, which would have put Lucchesini into a dither of a dilemma: whether or not to burst into the room in order to interrupt the incident. He was less concerned about the king's retaliation towards him than about his own sense of propriety. His patience, in the end, won out, and, to our advantage, gave us more indications of the types of conversation Frederick had with Zénobe.

Here follow some of these chats, preceded by the specification of their source.

---

77   Eldest son of the Tuscan *marchese* Lucchesini of Lucca, Girolamo traveled to Prussia to seek an audience with Frederick II whom he admired greatly. The Italian's diplomatic talents and his literary connections with Tuscany prompted Frederick to keep him in his court as chamberlain. He was also the Prussian king's de facto librarian following the untimely and tragic death of his previous librarian. (For more details please see footnote no. 83.)

Excerpt of a letter written by Zénobe to André, dated December 3, 1778:

> Frederick: What do you think then of art?
>
> Zénobe: To me, art is the result of man's need to create, to emulate the idea of god, who doesn't exist, but whose mythologies have made their mark on man simply because he was desperate to turn his imagination on creating something larger than himself.
>
> F: Well, God is certainly larger than man himself, but if God is indeed just a creation from the mind of man, is God, then, art?
>
> Z: I think god is man's greatest creation. A whole universe has been concocted to accommodate this central character in a tale that doesn't seem to have an end because it is now self-generating. Art is usually created for pleasure, as an emanation of the idea of beauty, or as a clarification—or, perhaps, a crystallization—of truth, but in the case of god, the creation got away from the creator. It's like the sculptor Pygmalion who fell in love with a sculpture he had carved, Galatea. He made her so beautiful, so graceful, so appealing, that he longed for her to come to life. In his half-crazed mind, she did come to life. The myth-tellers, however, leave out the part of what happened to Pygmalion's dick when he tried to make love to her. Marble is unyielding; flesh, no matter how turgid, is weak. In the same way, man keeps banging himself onto the rock of god. He will break himself onto that hard, unforgiving visage for the rest of eternity. No amount of frenzy, no amount of breast-beating, no amount of howling will make god come alive. So yes, Your Majesty, god is art, so compelling, so necessary, so immediate to man's desires that it has escaped man's control and now controls him. Galatea controlled Pygmalion until he went mad with lust, and grappling with the statue he had lovingly chiseled and shaped, it came crashing down on him and asphyxiated him.[78]
>
> F: Great Zeus, but what imagination you have!
>
> Z: Art is all about imagination. That's all man has, in his lonely world: just his head and what's in it. He peoples his world with beings bigger than he, stronger, more powerful than he, to explain the unknown, where he comes from, why he is here, where he is going. He creates because he must. With the passage of centuries, his beliefs about the intricate imaginings which he has called forth from his mind, leave the aegis—the shield of Zeus—of religion and are placed to moulder in the dark recesses of his mind as myth, as new creations appear and hold his attention. Man will always create new dogma to support and new beings to worship; that is his weakness. I'm just clear-headed about all of this: I want to move all these imaginings into the aegis of archaic—and useless—knowledge, and get on to science, which is exterior to us, and is the only thing that can help us. We don't create science, we discover it, piece by piece, for it is out there, outside

---

78   The source of this story, Ovid's *Metamorphoses*, has Aphrodite breathing life into Pygmalion's statue out of compassion for the sculptor's love of Galatea. They marry and have children. In Zénobe's version, there can be no deus ex machina.

of our imagination. It is in the whole universe that surrounds us and we need to uncover her secrets. The god stories have only impeded us from seeing this clearly; they obstruct, disturb, hamper us. Many times they even kill us. The Truth that will eventually set us free is not in the god stories, though that's what the god believers want you to think. Truth lies in science! Think of it, the descendants of Abraham claim that the freedom which Jesus mentions is freedom from slavery. Idiots! The freedom I'm talking about is freedom from god.

Excerpt of a letter written by Zénobe to André, dated December 4, 1778:

Frederick is to all intents and purposes a hermit. He told me he might as well be a recluse, like the Trappist monks. Only his mornings are dedicated to the functions of state, and the throne room, on the complete other side of the palace far from his living quarters, has the single function of administering to state affairs. It is there where he meets with government functionaries, with military chargé d'affaires, with all sorts of international envoys and plenipotentiaries and it is there he begins and completes his tasks and duties as sovereign. Arthur Lee, the American, was recently here by the way, trying to push Frederick to sign an alliance with his rebellious colonies. The king didn't have him stay long: the British envoy, Hugh Elliot, broke into Lee's apartment to steal sensitive documents. It is because of this insane silliness that once he leaves the throne room, no one is allowed to mention any affairs of state, under threat of spending the night in the stockade. Neither does he host soirées any more, nor afternoon tea parties or socialization of any kind. "At my age," he says, "the only parties that agree with me are good books." He has become a misanthrope who, although never sacrificing his obligations to his people, has concluded that he deserves some repose and solitude in which to carry on his other important tasks, writing his memoirs, writing an essay on German letters, and intellectual pursuits of that nature. I suggested to him that he write a treatise on the Art of War, since he is so good at it. I think he'll take me up on it. He told me that it pains him to think that two thirds of his life was spent on either organizing for war or waging war. If instead of having had to waste his time on war he could have spent all that time on poetry and music and the arts, he would have been a much happier man. But he wasn't born a man, he was born a king. And kings must wage war, unfortunately. It's either that, or be deposed and lose one's country. To think that even after he dies, his successor can lose in a few years everything he spent his lifetime fighting for. He spends a lot of time thinking of the precariousness of Prussia's standing in Europe.

Journal entry of *il signor* Lucchesini, Frederick's Italian chamberlain, not dated:

Having been dismissed by His Majesty, I was still in the *salon* preparing to take my leave when His Majesty asked the young man a straightforward question about his credentials and about his lineage. With quite a bit of shock I witnessed the beginning of master Zénobe's response and, because I couldn't be dragged away, I lingered at the door to hear the rest of it. Afterwards, I didn't close the door quite all the way, and witnessed a most unusual scene. It was clear to see in a flash that *il signor* Bosquet had never learned the protocol, the rules of deference, the physical attitudes of obeisance, that are the due of a sovereign. This was puzzling as I knew he emanated from Savoy, which is a country steeped in tradition and noble convention. Brash and unceremonious, the young man, who was standing, had leant against an armchair placed next to the one in which His Majesty was seated so that the young man was half-sitting on one of its arms. I found this most shocking and disconcerting. I will have to speak to this *signor* Bosquet. His Royal Highness might not put up with such insolence for very much longer.

Here, as far as I can remember, is *il signor* Bosquet's response, which was also disconcerting in its frankness, its length and definitely in its import.

"What does it matter? I am no king, nor duke nor marquis. My genealogy is of no consequence to anybody, especially to me. My knowledge of my ancestry stops at three of my grandparents. I never knew any details about my father's father, for my father himself seemed to want to repudiate all remembrance of him. I respected my father's wishes and asked no questions. Beyond all of that, who cares? Certainly they were all commoners with no imagination, no courage, no strategies, no incentive to extricate themselves from the hoi polloi into which they were born. So what does it matter who they were? They do not deserve to be removed from the oblivion to which their fate assigned them. Indeed, even a king's forebears at times deserve to be forgotten. Weak kings, deceptive kings, tyrants who bring to mind the Pharaohs of ancient Egypt. They took their people back to those times—they regressed!—treating their subjects like pawns, like cattle, not at all like members of a mutually-accepted pact."

His Majesty responded: "Reminds me a bit of my own father."

Il signor Bosquet: "Pardon me, Your Majesty, I in no way was imputing the reputation of your father. He was an angry person, to be sure, but he felt deep responsibility for the welfare of his subjects. He attempted to instill in his subjects all the old virtues in an attempt to redress their morals, to raise them to a high standard of which he was the keenest representative: sober, thrifty, healthy—"

His Majesty: "Callous, cheap, sordid, and a complete hypocrite, that's what he was. He certainly had no deep-felt sense of welfare for his own first-born son. He insulted me, struck me, kicked me, especially in front of the whole court, in order to make my humiliation as momentous as possible. He threw things at me, whatever was handy, including food and drink at the dining table. He was never satisfied with what I did, with my intentions, with my desires to improve myself; he sent his cruelest soldiers to be my preceptors in order to teach me the savage ways of the army, an army that might as well have been Sparta. I wanted nothing to do with his army, not even with his brigade of giants. They were his giants, his own to play with; they never tempted me. But he knew they could tempt me. He never let me have them.

"Ah, Father, you always wanted to break me, but you never did. You knew I felt nothing but contempt for you, never any respect or admiration. How could I desire that brutish military life, waking up before dawn to do maneuvers in the dark, in the rain. As if, as if... Just because I was a dreamer, because I was interested more in art than in the military. I'm still more interested in art than in the military. Not that I abandon my kingly duties, but that's what my generals are for. They're like my bookmarks. They will continue to hold my place until I get back. Father, no need to worry; the country won't be going to the Austrians, certainly not to the Bavarians. We shall take over the Bavarians, eventually. There might even be a time in history when the Austrians themselves shall fall beneath the tutelage of the Prussians. All of us united, the way we should be. See, Father, you needn't have worried so about your son. I came into my own. At a price, but I finally came into my own, Father."

Il signor Bosquet: "The price of which you speak... It's loneliness, isn't it?"

The complete silence that reigned for seconds after that one question was asked, proved to be the proof that His Majesty acquiesced to its accuracy.

His Majesty responded by reciting from memory a poem he had composed for his beloved Catt:

> *O Catt! nos jours, nos ans s'écoulent,*
> *Qui peut, hélas! les arrêter?*
> *Le Temps, les destins qui nous roulent*
> *Ne cessent de nous emporter.*

[Oh, Catt! Our days, our years flow by,
Alas, who can stop them?
Time and destiny who make us spin
Cease not to sweep us away.]

Imagine my surprise when the lad from Savoy answered back with another verse from the same poem!

Être heureux, c'est la grande affaire,
Et dans ce séjour imposteur
Où tout est fiction et songe,
Qu'importe qu'en nous le bonheur
Naisse dans le sein de l'erreur?
Chérissons-en jusqu'au mensonge.

[To be happy, that's the important thing,
And in this impostor life
Where everything is fiction and dream,
What does it matter if within us happiness
Is born from the breast of error?
Let us cherish even that lie.]

After that I heard a rustling and a scrape on the floor, as if someone had sat down hard on a chair. *Il signor* Zénobe's voice continued:

"I know it must be loneliness to be a king misunderstood. All I have to see is this grand palace, so vast, so beautiful, where most of the grand rooms go unused. There is hardly anybody here. In the evening, even the valets are gone. I know you do this intentionally. Loneliness presses on the soul harder in inverse proportion as the number of people around you increases. When everything is quiet and solitary, one's thoughts fill in the void much better than bustling crowds. That is, if one has thoughts. Monarchs like Marie Antoinette and Louis love to be in the maelstrom of frenetic activity, for they couldn't hatch a single thought between them."

The King laughed at this. I then knew that His Majesty was in good hands with the commoner from Savoy. *Il signor* Bosquet was right! Who cared who his ancestors were if he could make His Majesty laugh! I quietly closed the door tight and went back to my chambers.

A few entries after this one, also not dated, Frederick's chamberlain wrote a paragraph about Zénobe that might have some bearing on the king's opinion of the young man:

When I thought again of how unimportant *il signor* Bosquet held genealogy, I was shocked still. How could he so easily, so unconcernedly, admit to his coarse origins? Most parvenus are worried about concealing their past and go through great lengths to have all vestiges of it remain forever out of sight. But here this young man was, in front of a king, revealing the very thing that would have kept him away from the royal court! Anybody other than His Majesty would have banished this commoner without a qualm, but here the situation is outrageous: the Monarch of Prussia keeps the man close to him, hears everything he has to say, and converses with him as if he were an equal! And I must be polite to the commoner, too, since I must do my king's bidding. I, the youngest son of my family, 'tis true, but the youngest son of a duke, must endure such topsy-turvy proceedings, but I must see to it that the man has everything he needs! What sort of scheme is this? I must, concede, however, that perhaps jealousy is playing its ugly part in my reckoning of *il signor* Bosquet. I do not really see the commoner in him. His ways are debonair, he knows his rules of etiquette, his apparel is always stylish, and his voice modulated to suit a king's *salon*. He is, believe me, no slouch. His destiny was to be born a son of the people, but at the last minute one of the fates seems to have turned a compassionate eye by bestowing on him a lovely countenance, an impressive anatomy, and a gaze at once penetrating but impenetrable, intense but inscrutable. I must endeavor to be sympathetic to him, without harboring any ill feelings, for of all the lovely aspects of his comportment that strike me the most, is that he is being very engaging and gregarious with me. There is nothing for which I can assign fault either with his person or his bearing. And the fact that he is Voltaire's secretary is the cream on the puff.

Excerpt of a letter written by Zénobe to the *marquis* de Thibouville, dated December 6, 1778:

Frederick is a lonely king, although his mornings are rife with roiling matters of state finances and intricate diplomatic affairs with quarreling ministers who can't stand to be in the same room together. As soon as he is on the other side of the palace, however, in the private wings, he gives vent to his solitude. This is the real Frederick, not the one in the throne room. He might be called Great for what he has wrought in the throne room—Voltaire called him enlightened and modern—but, far from observing eyes, his other type of labor begins. The importance of art is what he tries to communicate. War destroys, war disrupts the progression of man, yet man must regain control of the creation of art because that is what matters the most. What do a few more acres of territory mean if one has lost masterpieces, or worse, if one has lost the artist. He laments the death of artists who never again will take up the pen or the brush to render immortal poetry or unforgettable paintings. What has the world seen destroyed for the sake of lucre or economical advantages! Those losses can never be recovered, artists can never be brought back to life, and the world becomes a poorer place.

Excerpt of a letter from Wagnière to Her Imperial Highness Catherine the Great of Russia, dated December 7, 1778:

It is with great concern that I write this letter to Her Imperial Majesty to impart the knowledge that I, my assistant secretary, and Voltaire's library, have been for the past week detained in Potsdam at the request of His Highness Frederick II of Prussia. We are guests at his Palace of Sans Soucy, in spite of the fact that I repeatedly remonstrated to him that our timely arrival in Lübeck was of the essence, in order to board the packet boat that you have so generously provided for our transport to Saint Petersburg. My fear is that the captain will not wait for us forever, and that we will then be forced to make the trip on foot. This will add much hardship to our voyage, and much more time, especially as winter increases its icy grip on the northern lands. I realize that my letter might not reach Her Highness in time to send instructions to the captain of the boat; at least she is made privy of our involuntary sojourn with the King. As has been your keen observation in times past, of this I am sure, Frederick Rex possesses certain personality traits that are extremely persuasive, and I would not place bets on those who would attempt to foil his expectations. His Highness has shown much interest in my assistant librarian who, as *monsieur* de Voltaire's last secretary, certainly has much to offer the book connoisseur and devotee of Voltaire's philosophy. Still, as has been made clear to us during our stay here, the War of the Bavarian Succession competes for His Highness's attention, and it is only a matter of time before he must repair to the theater of war. I am certain that we shall be released from our visitation in a matter of days. Please be advised that Frederick Rex has shown no interest in examining *monsieur* de Voltaire's library and that the seals on the crates remain unbroken.

Please receive from your humble servant manifestations of gratitude for the consideration and assistance that Her Imperial Highness has conferred on those who would render her service for no remuneration at all. We act in accordance with the sacred charge entrusted to us, the protection of *monsieur* de Voltaire's library and safe conveyance into the hands of the Empress of all Russias. This we do both for the love of our dear departed friend but also for the deep esteem in which we hold a Sovereign steeped in enlightened rule who has never forgotten her sympathy and humanity for those engaged in our philanthropic undertaking.

Signed, Jean-Louis Wagnière

Excerpt from an entry in Wagnière's journal, dated December 7, 1778:

Catherine the Great waits for us and for the world's most famous library and here we are like mice bound in the velvet ropes of Frederick the Great. We may not be captives in the dungeon, but tarrying in this great luxurious cage of a great potentate as we are, our destiny is no longer under our own volition. Was it ever?

We are the guests of the King of Prussia, to be sure. Nevertheless, I could not have been clearer with His Majesty about our haste in getting to Saint Petersburg. He should have provided us with an armed escort to hustle us through the northern Empire. Instead, we while away the hours, the days, waiting for his good graces and hoping that he soon has his fill of Zénobe.

I certainly cannot fault Zénobe for this delay because I remember those heady days of my youth when it was my turn to meet all those kings and queens, the powerful and influential who steer history this way and that. Those people are well in possession of their destiny and they carry on their chariot whole lands along with their entire populations who must move along with it. No, I cannot disapprove of Zénobe's infatuation with Frederick Rex because it is an experience he is likely never to forget. Besides, it is good for him to know and receive solicitude from someone like the King of Prussia. Evidently Zénobe has made quite an impression on His Majesty and I am sure that Voltaire would have approved of this friendship. In this world one must maintain relationships among the high and mighty for only they can come to your rescue when you've come into a predicament. And knowing Zénobe the way I do, I guarantee that he will come into multiple predicaments in his life. He is destined for them! Indeed, he almost didn't escape his trouble with the Inquisition. With his revolutionary way of thinking, added to his idealism and impatience, he will send himself along the highways of destiny scraping against all barriers and obstructions, instead of trying to go around them. But he is a good lad, and his heart's in the right place. Except, perhaps, for the fact that his youth and inexperience are sending his heart into places where his heart has no business being. I sit silently during supper and observe my three companions, feeling left out most of the time since hardly anyone throws me a glance, except when the conversation comes around to Voltaire. I watch their eyes, the bold blue eyes of Frederick Rex, his chamberlain *il signor* Lucchesini's dark brown eyes, and little Zénobe's sky-blue eyes, and their glances signify more than I can convey with mere words. It is like music rather than just the words of their conversation, not only because of the frequent accompaniment of some sort of mirth, either laughter or chuckles or titters, with corresponding changes of pitch and rhythm, but also because their sentiments reflect off the surface of their eyes. After all, they say that music is a language, one that transmits non-verbal communication in the form of emotion and passion; laughter, too, makes other feelings accessible, and corresponding eye-movements express the rest. I observe in those three a symphony of looks: His Highness will contemplate Zénobe in a regal manner, without blinking, as only he is allowed to do, and Zénobe will return the steady gaze with quick peeks in-between phrases; *signor* Lucchesini will scrutinize Zénobe while Zénobe's attention is on the king, but when Zénobe momentarily turns to the chamberlain, *il signore* will glance at the goblets and tableware. Every once in a while, Zénobe takes the liberty of viewing the chamberlain's face, in the guise of considering his expression, but will squint a bit too closely at his eyebrows, or his beard, or his lips. This music of laughter accentuated by the staccato and legato articulation of the play of their eyes, is a language all its own. I dare not join in it, but for the sake of Zénobe, who is learning so much from these pleasant soirées, I sit with them, but slightly on the side. I do marvel at how far Zénobe has come. He is fluent in this type of conversation, knowing instinctively to let Frederick Rex direct the conversation, but providing many interesting and entertaining anecdotes.

Still, the days tick by, and we'll have the volition of another sovereign to deal with, and Her Imperial Highness Catherine II is not known for her patience. What a quandary to be in!

The last page of a letter that Zénobe sent to *monsieur* Maurel, dated December 8, 1778:

[…] Please give my love to the whole staff. I imagine the *marquis* de Villette is back from his trip to Ferney, but at least they had a holiday from him while it lasted. I am sure he will keep going back to Ferney since Voltaire's château and village are now his, so he will keep going back to make sure he demolishes all the good work Voltaire ever did there. Did I tell you he was raising the rent on the clock- and watchmakers? "They sell to the crowned heads of Europe!" he declared. Didn't anybody ever tell him that royalty, like all aristos, never pay their bills in a timely fashion? With the exception of Catherine of Russia. She always pays quickly, and handsomely. Frederick told me that the 30,000 rubles she promised *madame* Denis for Voltaire's library is already in that biddy's hands, along with the fur coat, the portrait of the Empress encrusted with diamonds, and sundry other little gifts that prove to the niece how much the Empress loved the uncle.

How is le Nouvel André dealing with the new responsibilities he inherited when he became the *marquis* de Villette's librarian? How much I envy his visits to Panckoucke's bookstore, although I did credit to myself, while using credit for the first time, when I visited Panckoucke's store in Geneva. I bought every single prohibited book he had! By the way, I tell you in all secrecy that Frederick King of Prussia insisted that I return to Potsdam after I'm done with my duties in Saint Petersburg. He said that he would love it if I considered becoming his librarian in Sans Souci. I thanked him, of course, for the honor of this request, but that it all depended on *monsieur* Wagnière and his plans for Voltaire's library. It seems that right before we left Ferney, Catherine hatched the wonderful idea of building an exact replica of Voltaire's château in Russia. Wagnière is carrying *monsieur* Racle's architectural plans in order to have it built over there. It seems that Catherine wants the whole house to be just as Voltaire intended it, and she wants Wagnière to remain until he can place Voltaire's books on the shelves just as they were in Ferney. Quite a project, don't you think? How long do you think that will take? I don't want to take up residence in Saint Petersburg. This is supposed to be a rapid voyage just to make sure the library arrives safely. I've been dying to see you, and you can imagine how badly I've been wanting to see André again. I know that he's been busy on the family farm in Normandy, but I gather *monsieur le marquis* de Thibouville is still there. I hope he's not pestering André that much. Aristos have too much time on their hands. While the rest of us have to work for our living, they interrupt us, crimp our plans, and waylay our best intentions. I am already looking forward to writing you the letter where I can give you a rendezvous at the Corday's farm. We will meet there and be a happy family again, with you, our adoptive father. Meantime, we still have to take leave of Frederick, who needs to return to his war, and rush to Lübeck where we're supposed to take Catherine's packet boat to Saint Petersburg. I hope the boat will still be waiting for us there when we arrive! I shall be so nervous to have Voltaire's library floating on the Baltic Sea! I'll be nervous for myself floating on the Baltic Sea! I've never been on a boat, and I've already begun to have nightmares about it. But let's not let our imaginations take away our power to reason. We must practice forbearance and garner our courage to do the things we must. Voltaire's library must get to Saint Petersburg, dry and in one piece.

A thousand embraces, my friend and father! From your son who misses you and ardently wishes to see you before long,

Zénobe

The Sources of Poetry

"**A**nd what did you learn from meeting a king?" asked Wagnière as soon as they had left the palace grounds.

"I learned that a king can be a poet. I learned that not just anybody can be a poet. A king can be a poet only if he is born with, with that... what is it, *monsieur* Wagnière? What is that thing a man needs to be a poet? Or a woman, for a woman, too, can be a poetess. Women as well, yes, and kings, but only if... only if... there's that fire. It's a fire that burns, that burgeons forth from inside. But one doesn't become a poet; one is a poet from birth, and then you have to study and to train and to practice in order to become a great poet, but the affinity must already be there, you see? I will never be a poet for I don't have that dying need to write poetry. Other people have this desire to be admired—you know I'm thinking here of the *marquis* de Villette—and they write and they write, and they write what they feel and they feel a desire to be admired, and that's what comes out in their poetry, for they wind up spending their lives spilling ink on paper, but they don't have what it takes to be great poets. You must be born with this hunger, a hunger that never goes away. You don't even need readers to keep you going. You write because you must, just like our own Voltaire who wrote because he needed to act, to show the world its imperfections and injustices, yet, I suppose in the end, even he needed readers. He could not write to a void. Had he had no readers, his pen would have been stilled and the awareness that he could not help people would have come over him and that would have been fatal. He was a writer with a purpose and with an audience. But a true poet needs no exterior motive to write. The wonder of life, and the awe of language to mediate that life, is enough to get him to have callouses on his fingers and to get his fingers eternally black with ink and his sight that dims prematurely with all that scratching on paper by candlelight!

"I knew a woman, once, in Annecy. She was an ordinary woman, with two merry daughters, a husband who was jovial, and she had a household to run. She kept cats. She liked cats. Her husband was a joiner, successful in town, known all the way to Chambéry, who belonged to the guild and who was very sociable. She had every reason to be satisfied with her life as it was. But she had this... this strange... maybe not strange... this uncommon desire... this compulsion to write, and she spent a lot of time writing. I think breathing would have been second to her, after writing. So compelling was this that she would gather her lady friends around her in her tidy *salon* and they would read to each other. That was innocent enough. There were always plenty of common folk who wanted to imitate the aristos in everything they did, and the aristos enjoyed filling their *salons* with poets and artists and musicians. Everybody in town viewed our ladies with indulgence. Every fortnight it was the 'Evening of Poetry' and they would send their husbands off and, having baked for days, would have themselves a feast, a feast for the stomach, and then another one a bit later for the soul, or whatever it is that enjoys the recitation of poetry.

"You know, the precious savant ladies that Molière made fun of because they wanted to be viewed as learned, as cultured, as knowledgeable about stanzas and rhyme schemes and caesuras, they were ridiculous, according to 17th-century rules. The counterpoint lady, the one not ridiculous according to Molière's point of view, Henriette, the only one who has no high ambitions to become a professor at the Sorbonne, all she wants is to get married. Molière made fun of his learned women because they were women, and so should have been giving their time to their babies and their husbands, spending their time in the kitchen and doing their laundry by the river, or at least sending their servants to do so. But I think Molière was wrong to try to take away from women the desire to share in the production of what society deems the imaginative, or the aesthetic, or even the intellectual. We in the countryside, down to the humblest of peasants, knew that every man and every woman needs art. Look at music, look at singing, which, according to Rousseau was our primitive way of communicating. Doesn't the shepherd, usually mute in public, sing to his sheep in a beautiful baritone that can be heard from the other side of the valley? Doesn't the graceful thresher who, as she moves her van to a rhythm going on in her head, hum a haunting tune? A mother calming her baby: what lilting cadences she creates, half speech and half melody, to convey a natural lullaby! What about the farmers removing a tree stump in unison? They sing a song, usually of their own invention, simple and repetitive, to be sure, in order to unify their forces and synchronize their movements. Same manifestations with dance: why does the street peddler sway her hips and tap her feet as she recites her wares? 'Carrots, turnips, curds and whey/apples, pears, eggs and sweet bay!' A funeral procession goes by, the grievers swaying while stepping in unison to the drone of the dirge that tugs at your heart. People who are indifferent to this natural evidence of art, who cannot be moved or inspired, cannot live to their full human potential. Part of them is dead to the world!"

By this time in their conversation, the secretaries' wagon had left the grounds of the palace and was moving onto the main avenue towards the north and out of town.

"I've heard you humming to yourself as you read," observed Wagnière.

Zénobe looked at him as if he had said that there were inhabitants on the sun.

"I do not hum to myself as I read!"

Wagnière held the reins, so he could only roll his eyes heavenward and shrug his shoulders.

After a few moments, Zénobe asked, "Really? I hum when I read? I did not know this. Why should I hum when I read? And do I hum if I'm reading an amusing book? A tragedy? Philosophy?"

"That I did not observe, but next time I catch you humming, I will consider noticing the title of your book."

"Well, declare me an infant! One is always learning new and astounding things about oneself!"

"By the time you get to be my age, master Zénobe, those things get fewer and farther between!"

A few minutes passed in silence as faster vehicles passed them by.

"Well," asked Wagnière with impatience. "Aren't you going to get back to your story?"

"My story? Oh, yes! My poetess. I knew her rather well because the stall next to ours on market days belonged to a bookseller. They weren't particularly good books, mostly sturdy classics like Molière and La Fontaine and La Rochefoucauld. But she would come every Tuesday and every Saturday to look at those books. She would buy from us as well, but she took a turn down that street primarily to look at the books.

"One day as she was rifling through the stacks, she let out a little screech. We all turned to look at her. One of her hands had gone up to her head, her fingers to her temple. The other held a small volume, prettily bound in leather, pages edged in gold, not just on top but on the side and bottom as well. I believe the hand that held the book as if it were a captive bird trembled a bit. She emitted a little moan as she read and reread the title on the spine.

"Since I was the person closest to her I asked, 'Madame Leclerc, is everything all right?'

"She looked at me as if coming out of a dream, and replied, 'Yes, oh yes… oh yes oh yes oh yes. It's just that I found, I found here, in these stacks today—lightning fulminate me now!—a special treasure, a very, very beautiful book, indeed.'

"I was already old enough to be interested in books. As a matter of fact, my instruction had already begun with Father Anselme, so I looked at this book in her hand with much curiosity.

"She opened the book to the title page and read out loud with a quivering voice for all of us to hear. '*Œuvres de Louïze Labé, Lionnoize, revues & corrigées par ladite Dame.*'[79]

"Since nobody recognized this title, *madame* Leclerc explained, 'Louise Labé was a poetess, from Lyon. She was a friend of Ronsard.' She let out a quick laugh as if to signify her luck in finding this book in the village market of Annecy.

"Everybody emitted a noise of recognition at that. Who would not know the name of the most celebrated poet of the Sixteenth century?

"I had taken a step closer to *madame* Leclerc the better to see the beautiful book. It was indeed a treasure, still in very good shape, the binding sturdy and the pages crisp. When she perceived my interest, she opened the book and said to me, 'Wait, young man, just wait and see what this poetess is about. Let me read to you my favorite poem by Louise Labé.'

"In a few moments she had located the required verse, and she read, after having cleared her throat a bit, in a very mellifluous, well-modulated voice:

" ' *Je vis, je meurs; je me brûle et me noie;*
J'ai chaud extrême en endurant froidure:
La vie m'est et trop molle et trop dure.
J'ai grands ennuis entremêlés de joie.'[80][81]

She read the whole sonnet to us, which I won't recite to you now since you already know this famous poem. But to us at that time, it was the first time we had ever heard it. It was music to our ears, and poetry electric, to use Benjamin Franklin's word, because it stunned us into silence, and in wonderment we meandered inside our own heads trying

---

79 *Works of Louise Labé, from Lyon, edited and corrected by said Lady.* Originally published in 1551, this book enjoyed sporadic new editions in the Eighteenth century.

80 [Translation by the author] I live, I die; I burn and am drowned; / I feel extreme heat while enduring cold: / Life is for me too soft and too hard. / I feel such great troubles mingled with joy.

81 [From the fact-checker] There are better, more poetic, translations on the Internet.

to grasp the beauty and the sense and the associations. We immediately beseeched her to read it again, which she did, with even more emotion, and some of the farmer ladies had tears in their eyes, and I declare to you that, even though I was but a little boy, I had a lump in my throat the size of one of our *pain à lardons*.

"From then on I held *madame* Leclerc in high esteem. She was a lady who felt, I saw, and who felt deeply. And supposedly, she was a poetess herself, so I knew she wrote verses, and when she invited other ladies to her house for an 'Evening of Poetry' she would recite them. I became very curious, and I wondered how I would be able to have the courage to ask her if I could hear some of her poetry. Finally I told Father Anselme about my dying curiosity to hear some of *madame* Leclerc's poetry. He laughed out of surprise when he heard this, but seeing that I remained serious he told me that he would take care of it. Imagine my surprise when, after only a few days, he told me that *madame* Leclerc had accepted that I visit her at her home. Father Anselme asked her during confession, you see, and, even though it was a strange request at an even stranger occasion, she acquiesced."

Wagnière was laughing to himself as Zénobe told him this last. Zénobe supposed that his early interest in poetry was a bit amusing, or perhaps the strange request passed during a confessional was comically out of the ordinary. Zénobe chuckled, too. It was many years ago that this had happened, and as his thoughts traversed the mists of time it felt as if this had happened to someone else, to another little boy, in another village called Annecy.

Zénobe looked around him and saw that the frequency of passing vehicles was diminishing. They were gaining the outskirts of Berlin. The sun was climbing up higher in the sky and did its best to warm up the earth, but to no avail.

"I suppose her self-esteem was elevated because the request came from such a young lad," observed Wagnière.

"Perhaps you are right. I must have been eight or nine, I suppose. The fact that I was a boy, too, as opposed to a girl, might have added to the increase in her self-esteem."

"Were you invited to one of her poetry soirées?"

"Not at first. On the contrary. I was invited to a tête-à-tête with *madame* Leclerc. When I presented myself at the appropriate hour, I saw that nobody else was about. She and I were completely alone in her *salon*. She had prepared cake for me. I had never ever had cake before. I didn't know what it was. When I ate a bit of it, I suppose it made me so very happy that I blurted out, 'Your cake is as delicious as your poetry!'

"She laughed and laughed at that, but she gave me more cake. Then she said, 'Well, the other day in the market, what I read to you there was not my poetry. It was that of Louise Labé, a friend of Ronsard's and an impressive poetess in her own right. Today I was thinking that I would read some of my very own poetry to you. Do you think you would like that?'

"With a mouthful of cake I could only eagerly nod my head up and down several times.

"I wish now that I had kept some of *madame* Leclerc's poetry. I should have asked her to copy some of it down for me. I never thought that I would ever be separated from her, I suppose, and that I wouldn't always be able to go back to her house whenever I wanted and have her recite to me. The only thing that I can tell you today, with the judgment of my older self and improved skills to recognize the value of art, is that the beauty of her verses was not conventional. I don't even remember alexandrines or rhyming couplets. There must have been meter in her verses, for they were very musical, and the themes were lovely and lyrical, but she enjoyed playing with the rhythm, or perhaps I should say cadence, evidence for which lay in the fact that she used shorter verses intermittently with longer ones. There were no measures of six or twelve feet; it was more like three and nine: either very little, or too much. She also loved to use inner rhyme, as opposed to ending verses with it. It was a jumble, really, quite experimental, and some of the words she used would have had her thrown out of La Pléiade by Ronsard himself.[82] You know, with Ronsard, only elegant words could be used, words with cachet that had an equivalent in Greek. But *madame* Leclerc's poetry was also beautiful in its own way, and intriguing, with a musical quality all its own that came mostly from choice of vocabulary rather than scheme of meter or rhyme. I remember one of her poems was about a group of ducks that she observed by the pond, hardly a theme deemed worthy by the Academicians! Yet, it was magical, it was delightful, for the ducks were enjoying their encounter with the water that splashed on their backs and caught the sparkles of the sun. But all along, underneath the undulating surface of the water, underneath the surface of the text, there rippled an underlying dread. While the little ducks swam and dove, the water itself seemed to veer off to one side as if crouching, gathering its forces to become their predator. Even the poetess herself could foresee the pond veering off one day towards the shore where she stood, in an attempt to get her, and by extension, me, listening to the poem. She easily transmitted the unease at being so close to the edge. Mind you, we were in her house, in her *salon* sitting on comfortable armchairs, not at the edge of the pond. Even now I feel that disquiet, especially after having almost drowned in Tonnerre. Her poetry was powerful, emotive, teeming with novel visions. It was a transfiguration of nature, and a reminder of how humankind cannot ever detach from nature, and I enjoyed it tremendously.

"She was my first experience in the domain of how literature influences a person. There was something vastly heroic in the way *madame* Leclerc wanted to transcend her position in society, to go beyond the confines of her lot in life. Did she believe in the mythology of poetry, in the *furor poeticus* of creating verses worthy of Parnassus? Did she believe that she was necessary to society, to be taken as its keen observer, or to nature, as its earnest steward and able interpreter? I've no idea. She was quiet about her writings, quiet and subtle. On her poetry evenings she read just one or two of her own poems and allowed other ladies to recite their own, even though theirs were more traditional and therefore lackluster.

"In spite of her influence, it didn't do anything to turn me into a poet. I could enjoy her poetry to a great degree, but I didn't rush to Father Anselme's little classroom by the belfry and jot down my puerile little verses. You see, I wasn't born with that… that thing, that desire, that burning obsession, to write."

Wagnière turned in his seat to look at Zénobe. "But you wrote a play! In verse!"

Zénobe groaned. "Oh, that! Speaking about puerile little verses! It wasn't much of a play, I assure you. Even Voltaire thought it unpresentable."

"But didn't the *marquis* de Thibouville have it printed up for you?"

"Only because he wanted to ingratiate himself into my favors! He wasn't after the publication of high literature, far from it. He was after one thing and one thing only."

"Your gratitude," was Wagnière's response, quick and correct.

---

82   La Pléiade was the poetical group of which Ronsard was the titular head.

"Now that I am older, and supposedly wiser, I should go back to Annecy and ask *madame* Leclerc to publish her poetry. Hers deserves to be disseminated throughout Europe. It would be influential, and it would be revolutionary."

"But who would listen to her?" asked Wagnière with a sigh. "Is the world ready for a poetic revolution?"

"I say it is. The world is ready for all sorts of revolutions. It's all simply because the world revolves and the new keeps coming up to replace the old. And in this respect, don't you think, we lurch like a drunken pendulum into progress? That is, if we're to keep Voltaire's optimism."

Wagnière smiled while looking into the distance. The pain of having lost Voltaire was slowly dissipating, and in its stead both secretaries were finding a modicum of solace in his philosophy.

Kings become poets, women become poets, and poetry becomes revolutionary. That was a part of the world that was more than adequate. It was reasonable, even.

A Detail Slips Out

A s the pair traveled north and winter progressed it became colder and colder. The worry about Catherine's packet boat still waiting for them at the harbor in Lübeck also seemed to increase. Still, all they could do was continue moving, and continue conversing.

"Are you seriously going to consider Frederick's invitation to return to Potsdam to become his new librarian?" asked Wagnière.

Zénobe mulled this question over with a few stretches of his facial muscles and a scrunching up of his brows, opening his mouth a few times as if to speak, but then reining in his words at the last second.

"I see you are torn in two about it," continued Wagnière. "On the one hand, there is that beauty of a library. I've never seen anything like it! Gorgeous! Magnificent! It's as if the gods of Olympus brought down the beams of the sun and lit them aflame inside a room! But I know your heart is longing for André, and it's been months since you last saw him."

"I know, I know! Why does destiny throw us these dilemmas? In the meantime, I so much as gave a promise to Panckoucke to go to Kehl and help out with the publication of Voltaire's complete works. I wish André could travel to Potsdam, or to Kehl, to meet me in one of those places after we're done with Catherine."

"With Her Imperial Highness of all the Russias, you mean," gently chided Wagnière.

"Yes, *monsieur*, of course, whatever you say."

"We have no way of telling how long Her Highness will want our presence in her country. She has plans, apparently, for the library, for the reconstruction of Voltaire's château, for us. She has promised me a yearly stipend as librarian to Voltaire's library."

"Ah, Wagnière, we are both to be librarians, then? What prodigious enjoyment is that? We shan't be together, for you'll be in Russia and I in Prussia, but we'll both be doing the very same thing: librarians to kings and empresses! Is this not the apogee of pleasure on earth? Are we not lucky in that we've both been chosen for our skills and knowledge and, above all, our expertise in organizing books? We've always been bibliophiles, you and I, and here we have this wonderful opportunity forever to be among books. I can't think of anything I'd rather be doing. To read them, to discover their secrets, then arrange them methodically on a shelf; the feel of them, the luster of their covers, the feel of their pages, the scent of their interiors. Even when unbound, I love books. Then, to carefully choose the red morocco, to experience the gilding of the spines, to see the royal seal stamped on the front cover. All of Frederick's books come in unbound, and then the correct binding is chosen for them."

"Don't you mean His Royal Majesty of Prussia? Zénobe!"

"He can't hear us!"

"But one day you're bound to make a mistake in front of him, and miff him and he'll send you to the dungeon."

Zénobe laughed. "His Royal Majesty Frederick The Second is not like that. He's one of us."

"What ever do you mean by that?" Wagnière thought of all of the ways that the three of them, Zénobe, Frederick and himself, could be bound together under the same designation: bibliophiles, intellectuals, handsome men…

"I mean that he looks at a person and judges him by the content of his mind, not the credentials of his pedigree. Louis XVI would have had me ejected forthwith from his library if he knew of my origins. Frederick welcomed me there, we spent hours chatting, sharing ideas, telling each other about books we've read. We instructed each other, and we entertained each other as well. I learned much about the art of war that I would never have discovered on my own, or even through books. I convinced Frederick that he should publish his own rendition of the art of war. I believe he'll follow my suggestion. The only thing Louis XVI could have taught me was how to pick a lock!"

Wagnière chuckled. He then asked, "Did you notice His Highness Frederick the Great does not have an immoderate number of books in his library?"

"Yes, I noticed it right away. For a kingly library there aren't that many books. At one occasion, he took me to see the annex, which is where he keeps all the books that are not on display. That room is huge and looks more like a storeroom. He likes only a select few in the actual library, mainly those that he is reading or that are in line to be read. What a difference between Frederick's library and l'Arsenal, remember? The *marquis* d'Argenson's library he was allowing me to use? That room, which was indeed a storeroom once, for mortars and cannon shot and muskets and such, was transformed into a library, but it remained a library with two souls. D'Argenson intentionally wanted to keep the idea of the power of the first design: books are bombs. They propel explosive information forward and drive public opinion into new revolutionary directions that pulverize old worlds. That room was a cavernous rectangle, seeming even taller with the stacks of books that rose to the rafters. Somber, sober, a bit stark, it meant to overpower the user, to show him the strength of the books and the fragility, the aloneness of the individual. In this way, it was identical to a cathedral because it, too, wants to make the single person feel like nothing, because god above is so huge and overwhelmingly omniscient that there's not a damn thing the person can do about it.

"At l'Arsenal, the library is a symbol of the enormous task that awaits the individual in his struggle to learn. While around him and above him knowledge keeps getting bigger and bigger, he must still command the courage to continue in his endeavor and not drown in all that knowledge. He must assault knowledge, attack it head on in order to assimilate it and have it become part of him. The lonely reader is in effect leading a military excursion in the field, conquering left and right and enlarging his domain, book by book, to hold the power of books in his head. It was a heady feeling, to be in that library. The *marquis* d'Argenson was an angel who allowed me that pleasure. And yet, and yet… Every once in a while I would ask myself: 'What does a person do in front of an uncontrollable growth of information?' He will be squashed by all those books! Try as he can, but still he will need to accept the inevitable—he is doomed to failure because he cannot learn it all. The size of the library was staggering as was its task.

"This is why educating people in society is making them become more and more separated from one another: the physician must delve deeply and minutely within the study of the human body; the astronomer reaches out farther and farther to places in the cosmos; the solicitor seeks better defined laws and more consistent judgments in the field of human activity. Where do they all meet? They meet in some central nucleus of knowledge that is common to all of them, that joins their humanity in spite of their diverse and far-flung skills. This common center is in the arts, for all individuals must have at least a rudimentary understanding of what the arts entail: literature, philosophy, languages, poetry, music, dance, painting, sculpture; and a smattering of the history of art would be good to command as well. There are people who say that the arts are not necessary, for they don't put bread on the table or wine in your cup. They neglect two very important things: first of all, true artists must create, no matter what remuneration they can scrape up, and second, the arts are what hold us together. It is through art that we are able to come together into a common cause, that of living on this godforsaken earth and trying to make a go of it, for everyone, understand. Not just for the people at the top. At the end of the day, the coal miner, the apothecary, and the surveyor get together at the pub and tell each other stories. They sing and dance, recite verses of exploits, reminding themselves that it is struggle to communicate universal truths about their humanity, and these stories, these songs, this art, is the glue that attaches us to one another, and to that common humanity.

"Just look at Frederick and me! I mean, His Royal Highness and me! His lectures on military strategy took us to engagements in battlefield tactics that were stultifying, yet when he told me stories of his soldiers, those who showed uncommon bravery or those who deserted, those on whom he pinned medals and those whom he ordered to be shot; when he told me of the enemy civilians who had nothing to eat because the Prussian soldiers had eaten everything in their storerooms; well, I felt I was there, in the field of battle, in the granaries, in the camps. They're calling this war the Potato War, since that's all his soldiers can find lately. When my mind came back from these sorties to distant outposts I was very surprised to find ourselves sitting in comfortable armchairs, the king and I, in his beautiful library. It was the same feeling I'd get coming back to reality after having been ensconced within the pages of a book."

Wagnière nodded because he knew that feeling very well.

"Ha, ha!" jested Zénobe. "Stories are like military sorties: you leave yourself, go take a look about, but when it gets to be too dangerous you run back into your armchair."

Sunset was not too far off, but luckily the next village they would hit was already in their eyesight. The temperature was falling considerably, and it came to Wagnière's mind how much worse it could be if they were soldiers in a camp tending to their frugal meal of potatoes. At least they had an inn in their near future.

Zénobe had one more thing to say on the subject of Frederick's library.

"You were right in saying that His Majesty's library at Sans Souci is both brilliant and small. Well, small in comparison to l'Arsenal. Still, it is a big room, largely because it needs to be commensurate with the palace of a king. But the size does not overwhelm. It's brightness, however, does: all the tricks of architecture and decoration have been used to intensify natural light, but in the evening there are chandeliers and candelabra and sconces from which hundreds of candles shine and reflect their light on the mirrored walls. Ebullience is the word that comes to mind, for there is cheer and energy in that room; there are no shadows of any kind where negative thoughts may lurk. There is a spirituality in this library, there is optimism, and there is extreme comfort. One is not squashed by an inordinate volume of books. On the contrary, this is the library for the person who knows what he likes, who has chosen the types of books he wishes to keep around. He has banished from his collection those books that don't interest him and cares not a whit that someone might call attention to their absence. For instance, Frederick may have a few books written by Newton, but only for the historical importance of these seminal books of science, and he keeps a few books written about Newton, at least those that were penned by his friend Voltaire, and this for sentimental reasons. It does not mean that His Highness would be interested enough in the subject matter to actually read them.

"The majority of the books in the king's library lie in the arts, in what I was talking about earlier on. Literature, painting, music—Frederick does keep some of his flutes in the library and when the Muse strikes his fancy to play, they're at hand, even if it's just when he's there by himself. He's in there by himself a lot of the time. He is so like us: a book will be his sole and trustworthy companion for a whole afternoon and into the evening. When along comes one of us, he truly loves to share in the pleasure of speaking about books. He is a good listener as well. I've been the cause of more books being brought over from the annex as any of his previous librarians, including Winckelmann, I think!"[83]

"Oh, poor man! Why, oh why, didn't he stay put as Frederick's librarian? He would be there still, instead of having been stabbed to death in Trieste by an angel of the Lord."

"What?" was Zénobe's single interrogative that was more thrown at Wagnière than voiced.

"Oh, I'm sorry, that's what people say. I was just repeating it. It's just that, by a strange coincidence, the person who stabbed him to death was called Angelis."

"That's what that murderer called himself. His real name was Arcangeli, not that that's much better. Furthermore, the people who say that this was an angel called to do "the Lord's bidding," feel hatred for men like Winckelmann who, as talented and brilliant as he may have been, had the unfortunate habit of desiring men. That was, I am sure, the reason he became obsessed with the ideal of masculine beauty among the ancient Greeks. Everything about Winckelmann, his life spent researching the history of art, appraising it and inventing new categories of human endeavor, that of aesthetics, that of archaeology, none of that mattered to those who found his sexual nature contorted and twisted and morally decrepit. So you see, Wagnière, so-called turpitude trumps everything else in life. Nothing stands before it. In the end, the man deserved to be murdered, so idiots say, in spite of the gifts he gave to mankind. Society always has its final say, for ignorance and prejudice define what is turpitude."

"Do you think, master Zénobe, that Winckelmann and His Royal Highness were lovers?"

"I think Frederick's appreciation of Winckelmann went higher than that; why be lovers when they were intellectual companions?"

"Enlightened Platonic companions?"

---

83 Johann Joachim Winckelmann, as the first Hellenist, was indeed the creator of the disciplines mentioned by Zénobe later in this scene, including, most prominently, the history of art. In 1765, he was offered the post of Royal Librarian by Frederick the Great but left soon after to continue his research of ancient Greece and Rome, including the newly discovered sites of Pompeii and Herculaneum. In spite of his celebrity, his prodigious research, his authoritative publications and profound influence on the literati and artists of the time, the Nineteenth century did its level best to neglect him, all because he also desired to resuscitate Greek love.

"I think so. I can deduce Frederick's relationship with his librarian Winckelmann from his treatment of me. We sat within arm's reach of each other for hours, and not once did he try to abridge that gap. His snuff was always drifting on me, we were that close. But other than a finger posed on my arm or hand for emphasis about a point he was making, he never touched me, nor I him. Mind you, I wouldn't have been adverse to a bit of, a bit of... I don't want to shock you or embarrass you, *monsieur* Wagnière... But I wouldn't have been adverse to a gentle caress or a kiss on the hand. That's what his chamberlain, *signor* Lucchesini was always dreading, that something of that nature would occur between his monarch and me. I could observe his jealous streak by how he gave us sidelong glances as he walked to another room. And he never shut the door properly. Whenever His Majesty rang for him, he always materialized within a couple of seconds. I didn't care. Having sexual relations with the king would have complicated matters. I wanted the king for his mind."

"Do you think that *signor* Lucchesini is Frederick's lover?"

"I don't think it; I know it."

Wagnière elbowed Zénobe's arm. "Do tell, then, do tell. Don't keep me in suspense!"

"But you must promise me that you won't tell a living soul!"

"Anything, I promise anything and everything!"

"Well, *signor* Lucchesini told me all about it. I don't know if you knew: he first arrived in Potsdam just over a year ago, as a diplomat from Lucca. It was all innocent at first, and Frederick took a liking to this young diplomat who was smart and handsome. They discovered they had favorite books in common. Their late night tête-à-têtes lingered until way past midnight, and then it became but a formality to ask Lucchesini if he would prefer a suite of rooms closer to Frederick's own bedchamber. The prize of chamberlain was given him for his devotion and faithful service. Apparently, he is very clear-headed in a crisis, and no concierge can be better than an Italian one, for he takes it upon himself to know the business of all inhabitants of the palace."

"Why would *signor* Lucchesini have told you that they were lovers and risk His Highness' displeasure?"

Zénobe recognized—and admired—Wagnière's logic and forward thinking, but his expression of admiration quickly gave way to timidity. His cheeks, already ruddy from the cold, flushed with a pink that rose all the way up to his cheekbones. He quickly looked away to inspect the village in the distance.

"Say it isn't true!" commanded Wagnière.

Zénobe turned to his companion seated beside him and gave a little smile, his shoulders shrugging and staying high, his head sinking in bashfulness.

"Oh, but I feel envious of people like you!"

That was excessive of Wagnière, thought Zénobe, to say he was envious of people like him. "How so?" he asked.

"Please, don't get me wrong, but since you're already supposedly treading on ground that has been called "moral turpitude," to hurl aside other principles of morality is quite easy. Once the bigger transgression is breached, minor ones follow like ducks in a row. Why not bed a man even if by so doing you are being unfaithful to another man, simply because the new one is attractive and readily available, and the other one is far away in Normandy? No need to spend much time perusing the list of rules and regulations that put a damper on us who prefer damsels. I mean, you folk don't even need to worry about virginity, fidelity and all that other rot!"

"All that other rot?" Zénobe could not believe his ears that a protestant, a lutheran protestant at that, was espousing these extraordinary ideas.

"Well, yes!" argued Wagnière. "Once you have dispensed with an important commandment, like "Thou shalt not lie with another man," the rest of them come tumbling down all by themselves, don't they?"

"I suppose you're right," Zénobe answered. Logic had it that all those injunctions on sexual behavior were absolutely worthless, seeing that they came from religion. Within his thoughts he prolonged a soliloquy that he decided not to share: 'Why continue to observe the minor rules when the big one is no longer pertinent? Constancy and virginity and, what else, obedience, chastity, I don't know, all those virtues are no longer needed, if the first premise has been broken. I shall lie with other men, and they with me, and no one will define this as moral turpitude because that definition comes from religion which will be the first to fall in the revolution to come.'

Still, Zénobe was bothered about Wagnière's allusion to André. He knew Voltaire's longest-lasting secretary to be wily and astute. All of a sudden he thought that Wagnière might have set him up with his conversation. Not only was it possible that Wagnière had surmised back in Potsdam that Zénobe had had a fling with *signor* Lucchesini, but now he wanted to punish him by making him think of André.

He turned to Wagnière, but Wagnière was driving them through the gates of the village and had already turned his attention to finding an inn.

Last Stop in Germany

They found an inn suitable to their needs, not in Lübeck proper but close to its harbor, located in Travemünde, a borough to the north-east.

But as they went through Lübeck itself, they saw a town very different from what they had heretofore experienced. This town was effervescent with the animated movement of pedestrians and vehicles that criss-crossed the streets in every which way. It was late in the afternoon and the sun was already setting, and myriads of sparkling lights had begun to appear along the avenues and inside shop windows.

"Oh, how pretty!" admired Wagnière. "It looks like some of the constellations have fallen to earth to light up the town!"

Zénobe was also impressed by the twinkling of the flickering flames which were not candles, but seemingly tiny oil lamps, similar to the bigger ones used to light up Parisian streets and the Tuileries gardens. Peering into the vitrines he could see adornments and scenery set up to convey wintery panoramas of tiny villages blanketed under snow, and everywhere there was portrayed a fat man wearing a full-body red suit and a funny hat on his head. This man was always smiling, or laughing, and in several of the windows where the fat man was real, children flocked around the big man with hands outstretched towards him.

Zénobe asked Wagnière if he could identify the fat man in the red suit.

"I believe that is Father Christmas," answered Wagnière, "the one who brings sweets to children for Christmas."

"Why should he bring sweets to children, especially for Christmas?"

"Well, it's supposed to be a joyous occasion, and I suppose the people want children to look forward to it."

"You mean, it's a way to indoctrinate them and accept the birth of their Savior as something to feel joyous about!"

"Oh, I think it's more innocent that than. Look how mobbed that store is."

Wagnière was pointing to a store with a big sign jutting out from its second story marked with big bold lettering. «Maret Confectioners», it said. Underneath, in smaller lettering, were the words, «Best Marzipan in Lübeck».

"What's that?" asked Zénobe.

"What's what?" responded Wagnière as he slowed down in front of the shop.

"Marzipan." Zénobe wasn't quite sure how to pronounce it.

"I've no idea what marzipan[84] is!" exclaimed Wagnière, seemingly delighted with the crowds of children gamboling about the vitrines looking at the displays. In one scene, Father Christmas was pouring out objects from a big red sack onto the waiting hands of the delighted little children. Zénobe presumed the objects were marzipans.

"Well, there's only one way to find out!"

Wagnière handed the reins over to Zénobe, and in seconds was inside the store pointing at things and, presumably, asking about the different products. In a few minutes he was back with a box that he handed over to Zénobe. It was a pretty red box tied with a silvery ribbon that did not remain untied for very long. Inside were curious objects made to look like miniature fruits, simulating apples and oranges and pears, but some of which he could not even identify, like an elongated yellow fruit with black edges, another yellow fruit, almost square, but more mottled than the previous yellow fruit, with a crown on one end, and a round fruit with a small appendage at one end that reminded him of a question mark.[85]

Zénobe took one of these last ones, biting into it carefully, but then plopping the whole sweet into his mouth. It was outrageously good, and in an instant, a miniature apple followed it.

Wagnière was taking hold of the reins but Zénobe told him to wait. In a moment it was his turn inside the shop, and he turned from one basket of sweets to another. This time he chose miniature vegetables, little carrots and onions, red beets and fennel bulbs. His red box was a lot bigger than Wagnière's, and it was all Wagnière could do to keep Zénobe from eating the contents of both boxes.

"You are going to spoil your supper, master Zénobe!"

"I am aware of this, but this marzipan is just so good! I'm having the same reaction as I did the first time I ate—"

At the last second he stopped his mouth from finishing the sentence, "the first time I ate chocolate!" But at the *hôtel* de Villette they never ate chocolate, only drank chocolate, hot chocolate in a cup. Would Wagnière become curious about how Zénobe ate solid chocolate? This was rather rare, and he was afraid he would have to explain the episode of the *marquise* de Polignac in her carriage and what he had been doing there. Coming so quickly after the revelation of his affair with Frederick's chamberlain, Zénobe feared that Wagnière would truly think him a whore, and a whore who was paid with chocolate. He quickly remembered that he had eaten American pumpkin for the first time at the *hôtel* de Villette, cooked by Voltaire's chef Le Parnaud, and finished his sentence after pretending to have forgotten the name of the rare fruit: "...the first time I ate, uhm, what was it?—pumpkin!"

"But pumpkin isn't that sweet, and it's a vegetable, isn't it?"

---

84   As the most important northern port of the Holy Roman Empire, many exotic foodstuffs came in through Lübeck, including imports from the East. One of the items was marzipan from Persia and Turkey, but the inhabitants quickly learned how to produce their own marzipan, using the basic ingredients of sugar, honey and almonds. In other words, they learned to produce, and improve on, the confection of a substance of which two out of three ingredients were not indigenous to such a northerly region. Marzipan was still very expensive to manufacture, since both sugar and almonds came from faraway lands, and as such was affordable only to the higher classes. Shops like the one belonging to Maret, who will sell his store to one of his employees, Johann Georg Niederegger in 1806, were effective in lowering the costs and democratizing this luxury.

85   Neither bananas nor pineapples nor the fruit of the cashew had yet to be exported in large quantities to Europe. As a matter of fact, the fruit of the cashew has yet to become widely known in Europe.

"Yes, I believe you're right, although technically it is the fruit of the plant. Remember what we learned, that it is allowed to grow rampant on the ground."

Zénobe was happy not to have revealed the Polignac episode to Wagnière. He realized, however, that Wagnière was in some strange way acting as Zénobe's conscience. This protestant was going to make sure that the young man was going to remain faithful to his love back in Normandy. That his love was another man seemed to matter not that much to Wagnière. For that, Zénobe was thankful.

Wagnière and Zénobe learned soon enough that no big boats could dock at Lübeck. It was a port city, but the docks were located in a borough to the northeast, past the mouth of the river Trave as it pours its fresh waters into the cold Baltic Sea. By the time they reached this borough, aptly, and with German precision, named "the emptying of the Trave," or Travemünde, it was too late to do anything but look for an inn. Where the sea was supposed to be, all they could capture was complete and utter blackness, as if the world ended there. Zénobe especially was impatient to see a body of water bigger than Lake Annecy. His imagination was having difficulty envisioning a horizon made entirely of water as far as the eye could see.

That night he had a fitful sleep, with disquieting dreams of large waves approaching a boat on which he was sailing, but never quite reaching it. André was with him on the boat as they were tossed on the sea. Zénobe kept asking him why he had come onto the boat. André would answer him that it was to make sure he was safe. Had he but known that it was the sugar from the marzipan coursing from his digestive system into his brain that was depriving him of a quiet, deep slumber, he would have sworn off eating it, especially so close to bedtime. It wasn't until shortly before dawn that he had his last dream of André. André had finally gotten tired of Zénobe's infidelities and gotten off on some rowboat that he found, saying not a word, but demonstrating that he preferred the solitude of a dangerous sea to staying on board with a faithless lover.

A couple of hours later, Zénobe was quiet at breakfast in abashed cerebration of the meaning of his dreams. Wagnière noticed, but said nothing. He hoped that Zénobe's ruminations meant the birth of his conscience, at least where constancy to a loved one was concerned. Somebody had to teach the boy some morals, and who better than a lutheran to do it?

But Wagnière kept their breakfast to fifteen minutes. He was impatient to see if Her Imperial Highness's packet boat was still moored someplace in Travemünde. In five minutes they had walked to the sea, and Zénobe thought that he had walked into one of his dreams.

"Look, *monsieur*, 'tis true! A horizon made entirely of water. There is no land on the other side, just a continuation of the sea, as far as we can see. Look over there, in that direction," he exclaimed excitedly, pointing to the northeast. It is difficult to tell the water from the sky, it looks like the faintest of seams. The boat will sail into the distance and up into the sky!"

Wagnière laughed at Zénobe's childish comments.

"I hardly think so! Remember, Sweden is in that direction. It is just too far away to see. Due north is Denmark, and on a clear day you can see some of its islands."

"But even knowing these facts it is still a thrill, and still frightening, to envision a sea that never ends. I can certainly understand now how Columbus's men felt when they couldn't encounter land."

"And yet they finally did! You see, there is nothing to fear."

"And look over there!" Zénobe's eyes had traveled towards the west on a sliver of land jutting into the sea. Assembled on the beach there were rows upon rows of strange wooden boxes with benches sloping down one side to rest on the sand. Zénobe and Wagnière walked towards the contraptions out of curiosity. As they came closer, they could see people stretched out on the benches, displaying their bodies towards the morning sun.

"How queer!" declared Zénobe. "What are they doing?"

"I've no idea!" responded Wagnière.

"They are all facing the same direction. It's like a field of heliotropes, all turned to look at the sun. They're even the same color, too!"[86]

"Why, they're toasting themselves under the sun!" surmised Wagnière. "But to get that toasted, they must have been lying in the sun for days!"

"How curious! Let's ask them what they're doing."

"Right, go ahead," said Wagnière encouragingly.

"Well, you better ask. My German is not up to it."

"And you think mine is?"

Between the two of them, they managed to convey the question to a couple who were dressed in comical outfits that revealed their whole arms and most of their legs.

"*Gesundheit!*" they answered, looking at the sun and smiling broadly. "*Für unsere Gesundheit!*"

"For their health," said Wagnière, turning to look at Zénobe. "They are bathing in the sun for their health!"

"Very funny," was Zénobe's conclusion. "It reminds me of Benjamin Franklin sitting naked in his garden at night. He called it an 'air bath.' "

"A sun bath sounds just as preposterous. What people will do is always astounding!"

They thanked the sun baskers and walked to the piers. After a short inquiry they found out that the Russian packet boat was still there, after two entire weeks. Nobody could understand the Russians, and nobody knew what they were doing there. Wagnière explained that the boat was there to take them to Saint Petersburg. He didn't explain that they were Voltaire's librarians accompanying his library to the Empress of Russia.

With the instructions to find the boat on the busy piers, they found what they were seeking with difficulty. They had been looking high, mostly at the larger boats in front of them. Beautiful brigantines with a foremast and a mainmast; two-decker frigates with three masts; fleet cutters and sloops with only one mast, but a very tall one. They finally learned the meaning of packet boat: slow, small, and cumbersome, made primarily for the transfer of freight, domestic mail, and whatever passengers could be made to squeeze among all those packets. A more amplified description of the Russian packet

---

86   Heliotrope, a flower from the family Boraginaceae. Please remember that Zénobe, being daltonic, would have difficulty differentiating the sunburned color of pale Germans with the purple color of the flowers.

when they finally found it could have added the words 'unpretentious, drab, and a bit shabby.' The description 'sea-worthy' did not come at all to their lips.

A couple of the sailors on board saw the two men staring at their vessel from the pier and called out to them.

Neither one of them could answer at all, Russian being such an exotic tongue to them. All they could do was shrug and raise their hands in the air to signify that there was no understanding them. One of the sailors held out both of his palms towards them, as if asking them to wait. In the meantime, the other sailor went off, hopefully in search of someone who could speak the King's French. Eventually, a taller man appeared who smiled at them and asked, "*Vous êtes les bibliothéquaires du philosophe?*" (Are you the philosopher's librarians?)

With great relief Wagnière responded in French that yes, they were. He added that he was very happy to see that Her Imperial Majesty's boat was still waiting for them.

The answer came back that he, for he was the captain, had decided to leave that very day. "You were supposed to have been here two weeks ago!"

"I know, I know," said Wagnière, making dramatic gestures with his hands that, he thought, would signify chaos and turmoil. "I shall explain later when we are on board. We are here, and the library is here, at the inn."

It was a matter of a few hours to send enough men with wheelbarrows to the inn and transport all of their baggage, trunks and crates back to the boat. Wagnière left their carriage and horses to the innkeeper, who in exchange gave them a gift of a basket filled with marzipans.

It wasn't until they were on the boat about to sail off that Wagnière asked the captain to translate the meaning of the boat's name. What he could see, буря, was illegible. The captain pronounced it proudly for them, "Burya, which means "sea tempest."

Both Wagnière and Zénobe hoped that the nomenclature would not tempt the gods of the sea into sending them a "burya" or even a fine mist of rain. Zénobe especially was worried, for he had never before been transported by sea.

"What have I gotten myself into?" he kept asking himself as he observed the deplorable condition of the boat he was on. When they were finally liberated from the piers and headed out to that infinity of horizon that he could see to the northeast, Zénobe had to gather all the bits and pieces of his courage to refrain from jumping overboard to try to swim to shore, although even that was not possible, considering he had never learned how to swim.

Interstices Addendum

December 12, 1778

Response to the Letter from Diderot

It had taken Zénobe quite some time to respond to Diderot's letter about Catherine. It may be surmised that the philosopher's letter, which unfortunately has been lost, was not merely a tableau of descriptions of the Empress and of her court. It also must have voiced a collection of warnings about the Russian empress with her full panoply of royal idiosyncrasies, tempestuous inclinations and capricious temperament. Diderot could be trusted to have inserted even more serious warnings about her courtiers.[87] It is clear from Zénobe's response that Diderot did not neglect to mention the Queen's quick temper, her impetuosity, and her utter heedlessness about the opinions of others, her subjects' least of all. No one dared give her advice.

Even though she was sovereign over all Russians, she was not Russian herself. Diderot must have suggested the idea that Catherine, being German, felt keenly her superiority over the uncivilized masses of this backward monolithic Eastern nation. From her own perspective, she was their Messiah, not just their head of state, there to drag them into the Eighteenth century, and as such, felt her inevitable mandate to an even greater degree than any ordinary king or queen. Monarchs were plentiful during the Age of Enlightenment, and even though the *philosophes* kept busy and even traveled to faraway kingdoms to try to bring a modicum of that enlightenment to the monarchs in power, Diderot having spent a few months with Catherine, for instance, and Voltaire a couple of years with Frederick in Prussia, the idea of power was too inflexibly affixed to a potentate's nature to be budged by much. The idea that God has placed one on the

---

87   Catherine's courtiers, with one exception, took an intense dislike of Diderot: not only were they envious that a foreigner had daily access to their Empress, but that a self-avowed atheist had influence on her was considered repulsive. The only exception was General Betzki who, like Diderot, was interested in Catherine's directive to acquire international art for her imperial collections. Diderot was shunned and excluded from the best houses of the nobility. He retaliated by waxing philosophical and declaring, "I am the guest of the Empress in her house and I am accountable only to her; it is she whom I care to please and I care not a whit for her servants."

throne is too delightful to be given up easily. Besides, if the subjects themselves believe this to be true, who are they to disabuse their own monarchs of it? Of all the crowned heads, however, Catherine must have doubted that it was God who had lifted her up to absolute power for the simple reason that numerous times she had had to take matters into her own hands and in point of fact help God to put the crown on her own head. It was she who helped God to help her. A week after her coup d'état to wrest power away from her husband Peter III, the dethroned king was murdered. That historians have not uncovered verifiable proof of Catherine's complicity in this regicide is a testament to her caution and attentiveness to details, not to deficiencies in the art of the historian.

Please note in his letter to Diderot, Zénobe's assurances of vigilance and prudence in his future dealings with Catherine. It is doubtful he would have made so many remonstrances to Diderot had the *philosophe* not warned him in his letter about Catherine's lapses into treachery and hypocrisy. Zénobe's cavalier attitude, and his strange parenthetical comments about already being cognizant of aristocratic women's "duplicity and dissimulation" say more about his youth and inexperience than his ability to not just recognize deceit in others, but to be able to deal with that deceit in a way that would enable him to keep on living.

Diderot must have been alarmed when he received Zénobe's response. The young man's naïveté and ingenuousness were no match for royal wiliness and power. Unfortunately, the philosopher, who considered the Russian empress a friend, was not in a position to help his young friend who journeyed ever closer to her court. How would Catherine the Great react to such an innocent? Would she even notice him? For Zénobe's sake, Diderot thought, perhaps not. After all, it was Wagnière who was Voltaire's secretary and librarian. It was he whom Catherine had invited to her court. Zénobe was just an assistant, a young man with the physical strength to carry books and place them on shelves, to construct the shelves if need be. Diderot put great faith in Wagnière, and hoped that the older librarian would be diplomatic enough to keep both of them safe.

[letter not dated]

My dear Diderot,

It is with much pleasure that I finally send you an answer to your extensive and methodical letter about Catherine the Great. I realize that she is no easy subject; I realize that Russia is no easy kingdom. With trust in your direct observations and subsequent surmises, I promise you both caution and circumspection in my dealings with the Russians. You have been corresponding with Catherine for decades, as had Voltaire, and I promise I will not take your advice lightly.

Please take into consideration my experience with aristocratic women. There were plenty on hand at the *hôtel* de Villette to observe and analyze. I daresay these noble ladies are interested in power as much, if not more, than their men. They have more ground to cover; they don't wish to end up like the omega hen in the barnyard, pecked by all until her feathers droop and her head becomes bald. I have seen these ladies in social chitchat where utterances become tools of rank and status, at the expense of all the other ladies. Only *mademoiselle* d'Éon, bless her heart, stood apart from these inanities of a hierarchical system where everybody fights constantly to scramble up to the top. Her Croix de Saint Louis made sure that she enjoys a place of permanence at the apex. Think of it: What other lady could have been so intrepid, so valiant, at the battle of Minden?

Moreover, I have direct experience and association with another lady of high rank.[88] [89] My scrutiny of this lady has been such that I have learned much about the duplicity and dissimulation that reign in the hearts and minds of all of her class. I fear that the ultimate prize that they are after, access to the King and Queen, makes them experts in subterfuge as they use everything in their power not just to keep their social position, but to lower everybody else's by maligning them and even slandering them. Hypocrisy is their best tool. Rumormongering comes in as a close second. Cruelty is but a consequence of their actions, and enjoyment of others' suffering is but an added boon. The *marquis* de Sade could have come only from the aristocracy.

La Rochefoucauld was right: the noble class is a seething mass of callous humanity where everyone wishes to rise to the top of the mountain by stepping over everybody else, even flinging them to the bottom and enjoying their rapid descent. I do believe, my dear Diderot, that this noble society will not be swept clean until the King and Queen themselves are toppled.

But to get back to Catherine, who was she but a German princess, one of many, who merely added subterfuge, treason and murder to her arsenal of tools? Her ambition took her far. She was not content to be the dutiful wife of a tsar, however inefficient and stupid he might have been. Look at our own Marie Antoinette! At least she does not make any moves to assassinate her husband, which might after all be best for the country. Except that the Austrian princess never learned from her mother what it takes to run a country, and now as queen she prefers card games and concerts. Still, how can Catherine be admired for such ruthlessness? This is an answer I know. Because violence itself is a way to power, and in the end it is power that is universally admired. Neither you nor Voltaire ever seemed to mind that Catherine got to her position by transgression and high crime. I do not in the least blame you: No one else has, either. We just look at the power she has garnered for herself, a woman! Any outrage of her past is stifled by the dominion she holds over her territories. Marie Thérèse can only hope to be as ruthless, but she is not a shadow of Catherine's thumb, and her daughter Queen of France even less. Marie Thérèse wept over the partitioning of Poland—wept!—even as she received her pieces of gold. I do not believe that Catherine shed a single tear over the demise of her husband. Perhaps a tear of joy.

Another important difference between Marie Antoinette and Catherine the Great: the Queen of France adores her mother, and listens

---

88   Reminder to the reader: Zénobe is of course to the *duchesse* de Polignac referring.

89   [From the author] Reminder to the fact-checker: the *marquise* de Polignac was not yet a *duchesse*. She is still engaged in her struggle to rise in the ranks. Moreover, I am sure that the kind reader remembers this important detail from the first volume.

to her prattling advice which she follows as best she can. Catherine rose to her stature as anointed Queen of Russia because she despised her mother. Her mother gave preferences to her two sons over her firstborn daughter precisely because they were boys. The daughter was cast aside like so much detritus, scorned and neglected. More intelligent than her brothers, more intelligent than her parents and a whole lot more intelligent than her husband, she felt she had to take over, to save herself, to save Russia.

Even though in other ways I would find pleasure in denigrating the Empress of Russia, there are many reasons for which I can admire her. Still, I sincerely doubt your statement that all Catherine ever wanted from you was for you to be her mouthpiece in Europe and have you serve as her interpreter. It is true that your accolades of her served to influence public opinion back home, and that your admiration of the few inroads she had wrought on a vast feudal dominion colored the opinions of the inhabitants of freer nations. However, Catherine's other deeds, such as the war on Turkey, the brutal suppression of the Pougachyoff Insurgence,[90] and her refusal to free the French officers who were captured fighting for Poland against Russian hegemony, all worked against her in the sphere of public opinion. I truly believe that she invited you to her side because she loved you, appreciated you, and wanted some of your goodness and wisdom to rub off on her. Once you were there with her, she realized that both of these virtues were too liberal for the good of her country. Were she to diminish her dominance by a few degrees, were she to grant more authority to her aristocraps, she would have a hundred insurrections on her hands, and her noblemen and ladies would all be clamoring for even more power, if not clamoring to see her off to the same fate as befell her dear spouse.

She believed in both your goodness and in your wisdom. She said that sometimes she thought that you were a hundred years old, and sometimes only ten. Well, where sagacity and experience and knowledge of the arts and sciences are concerned, you are a hundred years old. But where optimism and hope and belief in the fairness of humans and in the compassion and mercy of others is concerned, you are but a child, my dear Diderot. I do not mean that as an insult, for you are not an unsophisticated, unimaginative simpleton. Far from that! Your goodness and honesty are so strong, your sense of justice and fairness so keen, that you think all of mankind holds the ethical and the moral in such high esteem. You tried to convince Catherine to moderate the laws of her land, so that the serfs could no longer be called slaves. Catherine's response sent an important signal: "There are no slaves in Russia. The peasants in Russia are simply the most attached to their land than any other peasant class in Europe," she explained. She makes it sound as if they are attached by gossamer threads of joy

---

90   Today the standardized spelling of the name of this rebel who tried and failed to improve the lot of serfs in Russia is Yemelyan Pugachev. His name in Cyrillic is Емельян Иванович Пугачёв.

and satisfaction or sweet feelings of nostalgia. I, who come from the peasant class of Savoy, know how the masters justify our slavery: they claim that we love our land, that we need the whip for our own good, that we remain as children under the warm paternal protection of our overlords. Without them we would have no direction, we would forget how to plant and harvest; without them we would just keel over and die. According to them, we desire nothing more than to remain unencumbered by the onerous responsibility of making our own decisions, especially those that would change our destiny, and therefore theirs! We need to remain as tillable as the land, as coarse as mud, as low as dirt. We are the dirt people, the stifled and the beaten down, who cannot raise our dispirited heads except to look towards those who flatten us and we are forced to thank them for our existence, even though they barely keep us alive and frequently let some of us die. We are the cur who licks his cruel master's hand. We have no voice, no impetus, no strength, no direction but down. When we die, our blood fertilizes our furrows.

But you know all this. You went to Catherine with a thousand plans and a thousand hopes to soften her sovereign hand. But she knows that this will not work, for she knows, better than her Russian subjects, what the downtrodden will do if they are allowed to rise to the level of blades of grass: they will sweep across the land and destroy everything they pass over. They will usurp the freedom of the locust and swarm everywhere to kill everything in their path. They will gust across the steppes, blowing down villages and cities, razing houses into sand, people into memories. Since no one ever took care to educate them, they will fail, if they ever get into a position of power. They will fight amongst themselves, and the law of the barbarian will have sway, for that is the only thing they know, the justice of the bible, where the intent is to massacre entire peoples, to exterminate every single living thing, down to babies and old people and even farm animals. They will carry on the law of god, who teaches the believer to be merciless in his slaughter. Nothing will remain but empty wasteland, as if tornadoes had carried everything off.

My philosopher friend, you tried your best, but Catherine is a tough nut to crack. I have decided that I will not even meet her. Her invitation was for Wagnière, and it is Wagnière who will present Voltaire's library to her. It is he who has the knowledge to instruct her as to the dimensions and disposition of the library as it was in Ferney when our friend was alive and well and working away in it. Remember, Voltaire also made a big effort to make a dent in Frederick's thick skin, and he served in his court for two whole years. How well did he succeed? Frederick has the gall to think himself an enlightened monarch, but in spite of his natural intelligence this self-description is delusional at best, willful deception at worst.

I shall accompany Wagnière to Saint Petersburg, but I will remain in the periphery, hiding in the shadows, as it were. I shall be more the postillion than the attendant squire. Catherine need not know I exist.

Who knows, were I to meet her, I might plunge a hot poker in her eye, or tongs in her ears. I've had experience with aristocratic ladies, and they will not take advantage of me ever again. I will submit neither to their cajolery nor to their seductions. You mention Catherine's proclivity to become intimate with a stranger on first meeting, that she is hospitable like no other and that her concern for her guests' comfort is nonpareil. Well, I'll let poor Wagnière deal with all that. I shall keep a low profile. The Empress of a foreign court has no jurisdiction over me. I am merely the librarian's assistant. I shall keep to the books.

Thank you from the bottom of my heart. Your experience with the Empress is invaluable, and I shall share it with Wagnière. He is, of course, a brilliant secretary and librarian, but I don't suppose he will be interested, like you were, in a personal relationship with Catherine. Wagnière takes pride in his earnest professionalism and frankly has no time, perhaps no inclination, for warmth and cordiality. He will have to be careful because Catherine is devastated with the loss of our philosophical friend. Voltaire sustained her during dark and terrible times, and they were intimate friends who shared all their interests. They bared their soul to each other. I daresay that is why Catherine wants her letters back. What I fear is that Wagnière might be put in the position of simulacrum of Voltaire and that Catherine might find him wanting. Will she be disappointed when the secretary doesn't come up to the same standards as the master? Wagnière carries Voltaire's books; he doesn't carry his wisdom. Nor do I, mind you, but I shall try to help Wagnière to reconnoiter the shoals and reefs that may lie in shallow waters.

I am forever in your debt and have the honor to call you friend.

Zénobe Bosquet

Part 4

Sailing on the Baltic

Discussing Morality

Zénobe did not exactly turn out to be a seaworthy passenger. It was not that he became seasick, yet the constant pitching and rolling was bothersome to him while he read to himself, or wrote letters, or particularly when it was time to eat. The wine in their glasses proved a constant indicator of gravity, like liquid gyroscopes placed on the table, all identically showing the constant movement of the circular plane at the surface of the wine, now aft, then swirling around to fore, spinning the liquid round and about to soporific effect. Zénobe continued to feel this movement in his stomach after he had drunk the wine.

He would go on deck to inhale the cold Baltic air, but seeing the rollicking of the *Burya* on the waves seemed to make the movements worse. After a few minutes he would go back down into the hold and try again to read, or to write, but taking a nap was out of the question. Indeed, going to sleep at night had to be when he was too tired for anything else, for their beds were mere hammocks strung up and free to vacillate unsteadily between the cardinal points. All was in perpetual oscillation, unsteady and erratic. The horizon shifted to and fro as the packet boat rose up and down. Zénobe quickly became tired of walking because his feet felt unbalanced and his line of movement described a wobbly line, as if he were drunk. Yet he marveled at the sailors who walked back and forth on deck and up and down on the stairs with even steps and never needed to grab on to walls or objects to steady themselves.

Zénobe's favorite activity became conversation with Wagnière. That was the only productive way to pass the time. Since Russian was an unfathomable language to them, and since the captain was always too busy save for polite salutations every time he saw them, the two secretaries felt as isolated as they had been during their long trek to Lübeck.

Zénobe unfortunately chose as a first topic of conversation a subject that led to such choppy disagreement, such a spiraling altercation, that the two friends almost came to blows. But Zénobe had had it with Wagnière and his holier-than-thou protestant ethics. The elder's needling comments about Zénobe's infidelities had had their effect, they had cut under Zénobe's skin and festered and prickled. The young man felt he needed to bring up the subject and clear the air.

"*Monsieur* Wagnière," he began, "I do not like it when you become critical of certain actions of mine, and judgmental about my dalliances with people other than André."

Wagnière put down the book he had been reading, his eyebrows raised in surprise and dismay. "Dalliances, you mean dalliances in the plural? I thought there was only the one with Frederick's chamberlain!"

Zénobe's expression took a turn to register dismay. Still, he was not about to let a protestant get away with judging his character. Zénobe thought himself to be highly moral, tolerant, and benevolent. Unvaryingly benevolent.

"What does it matter," he responded with escalating volume, "if there's been one, three, or ten?"

Wagnière let out a guffaw. "*Gott im Himmel*! I take it, then, that there were three! Three instances of you being unfaithful to your André!"

Wagnière looked to the heavens while he thought of Zénobe's disloyalty and added, "How did you even have the time, or find the circumstances, to stray from the moral path of fidelity?"

Zénobe was taken aback. He never actively sought the circumstances; they had come to him! He made a strangled noise of impatience and decided to confess it all.

"Well, if you must absolutely know, yes, there's been three.[91] The chamberlain, Gil Blas, and the boy who replaced André after he was kicked out by the aristos at the *hôtel* de Villette. You had already returned to Ferney so you never met this fellow. His name was also André, so I called him *le nouvel* André. He was placed right in my bed; I had no say in the matter! I couldn't very well ignore him! He was there, physically, and even though he was a bit short, he wasn't ugly. Nevertheless, I never loved him. It was just a physical dalliance, a parenthetical interlude, one that never attached itself to my heart or mind."

Wagnière spluttered in response for a couple of seconds before correctly constructed words could follow. "Well, that makes it even worse! If there was no passion there, no emotion, no love or affection, if it was just a mere physical tryst, then it was an instance of fornication, a bout of lechery, just to assuage your concupiscence without even a tiny bit of tenderness or spirituality to counterbalance a desire to satisfy your lust!"

"There are so many things about your statement that are grievously in error, I... I... I just don't know where to begin. But let me respond to you by asking you, what would you have done if you found in your bed one night a short but pretty woman who was not your wife?"

"I usually have more control of who gets deposited in my bed, but I will nevertheless answer your hypothetical question. If an unknown woman, short but pretty, ended up one night in the bed where I was supposed to sleep... I... I would ignore her, and, if I couldn't get her to leave my bed, I'd go right to sleep."

"Well, I did ignore *le nouvel* André the first night, the first few nights, as a matter of fact. But after a while I got used to him, and the bed was so small it was hard to ignore him. And then... it just... it just... happened. One night it just happened! I think we were both still asleep."

"Lovemaking cannot happen in your sleep!"

"I tell you it can, and it did! It was just a physical reaction to a situation of proximity and convenience."

"My! You really suck out all the romance and the thrill!"

---

91   For some odd reason, Zénobe leaves out d'Éon's young tenant farmer in Burgundy, Étienne Étamble. Perhaps he thought that a one-night stand was not even worthy of the meaning of the word he himself chose to describe his affairs, 'dalliance.' Perhaps if he had chosen 'escapades' or 'peccadillos' or, to use Casanova's term, 'romantic entanglement,' that fleeting romance would have become the fourth instance of Zénobe's unfaithfulness. He also rather conveniently disregarded the torrid affair he conducted with the *marquise* de Polignac, even though it came rather early in his relationship with André. Also, perhaps, an affair with a woman did not, in his mind, count, for much.

"Because I tell you that there was neither romance nor thrill! We exchanged no vows of love everlasting; we didn't look longingly in each other's eyes and promise each other fealty! It was nothing, and it was nighttime. It was pitch black in that little back room and we couldn't see a thing, and we couldn't say a thing because of the people in the other rooms. I swear to you that there was never any fornication, whatever that means! Not even direct contact. It all took place through our night shirts and bed sheets. It was just friction through the fabric, friction through the fabric."

"Oh, that is just a lexicographer's facile exercise in substitute synonyms! The deed was done and you got to know *le nouvel* André in a Biblical way!"

"I certainly don't know what that means, either! I mean, I've read it, but what does it really mean? Usually when the bible people get to know each other, you know, *know* each other—how about that word as a euphemism?—after they *know* each other there is usually a child born of it. That means there was penetration, then ejaculation. Well, people like you always take it for granted that people like me also want to do the same things you do. Well, in our case it is not possible. And some of us don't like to imitate the Greeks who subdued and emasculated their lovers."

"I do not care to discover any more of your carnal proceedings. All I know is that you were intimate with someone who was not your wife, I mean, your beloved. André back in Normandy is your beloved and every time you have intimate relations with someone else you inevitably steal something away from him, for he is your true and only."

"What, pray tell, is that? I can't be taking anything away from my beloved André because he doesn't even know!"

Wagnière was stumped. Yet, he needed to continue his lesson on morality.

"If you steal from a friend who doesn't know, you've still stolen from him. You think that this is perfectly acceptable?"

"Of course not! You stole something from him. I repeat, what is it that I stole from André?"

"You stole your faithfulness, you stole your loyalty, your love and concern and tenderness!" Wagnière was spluttering again.

"But all those… those virtues, and qualities, and emotions, they're all on my side. André will not know that they've been diminished. I'm not sure that I can tell that they have been diminished. I find my love for my true and only, for my beloved André, to be intact. All my love and concern and tenderness are still intact. They're all still there, and I miss him a great deal. What if I were to have contact with one of these Russian sailors? I couldn't even tell him anything—we don't speak the same language. It would just be a physical, ephemeral, non-invasive contact. No feelings, no emotion, just… lust, as you said. Why make of it a moral morass? It's just nature at its simplest, and its strongest."

"Well, promise me that you won't have any 'contact' with a Russian sailor on this boat. If the rest find out about it they might just decide to throw both of you overboard. That's nature, too, at its simplest, and strongest."

"I shall refrain from any onboard tryst, for what you have just said makes the most sense of all. However, I disagree with you. The sailors throwing overboard a couple of *anti-physiques* has nothing to do with nature. That is all culture, and culture very frequently gets things wrong. Intolerance to what is out of the norm is taught, and just because it has been taught for generations it still won't make it right."

Wagnière had become more subdued. "We have come very far from the ancient Greeks, and sexual mores have changed drastically. Still, I persist in thinking that questions of conjugal fidelity are involved in all instances and for all types of people, including those whom you represent. If I'm being judgmental, forgive me, but this is something that has been inculcated in us protestants from the time we were children. I am aware that philosophers like Diderot wish society to think, and rethink, about the apparent absence across the world of universal and absolute truths concerning sex, but when we live in a society that looks askance at certain practices, it is necessary, I think, to keep a low profile."

"I understand what you are saying," said Zénobe, also bringing the vociferousness of his voice down to a lower level, "but if those who differ in their opinions were eternally to keep a low profile, there would be no social progress. Look at *mademoiselle la chevalière* d'Éon. She will not keep quiet, she will not keep a low profile. She demands of society that she be allowed to live her life just like she did when she was a man. I believe that she is doing this for all women, not just herself. I love her, and I admire her. Look at the *chevalier* de Saint-George. He is a bit more measured in his fight for equality, but he ardently works for tolerance towards the black man. He himself, just like *mademoiselle* d'Éon, is an exemplary individual worthy of emulation. I wish the same equality to apply to *anti-physiques*. We are worth no more, but no less, than anybody else."

"So you need to become an individual worthy of emulation. In your character you must instill all the qualities and virtues that your own society demands of exemplary persons. You should seek nothing less than to become a paragon of society, a representative of your type of people, and as such, they would be compelled to see in you a principled and respectable human being."

Zénobe knew that Wagnière was right. A high-minded leader had to lead from a position of meritorious conduct, for any failures would be seen by society as a justification to perpetuate their intolerance and rejection of what the leader represented. He liked the idea of himself as a paragon.

Zénobe nodded to Wagnière but said nothing. He was thinking of André. How far away he was, and getting farther with every league they sailed east. When would he see him again? In the interim, he was approaching the court of Her Imperial Highness Catherine II. Zénobe was certain that she would not be able to refrain from making sexual overtures towards him. This was her reputation, and her autocratic power allowed her to circumvent all questions of paragons and virtuous individuals. She could be promiscuous to her heart's content. Kings and queens were exempt from what ordinary mortals had to deal with. If she wanted him, she would be able to have him. He decided that he would not show his face to the Empress. It was Wagnière whom she had invited to attend to Voltaire's library. Zénobe would keep a low profile. Humble and lowly he would be, a mere servant, too inferior for a queen to hold interest in him. He would hide under modest attire, be but a paltry lackey to the librarian. He felt he could slip under the attention of Catherine by acting like a drudge. He would be a good drudge, a great drudge. After all, a little over a year ago he was drudging in the fields of Savoy. It would be easy for him to return to that frame of mind.

Wagnière, who was still looking at his friend, marveled at the activity that must be taking place between his ears. All of a sudden in front of him, Zénobe looked diminished, reduced in size. But the secretary attributed the change to an erroneous reason: he thought that Zénobe's conscience had finally been victorious and was making him feel contrite and repentant. This, to a protestant, is a thing of beauty, because Zénobe's remorse, he knew, would make him more virtuous, and more apt to one day receive the grace of God.

Of Storm at Sea

After a morning of swirling gray clouds playing havoc with the sun, a darker blot appeared on the western horizon and got bigger by the hour and more menacing, lit from within with recurrent flashes of light followed by tremolos of low-pitched rumblings. It looked like another sun that was being held captive amidst ragged shrouds of cumulonimbus and was fighting mightily to get out. Even though the *Burya* was sailing in the same direction, the fast advance of the storm made all the sailors jittery. Zénobe, who spent much time on deck, observed that they only had eyes for the advancing blot and seemed to accept that it would overtake them. Everything that could be lashed was lashed with thick rope, the sails were trimmed way before any squalls arrived, and, more ominously, the captain allowed supplemental rations of vodka to be distributed to the crew. At the last minute he turned the *Burya* around and pointed her bow into the first waves that began crashing against her.

Zénobe did not have the heart to tell Wagnière, who hardly ever came up on deck, what was about to befall them; he would soon figure it out on his own. He didn't tell him either about the crew imbibing impressive quantities of vodka so early in the day. But Wagnière had noticed that they were now facing the opposite direction and that the seas were rougher than usual. Their dinner that afternoon was late, and cold; the fire in the galley had been doused early, for fear that a rogue wave might hit unexpectedly.

Zénobe admired the captain for taking such timely precautions, except perhaps for the vodka. Maybe it made the men more courageous. Wouldn't it make them more careless? Perhaps it was to make them more indifferent to calamity. In any case, thought Zénobe, it was a good captain who took preventative measures to keep his ship and crew safe. Then he thought that the dilapidated condition of the *Burya* warranted these strict safeguards in the first place.

How could Catherine the Great of all the Russias, the wealthiest queen alive, have sent this ancient ramshackle mail packet to retrieve Voltaire's library? Had she wanted it to sink all along so that she would forever be free of her correspondence with the philosopher? Did her letters to him truly hold such secrets that their dissemination would embarrass her on the world stage? Had she not thought of the fact that Voltaire's librarian would also go down with the ship? How could she doom poor innocent Wagnière to such a horrific fate?

The storm was upon them full blast right before sunset, all the more to enjoy in the complete dark the volleys of rain and spray and the mountains and valleys of a turbulent sea, lit sporadically by fusillades of lightning. The thunder, combined with the pandemonium from within the bowels of the ship, was enough to frighten the cockiest of sailors. Wagnière and Zénobe stayed in the galley behind one of the tables that were, of course, nailed to the floor, their arms and legs wrapped around each other.

As wretched as they felt from the shrieking of the wind and the rolling of the *Burya* on the chaotic sea, their perspective worsened when foam-flecked water started trickling, then pouring down from above. This drove them wild with fear: how much water could the ship take on before it foundered? How much shaking could the vessel take before it shattered into pieces? When would the call be made to lighten the ship, to throw overboard all the boxes, crates and mailbags in her hold, including those holding Voltaire's library?

Voltaire's secretaries were afraid for their survival; they were, however, even more distressed about the possibility of Voltaire's library going down into the depths of the North Sea. Had they come all this distance just to see their prize lost forever to a cruel indifferent Nature? Zénobe remembered the harrowing experience when he almost drowned in the well at Tonnerre. He understood why the naïve minds of the ancients had created the basilisk creature to explain the treacherous currents within the well. Now he felt that there were a thousand monsters beneath their paltry *paquebot* wrenching it in a thousand directions. To Zénobe, this was Nature at her most merciless detachment, uncaring for the hapless souls on the *Burya*, rocking them to madness, thrusting on them unbearable trauma and the inevitable threat of imminent obliteration, like a cat playing with its mouse for hours on end, before finally tearing off its head. Why did they have to go through so much torture before the storm sent them down to a ghastly death? Numerous times, as he held on to Wagnière for dear life, he would will the descent to begin, acceding permission to be devoured, for he could not take one more minute of this ordeal. He promised God—no, not God—the world, life, existence, that he would never ever again set foot on a ship. What a fool he had been to trust a rickety boat that was tossed around like a plaything on the dark and turbulent sea.

Zénobe glanced at Wagnière whom he held tightly to his bosom. The poor old scribe had his eyes closed and his mouth open—Was he moaning? His head was bobbing on his neck to the movement of the pitching. Zénobe stared at him. Was he dead? Had he died of fright? Zénobe brought a hand up to Wagnière's throat to feel for a pulse, but with all the thrashing and plunging and swooping back up, along with the clamor of the tempest, he could not verify that his companion was alive. It wasn't until Zénobe took his friend's head in both of his hands that Wagnière reacted and opened his eyes wide with fear. Relieved, Zénobe pressed his head to Wagnière's as, all alone in the galley, they continued to ride out the storm.

It is a shame that they were unaware of the tenacity of both the *Burya* and her captain, Nicolai Shounine, who had much experience and intimate knowledge of his ship, which after all was named "The Tempest" in a direct attempt to placate the gods of bad weather. Shounine had run through storms like this before, and it never occurred to him that the *Burya* was ever in danger from this one. He never even considered ejecting jetsam. He could sense that his men in the hold were holding their own at the bilge pumps. During the worst part of the storm he had ordered the crew to heave to, and the *Burya*, which never rode very high in the first place, was also holding her own against the raging sea. He surmised that his landlubbers were anxious about the storm, but he had no time to go down into the cabins to hold hands and appease fears. They would probably hold him in higher esteem the next day, anyway, for having thwarted death's icy grip on them. When the fast-moving storm began to abate, about an hour before sunrise, Captain Shounine sauntered down and found his landlubbers clinging to each other, and asleep, in the galley. He smiled and left the galley to his cook who was about to begin the daily chores. The seas were still a little rough and the wind still whistling when Wagnière and Zénobe woke up to clattering on the stove and mugs of coffee thrust in front of them.

It was the tastiest coffee they had ever experienced. They felt reborn.

A Discussion on Free Will over Breakfast

I no longer believe in free will, said Zénobe unexpectedly to Wagnière who gulped his coffee and answered, And why is that?

Z: Well, just look at that storm from this night. Nothing we could have done, nothing we could have thought of doing, nothing that we were capable of doing, would have changed anything about it. We were tossed upon the waves like a toy boat. Those waves were completely indifferent to our fate. We could have gone down, and nobody would have known what happened to us. We would have disappeared, and months would have gone by before it would dawn on people, only certain people, mind you, that we were gone. Forever lost. Never to come back again. We would have been memories in people's minds, and only very few would have cared anything at all about it. *Madame* Wagnière, André, *monsieur* Maurel, *la marquise* de Villette… Just a handful of people would realize that we had slipped under the dark surface of the sea, entombed in a watery grave.

W: What makes you think that no action on our part had any sway in the bigger picture of the storm? Yes, the storm was indeed overwhelming, but had our captain not taken the precautions he did perhaps our ship would have been swamped and relegated to the depths. His experience counted for something, and it modified his actions which had a direct import on our destiny. Here we sit drinking coffee, waiting for eggs and sausage, and we quite possibly may have the captain to thank for it.

Z: I'll accept your claim that perhaps the captain's actions influenced the outcome of the *Burya* and us, but your free will, and my free will last night had absolutely no bearing on our fortune. We could have gone down into the hold, we could have gone on deck, we could have done anything we pleased and it wouldn't have changed a thing.

W: You do not know that, Zénobe. Had we gone into the hold, we would have perhaps been asked to man the bilge pumps. Had we appeared on deck, a wave could have swept us out to sea. In view of our inexperience on boats, that would have been a probable event. True, by doing nothing and being frightened out of our minds we remained in the galley and probably saved our own lives out of ignorance. Inaction is also a decision, whether or not we made it through Cartesian methodology, or through a roll of the dice; at times it is the best decision. We are alive, we are enjoying our coffee, by the grace of God, and anything else could have ended up with us at this very moment at the bottom of the sea.

Z: Well, if you want to bring God into the picture, aren't you as a lutheran committed to believing in predestination? It is God who moves all the strings, and you are but a marionette ceding to every tug and drag.

W: We are taught that our salvation is predestined by God and not by any collection of good works. But we are not taught that damnation is predestined. That is the destiny of unbelievers who reject the forgiveness of sins.

Z: Wagnière, you are my friend and I would die for you. However, you know that this talk of God annoys me to my very core. Where is the idea of determinism in a god-less universe?

W: Well, a moment ago you were saying that you had no free will and that you were being tossed on the waves of life like a plaything. The tempest becomes a metaphor for existence, which we all know is no easy thing in this world. In your young age you have already ascertained this time and time again. But if you wish to argue for free will, be my guest. I'm curious as to how you will express it.

Z: Storm-tossed or not, we act; we thoughtfully decide on our actions, and these actions may break on the hard indifference of this world with nary a result, or at least the result we desire. So we act with an increased effort of our volition, with more strength, sometimes with violence, and that still might not budge the world. I think that it is only when many of us are acting in support of each other, with violence, that we can see our desired results take hold and move the world. If the volition of our opponents isn't stronger, that is. So, I think I am making a case for the free will of the masses, who wish to free themselves of oppression and prejudice.

W: Ah, you are avoiding the issue. We are talking about the actions created by the free will of the individual. One man, one free will.

Z: Well, you'd have to have the influence of a Voltaire to sway the world!

W: Ah! He was the expert! He had the wherewithal to sway so very many people. But you are just starting out; you might sway just one other individual, and then another and yet another. And those could pass on your message to others, like ripples in a pond. Still, the free will of the hordes is difficult to direct. Individual conscience gets swallowed up by the mob, and anarchy results, each person following along because the others seem to be in control of the action, but in the end, there is no control.

Z: Still, I do prefer the idea that I am free to do as I wish, with my conscience acting as my guide, for I don't want to view myself as being impotent, as being limited in my actions. Besides, I think that someone who believes in determinism would, after a while, become a listless fatalist who accepts all that is thrown at him, and lingers in doubt and irresolution. I like the idea of creating my own destiny. That is what *mademoiselle* d'Éon holds to be true. But I realize that this may be a false premise, an illusion. Just like those who love the idea of a god who loves them and protects them and answers their prayers, that desire for a god will not produce that god. My desire for free will might not be enough to produce it. For all I know, I am borne by the winds to my destiny, and nothing I can do will break my fate. Still, I will act as if I were in possession of my own volition that is independent of others'. I may be making the same mistake as those who wish to believe in God because it makes them feel better. Well, believing in free will makes me feel better.

W: So your statements a few minutes ago were spoken out of fear and a sense of fragility?

Z: I'm afraid so. I thought we were all going to die. Doesn't your typical man call out to god in the midst of peril? Well, in my case, I cannot call out to god, but I cry out to the indifferent heavens that I am but an atom swirling in the ether. It felt as though the sky and the sea were going to squash us like insects and submerge our insignificance forever. But now, in the light of day, on a calmer sea, my inner torment dissipates with the tempest. With calm I regain my wits, and therefore my beliefs. You do realize, even Voltaire would have been very worried last night.

W: Is this what you think? He would have been worse off than either of us; he would have been in hysterics. But now he would be regaling us with bons mots and jokes.

Z: If he were still alive we would still be in Paris, listening to his witty jokes to Parisian society. We would not be on this leaky boat on a godforsaken ocean to deliver his library to the Empress of Russia. But there is our answer, proof of the fact that we are not in possession of free will. That proof is manifest in our death: free will is but an illusion because it cannot stave off the Grim Reaper. Perhaps because of our frantic actions we may defer it for a while, but eventually, we go under, and our false ideas of free will go with us.

W: Grim indeed, grim indeed. All the more reason to be active and try to improve this world. We have Voltaire as our model. He never stopped writing to try to destroy the evils of the world. He acted, willfully and powerfully, with every word he wrote. We in turn act to keep his library, his legacy, together so that future generations can look into it and admire the man, and revere his works.

Z: And love him, the way we love him. I cannot lose sight of the fact that he is our guide and we are his disciples. We voyage for a reason. We are on this boat for a reason. We will succeed in our mission and deliver Voltaire's library to the "Semiramis of the North," as Voltaire called Catherine. The original Semiramis founded Babylon. What will Catherine found? I cannot help but dream that she will found a new civilization based on the sound political and social principles of Voltaire and Diderot. She will see the light after she has read the books in Voltaire's library, and Diderot's as well, when she gets it. See, my dear Wagnière, in the calm of the sea I feel more hopeful, I become an optimist, although, since Voltaire warned us to be temperate, it is an optimism mitigated with philosophy. This will truly be a force to be reckoned with.

W: May God bless this force, and the desire for enlightenment of all monarchs.

Z: If not god, then fate, which will give us the free will to engage and persist in our task!

Dead Calm

Zénobe would not have so readily praised the calm sea had he known what it could lead to.

The doldrums arrived, with not a wisp of air catching the sails of the packet boat. With all sails aloft, the boat looked as dispirited and downcast as all of the occupants. The first day was not so bad, but after the third or fourth, the crew was jumping out of its skin in impatience and exasperation.

Zénobe and Wagnière continued to read, which was their salvation, of course, for they had discovered the marvelous secret of reading: one was transported to different places and times, entertained by foreign adventures and thoughts and concepts, intrigued by diverse people who lived in the pages of books. Still, it was an eerie silence punctuated by the gruff voices of the crew as they began to fight amongst themselves, out of boredom and the need for something to do. Neither one of them could stay enthralled by his book for very long. The many interruptions made the two librarians decide on a tactic that they felt was the best thing to do in this situation. After having sought and received permission from the captain, they set themselves up on a couple of chairs on the sunny part of the deck, instructed the crew to array themselves before them, and proceeded to perform a dramatic reading of scenes from *Candide*. Captain Shounine provided the simultaneous translations from French to Russian. Wagnière and Zénobe were impressed that the captain displayed a modicum of talent for the flair of the dramatic.

Voltaire could not have asked for a better, more pliable, audience than these rough Russian sailors in the midst of the doldrums. They were fascinated by the story of the young Candide who goes from misadventure to tragedy to total loss to a grudging sort of happy life. They roared in laughter when the Old Lady, along with all of the women, each lost one of their buttocks so that the Turks, their captors, would not die of hunger while they were besieged by the Russians. They also laughed when Candide rescues his beloved Cunégonde from the clutches of a Jew and an Inquisitor who have been amicably sharing her charms on alternate days, by running them through with his sword. But when Candide is obliged to kill Cunégonde's brother because he refuses to agree to their marriage, the crew was rolling on the deck, arms to bellies, tears of mirth rolling down their cheeks.

"Alas! My God!" cried Candide. "I have killed my old master, my friend, my brother-in-law; I am the mildest man in the world and I have already killed three men, two of them priests!"

During the scenes of El Dorado the men were filled with astonishment at the description of the pebbles (emeralds and rubies) and yellow dirt (nuggets of gold) found all over the ground of this mysterious mountainous land, of untold wealth in a place where the inhabitants did not pray to God for they had been given everything they ever wanted. The sailors groaned every time one of Candide's red sheep, each one of them laden with treasures, met its demise. They were strangely quiet during the scene in Venice with the six kings all staying at the same inn, including two competing ones from Poland, who had all, by an unhappy reversal of fortune, been dethroned. Their own Russian Emperor, Ivan VI, who had been deposed as an infant still in his cradle, figured in the group, all having come to spend the Carnival in Venice. No mirth here, just introspection as it dawned on the sailors that the grand Wheel of Fortune was applicable even to kings. But their laughter returned, with more intensity, when Candide finally finds his beloved Cunégonde, never having abandoned the search for her and after having spent the whole book with much arduous scouring across continents and oceans. His voyages have taken him to Constantinople where Cunégonde is the slave of a Transylvanian monarch living in exile among the Turks. After all this time, after all their travails and calamities and scourges, Candide is exhausted, and Cunégonde is ugly. Her legendary beauty has been replaced by a sunburned face, red eyes, wrinkled, chapped skin, sagging breasts and red, scaly arms. The sailors laughed in disgust as Candide vows to marry her anyway. The end of *Candide*, which is very philosophical, left the crew in a brown study. There was much to digest in this slender book; Voltaire had thrown into it all of his concerns, all of his ire against the injustices of the world, all of his ranting against man's inhumanity and depravity. Still, the irony, the sarcasm, the satire of this expert of satire, infused the story with the laughter of recognition that man, always duplicitous, always cruel and brutal, deserves the fate he has carved out for himself.

At the end, the crew applauded with much enthusiasm, praising their French guests for their magnificent presentation, accompanying it with all sorts of boisterous whistles and calls, and warmly praised their captain for his stellar performance as translator and actor. Who knew that captain Shounine had such talents? During the remainder of their forced inactivity, members of the crew approached Shounine to ask questions about the novel. If the captain did not know the answer he would in turn ask Wagnière or Zénobe who were only too happy to respond. Interest and curiosity remained so high that a repeat performance was requested for the following day. Voltaire's librarians were delighted and their second reading was even more dramatic than the first. The second time even the cook came to watch, and nobody minded that supper that evening was bread and cheese. Feeding their minds had come first.

The Captain Relates His Story

A few days after the winds and breezes had returned, Captain Shounine was sharing a mug of vodka-laced coffee with his French guests in the galley late at night. Wagnière and Zénobe had repeated their accolades to the captain, declaring that he had missed his true calling by not offering his talents on the stages of Saint Petersburg. Even in Paris he would have an audience, they told him, for he could play the parts of foreigners in those plays that called for them. With his slight foreign accent he could be, of course, a Russian prince, or a Turkish pasha, and Indian Brahman or even an Egyptian priest. French audiences would become besotted with him, for his looks were not bad, not bad at all.

Captain Shounine looked abashed, but pleased. "Well, I would love to go to Paris one day. See the sights. See the ladies. Everybody has heard of the French ladies! And also those who are not ladies! Would love to meet them! Who knows if I could be in theater? I love world theater! The whole world is theater, no?"

Wagnière answered, "According to many authors, yes! Including Shakespeare in *Macbeth* where he says that 'life is like a poor player who struts and frets his hour upon the stage and then is heard no more.' The Spanish dramaturge Quevedo wrote that 'life is a comedy; the world is a farce of which we are all actors.' "

The captain looked up into the air like a good actor who is trying to find inspiration in the motes and wisps floating therein, furrowing his brow and smiling forlornly, with an accompanying sigh, "I've been an actor my entire life." Then, looking conspiratorially around him to ascertain they were alone, he intoned, "My name is not Nicolai Shounine."

Wagnière looked at Zénobe, Zénobe looked at Wagnière, then they both looked at the captain who seemed to be ready to explain this mystery to them.

"I was not born Nicolai Shounine. This is a name conjured up for me by a queen, to hide my real identity. It is a pseudonym behind which I have been hiding for two decades. Nor was I supposed to be a sea captain. I had never before set foot upon a boat until the day I was made captain of this one. Believe me, this is why I am the captain of this third-rate floating wreck. 'Twas to lie low. Low in the water. Low in life. To pass by unnoticed. Therefore unharmed. Nobody sees me. I am not enviable in any way. I go back and forth between Saint Petersburg and Lübeck. I stop in Tallinn, in Riga, in Klaipeda, in Gdansk, in Lübeck. Then I do it again backward. To and fro, that is my life. The Baltic Sea is now my domain. This is where I now strut and fret. Would you like to know where my previous life took place?"

The captain saw on the expressions of his companions a look of enthralled attention. He took a moment to collect his thoughts, and began a dramatic rendition of the story of his youth.

"My real name is Pyotr Antonovich Ulrich. I was born the bastard son of Duke Anton Ulrich of Brunswick-Lüneberg in the prison where he was being held captive. It was he who, in his youth, was sent to Saint Petersburg to be married to the niece of Tsarina Anna Ivanovna, the Grand Duchess Anna Leopoldovna of Mecklenburg-Schwerin, who cuckolded him from the very beginning of their union with Count Moritz Karl of Lynar. My father, of course, was outraged, but since he was rather docile of character he learned to live with this disgrace. Besides, when the tsarina died, his infant son, my half-brother, became tsar himself, and Anna Leopoldovna became regent."

Wagnière interrupted. "You mean, you mean... Never mind, go on!"

"But Anna Leopoldovna was as bad a regent as she was a wife. All she cared for was her lover, Count Lynar, and soon she had another lover, her favorite lady-in-waiting, Julie Mengden, whom she married to Lynar, so both of her lovers were conveniently united. It did not help matters when my father, Duke Anton Ulrich, also fell in love with Julie Mengden. It was a complex state of affairs. They say that the regent Anna Leopoldovna never dressed properly, appearing in court with her buttons unattached, the easier to dispense with her clothes as soon as she returned to her boudoir to be with her lovers. Affairs of state were left unattended to, ambassadors and chargés d'affaires were neglected, and people began to grumble. The Russian Imperial Guard turned their attention to Elizabeth, daughter of Tsar Peter the Great, and decided that she would be a better leader than the regent Anna Leopoldovna. They helped Elizabeth to stage a coup d'état, swift and bloodless, that left both Anna Leopoldovna and my father, Duke Anton Ulrich, imprisoned in the citadel of Riga, from which they were transferred to the fortress of Dünamünde, then to the fortress of Ranenburg—"

Wagnière abruptly stepped into the captain's conversation. "Then Ivan was separated from his family and sent to Kholmogory on the White Sea!"

The captain smiled. "You know your history, *monsieur.*"

"It is just that our dear friend Denis Diderot was always interested in what happens to people when they are isolated, and he was horrified at the idea that an otherwise normal child was limited to seeing only his jailer. The boy couldn't take that frightening solitude and eventually, uhm, eventually..."

"Eventually, he went out of his mind," finished the captain. "My half-brother became a blathering idiot."

"Your half-brother!" said an astounded Zénobe who had not quite been able to piece together the intricate intrigue of this Russo-Germanic aristocratic family. "Your half-brother was a tsar!"

"Yes. I came years after, when my father was imprisoned in Dünamünde. Well, he found enough liberty to get a servant girl pregnant, not that Anna Leopoldovna cared. She spent her days regretting not being regent. No more nice life. No more luxuries. Now she was forced to lead a simple life, with no one to visit. No more grand balls, no evening gowns, no nothing. Simple life. A very small château. Small garden. Hardly any servants."

"So what happened to your half-brother Ivan VI, Emperor of Russia?"

"He was emperor only for a year, from when he was two months old to when he was one year and two months old. In 1756, when he was but a young man, he was transferred to an even more stringent prison, the fortress of Schlüsselburg, by the Neva. But even there word leaked out, and a few old army officers tried to rescue him. Catherine, the new Empress, had left instructions that the jailer murder Ivan if ever there were an attempt to rescue him. Which is what happened. His rescuers rescued a corpse. They became corpses in turn. There ends the story of Ivan VI."

"No wonder you translated that part of Voltaire's story with so much conviction and emotion!" said Zénobe. "In reality, however, your half-brother never left his prison. Voltaire simply used him in his story as one of the multitudinous examples of sovereigns who are deposed, dethroned, ousted and relegated to the status of commoners, or kept in the dungeon. What about his siblings, your half-brothers and sisters?"

"They remain to this day in Ranenburg. Father died four years ago. He went blind before he died. And his wife had died years before, giving birth to their fifth child."[92]

"But why did you have to change your name?" asked Zénobe.

"By direct order of Catherine. She said I had to repudiate all ties to Brunswick-Lüneberg or to Mecklenburg-Schwerin, although Anna Leopoldovna was not even my mother. My true mother was the maid responsible for bringing flowers and comestibles into the prison, which was a very nice house, by the way. There were no bars on the doors or windows. But there was a high wall built around the perimeter of the premises. It provided a very visual out of bounds for the royals. A garrison was provided for and they knew very well who could not step out of the gates. My mother and I could walk in and out a hundred times all day. But my half-siblings could not. My father could not. Anna Leopoldovna could not. Before Ivan was taken away, he could not. I knew I was the bastard son of a duke. I knew my place. But I had more freedom than my father. He was shut in. I could walk into the village when a fancy took me there. Deep down I felt superior to my father.

"Catherine knew of my existence, and when I was old enough to understand, she told me I had to forget my father was a duke. She said that there were enough pretenders to the throne of Russia. Every year there is another young man presented to the court as Ivan VI. But we knew where the real Ivan VI was. He was languishing in prison, bored out of his mind. Catherine gave me my new name, she gave me my career, she gave me my boat, she told me to forget I was the son of a duke. I did as I was told. I took my new name, my career, and my boat, and I forgot all about the past. All I know now is this packet boat and the places where I dock, as I come and go between Lübeck and Saint Petersburg. Of course, my crew know nothing of this, and you could not tell them anything even if you wanted to. But I know that you will keep my secret. You would not get me into trouble with Catherine. She is good tsarina. Good head on her shoulders. She has balls of a man, too. Good head, good balls; that makes for good tsarina."

Both Zénobe and Wagnière assured him of their secrecy. Besides, who would have believed such a ridiculous story? The ambitions of the aristocrats were equal only to their follies. Captain Shounine was saved only because his mother was a servant. His freedom was due to the humble social circumstances of a flower girl. He posed no threat to the Empress. Within the modest confines of his lot in life, he enjoyed much

---

92 Anton Ulrich and Anna Leopoldovna's children were not released from their prison until 1780 when they were handed over to their aunt, the Queen Dowager of Denmark, Juliana Maria of Brunswick-Wolfen-büttel, who kept them under house arrest, their room and board paid for by Catherine the Great.

more freedom than his father did for the entirety of his life: attached to the Court, attached to an arranged marriage, then held in captivity at the whim of two empresses.

When asked if he himself had ever married, the captain answered, "I am wed to the sea. The sea is my mistress. Besides, I have lady friends in every port, in Saint Petersburg, in Tallinn, in Riga and in Klaipeda. None in Gdansk or Lübeck. I'm seeing to that."

Still, Zénobe shuddered that night as he went to bed thinking about the lot of Captain Shounine's half-brother, Ivan VI, the toppled Emperor of Russia. He had been the innocent victim of his parents' ambitions. The thought of the young boy spending all his days alone in a cell was horrendous. How can that be done to a human being? Well, it was Elizabeth, then Catherine, who were responsible for that. But who has the courage to tell a Queen that she has committed an atrocity? Zénobe brought this up with Captain Shounine a couple of days later when they met in the galley, and the captain, draining a glass of vodka and then pouring out another, answered, "Everybody in court is so spectacularly occupied with self-preservation and self-importance that there is no compassion for those souls who get lost in the shuffle. Everybody learns: nothing but pleasantries and congratulations and adulations go to the Queen. No complaints, no doubts, no reproaches. Those can land you in jail, my friend. Or at least under house arrest. I have seen enough of that with my own two eyes. I didn't want it for me. I comply, you see, I comply. Why rock the boat?"

This last he said with a wide grin, showing a double row of even, white teeth that were almost clenched shut. It was a smile that all at once showed grit and pliability, endurance and resilience. No wonder his crew loved him.

Zénobe turned meditatively away and inwardly agreed with the captain. Nor would I wish it for myself, he thought. Nevertheless, his inward voice also said, "I just find it so hard to comply. Especially when the injustice is leveled at me. Even if the injustice is leveled at somebody else."

He very much admired the captain, and would have wanted to know more about him, but a completely unexpected adversity arose that claimed the attention of everybody on the packet boat as they sailed on the Baltic Sea, approaching their first stop, Gdansk. It was to be their biggest obstacle yet.

A Medical Emergency

In Gdansk it was necessary to execute a search for a physician. Wagnière could not get out of his hammock that morning. He was feeling exhausted and did not want breakfast brought to him. The previous evening he had complained of fatigue and had retired early, before supper. Zénobe understood that refusing food was a part of being ill. He brought Wagnière a cup of sweet black coffee from the galley, feeling hopeful that his friend could at least drink a bit of it. When he approached the listless Wagnière and looked into his eyes he started. Wagnière thought he had burned himself on the metal cup.

"No, no, it's not that hot," Zénobe answered. "See if you can take a few sips of this."

As soon as Wagnière had taken hold of the cup, Zénobe rushed out of the berth deck. He found the captain out on deck looking towards the city of Gdansk approaching in the distance.

"We'll be there in no time," he called out to Zénobe as the young man approached him. "I know you've been dying to—" His statement died on his lips when he identified concern writ large on Zénobe's expression.

"It's… it's Wagnière," said Zénobe.

Captain Shounine quickly followed Zénobe down into the berths. As soon as he saw Wagnière's eyes, he had a diagnosis.

"О, это я знаю!" he exclaimed. "О, несчастный человек! Our friend has jaundice."

"Jaundice!" cried out Wagnière and Zénobe in unison. "Jaundice?"

They both knew what jaundice was. Wagnière's sclera were a dark yellow. That also explained his fatigue and his apathy about food. There was one more symptom to inspect. Zénobe reached for the chamber pot and Wagnière, too worried to think of being bashful, urinated into it in a flash. All three of them groaned. The urine was stained a dark brown.

"Oh, no!" moaned Wagnière. "What are we going to do now? I have jaundice!"

"Do not worry, my friend," said Captain Shounine. "We are right outside Gdansk. We shall find a doctor for you, fast!"

"A doctor in Gdansk?" asked Wagnière forlornly.

"They have good doctors in Gdansk!" assured the captain. "We shall get you the best one. Please do not worry."

The captain left them, and Wagnière turned to Zénobe. "The best doctor in Gdansk." He shrugged. "I would feel better if we found the appropriate volume of the *Encyclopédie*! I want to read the article for "Jaundice."

"I'll see to that myself," promised Zénobe. "I will scour Gdansk for a copy of the *Encyclopédie*. Surely they have a library somewhere in the city with a set of the *Encyclopédie*."

Even before the bundles of mail had been delivered to the city of Gdansk, quests for a physician and for a book were arranged. The physician, an expert on diseases of the head, was found having dinner at his home, and the required volume of the philosophers' books of knowledge, number XVIII, was discovered in the personal library of a gentleman named Sellius whose cousin, Gottfried, had had a hand in the translation of Chambers' *Cyclopaedia*, precursor to Diderot's *Encyclopédie*, into French. As Zénobe ran back to the docks with the precious volume in his embrace he thought that Prussia should never have shared in the partitioning of Poland, yet he couldn't help admitting that the protestant Germans were much more tolerant than the Polish catholics, accepting of a citizen keeping a set of the *Encyclopédie*, the product of French atheists.

Both book and healer boarded the *Burya* at the same time. Once in the berth-deck standing by the patient swinging in his hammock, the Polish doctor, who announced himself, in passable French, as *Doktor* Georg Blumenthal of the Gdansk Medical Institute, took a look at the big, heavy book in Zénobe's hands and said categorically that it would not be necessary to rummage through it. His own knowledge was both apt and sufficient.

Wagnière and Zénobe exchanged glances of dismay and then panic.

"What is this that you are drinking?" asked Dr. Blumenthal of the patient.

"In the cup there is coffee," explained Wagnière. "I took a couple of sips, but it tastes too bitter. In the glass there is vodka, given me by our captain who said it would perk me up."

"Either that or put you down, permanently," asseverated the physician with grave modulation to his voice. "Take those away," he instructed Zénobe who had to put the book down on the hammock beside Wagnière before he could remove the offending liquids from the site. The doctor ignored the tome and proceeded to auscultate his patient. He started with Wagnière's head, thumping it as if were a gourd, giving it a thorough examination, especially the areas around the ears. When Zénobe came back, the doctor was still squinting at those areas, asking Wagnière if he had received any blows to the head recently. Wagnière thought about it for a few seconds, then gave a negative response.

Dr. Blumenthal started swaying the hammock to see how far it would go, ascertaining that it hit both the hull of the boat on one side and the neighboring hammock on the other.

"Who sleeps in this hammock?" asked the doctor.

"I do," answered Zénobe.

"Is your head on this side, parallel to the head of the patient as he sleeps?"

"Yes, sir."

"Have you noticed your heads banging together when the seas are choppy?"

Wagnière and Zénobe remembered the storm when they thought they would be drowned.

"Yes! There was a terrible storm," explained Wagnière. "I suppose that our two skulls were clacking together for hours," as he put a hand next to his temple.

"*Eh, bien, voilà!*" exclaimed the doctor with conviction. "That is the culprit, and that is why you now have jaundice, *monsieur*.

With both respect and trepidation Wagnière remarked, "But I thought jaundice was a disease of the liver."

"In this you are correct, *cher monsieur*. Quite correct. But it is blows to the head that, in spite of the distance between the seat of intelligence and the liver, instigate maladies of this fragile organ. The head is fragile, too, and there is a natural sympathy between the head and the liver, an affinity, let's say, or connectivity, that when the head is struck it excites—and sometimes damages—the internal organ."

The doctor then proceeded to press on Wagnière's abdomen, none too delicately, to attempt to deduce the size and resilience of his liver. Wagnière complained with a yelp of pain, which the doctor duly noted.

"Did you save your urine from this morning?"

Zénobe picked up the chamber pot and brought it for the doctor's perusal.

"Typical," he announced. "Quite typical."

He ordered Wagnière to turn around in the hammock and proceeded to check his kidneys. "I see your kidneys have not yet been affected. Let's see if we can keep it that way."

When Wagnière was again face up, the doctor gave his prognosis. "You have a serious case of jaundice, provoked by a blow, or most probably, a series of blows to the head, which has led to spasmodic retrenchment of the liver tissue. In order to get this tissue to become supple again, we must instruct you to stay in a supine position, preferably in a bed that does not move. Therefore, we have to get you off this boat and to a bed that is affixed to terra firma. We must bring blows to the head to zero. Under no circumstances are you permitted to drink coffee, vodka, tea or any infusions that function as diuretics. Your liver and kidneys must be used as little as possible. You may drink only pure water until the yellowing of your sclera dissipates. You may eat what you wish, but no overeating please! Breakfast and dinner only. Skip supper as I would rather have you sleep with no pressure in your abdomen. Avoid all foods that produce flatulence, and avoid all yellow or orange foods, so no egg yolks, no carrots. Jaundice is a serious ailment and your complete compliance to my instructions is of dire necessity. Your life may depend on it. Is this understood?"

Wagnière smiled weakly and answered, "Yes, *monsieur le docteur*. All understood."

No sooner had *Doktor* Blumenthal left that Zénobe grabbed the volume from the *Encyclopédie* and turned to the article «*Jaunisse*». He read its contents out loud to Wagnière:

> «Jaundice is an illness whose characteristic symptom is the change of the natural color of the body to yellow; it is also called in French *ictère jaune*; in Latin *icterus flavus, aurugo*, or *morbus regius*.
>
> Several kinds of jaundice may be distinguished, with respect to the variety of symptoms, to the difference of the causes, & to the manner of the invasion; e.g., there is a known type that is considered to be periodical in nature. In another, the yellow discoloration is only observable in the eyes and face; in others it is observed all over the body, indeed, opening the cadaver shows the interior parts also tinted the same color, in certain cases, even the bones have been infected.

Wagnière made a gesture and an expression that communicated to Zénobe that he should skip this part of the text. He sped-read to a less disquieting section:

> At times, the color of the eyes is so altered that sight is weakened and diminished. Objects appear yellow to the patient, and in the same

way, by the effect to the tongue, all foods seem bitter. Beyond this discoloration, one observes in the majority of the jaundiced other symptoms such as vomiting, cardialgia, anxiety, difficulties in breathing, lassitude, fainting spells. The patients complain of a compressive pain in the environs of the heart & towards the inferior region of the ventricule, of a discomfort, of an obscure tugging or tearing or sometimes an acute pain in the right hypochondrium.

Zénobe interrupted his reading to ask, "Where's the hypochondrium?"
Wagnière shrugged. "Someplace in the abdomen, I think."
Zénobe looked at Wagnière's abdomen. Wagnière reacted, "I have no pain anywhere in my abdomen. When the doctor pushed into my organs here, he pushed hard. It would have hurt anyone. But keep on reading."

[Jaundice] is principally excited by the passions of exuberant living, by excessive work, by long voyages under a burning sun, by aromatic liqueurs, by the inflammation of the liver, by ardent inflammatory fevers, by too strong an emetic or purgative, anything that causes the bile to flow more abundantly from the liver. The passions of the soul of those who languish in a meditative, sad or melancholy life; coerced work, especially after a meal; these are also some of the more frequent causes of jaundice. But then so are the bites of several animals, such as the viper, spiders, or rabid dogs, & the exhalations of toads, of any plants from the family Aconitum, known as wolf's bane or devil's helmet, & of several other poisons, all of which may also produce jaundice. Many of these causes provoke obstructions in the liver & bilious calculi. [...][93]

The appropriate medications recommended for the jaundiced patient are tamarinds, manna,[94] rhubarb, & a little bit of *scammonée*.[95] Purging is not recommended for the patient as this might augment the trouble. Another substance with eminent properties has been identified in the aloe plant, along with fumitory, or fumewort,[96] and celandine, or swallowwort.[97] Finally, mineral waters that are acidulous are to be recommended, such as those from Vals, from Passy and from Forges.

Wagnière reacted immediately after Zénobe put down the big tome.
"Well, we're a bit too far from Vals, Passy or Forges. I am sure we can find some of these other items in Gdansk. Also, it is good to know that I am staying on the boat. The fine doctor from Gdansk does not know what he is talking about. There is absolutely

---

93 Much of the article has been suppressed here, leaving only the major points that would have been for Wagnière's case pertinent.

94 In this context, manna refers to the dried exudate of the Eurasian ash *(fraxinus ornus)*, which contains mannitol and has been as a laxative and demulcent used. A demulcent relieves inflammation or irritation in the body.

95 The root of the plant *convolvulus scammonia*.

96 Herb from which fumaric acid is extracted.

97 *Chelidonium majus*, an herb recognized as a useful detoxifying agent. The latex of the plant is also used for getting rid of warts.

no mention of blows to the head in the article of the *Encylopédie*. I would much rather put my faith in the works of Diderot and his friends. Where does this Pole get his information from?"[98]

Captain Shounine was not in the least derelict in his responsibilities to his sick passenger. He sent ten of his men to scour the markets of Gdansk and it is to their assiduity that all of the ingredients needed for Wagnière's convalescence were found and brought on board. Tamarinds recently imported from the Ottoman Empire (in today's Turkey) were found in such numbers that the whole crew got to taste them, thereby unintentionally preventing scurvy to all aboard. It was easy to tell who was sucking on a piece of tamarind in his cheek. His expression was a scrunched up mouth and knitted brow due to the extreme acidity of the fruit. At times it seemed that the whole crew was coincident in a disagreeable sour mood, all conducting their duties with a foul mien.

---

98   The theory that blows to the head adversely affected the liver continued well into the Nineteenth Century, and was even by some French doctors advocated. For instance, jaundice is still discussed under the heading of head lesions in the fourth edition of M. le baron Boyer's *Traité des maladies chirurgicales et des opérations qui leur conviennent,* in Paris in 1831 published! [For those readers who are interested, see the section under the heading *«Des Abcès au foie à la suite des plaies de la Tête»,* tome 5, pp. 149-153.]

The Days before Christmas, 1778

The Patient Worsens

In spite of the daily rhubarb, the constant sucking on tamarind, the infusions made with aloe, fumitory and celandine, Wagnière's health seemed to deteriorate. The sclera of his eyes became the color of copper. His energy waned to the point that he could not even tolerate Zénobe reading to him.

Zénobe hovered over his patient, not knowing what to do, not knowing what not to do. Just in case there had been a modicum of truth to the Polish doctor's theories, he had placed wadded cotton on either side of Wagnière's head. He had to force feed him the medicinal ingredients, and could not convince him to eat anything that was regarded as food. As a result, with the passage of days, Wagnière became emaciated. His dry sallow skin began to wrinkle, especially on his cheeks and arms, so that he looked as if he were aging in some dreadfully accelerated fashion. Every time Zénobe approached his friend to ask him what he wanted, he was greeted by an expression of dire fear. Wagnière could feel himself being dragged towards death, an ineluctable drift into the end of his life, and he was terror-stricken. In spite of Zénobe's constant administrations, he felt so alone. He was going alone to a place unknown, and unknowable, and, good solid lutheran that he was, he tried to bring up every bit of his religious teachings to sustain himself, but his physical condition of lethargy seemed to drain even his spirituality. The image of God Himself kept being eclipsed by involuntary movements of his exhausted body and mind. How could he call upon God to help him in his time of need if God kept withdrawing behind veils of anguish and black despair? Where was the light he had been promised? He would have wanted the light of succor, the balm of love, to come to him in a spurt of illumination, but in his exhaustion even memory waned. The scripture he had thought unshakably ingrained in his memory tore out of his mind like a book shedding its paper in flakes as if they were the scales of a rotting fish.

Zénobe was in anguish for his friend. The days passed, the *Burya* made its scheduled stops in Klaipeda, Riga and Tallinn, and in each town Zénobe left the boat to seek the counsel of other doctors, but the only commonality among them was the discordance of their opinions. Mutually exclusive, oxymoronic, reciprocatingly contradictory, each deprecating, denouncing the advice given by the others, the doctors diminished his hopes that medicine would one day be universally uniform in its diagnoses and prognoses. The crushingly sad result was that each time Zénobe came back to the boat empty-handed, empty-minded, he had no hope to offer his friend. He could only look on as Wagnière's condition deteriorated seemingly by the hour.

The time came when Captain Shounine broached the subject of Wagnière's burial at sea. He explained how it was done and Zénobe nodded his understanding and approval. Yet, he could not bring himself to accede to his friend's departure from earth. He still could not even believe how a healthy person could in the space of a week tumble into an illness that was withering his body from the inside. What was it that was surreptitiously attacking his organs, that was sapping the very life from his veins? Since it could neither see nor understand what was undermining Wagnière's body, Zénobe's mind flailed about to such a degree that he realized the strength of fear and of anguish that pushed people into believing the most outlandish of things, based on the flimsiest of notions far distant from rational thinking. Even he started suspecting vapors rising from the sea, gases falling from the sky, spirits and pixies crossing through the hull to ply their black magic to the Keeper of Voltaire's library. They wanted him to fail in his attempt to bring light into Russia. They wanted him to keep out of a huge region of the earth, east of the Urals, still relatively untouched by the awakening that was going on in Europe, by the advancements of science that were dispelling superstition. The jealous spirits of Russia wanted to keep that land free of knowledge and insight. Zénobe realized his moments of weakness sprang from his drowsiness but he could only sleep for an hour or two before he had to see to Wagnière's needs.

Their next stop was their destination, just a few days away. Zénobe was unsure if Wagnière would live long enough to make it into Saint Petersburg. Would they have to disembark only to seek sepulture for Wagnière's body? Catherine had been counting on the librarian to build her a library, nay, Voltaire's whole château, with the library at its heart, in order to bring the Enlightenment into her dark feudal state. Wagnière's death would put a stop to all of that. What would Catherine do? What could he, Zénobe, do to replace Wagnière?

Zénobe was certain that he could not realize what Wagnière had been planning to undertake with Catherine. This was an elaborate project that was slated to take much time and effort. Its organization was all in Wagnière's head, and his head was not in the least accessible to accomplish work of such complexity. It was difficult enough to make him understand the importance of swallowing the medicinal concoctions that Zénobe prepared several times a day and night. Catherine and the disposition of Voltaire's library were no longer within the grasp of Wagnière's understanding, which kept decreasing by the day. It was dedication to the last remaining vestige of Wagnière's intellectuality that Zénobe decided to continue his objective. So long as Wagnière was awake enough to conserve that tiny piece of his mind through which he could still struggle for survival, he as his friend and caregiver would continue to aid him. Even when Wagnière ceased to speak, no longer able to mumble, Zénobe would peer into his yellow eyes and recognize a glimmer of rational thought. It was this last bit of intellect, this final scrap of reason eking out of Wagnière's eyes that sustained Zénobe's hope, and also his wits.

Arrival in Saint Petersburg

Captain Shounine turned out to be a fine friend. When they arrived in Saint Petersburg, he had Wagnière carried to his home in a litter. There, his passengers became his guests, using two rooms on the second floor. The captain had only two servants, a valet and a cook, but both were instructed to be at his guests' beck and call, day or night. For this, Zénobe was extremely grateful and remained in awe of the captain's altruism and generosity.

The crates holding Voltaire's library were taken to Catherine's country estate at Tsarskoe Selo, Captain Shounine himself alerting her to Wagnière's precarious condition. She immediately sent two of her physicians who, by the miracle of Catherine's influence, were in complete accord with the treatment of jaundice as stipulated in the *Encyclopédie*. This was the woman, Zénobe remembered, who very publicly had herself, and her son the prince, inoculated by English doctors who had brought to her country the vaccine for smallpox, thereby convincing her courtiers that it was safe enough to follow her lead. Up until then, because of the mystery that still shrouded most maladies, the devout thought it best to leave medical treatment to the intercessory influence of priest, saint, virgin and god, since illness was still considered to be divine retribution for sins and other offenses against god's holy laws. Catherine was a learned woman who accepted the advances of science and medicine. Even so, Russians waited a few days after the inoculation to make sure the Empress and her son survived.

Catherine sent back word that Voltaire's library would wait for his librarian to recover his health. Only he could reconstruct Ferney and because she wanted him to recuperate fully she would wait patiently for nature and the art of medicine to do their intended work. For her, this was the ideal: nature in tandem with human wisdom to alleviate the ills of mankind.

The Empress of Russia learned that Wagnière had a compatriot who was taking care of him. Through Captain Shounine she ordered this man to write her daily dispatches to keep her apprised of the condition of the patient. Zénobe accepted this order with no sense of apprehension, even thanking the queen, again through Shounine, for her solicitude for and attention to *monsieur* Wagnière. It never dawned on him that these daily letters, as innocently as they arose, were to be the catalyst that altered his destiny concerning his sojourn in Saint Petersburg, home of Her Imperial Majesty Catherine the Second.[99]

Once again Zénobe was taking care of a dying man. Once again there were two doctors, Dr. Sergey Sergeyevitch and Dr. Solomon Ashkenazi, but they seemed to work in tandem much better than doctors Tronchin and Lorry had in Paris. They both gave orders that never conflicted with one other, and their cooperation lent amicability and tranquility to the proceedings. It was clear that neither doctor wanted to usurp the other one.

A great difference in the treatment of the patient was also readily apparent when the doctors instructed that a small window in the room always be kept open, in spite of the bitter cold outside. Doctors Sergeyevitch and Ashkenazi both propounded the idea that keeping a sick room hermetically sealed was detrimental for the patient. In Paris, Voltaire's room had been kept airtight, with foul odors emanating from the patient compounding daily so that it was difficult for people to come in without gagging. The Russians observed that a replenishment of air in the sick room was advantageous, and even crucial, to the improvement of the patient. With a fire going in the fireplace the temperature of the room remained comfortable, and the brisk air brought fresh oxygen into the room.

In this manner Wagnière began to improve, ever so slowly at first, but as the days wore on his condition visibly ameliorated. His dry sallow skin regained a bit of color, the sclera of his eyes lightened, his body no longer seemed so limp and lifeless. After a few days he was able to sit up in bed, after a few more he had energy enough to walk a few steps in his room, and in time he was able to use the chamber pot by himself. But to Zénobe, there was no sign that Wagnière was improving that was as great as when he asked for a book to read.

---

99   As reluctant as I am to insert this particular note at this time, for fear of offending the intelligence of the reader, I nevertheless feel that sometimes it is necessary to err on the side of caution and state the obvious. All conversations and all written communications between the upper classes throughout Europe were eased by the fact that the lingua franca was, of course, just that: French. When Voltaire wrote to all the crowned heads of Europe they responded in his same language. The nannies, governesses and preceptors of the royal children in courts from Portugal to Sweden were mostly French. It is said that Marie Antoinette spoke French with an Austrian accent; I disagree with her disparagers. The mother tongue of her father, François III, *duc* de Lorraine, *grand-duc* de Toscane, later becoming François I, emperor of the Holy Roman Empire, was French, spoken fluently as well by her three consecutive governesses, the *comtesses* de Brandeiss, de Lerchenfeld, et de Trautmaussdorfft, not that they did well by their pupil in other subjects. Little Sophia Augusta Fredericka of Anhalt-Zerbst, the future Catherine the Great of Russia, learned French from her French Huguenot governess, Elizabeth Cardel, whom she called Babet. The education given to little girls during this era, even to aristocratic little girls, was attentive to poise, painting, singing and dancing, while science, history and mathematics were considered a waste of time for girls, but the lessons in French were inescapable and routine, since everything else was taught using this language.

Zénobe looked to the heavens as even atheists do and in silence commended the care and support of Russian doctors. Quickly rummaging through his own books he found one that Wagnière could read with great advantage: it was Molière's *Imaginary Invalid* and Zénobe knew that it would lighten the patient's heart. He did not stop to think that it happened to be Molière's last play: even as he played the primary role of the sick hypochondriac, the playwright was himself sick with pneumonia and died after the fourth performance. However, Wagnière must have also forgotten this biographical detail, and all that Zénobe heard coming from the patient's bed that evening was chuckles and guffaws, punctuated by remarks such as "Oh, the fool!" and "What an idiot!"

Once again Zénobe was in awe of the printed page. He thought: Books take us away from ourselves and place us in a different world, a world created by an author long gone. When we visit this world, the author comes alive as well, as he gives us his hand for us to inhabit his imagination. That is magic, and Molière comes back from the grave and helps my friend to forget about his own illness, inviting him to laugh in amusement and diversion. Medicine should be so effective.

He himself took out something to read and in an armchair beside his friend read a story of Russian princes of old and places faraway. It was a play, in manuscript form because it had not yet been published, that Catherine the Great had written about the founders of the dynasty of Russian kings, of Gostomouisl, and Rurick, and Vadim.[100] It was about the three sons of Oumila, daughter of Gostomouisl, wife of Lioubrat, king of Finland. It was about all of their ambitions, their yearnings, their conflicts, and about who would become the ruler of the Empire of the North. Zénobe once again was astounded about the hunger for power that defeated all other desires, even the one for love. What is it about power that makes men plot against even their own brothers? And once a man, or woman, is on the throne, he or she must guard it constantly, for fear of being deposed. Who wants to live in perpetual fear? And what is the attraction of power that leads kings and empresses to commit injustices? There was no answer, according to Zénobe. It was a question to be relegated to the category of the unanswerable: Why are we? Whence come we? What is life? What happens to us in death? Is there a soul? Why does power attract?

As a literary critic Zénobe liked the play, although it was a thorough romp in anarchy, with no regard to the three dramatic unities of time, place or action, with characters coming and going and the plot twisting and turning. But he realized that Catherine's style was simply following the vicissitudes of history, of the quirks of the dramatis personae who by their very flaws accelerated or retarded the action, or made it jump into a completely new direction. Real life was like that. A story that deploys conflicts between characters, takes them to a logical denouement, then solves everything in a neat resolution that satisfies everybody, is not based on real life. Real life is chaotic, digressive, with unforeseeable intricacies, and influenced haphazardly by random vectors. Zénobe realized that real life never satisfied everybody, and that Catherine's play, with its inconsistencies, its illogical turns, and its scenes that were in turn dazzling and dull, was rather good. Especially in its characters for the veracity of their actions. Fouler personages were never to be found, save for in the pages of the history books.

---

100   The name of the play, originally in Russian but translated by Catherine's command and oversight into French, is: *Imitation of Shakespeare, Historical Scene, without Observation of any Rules of Drama, Derived from the Life of Rurick.*

Between Christmas and the Festival of the Epiphany, 1778–1779

Letters Written to an Empress

Most of the letters that Zénobe wrote to Catherine II describing the condition of Voltaire's librarian, *monsieur* Wagnière, have survived. They were eventually found in Ferney, among some of the papers that belonged to the librarian himself. Why the Empress would have handed these letters to Wagnière is up to question, even though we may surmise that she, who was at all times working on the latest version of her memoirs, must have realized the importance of these daily reports on his physical condition. Wagnière eventually did write his memoirs in which he never mentions the letters. As a matter of fact, he never even mentions the fact that he nearly died of jaundice during his trip to Saint Petersburg. Perhaps it was too painful a memory to recollect; perhaps his very memory at that time was affected by the illness; perhaps he thought it unimportant or beneath the dignity of the librarian of the world's most famous *philosophe* to complain of mundane ailments or yet again, perhaps he felt it was nobody's business. Wagnière was ever the circumspect, diffident, and reserved fellow, who only complained when it came time vigorously to defend his master, Voltaire, especially against the *marquis* de Villette and *madame* Denis, whom he forever blamed for having caused his death by keeping him too long in Paris.

In any case, another reason why Catherine might have so easily divested herself of these letters was that, in truth, she was known to be rather perfunctory in most of her ventures: she seemed to forget all about Diderot as soon as that philosopher left Saint Petersburg in 1774. Some say even before he left. At the beginning of his stay, Catherine had so much enthusiasm about having the celebrated thinker and author right there at her court that she was calling for him just about every day; towards the end, Diderot was feeling rather abandoned and spent whole days alone in his room. It would not have been surprising to know that Catherine tired of Wagnière's efforts to duplicate Voltaire's château on the grounds of the Hermitage. Once she had access to the author's books and correspondence, the rest of the Voltaire project soon declined into a desultory endeavor which eventually was left stranded, for lack of resources, supervision, or even attention. One might say that, as Wagnière improved, his project developed jaundice, diminished, and eventually ebbed away to nothing. The librarian survived, but Catherine's project to recreate Voltaire's château in Ferney met a demise of extreme exhaustion.

It is of course not difficult at all to recognize *monsieur* Zénobe Bosquet's handwriting in the following letters. It is the same cursive as always, displaying his idiosyncratic small e's and o's, the forceful upward strokes where the nib sometimes carves into the paper with his b's, d's, f's, h's, k's, l's, t's and also with the tails of his g's, j's, p's, q's, y's and z's; and the panache with which he oftentimes closes the last letter of a sentence, perhaps with a curlicue or even a double curlicue, perhaps doubling back to underline the word, perhaps using the same final line of ink to return to the last word and cross his t's. With this series of letters, however, it can be observed that Zénobe took extra care to be neat and precise, skillfully maintaining strict horizontal lines and attempting to be regular and elegant in his strokes.

He had of course already written to Catherine, several times, as Voltaire's secretary taking his dictation. But now it was his own words he penned. He must have realized that these letters were, in a way, his introduction to Catherine since they had not yet met in person. As a peasant boy from Savoy, he wished to impress and oblige this queen who was so obviously solicitous about the health of his friend, Wagnière. Perhaps his previous notion about avoiding her altogether was adapting to this new situation.

26th of December, 1778

Madame:

It is with utmost gratitude and undying appreciation that I write you this memorandum, first of a series, to keep you apprised of the health of Voltaire's librarian, *monsieur* Wagnière, who, as indisposed as he is, nevertheless belabors the notion that he would much rather be employed in the project of replicating Voltaire's library in Ferney than remaining immobile and unoccupied in bed. He regrets wasting your time and patience while we all have to wait for the amelioration of his health, and trusts that in a short while, with the reinforcement of the generous aid of your own doctors, the restoration of his health will be swift and certain.

Meantime, the coloration of his skin and sclera has become less stridently yellow; he can now sit up in bed and sup on soup and soft bread; his speech is rather less slurred; his memory is much improved; and his ability to complain about his aches and pains is reassuringly more spirited than it was a few days ago.

I thought we were on the verge of losing Wagnière. Thanks to the care which you are providing, through the beneficial supervision and effectiveness of your doctors, especially that of Dr. Sergey Sergeyevitch,

who is in reality an angel sent from heaven, and the daily kindnesses
with which you regale both the patient and myself, I am confident
that the patient will lose no time in achieving a complete recovery
of body and mind withal. Thank you for the profusion of fresh and
dried herbs which allow us to give to the patient every hour a different
tisane. Thank you also for the food we receive daily: besides delicious
sustenance for our bodies it also gratifies us to know that you are our
generous benefactress forever vigilant of our health and comfort. Thank
you especially for the portrait you have sent us of yourself: despite its
miniature size it is clear to see your exquisite features from which
shine forth your altruism and your wisdom. Voltaire called you the
"Sémiramis of the North";[101] the reasons for this are abundantly clear.

I have the honor of being your complete and faithful servant,

Zénobe Bosquet

27th of December, 1778

Madame:

I am in awe of Dr. Sergey Sergeyevitch's care and compassion for
monsieur Wagnière. He has explained to me why he refuses to bleed the
patient, saying that weakness is exacerbated by removing the vital fluid
of life. I have a tendency to agree, for I saw the effect that measured
exsanguination had on Voltaire, even if it was just a few ounces at a
time. Still, he became quite lethargic and languorous. His doctors in
Paris were Dr. Tronchin and Dr. Lorry, and they both seemed pleased
that Voltaire's normal vivacity was sapped to the point of listlessness. I
frequently thought that they were jealous of the frenetic physical activity
and mental acuity that their 84-year-old patient routinely exhibited.
They preferred that he be torpid of both mind and body so he could
no longer be the paragon of initiative and drive for which he was
universally known. Voltaire always had several projects operating at
the same time, and he could exhaust two or three secretaries in one
afternoon, seamlessly careening from one project to the other without
faltering or becoming confused. But when he was bled, he became
torpid, both mentally and physically, and in need of rest. It would take
him days to recover. Towards the end, a combination of being bled
and taking laudanum sapped his strength to such a degree that he
was not able to recover.

It is a most happy circumstance that Dr. Sergey Sergeyevitch is of
this opinion, that bleeding should be relegated to illnesses that incite
the patient's blood and inflame their aggression. Poor Wagnière is
so enervated already that he needs to retain all the blood that he
possibly can.

I have the honor of being your complete and faithful servant,

Zénobe Bosquet

---

101   The original Sémiramis was Queen of the Assyrians who, 800 years before Christ, successfully made
Babylon great again, adding many lands to her empire.

28th of December, 1778

Madame:

It is with praise and admiration that I write you about Captain Nicolai Shounine, whose hospitality with two relative strangers has been superlative. When we were in his packet boat he could not do enough for us, assuring himself personally every day that we were comfortable and well cared for. But ever since Wagnière fell ill, he has truly redoubled his efforts to provide for us, even sharing his private home and convincing us that it is now our home as well. Such generosity of spirit, such Christian charity, as overwhelming and touching as it is coming from one man, clearly emerges from a larger, wider source, and from my perspective, it comes from that man's society, and that man's sovereign. It is her largesse, her philanthropy, her openness with foreigners, that flows forth at her instigation and suffuses into all corners of her realm. Captain Shounine had been a superb host at sea; he didn't need to continue providing for us on land, and yet, here he is, constantly by our side, attentive to everything large and small.

Such lavish and reassuring concern for our well-being redouble our feelings of gratitude and indebtedness, not just for Captain Shounine, but also for his Queen, whose generosity fills the hearts of her subjects to such an astonishing degree. It is not surprising that Wagnière's health improves daily. This morning I lauded the stars, with you in their midst, that he was sitting up in bed with a book in his hand. It has been quite a while since he was able to plunge himself into a book. This, for a librarian, is our idea of heaven.

I have the honor of being your complete and faithful servant,

Zénobe Bosquet

(?)29th of December, 1778

This letter is missing the top half of a single sheet.

… told us that he studied medicine at the University of Padua for eight years before he went back to his home country of Lithuania. He speaks with pride of how he came to be in your employ and calls your court a 'New Golden Age' for Russia and the countries surrounding it.[102] I myself must add my steadfast assent: it is indeed remarkable that you have surrounded yourself with talent from so many lands: a Jewish doctor from Lithuania, statesmen from England, artists from France and Rome, architects from Tuscany. You gather unto yourself the expertise and artistry of multinational guests whom you accept, not just with tolerance, but with open arms. This is indeed enlightenment, and I am most happy to witness it. Indeed, Paris should emulate you

---

102   The identity of this person must be Dr. Solomon Ashkenazi, the second doctor that Catherine assigned to the care of Wagnière. He was indeed educated at the University of Padua and came from Lithuania.

in this, but Louis is far too myopic and, since he is too impotent, he allows the bigoted clergy to rule for him.

30th of December, 1778

Madame:

The patient continues to convalesce at a swift pace. Wagnière is now taking walks in his room and in the hallway outside, with help and support from someone to keep his balance, of course, but the steps he takes are his own. His conversation is back with a vengeance; his memory seems to have come out of the darkness with no apparent lacunae; more importantly, he speaks of the anticipated honor and pleasure of meeting Your Imperial Highness and getting on with the occupation that brought us to your country, that of putting up Voltaire's library in the same disposition they were at Ferney. On this subject, he asks if work has started on the reproduction of the château, and if the books will wait until the reproduction is completed, or if they will be put up somewhere else temporarily. They were well encased and the winter cold assures that humidity will do them no damage. Still, I think that our recuperating friend is becoming impatient to begin his work. One can't keep a Swiss lutheran down for long: work for them is their prime directive. Perhaps this is what sapped his energy in the first place. The prolonged exertion to organize and pack the thousands of books, followed by a strenuous voyage not devoid of danger and fright, most probably undermined his ability to fight off illness. The peace and quiet of his convalescence are, of course, still essential, even though it is his own consternation at being held confined that are now at times interrupting them.

"*Che 'l perder tempo, a chi più sa, più spiace.*"[103]

I have the honor of being your complete and faithful servant,

Zénobe Bosquet

31st of December, 1778

Madame:

On this last day of the year I have more good news: the patient continues to become stronger and his energy to last longer. He is now eating more solid food, not just soups and purees. However he still refuses wine, and like your physicians, I attribute this to nature's way of alerting us to what is best for the body.

He calls out your name several times a day, to laud you, to compliment you; he cannot thank you enough for your bounteous generosity. I, too, add my praises to his.

Tonight we will bring in the new year, not with prayer, for I do not believe in god, but with thanks. We feel so protected and so loved

---

103   "The wisest are those who feel the most sorrow at the loss of time." Dante Alighieri, from his *Purgatorio*, Canto III, v. 78.

beneath the balm of succor which you provide through your subjects. Captain Shounine, Dr. Sergeyevitch seconded by Dr. Ashkenazi, the people who constantly bring us delicious food and drink, they all reflect to such a degree the solicitude and sterling qualities of their mistress. To you we send our heartfelt thanks and our undying admiration.

We are far from home and far from our friends, it is true. But your welcome and generosity are so sincere and so overwhelming that we cannot help but realize that we are here also among friends.

Please accept, *Madame*, our most profound respect and our most enthusiastic gratitude,

Zénobe Bosquet

1st of January, 1779

Madame:

A few days ago I read your play based on the life of Rurick. This morning I read your play entitled *Oh! These Times!*.[104] I must say, one can understand why Voltaire was always extolling your talents and virtues, for there are so many gathered together in this one person who also happens to be an Empress. That you have literary skills among all those virtues is not surprising at all; what exhilarates me is your condemnation of false piety, nay, of false religion, for the principal character in your play is so well portrayed, so despicably painted in the true colors of the religious hypocrite, that it is clear to me that you hold such deceit in as much contempt as I do. I have not met such a wicked scoundrel since Molière's *Tartuffe*.

The fact that you also criticize the pervasive convention of prohibiting education for girls is also admirable. Young women, too, need to know history and science, mathematics and culture. Keeping half of the population in total ignorance might be a way to keep them under control, but I agree with you that it is also imprisoning their minds. Girls are curious, too, I can tell you this from experience since I have four sisters, and they need to expand their horizons to achieve what nature intended for them to be: partners complete in a society that provides them with intellectual freedom. My very good friend in Paris and in Tonnerre, the *chevalière* d'Éon, would be the first to congratulate you. She much admired your predecessor Empress Elizabeth when she served as a French diplomat in Saint Petersburg; today with Empress Catherine she would be in awe.

I have the honor of being your complete and faithful servant,

Zénobe Bosquet

2nd of January, 1779

This letter is missing, or was never written.

---

104   The titles in the original Russian are, respectively, Из жизни Рюрика (*From Rurick's Life*) a play in which she imitates Shakespeare in the dispensing with the three unities of classical drama; and О время! (*Oh! These Times!*, also translated traditionally as *Oh, Tempora!*).

3rd of January, 1779

Madame:

One of Captain Shounine's servants has taken the time to decipher for me the Cyrillian alphabet and teach me the rudiments of the Russian language. It is my honor that I can address to Your Imperial Highness a few phrases in your adopted language.

С Новым Годом! Всего хорошего! России замечательная страна! У меня плохо с русским![105]

I wish I could converse in Russian, but its accumulation of consonants trips up my tongue, and the «ы» sound is unfathomable. It is a vowel that seem not to be coming from the mouth, rather from the throat. In written language the «г» looks like a «p» and the «и» looks like a reversed «N»; the «Я» looks like a reversed capital «R». It is simply amazing, and I am so amused by this new language!

Wagnière can now sit at the desk and write. He is sending a letter to you together with mine. The patient asks when he can begin the enterprise for which you summoned him from Ferney. He is ready to begin the new Russian Ferney that, in his opinion, shall be the symbol of continued tolerance in the advancement of knowledge.

I have the honor of being your complete and faithful servant,

Zénobe Bosquet

4th of January, 1779

This letter is missing, or was never written.

5th of January, 1779

Madame:

Monsieur Wagnière and I wish to thank you for the carriage and four[106] you provided for us yesterday, and for the driver-guide whom you instructed to take us on a tour of Saint Petersburg.

Today we continue to speak of the extraordinary sights and the captivating sites of this marvelous and unique city. We have been thoroughly thrilled and delighted by it, this city founded by Peter the Great and augmented by Elizabeth and Your Imperial Majesty to such a heightened degree that it takes one's breath away. A city wrested from the marshy islands of the Neva and transformed into one of the most magnificent cities on earth, it displays the genius of its founder and of his successors! It is grand, it spreads practically to the horizon; its boulevards are wide, too wide for the number of vehicles one sees on them, but perhaps with a view towards the future and increased circulation; its public buildings are imposing, both by their design and by their monumental size. True, most of them are still unfinished, but their scale and splendor are readily apparent.

---

105 Happy New Year! Best wishes! Russia is a wonderful country! My Russian is bad!

106 A carriage and four horses.

In so few generations, Russians have gone from complete seclusion and isolation to an emerging nation with international associations and trade with the European nations. The vestiges of medieval barbarity and superstition have yielded to knowledge, refinement, and civilization. Peter dispelled the ignorance in which his people were enveloped, broke down the barriers of rusticity and gave them the arts and the refinements of enlightenment. True, despite Peter I's edicts, many beards are still visible on the faces of those men belonging mostly to the lower classes. Noblemen are almost indistinguishable from their European counterparts, save for the regional costumes you see on some of them.

The palace of Peterhoff took our breath away. Its extensive gardens that line the shore of the Gulf of Finland are the most beautiful we have encountered. They shame those of the Tuileries Gardens in Paris, and *monsieur* Wagnière says that they are more magnificent than the ones in Geneva by the shores of its lake. (I was in Geneva once but did not know any better and spent more time in the bookstores than strolling on the streets.)

The guide said that many of Peter's builders fell victim to the noxious vapors of the marshes surrounding the islands on top of which the city was erected. I find their sacrifice as courageous and honorable as those of soldiers who give up their life defending their country.

The most impressive landmark of all was *monsieur* Falconnette's pedestal on which he is erecting the equestrian statue of Peter the Great. The guide spoke of a 'rock' which did no justice to the immensity of this monolith. 'Boulder' does not do much better. 'Mountain' or 'cliff' begin to approximate the size of this behemoth, which, as explained to us, was moved from a distant location to be placed here. The statue itself is also impressive: Peter the Great is a figure full of energy and brimming with enthusiasm. Both horse and master seem to be in full movement, stopping only at the last instant before the edge of this cliff, with Peter's arm pointing to the Neva and the West as if to say, 'There, there we set our sights, there we reach out to join the brotherhood of man, to seek what is ours, and that is to share in the achievements of the West for those also belong to us, for we are no longer immured within the walls of our own sightlessness. We see, and we reach out, and we progress and advance to the horizons!" I still feel shivers of emotion up my spine when I think of this magnificent statue which you commissioned. What Peter the Great began, Catherine the Great continues, to the permanent benefit of her people. I find the inscription at the base of the statue glorious in its simplicity and impressive in its modesty: «Petro Primo, Catherina Secunda posuit, 177__». When it is finished, it will be one of the greatest achievements of mankind.

We were also impressed by the large number of Houses of Worship. It is certain that the Greeks like their domes, for they bloom like mushrooms all over the city: in each case four smaller ones encircling a large one, all of them covered in copper gilt, making them shine even on an overcast day. True, inside one finds lavish and costly ornamentation, to the point that every Virgin and every baby Jesus is dressed in sumptuous gold and silver thread. They seem imprisoned in golden fetters they are so overadorned. Saint Nicholas is also ubiquitous, and similarly garbed. One feels that the barbarous expense to dress the nakedness of statues would have best served society if the funds had been distributed among the poor. But then again, an atheist cannot truly judge the sacrifices made by the penitent. Still, the ancient Greeks preferred their statues completely unclothed. Why did their descendants not share the same preference?

We also visited the Church of the Citadel in which repose the earthly remains of the Czar. The unadorned simplicity of his tomb mirrors, I presume, the plainness and the austerity of the great man himself. He was unpretentious, for he was serious and direct about the way he led his nation. His successor sovereigns are also there, of course, save for Peter III, your late husband, who lacked the vision, and the concern for the Russian people, evinced by the other monarchs. We were told that he alone is interred in a monastery a few miles out of town. I believe that it is his just repose.

On the way back to Captain Shounine's house, our guide took the boulevard that follows the bank of the Neva. The parade of new buildings going up adjacent to this grand boulevard, with magnificent views of the river, is phenomenal. Our guide said that the row of buildings is only halfway done, that eventually they will stretch for two leagues. Even halfway done, this is a magnificent, an extraordinary feat of architecture. The Neva itself is beautiful: where it still flows in the faster current its waters are clear and perfectly clean, and on the whole, this project makes for the finest walk in the world. The Thames or the Seine or the Danube would be happy to be half as beautiful. I myself have seen the Seine and would find it difficult to call it scenic.

In general, it may be said that nothing looks old in Saint Petersburg. Everything is recent, or completely new. It is a city still in its initial growth, and there is everywhere construction and commotion. It is the energy of a new city, a new and uncommon metropolis that is the promise of a new Russia, a center of civilization and a beacon of hope for those of us enthralled with the idea of enlightenment. I for one cannot forget the fact that it is a collaborative enterprise begun by a man with great imagination, enthusiasm, and concern for his people, but that has now been undertaken by a woman with the same commitments, the same obligations, and the same love of her people, and I commend Your Imperial Majesty for it.

I have the honor of being your complete and faithful servant,

Zénobe Bosquet

6th of January, 1779

Madame:

This morning *monsieur* Wagnière had the distinct pleasure of receiving the visit of your architects, *il signore* Antonio Rinaldi and *Herr* Yury Matveyevich Velten, with whom he deliberated about the project to build a replica of Voltaire's château. Having brought all the drawings and plans prepared by Voltaire's architect, *monsieur* Racle, *monsieur* Wagnière asked if it would be relatively easy to build a Russian Ferney. The response was a swift yes, except that such a project would have to wait its turn behind all the other projects that Your Imperial Majesty has begun throughout the city. What with the expansion of several of the palaces, the improvements to the city, the erection of the monument to Peter, all of these works entail skilled workers and special equipment and tools, none of which can be in two places at the same time. Your architects suggested that Wagnière put up the books temporarily in a room dedicated to this purpose at Tsarskoe Selo, readily accessible to you and your librarians. The replica of the château may take a few months to build, but *il signore* Rinaldi could not now predict when such an undertaking could begin.

Monsieur Wagnière is ready to start with any proposal that Your Imperial Highness bids. He does tire easily, but it can be said that he is chomping at the bit. Voltaire's books have been in crates for far too long, and they need to be liberated.

I have the honor of being your complete and faithful servant,

Zénobe Bosquet

January 6, 1779, Festival of the Epiphany

Letter from the Empress

Monsieur,

I have made some inquiries about your person, mostly to *messieurs le marquis* de Juigné and di Fuoco, my ambassadors from Versailles and from Turin, but also to sundry artists and architects from the Italian states who have made Russia their home. I have been quite disappointed to see my queries stymied almost immediately. It is not in my habit to be thwarted thusly, which is why I bring my questions directly to you. When asked about your true identity, both of my ambassadors emerged with highly suspicious suppositions of your personal history. The only detail that I am willing to concede is that you are the bastard son of Victor-Amédée, since both ambassadors seemed to be of the same opinion on this point. *Monsieur le marquis* de Juigné, however, asserted that you served as one of Voltaire's secretaries during his sojourn in Paris, and maybe even before he left Ferney, and that once in Paris you had antagonized *monsieur* the Archbishop Beaumont. *Il Signor* di Fuoco was just as convinced that Victor Amédée had you imprisoned, his own son, in Turin for having attacked his priests in Savoy. This is not the first time a father has had a son incarcerated, of course: the *marquis* de Mirabeau has placed his son Honoré Gabriel Riqueti, *comte* de Mirabeau under lock and key, but all the son does is publish treatises against despotism. Whatever the case may be between you and your father, annoying priests is a penchant that I would expect from a follower of Voltaire, and I admire your anti-clerical stance. I myself have put the clergy of Russia in their place: it is as servants of Russia that they now enjoy their status in society.

Still, I am curious as to which of these two stories is the true one, if at all, and feel that only you can dispel my doubts. From your letters I have gathered that you are well-educated, well read, and well-versed in social protocol. You also seem to be highly independent in your opinions and beliefs: I have never witnessed anybody be so blithe about admitting to their atheism, not even *monsieur* Diderot.

I beseech you to appear before me tomorrow at 2 in the afternoon. Doctor Sergey Sergeyevitch will stay with our patient, *monsieur* Wagnière, while you are away from him. Neither ambassador will be present, so I expect you to speak at ease and candidly.

Catherine Regina

The French need not read this addendum since their culture, and the mirror of their culture, literature, abounds with amorous relationships between older, more mature women and young men intellectually their inferiors, but usually avid to learn at the altar of experience, sophistication, and wisdom. For the young man it is not necessarily the discovery and exploration of sex which is placed in a position of priority, although that, too, may receive some studious and grateful consideration. It is more than that, for the young man. It is a total learning experience to involve himself with the lady who represents a higher level of *savoir faire*, an added polish of social comportment, a sensitivity to human relations, a foot up on the ladder of aristocratic hierarchy. Any young man who would eschew such an occasion for guidance and advance would invariably deserve to remain unrefined and artless, a rustic with no ambition and no desire for improvement, a hick who merited the very ignorance that kept him supine and spurned. Zénobe had made such inroads since that fateful day a year ago when he had mustered the courage to present himself at the front entrance of the *hôtel* de Villette, that he desired to meet the Russian empress and receive instruction from her, in spite of his initial reluctance to do so. He was no longer a ruffian from the Savoyard peasantry. He had risen in the eyes of society to become the scion, albeit the bastard scion, of the Savoyard king. No matter that this was untrue, but the aristocracy and the edifice they had built for themselves was a European creation, and one leapt at the chance to climb a rung or two. Zénobe had ascended quickly to heady heights, with the help of others, to be sure, but he maintained his lofty level with the lessons he had picked up along the way. Who better to continue these lessons but Her Imperial Majesty Catherine the Second herself?

Nowadays, those who come from democratic places have a tendency to spurn the game of hierarchy, although in many of those nations, it is money that has replaced the old system of rank and caste. In 1779, in Russia, the social structure denoting one's place from monarch to serf was firm in all its inglorious vigor. Both Catherine and Zénobe were well aware of how the game of hierarchy was played; each knew the rules; each knew what was expected of each other; each knew how the game could, at any moment, be terminated by either one of them. Subtlety, intuition, keen observation, study of character, quick reaction, witty ripostes, and, finally, guile, would serve as their resources in the game.

May the best player win.

Part 5

The Throne of the North

January 7, 1779

An Audience with Catherine the Great

"**Y**ou are neither French nor Italian!" cried out the queen of Russia as she saw Zénobe walking up to her throne at the far side of the Hall of Audience. He had been announced simply as '*Monsieur* Marie-Jean Joseph Zénobe de Bosquet,' so Catherine asked while he was still quite far away, "And what about your aristocratic credentials?" Never had the walk to her throne seemed so long to her as the figure of Wagnière's assistant become more and more promising with every step he took. "My ambassadors are crazy! Hey, but you're Swedish!"[107]

Zénobe lost no time walking up the rest of the way and swiftly going down on one knee, his head bowed low.

"My queen," he said. "Today I am Russian!"

Catherine beamed as her ladies-in-waiting made little giggling sounds of approval. She tilted her head back the better to inspect him. The diamonds in her crown, her earrings and the pendant around her neck shimmered and sparkled. She was no longer young, but she was still quite an attractive woman, with her mischievous and friendly blue eyes, pouty lips that she kept in a semi-permanent sarcastic smile, and an expressiveness to her face that invited further glances of observation, not to mention of fascination.

Usually this great hall was teeming with courtiers, diplomats and army officers of all ranks. Today, only the guards at the doors and six ladies-in-waiting, poised around the throne on the dais, were in attendance.

"Please stand, sir, and come closer. You are one who is very young," she observed. "From the sound of your letters I was expecting someone closer to Wagnière's age, someone in his forties or fifties."

"I am twenty years of age, *madame*, and the rest of my years I devote to you."

Zénobe followed protocol, at least his idea of it, to its utmost. He kept his gaze down, his torso inclined towards her and his hands folded in front of his chest.

"Step up, young man, and I entreat you to look me in the eye. Your respect and deference have been duly noted." She glanced at her ladies and they all nodded their

---

107   Reminder to the reader: Zénobe still wears the only aristocratic clothes he has ever worn, the military uniform made for him by Maurel. The majordomo had chosen the Swedish colors for their exoticism and rarity on Parisian streets. The empress had been expecting a title of *marquis* or *comte* or even *baron* to be attached to his name.

heads in acquiescence. "You will see that I am a modern sovereign and care not for *démodé* ways. Come closer. Don't be bashful."

Her Imperial Majesty had given a direct command but it was still difficult for Zénobe who, with his lifetime of inculcation with behavior towards patricians, could only slowly raise his gaze towards the Empress' eyes, in case she changed her mind for his effrontery and had him cast his look down.

Catherine underwent an involuntary reaction as Zénobe's regard rose up the full length of her body to catch sight of the details of her dress, of her mantle, of her sash, all the way up her bosom and finally to her face: when the full blue gleam in the young man's eyes shone into her own, a watered-down version of blue, she underwent a barely perceptible intake of breath and a widening of her own eyes. Her pupils dilated and her heart rate increased, though these reactions none could tell.

"Are you then French? Were you Voltaire's secretary in Paris and did you in fact show disrespect to the Archbishop of Paris? Or are you Turingeois, held captive by the Duke of Savoy, who may be your father, imprisoned in his dungeon for having assaulted his priests? Or are you now a Swede, come to redress the injustices of the past meted out to your country by mine? After all, the spot on which we gather and chat amiably once belonged to your country, and this not too long ago. Are you come to take it back?"

After a slight hesitation, due to his surprise that Catherine already knew so much about him, coupled with the inability to choose where to begin his explanations, Zénobe decided to throw his fate to the mercy of the queen. He again dropped to one knee and bowed his head low.

"Oh, my queen, I am come to you an impostor in all but what has been said about me and Voltaire. It is true that I was *monsieur* de Voltaire's secretary in Paris. As for the incriminations about me and certain priests, some of them may be true, others false, still others grossly exaggerated. I do apologize for this last deception, for I am no Swede."

"Ah, what a relief," answered Catherine. "I was about to bring in my guards, young man. I felt for a brief moment that my safety might be in danger."

Again impatient at seeing Zénobe in a position of submission before her, she urged him to rise to his feet. Zénobe complied and saw that Catherine was all smiles and dimples and moving her shoulders about as if she were enjoying the moment. Her movements made the gems upon her head, those hanging from her ears, and the sumptuous necklace pressed on her bosom sparkle all the more. Rings on her fingers reflected the candlelight in myriads of rainbow shimmers. The queen was scintillating as if she were her own constellation here on earth, one that was in perpetual motion, twinkling in rubies, diamonds, emeralds, lustrous green silk and blue taffeta. Only one item, an armband high on her left arm, was dull and flat, made of matte black velvet.

An official audience granted to representatives of state usually elicited boredom from Catherine, due to the tedium of most business. Only when there was a rebellion to be quelled someplace in her realm, or when a visitor of the caliber of Diderot was come to her court, or when she was in the presence of one of her lovers, did Catherine become ebullient and exhilarated. The enthusiasm and liveliness of her youth seemed to bloom again. Today, it seems, had brought to her one of those circumstances that evoked the pleasure of discovery. This strange and beautiful young man in front of her certainly aroused her curiosity, but the additional element of the outlaw, of the miscreant, of a man who wantonly went around goading priests, only served to inspirit her to an even greater degree. However, the imperial throne room, which she abhorred, was not a place amenable to friendly conversation. It was too huge, too marble-hard, too echo-laden. She needed to be more comfortable for this interview. She waved to her ladies-in-waiting who, seemingly anticipating her wishes, surrounded Zénobe.

"Please, *monsieur*," said the queen. "Follow my ladies. We shall continue this chat but in a more inspiring location. The only thing that the throne room is inspiring in you is your passive docility."

Zénobe obediently followed Her Majesty's ladies down some long corridors, up a staircase, down another, across a grand courtyard, and into a medium-sized room. This was Catherine's antechamber, appointed with comfortable sofas and armchairs, not excessively adorned, but in a subdued style that was still rather feminine, peach and pink being the primary colors.

The ladies escorted Zénobe to a settee by the huge fireplace on one side of the room and deposited him among the cushions. One of them brought him tea and biscuits, another a goblet of red wine, still another a faceted glass of what seemed to be water but turned out to be vodka. Zénobe's sputtering as he gamely tried to gulp down the fiery liquid made the ladies laugh. Tears came to his eyes, but he laughed as well.

"Ah," he said, "this drink has to be sipped, not guzzled."

One of the ladies, a dainty brunette, explained, "Well, *monsieur*, it's still only водка (*vodka*)!"

Zénobe did not understand.

"*Vodka* in Russian is the diminutive of *vod*, which means water. So *vodka* means 'sweet little water'!"

Zénobe wondered, "Ah, then, will it make my garden grow better?"

The ladies were all twittery with amusement. The swaying of their candy-colored gowns was mesmerizing. Some of them hid their pretty faces behind fans which danced like butterflies in their hands.

"What are you doing with my ladies, young man?" asked Catherine as she appeared in the room from a *trompe l'œil* door. "You are debauching them, I gather?"

Zénobe immediately was on his feet.

"No, *madame*, I believe it is the other way around."

"My ladies are as pure as the snow outside this very palace."

Zénobe had seen the snow on his way in. The only thing it wasn't was white.

"And I very much admired it as I entered the palace. It reminded me of the "snows of yesteryear" and of the ladies from the past whom one continues to remember fondly and admire."[108]

The ladies, including Catherine, took delight in being compared to the celebrated women of François Villon's poem.

"Inasmuch as my ladies-in-waiting would love to continue hearing your flattering remarks, I do need to converse with you about a few, oh, shall we say, a few hundred items?"

Catherine's ladies took this as their cue to flee from the room and leave the two to their privacy.

Her Majesty took her seat besides Zénobe, who haltingly bent his knees to perch on the very edge of the settee. He noticed that she had no crown now, no clusters of diamonds hanging from her ears, no necklace with the huge diamond pendant. It was

---

108   This is an allusion to a famous poem by François Villon, in which the medieval poet speaks with affection and nostalgia of «*les neiges d'antan*» and of the vanished ladies of history who are worthy of being remembered.

her eyes that shone alone with the brightness of reflected intelligence. There was ruse there, but blatant enjoyment of life as well, and a bit of expectation that he would know how to play this game. The peasant from Savoy was all of a sudden aware that he was alone with the Empress of the largest country on earth.

"Please, make yourself comfortable," she told him. "Sit back, arrange the cushions behind you. Cross your legs, if you wish. Are you cozy?"

After gulping as discreetly as he could, Zénobe answered, "*Oui, madame.* Very much so. Your hospitality and your concern for guests are legendary, as experienced directly by *monsieur* Wagnière and myself, and as reported to me by our mutual friend Diderot."

"Oh," she cried out, "You know Diderot as well, then?"

"I had the pleasure and the honor of meeting all of Voltaire's friends. And quite a few of his enemies, as well."

"Oh, like that dark and evil Fréron![109] How I hated that silly, little man. And he being raised by the Jesuits, too! I'm not surprised. Priests are the most envious, covetous of beings who lurk in the shadows watching life parade by. They're supposed to have nothing and be satisfied with nothing, but they envy everybody else who is allowed to have things, and they want those things, too. They know how to get them as well. But it's like possessing beautiful things in secret and being fearful that some busybody will find out. That leads these priests to be grasping, greedy creatures who must hide their beautiful possessions, especially from each other. Well, I rectified that here in Russia. Now the priests have nothing, which is the way it should be. I forced them to imitate their Messiah. Now they are happier, for they are no longer hypocrites. You see, you can force people to be upright and honest. You just have to show them what is best for them!"

She laughed gleefully at her own temerity in cutting the clergy down to size. Zénobe joined in her mirth and his face dazzled the queen as he smiled. She needed to keep him amused and not let his smile wane.

"But tell me, how is our dear Diderot?"

"He is doing well, *madame.* Of course, we are all still grieving over Voltaire–"

"As am I," Catherine interrupted, glancing at the black armband on her left sleeve.

"Diderot has turned to his writings, which is, I gather, the way that many writers deal with their grief. Writing is a way to dissipate the gloom, to find your way in the dark and establish the optimism that brings enlightenment."

"Well, said, *monsieur.* This is why I love to read Diderot's works. And Voltaire's."

"Among the books and papers we brought to you, there are a few unpublished manuscripts from both of them. I hope you enjoy reading them."

"Indeed I shall, indeed I shall. I cannot wait to turn my attention to them. But I am also aquiver with the anticipation to find out your provenance and history. You are obviously well-read, intelligent; not just anybody can be secretary to Voltaire. The daily letters you have written to keep me apprised of Wagnière's condition attest to your knowledge, to your abilities, your skills of observation, to say nothing of the resourcefulness and intuition you display in providing for your friend. You could soon be a physician yourself, I can see."

---

109   Élie Fréron, one of the thorns in the side of the Enlightenment philosophers, tried to discredit and malign them at every turn. His journal, *l'Année Littéraire, The Literary Year,* was rebaptized by Voltaire as being *l'Âne littéraire: The Literary Ass.*

"Well, it is the skill and knowledge of your own doctors who have been instrumental in the improvement of Wagnière's health. All I have done is observe which of the remedies seem to have led to more salubrious consequences."

"Well, not just anyone could have dealt with that as successfully as you did. But please, tell me your story. Pray, do not leave anything out. I want to find out everything about you, young man. You are different from most. You are a Franco-Italian Swede, and you intrigue me."

Catherine's ways were so cordial, so natural (as Diderot, too, had observed), that Zénobe felt it was his duty to tell Her Imperial Majesty of all the Russias the complete truth about his background. He hoped she wouldn't be disappointed to know that he was no aristocrat. Yet, he left out three parts of his story that he instinctively thought might perturb, or perhaps disappoint, Her Majesty. He did not divulge the fact that he came from a family of land-tilling peasants, preferring to mention a background of vague burgher activities in trade and imported goods. He made no mention of André or his affection for him; and he completely failed to include all episodes of his interactions with *madame* de Polignac, Marie Antoinette's favored lady-in-waiting.[110] He explained with great relish how he had infuriated the priests in Paris and all across France all the way to Savoy and Turin. He regretted nothing of that, and gave the definite impression that he was proud of treating the clergy as the lowliest of creatures on this earth, akin to toads crawling in mud and filth or slimy worms eating dead things. They were the parasites of society and they wanted everybody to remain blind and ignorant.

Anti-clericalism was a good beginning for the relationship that ensued between Catherine the Great and Zénobe Bosquet. The fact that he wasn't gentry did not in any way diminish him in her eyes. Most of her past lovers had been military men from the class called the lower gentry, although, truth be told, some of them had acted as if they were commoners. Every time the boy sitting beside her averted his gaze away from her, she quickly looked him up and down and realized that Zénobe could never be taken as a commoner, however. If his lot in life had slated him to be a lowly country tradesman, he had long ago shed his rusticity. His education had raised him to the level of kings and queens. Mind, there were kings and queens who were rather stupid, obnoxious boors, like her own husband Peter III who had died for being so fatuous.

An item from this first interview comes to mind: When Zénobe mentioned his friendship with the *chevalière* d'Éon, Catherine the Great let out a squeal of pleasure.

Ah, *madame la chevalière* d'Éon! Is there no other creature on earth who is so wonderful, so vivacious, so splendidly generous with her mind?"

"Indeed not!" agreed Zénobe. He proceeded to tell the queen how generous the *chevalière* had been with him. He had to tell her, of course, of their encounter with Jean-Jacques Rousseau and how the writer had treated the poor *demoiselle* with disrespect. Another story to tell was how the *chevalière* fished Zénobe out of the well in Tonnerre as he was drowning. In turn, Catherine told Zénobe many stories of the *chevalière* d'Éon in her position as clandestine *ambassadrice* from France who was able to pass right under the noses of hard-line Russian statesmen and win direct access to the Empress

---

110   Please remember, dear reader, that it was *madame la marquise* de Polignac who had bruited around town that Zénobe was the scion, albeit illegitimate, of the Duke of Savoy. Had their romance ever come to light, it would have been better for her to have been known for a tryst with a bastard prince as opposed to a lowly peasant from the fields surrounding Annecy. This last she could never have lived down.

Elizabeth, who made her her *lectrice*.[111] As a genteel and charming lady, d'Éon eventually convinced the empress to view favorably an alliance with France, something that male French diplomats had not been able to do. Catherine and Zénobe's mutual admiration for the *chevalière* d'Éon led to other topics of conversation, which ensued in many other themes and questions and subjects. The afternoon passed so quickly that both were surprised to see themselves in almost complete darkness. Catherine rang for the maids who quickly lit candles and brought in refreshments, including more vodka, and in one evening a new friendship was born. Catherine found in Zénobe an ally, a confidant, a mind who could understand hers and remained nonjudgmental. This last was heaven-sent for it was Catherine's experience that most men could not help being censorious and patronizing with women. Zénobe was refreshingly amoral, accepting all her ideas without pronouncements or sermons as to their purported lack of virtue, honor, scruples, or even veracity.

For instance, when they were on the subject of social expectations of women, Catherine mentioned that she herself saw no use in accepting the fate of the individual as meted out by society's expectations.

She explained with utmost seriousness, "Women are supposed to know their place in the scheme of things and remain exiled to the edges of society and say, 'Yes, sir' and 'No, sir' and give advice obliquely to make the man believe he thought it up himself, well, no, no, no, thank you! I preferred to replace the man, why even bother being discreet and deferential, making oneself a victim of self-abnegation? I was in a position to replace a man, so I did! It was the easiest thing in the world to do! Of course, in this case the man who was so weak was Peter."

Zénobe's reaction was not, "There are those who think women should…" or "Woman was not put on earth to…" or even "Without the aid of your military, who were all men…" No, his response was, "And you are to be admired all the more for it. Peter III was clearly not made of stern stuff and was so gullible that he surrounded himself with sycophants and hypocrites. I heard that flattery was the quickest way to his heart. It was established by all objective observers that these intruders into your husband's good graces were running him, and therefore running the state."

Catherine was astounded to hear such an unfiltered opinion, especially one that was so incontrovertibly true.

"Yes, exactly! How do you know about the tsar's foibles?"

"He seems to be cut out of the same mold as the king of France. Louis XVI cannot make a decision on his own. He has to rely on a herd of advisors who have no experience or knowledge about how to deal with the cogs and levers of government. The advice that that man receives is useless, and sometimes even detrimental to the business of government. Yet he implements it with blithe disregard to the damage it consequently brings. Then, even in the face of the reports that start to come in of the harm to society that his practices are causing, he redoubles his resolve to continue in using the very same practices. Bad advice makes itself known quite rapidly, but the king of France is so afraid of being known as irresolute and a ditherer that he staunchly follows bad

---

111 *Lecteur*, feminine *lectrice*, was an attendant whose services included retrieving the necessary books from the library and reading passages from them out loud to the listener. De rigueur were a well-modulated voice, a talent for dramatic narrative renditions, and a strong constitution in case the recitations lasted for hours.

advice until the damage is so appalling that it can no longer be masked or justified by the king's men.

"I say, if you are going to make a man king, well then goddammit, educate him to be one. Teach him about economics (the *chevalière* d'Éon is an expert in the field and chomping at the bit to counsel her monarch!—but she is only a woman to him!); teach him about diplomatic relations; teach him about history; teach him about justice; and teach him about the dangers inherent in the union of state and religion. I should also be saying, 'Teach *her*' for a queen may also be groomed. Great sovereigns of the past have been women, and women make excellent sovereigns. Their empathy is all the greater for having been downtrodden. Their subtlety and perception likewise are greater."

After such a stimulating speech, all Catherine could do was stare at her interlocutor and sigh with happiness.

From that first interview, Catherine kept inviting Zénobe into her antechamber every afternoon. While Wagnière convalesced, his assistant consorted with the queen, holding entertaining conversations about everything under the sun.

Discussing Literature with Catherine the Great

"Have you read *Joseph Andrews*,[112] the novel by Henry Fielding, *monsieur* de Bosquet?" was the first question Catherine asked Zénobe as soon as they were seated in her salon, enjoying their first cup of tea, anticipating a few hours of the pleasure of each other's company. Catherine especially was thrilled and hopeful because she knew that they had a total of four hours ahead of them for this particular interview. Her ladies-in-waiting had been told that there would be no interruptions and for the ladies themselves to make themselves scarce. In addition, in case there were signs that the Empress might alter the afternoon's plan and repair to the boudoir, they were supposed to disappear completely.

Zénobe answered with pleasure. "*Oui, madame*, I have read it. Just a couple of weeks ago, as a matter of fact. Wagnière and I read it out loud to each other on the road. We used Voltaire's own copy."

"Oh, what a happy event!" Catherine exclaimed. "I read it recently as well, in English. Did you read it in English?"

"I am sure that our English is not as excellent as yours. Voltaire understood and spoke English, but he did have a copy of the novel that had been translated into French, which is what Wagnière and I used. Of course, on the margins were Voltaire's corrections of the translation, for he also had the original version in English. I believe that the only reason why he even bothered to acquire the French translation was to criticize the translator."

Catherine looked at Zénobe with a quizzical look.

"You see, *madame*, the translator was Desfontaines."[113]

---

112   The novel's complete title is *Joseph Andrews, or The History of the Adventures of Joseph Andrews and of his Friend Mr. Abraham Adams,* was published in London in 1742, and translated into French and published in Paris the following year. In both countries it enjoyed much popularity and critical acclaim.

113   L'Abbé Pierre François Guyot-Desfontaines (1685-1745) was always a thorn in Voltaire's side in spite of the fact that Voltaire saved his life. In 1724, Desfontaines languished in a cell of the Bastille, accused of sodomy, waiting to be burned on the Place de Grève. It was said that he had kept a group of young libertine men with whom he participated in scenes of debauchery. Voltaire, as a writer helping another writer, and knowledgeable of how lies were often fabricated as an excuse to throw intellectuals in jail, used his influence to have him liberated. Desfontaines showed his gratitude by authoring, anonymously, of course, since he was also a coward, a libelous tract, *La Voltairomanie,* in which he enumerated Voltaire's own scandalous anecdotes. Voltaire never forgave him.

Catherine burst out in laughter. "Oh, how rich!" she exclaimed. "Of course, Voltaire would love to have any occasion to criticize Desfontaines!"

"Men like Desfontaines are despicable."

Agreeing, Catherine grimaced with disgust.

Zénobe explained, "In the first edition of the French *Joseph Andrews*, Desfontaines hid behind a falsehood, as he was wont to do. On the title page, there is a statement that the novel was translated by a young English lady, who remains anonymous." Zénobe laughed at the idea of a repulsive old abbot disguising himself as a proper young English lady.

"Voltaire certainly made an error in judgment for having come to his aid," remarked Catherine. "Abhorrent! In France they stopped a long time ago burning people like that at the stake.[114] That was after Desfontaines was liberated. He should have met the same fate. You see what Voltaire's influence could do. That horrid abbot did not change his ways, however. In this country," she said, denoting Russia, "he would not have lasted too long."

Zénobe stopped laughing. "Oh, how so?" he asked nonchalantly. His secret was locked up tight within the recesses of his mind where no one could surmise its existence.

"Well, Peter the Great forbade them from being in his armies. It was an attempt to bring the military up to par with the rest of Europe. As far as I know, that law still exists. Personally, I am indifferent. Many of my artisans and architects are foreigners, Italian, French, English, and a lot of them are… that way. For some reason, being that way and being an artist go hand in hand. Perhaps it's the freedom of the imagination that takes them places where normal people wouldn't care to go, wouldn't dare to go. Whatever the case, they're my foreigners, therefore they are protected. But out there—" Catherine with a dramatic sweep of her arm denoted all the Russias. "Out there, the people, especially those weak enough to be influenced by the Eastern Orthodox Church, would rather castrate the deviants as well as burn them at the stake. You can't stop that; it's what they do. The religious leaders dictate, the unthinking masses do. What I don't understand is, why do more of those deviants step up and raise their heads after their predecessors have been tortured and killed? The fear of pain or death isn't enough to stop those poor imbeciles. They keep showing up and then society has to deal with them, too. It's incomprehensible! If only they remained invisible."

Zénobe said nothing. What could he say? This was the queen speaking, yet Zénobe understood that this particular queen realized her influence against the Orthodox Church was limited. Besides, it sounded as if she had to chose her battles carefully, and waging battle in defense of sexual deviants was not one of them. At least Zénobe felt, were his secret out, he would fall among Catherine's "foreigners," and therefore he would also be protected. He decided nevertheless that it would be in his best interest if he said nothing about the subject. This wasn't Paris. In Paris he would have to be invisible for being an atheist; in Saint Petersburg he would have to be invisible for being a deviant.

"To get back to the matter at hand," continued Catherine, "I want to pursue the theme brought up by Fielding in *Joseph Andrews*."

"Are you speaking of the theme that Voltaire incorporated into his own *Candide?*" asked Zénobe. "The theme of the hero being ingenuous, honest, but not worldly enough to save his skin?"

---

114   Bruno Lenoir and Jean Diot were the last homosexuals to be burned alive in France, on July 6, 1750,

"Oh, I didn't even think about that. But now that you mention it, yes, I see a lot of Joseph Andrews in Candide. Everything except Joseph's extreme obsession to remain pure."

"You mean, sexually pure? A virgin?"

"The idea of purity in a man is a bit draconian, don't you think?"

"Unrealistic, I would say," answered Zénobe.

"That's right! No healthy young man would reject the advances of his lady mistress, now that his master, her husband, was dead."

"But it is precisely in remembrance and in respect of his master that Andrews refuses to even acknowledge the overtures of his mistress. He is blind to her propositions, as circuitous as they may be."

"Yes," agreed Catherine. "I know how the game of seduction is played and the lady mistress's words would have needed to be a bit more forthright, especially with such an innocent and naïve boy. He does not understand ruse and deception. Nevertheless, her physical attitude, her looks full of yearning, her gazes full of promise, and her burning sighs of passion should have tilted him in the right direction. Nature is always bursting at the seams to get out, and hardly anything ever stands in its way, not religious exhortations, not feelings of respect for the dead, not consciousness of a difference in age, culture, or aristocratic rank. I mean, the lad is, after all, a servant. A tall, broad-shouldered, handsome servant."

Zénobe looked at Catherine who seemed to be doing a credible imitation of Lady Booby's sultry performance. Zénobe had this to offer: "I think the author was trying to be coy about the timidity of a young girl's sexual conduct. After all, Joseph Andrews is the brother of Pamela Andrews.[115] You seem to think it ridiculous that a young man should refrain from offering up his virginity to the practicality of experience; perhaps the thought of female virginity is also ridiculous."

Catherine's expression revealed shock. Gone were the heavy sighs, the half-closed lids, the licking of her lips.

"Dear God in Heaven!" she exclaimed. "You go in directions where Voltaire never went!" She put a hand up to her forehead. "I cannot conceive of Fielding wanting to say this. Wasn't he a proper English gentleman?"

"Yes, to be sure, I am convinced of this and would not want to besmirch his reputation. Yet, intellectuals are always interested in making people think. What is unmentionable previous to his book, is now—on the printed page in indelible ink—mentioned. What is inconceivable before, all of a sudden becomes a thought, which makes it henceforth conceivable. From being conceivable to being plausible is just a matter of time. From being plausible to being credible is also a matter of time, while the mind adjusts to the new thought and directs it to the world of reality. From being credible to being acceptable, and in some far-off future being admissible and then sustainable, is but a further series of significant steps. Female virginity is ridiculous. Think of it. What is its history, what is its purpose? After all, who invented it? Men. They invented it, created whole mythologies around it, invented dogma to coerce it, enacted laws to enable it to prevail, and even convinced women of the necessity of it. Why didn't men pay as much attention to making male virginity as important, nay, as essential a virtue for the male

---

115 In his novel, *Joseph Andrews*, Henry Fielding creates a hero who is the brother of Pamela Andrews, heroine of the novel by Samuel Richardson, *Pamela, or Virtue Rewarded*, published in 1740. The virtuous Pamela must thwart her master's repeated attempts to seduce her.

as it is for the female? Fielding is saying that it is time to think about female virginity as a falsity, as a fictitious commodity with which females must comply, on the pain of losing everything of importance in their life. What normal woman wants to end up either in a whorehouse or in a convent? Although Diderot would say there's not much difference between the two."

Catherine was looking at Zénobe as if he had descended from the heavens like Zeus disguised as a swan.

"*Monsieur,*" she said. "*Monsieur...*" She chuckled as she spoke, giving her speech a musical expression, like a chromatic scale becoming acute towards the end. "*Monsieur...* You startle me. I must tell you, indeed, the truth behind my choice of subject for our first conversation. You are much too intelligent, and I am not accustomed to this. I am not usually surrounded by men of this kind."

Zénobe became suspicious of, and not a little unnerved by, her use of the phrase "of this kind" to which he dared not respond. He did, however, display gratitude for her compliment with a bow of his head.

She continued. "I have friends, and favorites, with whom I am intimate, but they don't speak to me of literature as you do. Even Diderot, that beautiful soul, he and I would spend hours speaking about all sorts of subjects, those found in society, and those discussed in the parallel universe known as literature. But even he was a bit obtuse when discussing subjects that had much appeal to me. I suspect he did not want to offend my regal honor, but I assure you, I was never offended. I say, thoughts are too precious to waste. If you can coax a thought out of the mind by well-chosen words, then it cannot be obstructed; it must come out into the light. You tell me that female virginity is a fallacy created by men to further subjugate women, I agree... I agree, wholeheartedly! Along with this great feeling that I get from you, the joy of effective intercourse, is the realization that this thought you expressed was but inchoate in my mind, that I had not exercised it enough to verbalize it, to complete it. Before, it was a mere shadow, something else in a woman's arsenal in order to flail against men. Now, I possess it; I can use it to accuse men directly of their subjugation of women."

Zénobe, who did not think that his reading of Fielding was an interpretation too outrageous or far-flung from the reality of the text, did not therefore believe that he deserved these accolades from the queen. Perhaps the men with whom she was used to dealing were bereft of good, solid ideas when reading literature. Perhaps they had never come across Aristotle's *On Interpretation*. It is true that Catherine was surrounded mainly by military men, and Zénobe believed that soldiers always had other interests at heart, and other talents that corresponded to those interests. Carpenters would have another set of interests and talents, as would musicians. Would a hussar have the patience to read a novel the length of *Joseph Andrews* and then care to interpret the author's intentions? He did not think it possible. Zénobe knew his way around a book, and what he had just said may or may not have been true, but it was his sincere interpretation of the author's intentions. Perhaps he was imposing a horrendous fallacy against an innocent, God-fearing author. Nevertheless, Zénobe felt things when he read books. He intuited things based on the way that writers used their language. He had learned sarcasm and irony from the best there ever was, Voltaire, and even though the subjects discussed by that great man, and by other great men, were steeped in comedic banter and lexicological playfulness, the subjects at their core were deadly serious. Fielding's irony was perhaps not a hammer to be used to hit the reader over the head, yet it was gradual, subtle, and in the end, as potent as Voltaire's more muscular brand. Zénobe Bosquet loved Joseph Andrews, saw him as a comrade, a brother, a lover.

Catherine had continued in her perusals. "You are intelligent enough to perhaps realize why I had brought up the subject of this English novel in the first place. I wanted to throw at you a peculiar story of a young man who refuses to abandon the virtue of chastity, and spends the whole novel fighting to retain control over his virtue. Depending on how you reacted to the story, I would model my subsequent behavior on how best to seduce you. So you see, I had ulterior motives in discussing literature with you."

Zénobe was not surprised, although he had not seen this particular literary-based tactic coming. He thought that eventually Catherine would just make a physical advance towards him. He thought her more direct, more unequivocal. She was used to being queen.

"You are not the first to attempt to do this by using literature," was the first thing that he thought of saying.

"No? Who, then, and in what context?"

"The poet Ronsard, who invites one of his lady admirers to think of how in the future she will be admired and lauded, if only in the present she gives in to him and accepts to be known as his lover. This may perhaps be true, but in the end, I think, they will have used each other in a deplorable manner: he will have used her for his own pleasure in the present, leaving her payment for some future moment; she would have used him to provide more fodder for his unseemly poetry, and to gain for herself the reflected glory of a revered poet."

"I believe I know the poem. Is it one of the sonnets for Hélène?"

"*Oui, madame. La pauvre Hélène.*"

They both burst out in laughter. Poor Helen was a dolt if she believed Ronsard's entreaties couched ever so seductively in stunningly beautiful rhyming alexandrine couplets.

In a preemptive attempt to thwart a seduction on her part, Zénobe said to Catherine, "*Madame,* you do not have to seduce me. I am interested in your mind. That is so much more fulfilling, lasting, satisfying."

"In my mind? You are interested in my mind, you say? You are not interested in any of this?" She indicated with an abrupt sweep of both arms the well-appointed salon, the magnificent palace, the fantastic capital of Saint Petersburg.

"Are you intimating that ease and luxury are mine for the asking but only through you? I hope you are not disappointed, Your Imperial Highness, but a lot of this is duplicated, to a lesser degree, in Potsdam, in Versailles, in London—"

"God's thunderbolt!" she proclaimed. "Everybody else wants to live in the lap of luxury and they clamor for mementos of my friendship, little presents to serve as testimony of my gratitude, jewelled portraits of the empress, little dachas in the countryside, with accompanying serfs."

"I would gladly accept a portrait of the empress, but without the jewels."

"I don't believe it. Even *madame* Denis got a portrait of myself, surrounded by a hundred diamonds."

"But in return, you received the library of a great, wise man."

"Well, that cost me thirty thousand rubles."

Zénobe whistled his admiration.

Catherine's regal tone descended to the dimensions of the sofa on which they were seated. "You are not interested in this?" Her gesture indicated herself, from neck to thigh.

"*Madame*, you are beautiful; you are majestic; you are a woman whose charms are heavenly and legendary. How can a lowly plebeian like me ever be so bold as to risk the audacity to yearn for you even from afar?"

"Well, who said anything about it being from afar? At least you're a step above Joseph Andrews who claims not to understand his lady mistress's advances. *Monsieur*, you do yourself a disfavor. Are you not then the bastard son of the King of Sardinia and Duke of Savoy? Even a bastard son maintains a modicum of the nobility of his patrician father. That family's pedigree goes back even farther than my own family's."

"*Madame*, that I am the bastard son of a sovereign is but a rumor—"

"And a rumor that I have chosen to believe, *monsieur*. Moreover, your bearing, your education, your comportment, even your stance, *monsieur*, are worthy of the highest echelons of the aristocracy. Do not place limits on yourself, for you are no plebeian."

Zénobe was readying his response when the Empress raised a hand graciously in the air and in the same sweep of poise and finesse brought it back down to pick up a tiny crystal bell. It rang in a barely audible tinkle and noiselessly from several doors appeared ladies-in-waiting carrying pastries and fanciful victuals arranged artistically on silver salvers. Champagne was brought, flutes filled, silk napkins laid gently on laps. The curtains were drawn, candles were lit, the fire in the sumptuous fireplace was stoked.

In a few minutes, the ladies had disappeared again, and Catherine the Empress breathed a long and dramatic sigh. Zénobe remained quiet and motionless, trying to interpret it as being either an exhale of pique or a shuddering moan of vanquished lust. He could remember nothing in Aristotle that would help him with that analysis.

Late at night when he had finally gone to bed, after continued scrutiny of the Empress's enunciations and expressions and gestures, Zénobe decided that she had acted like a proper lady, but that she had simply deferred any more talk—or action—about seduction to a later date. He could read in her eyes an emotion, a desire, an intent to know him more intimately. She could be coy, deferential, playful as a girl, but there remained on her brow the weight of the Russian crown even when she was not wearing it. It was a look in her eyes, an angle of the head, an assertiveness in the corners of her mouth as she smiled, a tone in her laughter, no less mirthful for it. He was in the presence of a mature queen, a handsome woman with an intelligent mind. He decided that, since Her Imperial Majesty requested his presence for afternoon tea and conversation, he would not countermand their mutual pleasure at these encounters.

Having learned from Diderot's unintentional blunders of touching the royal personage, Zénobe decided that in the future he would never even reach for her. Their mutual philosophical friend had confused Her Royal Highness's keen interest and curious inquiries for intimate cordiality, and had poked an emphatic finger several times to her thigh in order to punctuate his thoughts, leaving bruises on her skin and apprehension in her inquisitiveness. As the days wore on, the number of her questions directed to the French sage diminished and she had to place a table between them. Diderot, poor thing, noticed, but the enthusiasm of his perorations to her never flagged, never wavered. He was conspicuously a philosopher to the very end of their discussions. He had kept up his end of the bargain. Zénobe, too, wanted to focus his meetings with Catherine on the intellectual, but more passively allowed her to change the subject at whim. He felt that she was testing him, waiting for him to decide that it would be a mutual diversion to participate in a more romantic liaison. To Zénobe, it would be more like a sordid entanglement. He had the Polignac tryst to remind him: with Marie Antoinette's favorite lady-in-waiting taking charge of their amorous fling, he had felt used, sullied, and when coin, along with chocolates, were thrown in to complete the bargain, humiliated. But perhaps, Zénobe thought, just perhaps, he was thinking like a virgin who wants to hold on to her virtue. The only difference was that his virtue was his love for André. Maybe Wagnière's persuasive appeals to his sense of morality were finally reaching fruition. Nobody likes to be thought of as a whore, and becoming lover to the world's most powerful and wealthy woman would escalate this quandary of whoredom to new and lofty heights.

As he heard Wagnière lightly snoring in the bed across the room, Zénobe could already hear his admonitions about being unfaithful, once again, to André. His love and appreciation for Wagnière at this moment knew no bounds. In return, he decided that he would do his utmost not to tumble into bed with the Empress of all the Russias. As he thought of his efforts to keep his virtue, he had to laugh. He recognized his proximity to Joseph Andrews who in the pages of a fiction had to fight through schemes and ploys, through traps and ruses, in order to hold on to his chastity. Zénobe no longer had his chastity to hold on to, but constancy and fidelity to André certainly were virtues to which he could aspire. With these positive thoughts, he fell asleep thinking of André on his farm, leading a simple life on the soft, green, rolling hills of Normandy, far from the intricacies and pitfalls of congress with omnipotent monarchs.

An Empress Impressed

O ne of the reasons why Catherine had more time on her hands and could arrange to see Zénobe every afternoon was that the latest of her favorites, Ivan Nicolaïevich Rimsky-Korsakov, was out of royal favor and on his way out of his royal apartments. The previous favorite, Simeon Gafrilovich Zorich, had not passed muster because of the severe paucity of ideas in his head and his inability to react to the ideas of others. Very handsome he had been, and a courageous warrior when fighting the Turks, but Nature had endowed him with a meager mind, and his education had not extended its elasticity. Now, his successor, Rimsky-Korsakov had fast lost his luster in spite of his own smoldering good looks, even though he initially exhibited a lot more: a musical talent.[116] He was an excellent violinist, and he had a lovely tenor voice. However, one could listen to the same Mozart pieces for only a few times before one had them memorized. He even made the same movements at the same places: a toss of the head at the end of a *pizzicato* passage; a deep sigh during a *ralenti*; looking towards the ceiling during a particularly mournful *legato*. Catherine laughingly explained to Zénobe the fiasco with the books Rimsky-Korsakov had ordered for the library in the rooms that she had given him: the elated bookseller filled the library with stunningly beautiful, thick, leather-bound books, that were all commentaries of the Bible, in the German language, and that he had not been able to unload previously. When Catherine interrogated the bookseller about these useless books, the sheepish merchant answered that the only instructions he had received from *Gospodin* Rimsky-Korsakov was to bring in tall books for the bottom shelves, medium-sized books for the middle shelves, and smaller books for the top shelves. "That's Ivan in a nutshell: gorgeous to look at, but eminently unusable longrun. Shortrun, he certainly was superlative, like a well-decorated piece of meringue, sweet and tasty, but not very nourishing."

Zénobe was no idiot: He knew that Catherine was looking at him as the wolf looks at the lamb. This is why he always made sure that he had enough themes in his memory that he would be able to discuss at length with the Empress during their afternoons together. Two hours was not very long, so this was easy to do. If he could flit from theme to theme, and keep Her Imperial Highness alert and eager to talk, any thought about the predator pouncing to claim its next meal was postponed, until the time was up and Catherine had to get herself ready for supper, to which Wagnière and Zénobe were never invited in view of their foreignness. (Diderot had never been invited, either.)

---

116   This is not the famous Russian composer of the Nineteenth century, Nikolai Andreïevich Rimsky-Korsakov (1844-1908), but rather a minor courtier who dabbled in music (1754-1831).

Zénobe had had enough experiences with aristocrats, his superiors, who thought nothing of incorporating him into their sphere of possessions. Nobles always thought that they owned the plebeians. Neither la Polignac nor Thibouville had ever said 'please' to him, and Villette was forever caressing and fondling him whenever they were in the same room together. What kind of behavior was that? Am I not master of my own body? Apparently not, according to the aristos. They felt free to procure for themselves the bodies of their inferiors, almost as if they thought that the lowlies would want nothing more than to be taken into their possession. How was that possible? It is true that for centuries the lord of the manor had absolute rights to the body of his newly-married peasant girls. It was for one night only, but it was a very important night, the wedding night. Voltaire had written a play about this, *Le Droit du seigneur,* in 1761, which meant that some aristocrats were, as late as that, unwilling to let go of this particular aristocratic perquisite. Perhaps it was hoped, by the nobleman himself who lusted after his peasant girl, that any child born of this fornication would be his, and not that of the peasant groom. Peasant girls were not the only ones to be molested, however. Peasant boys frequently became noble ladies' toys. Zénobe vowed that his body would not be used in such a humiliating way. The distance between him and an Imperial Queen was vast to an extreme, but he knew the worth of his self-possession, in the literal sense of the term, and he wished to keep himself to himself. He did not wish to be annexed by a tyrant who only thought of him as a foregone conclusion. He had the right to say no. He had convinced the *marquis* de Thibouville of the errors of his outmoded ways, and Catherine would have to follow suit.

He realized that his line of reasoning took precedence over Wagnière's protestations on the necessity of remaining faithful to André. But with one mode of behavior, he solved two problems. This particular afternoon, his third one alone with Catherine, he kept the conversation going with no flagging in either subject matter or energy. Catherine was enthralled, both by the breadth of Zénobe's knowledge and by his stamina. Here was the preceptor she never had, that she wished she had had. She would have learned so much, as a child, instead of being kept in ignorance, superstition, stagnation, and submission. 'Duty' was a horrible word for her, as was 'tradition.' She wanted to raise the lot, as well as the expectations and ambitions, of women. She had the chance to voice her opinion when Zénobe brought up the subject of women poets and novelists.

"Russian women," she said, "should be the intellectual equals of French women. Why shouldn't they be?"

"The same with German women," answered Zénobe who had not forgotten that Catherine was from Anhalt-Zerbst.

"I inaugurated a new method for the education of young women years ago, and so far it seems to be working."

"Yes, I have heard of this. Not only did you discard Rousseau's ideas of educating young ladies, you went so much further than any other pedagogical standards. I congratulate you, and I beseech you to continue this work with other women who might not quite belong to the nobility."

"Now you're sounding just like Diderot. Philosophers are impatient, this I know, and that is why society needs enlightened rulers who have the patience, and who accept the realities of the battleground. You would have me educate plebeian women, what, even before I educated plebeian men? You know very well how the men would react to their women being more educated than they. You've seen it for yourself with Molière. Even he, educated as he was, could not manage to garner much enthusiasm for learned ladies. Twice he made fun of those women who wanted simply to have access to learning,[117][118] but the edification of women is only possible when the men are so much better educated that they feel no threat from intellectual women. Diderot would have me change Russian society in a matter of weeks; I knew that what he proposed was a task that needed to be prolonged over the decades, if not centuries. Please, do not jump to any conclusions. I appreciate your concern for women. Would that all men share your opinions. But men, especially Russian men, are not capable of it. Russian women, too, are not ready to be liberated."

"At the very least, men need to accept the idea of philandering wives as much as they are guilty of adultery, in order to render the two sexes equal."

"That will never happen, so long as men consider women their property, not to be shared with anybody else."

"That is exactly my point. Women are not the slaves of men. Why should one sex be considered a possession, like goods and chattels? A couple should be two people united by mutual attachment, with no coercion, no duress, just two separate and inviolable psyches each harboring an individual volition that alone accepts the partnership. That, to me, is the ideal relationship."

"Well, young man, you would be excluding all aristocratic marriages for they are almost without exception beholden to property, status, money, or ambition, in different combinations and sometimes all four at the same time."

"As much under an obligation as your own marriage was, in order to grant the Russian royal line a geographic influence to maintain the peace between two heretofore warring factions. Austria giving Marie Antoinette to Louis XVI was a parallel, if not identical, alliance. You, *madame*, in all of your impressive royalty, were but a mere pawn for the vagaries of history."

"At least Marie Antoinette and Louis XVI found a modicum of nuptial happiness."

"I would call it mutual bovine contentment."

Catherine let out a yelp of startled disapprobation. "No wonder your father had you imprisoned!"

Zénobe could only remain silent. He had already made his peace with the rumor that he was the scion of a sovereign.

"But you know, you're not the only son whose father had him imprisoned."

"Indeed not! Mirabeau is at this very moment languishing at the Vincennes dungeon, the same one where Diderot spent some time. His father is in no hurry to have him liberated; he thinks that prison will make him more amenable to paternal counsel.[119]

---

117   In both of his wildly successful plays, *Les Précieuses ridicules (The Affected Young Ladies)* and *Les Femmes savantes (The Learned Women)*, Molière tried to discredit uppity women whose pretentious ambitions made them imagine that they were the intellectual equals of men, that they could attend classes at the University.

118   [From the author] Please, *Herr* Ralph! You make it sound as if you and I both agree with Molière's views on women. On purpose he created ridiculous woman characters who seriously lacked intellectual prowess. The most clear-headed of them all, Henriette, rises to the reactionary ambition of being a wife and mother. Why did it take so long to reach the likes of *madame* Gabrielle Émilie Le Tonnelier de Breteuil, *marquise* du Châtelet, mathematician and the love of Voltaire's life, or *mademoiselle* Jeanne Julie Éléonore de Lespinasse, *salonnière* and the love of d'Alembert's life?

119   Gabriel Honoré de Riquetti, *comte* de Mirabeau, spent a total of three years in the castle-prison of Vincennes, from 1777 to 1780. Diderot had been a tenant for several months in 1749. The *marquis* de Sade will be incarcerated there from 1777 to 1784, during which time he meets Mirabeau, but they develop a mutual dislike of each other.

All he's doing is creating a son who is more obdurate, more passionate, more resolved to bring liberty to all people. His father is teaching his son how to be a better revolutionary."

"And you?" asked a thoughtful Empress. "Who taught you to be a revolutionary?"

Zénobe smiled. "I am not sure that I am a… revolutionary. Was Voltaire one? Is Diderot? Condorcet? All I have ever done is to attempt to follow in the footsteps of those who hunger for the truth, who wish to destroy the myriads of ways humanity has devised to enslave one another, to bring justice, true universal justice, and liberty to the downtrodden, to the excluded, and these include women!"

Catherine could only smile and acquiesce. These were her dreams, too. Yet she did not consider herself a revolutionary. 'Revolutionary' was a word, then, used by others, to describe those who wished to overturn the status quo of injustice and injury to the powerless. She looked at Zénobe, as one firebrand to another, and took his hand and held it next to her heart. There were no sexual overtures in the movement, and Zénobe identified it for what it was: an acknowledgment that they were one of a kind, each in his and her own way, moving through history with a conscience to do good, and to rectify what evil plotted in the world.

With a wink and an impish smile, he whispered to her, *"Écrasons l'Infâme!"*

An Expensive Gift

As soon as Zénobe sat down to afternoon tea he noticed a small box placed on his side of the table, in front of the dish of biscuits. Catherine was speaking of the exploration of the remote corners of the earth that was going on by persons of note from different countries, such as Captains Bougainville and Cook, and she was voicing an opinion that Russian explorers should also be sent out to search for new lands and new civilizations, although she doubted there were any big land masses left to discover. Most of the new terrain being found and colonized were island archipelagos or, worse, single islands surrounded by thousands of miles of sea.

"It's a shame there's nothing left!" she said miserably, then sighed and popped a whole biscuit into her mouth during the top part of the sigh.

Zénobe consoled her by mentioning that the lands being discovered were certainly worthy, that the new people to be found there had such dissimilar cultures that they were teaching Europeans of other ways to live and worship, and that, since these new people were not talked about in the Bible, they offered proof that the writers of the Bible had certainly been limited in their scope and therefore should not be given the confidence to reveal universal truths. He had another thought, that world exploration was a very dangerous business and that Captain Cook had been killed by the natives in Hawaii just the previous year, but he kept that quiet. He did not wish to quell Catherine's enthusiasm about sending Russians on world explorations. It certainly went along with the desires of world domination of her predecessor, Peter I. If anything, colonization gave the world powers the excuse to export their wars to those newly discovered lands and force their inhabitants to choose sides.

In order to remain positive and a bit flippant, he said, "Imagine the lands that would be discovered in your name. But you could start closer in, by accepting England's offer to give you Minorca. It's not a new civilization, but it would give you a presence in the Mediterranean. It could serve your purpose to eventually take over Constantinople."

"How do you know of all this? Have you been talking to my diplomats?"

"Not at all, I've simply been a witness to correspondence written by people who know things. You can't be secretary to Voltaire and remain in ignorance about world affairs."

"Yes, this is true, but the secretary's role is to transcribe and send and receive letters, but then to forget what was in them. It could lead to dangerous ideas lingering inside the head of someone who cannot be trusted with them."

"I've never spoken to anybody about this, not even to Wagnière. It's not like I would have held a conversation with the *marquise* de Polignac and asked her her opinion about whether or not Catherine the Great should accept Minorca from the British in exchange for providing troops to send to America and teach a lesson to the recalcitrant colonies. Why should only the Hessians have that pleasure?"[120]

"You know the *marquise* de Polignac?" asked Catherine with genuine interest.

Zénobe's face turning a bright red told the Empress more than she had at first surmised.

Zénobe could not now look into her eyes. How stupid he had been to mention the *marquise*'s name! He should have talked about having held a conversation with Marie Antoinette who was even more inane!

"You *know* the *marquise* de Polignac. How interesting. How very clever of you. But before we turn our discussion to her, tell me this. Do you know why I didn't want to make a pact with George III over Minorca?"

After a moment's hesitation, Zénobe responded, "Because you don't trust the British?"

"Well, there's that as well, of course. That's no secret. However, in this instance, I was not even tempted by Minorca because I want the American colonies to be left alone. I have instructed my British ambassador to tell the English king to leave the colonies alone. They are gone, they have freed themselves from the British sphere of influence, they are out of George's reach. It is too late. The British bungled it. Now they must pay the price. Now they have to live with their bad decisions, going back years. America is a brand new country. I do not know if their experimentation with the creation of a government with no king will work. I doubt it will. Eventually, they will have to give themselves a new king, but an American one, not a German one. Someone who will understand what it is to be an American."

"I think it might work out for them," said Zénobe cautiously. "There's not that many of them. Democracy works well when there are fewer people."

"Yes, of course, especially when you ignore half the country!" was the regal rejoinder.

"Who do you mean, the slaves?"

"The women, *mon bon ami*, the women! Although let it be known that nothing is different in distant America: their women are also slaves! Slaves to men!"

Zénobe abandoned the field of discussion to Catherine, more for his blunder of having mentioned the Polignac woman than anything else. In the field of woman's emancipation, Catherine knew what she was talking about. She was a woman who ultimately could not be kept down by her husband, who managed to turn the situation around and completely subjugate him. Truth be told, Peter III hadn't been very smart.

Eventually the question that Zénobe had been dreading finally came around.

"So, tell me, *mon bonhomme*, how you know the *marquise* de Polignac, Marie Antoinette's favorite lady-in-waiting. Is she as beautiful as they say she is?"

"She was among the first guests to welcome Voltaire back into Paris. Her beauty rests in her eyes; they are of a color rarely seen."

"But clearly Marie Antoinette and Louis didn't want Voltaire in Paris. Why would they send *madame* de Polignac to welcome him?"

"The tide was too strong, *madame*. Do you know that hundreds upon hundreds of well-wishers showed up to see Voltaire, to touch the man, to touch his hem, to acclaim him and adore him? Had the king given the order to have Voltaire sent back to Ferney,

---

120   All this is true. England asked Catherine to send thousands of troops to America to help out in their imperialist cause but she politely declined. She might have need of those very same troops to send to Turkey! Think of the possible outcome of the Revolutionary War had the Russians joined the Hessians against the Americans and the French!

His Majesty would have been a laughing stock. How can you keep the sun from rising? How can you keep the winds from blowing? The French king did, however, refuse to see him, and he ordered his court not to go see his play. Marie Antoinette was the first one to disobey that order. Now that Voltaire is gone, His Majesty has prohibited anybody from putting up any of his plays for a full year. That's the extent of his power. He is petulant and petty, like a child who doesn't let anybody else play with his toys. Does he really think that people will forget Voltaire? He is truly an idiot if he thinks that. I am sure that on the first anniversary of a year and a day after Voltaire's death, many of his plays will be played on the stages of France!"

Catherine was astounded. "You called Louis XVI, a Bourbon sovereign, an idiot."

"*Madame,* I am sorry if this offends you. But how can it be termed otherwise? Was not your very own husband, Peter III, an id—"

"My child, don't you know that certain things must remain unsaid? Inside our thoughts we can have the supreme liberty to insult kings and queens, to torture our enemies with no reservation, to wish those who are against us to drop dead. But what passes through our lips, words that can be heard, overheard, whispered to others, and eventually used against us, will come back without a doubt to haunt us, and the very things we said about others will be said about us."

"My Queen," said Zénobe with intensity. "Nobody could ever say with veracity that you are a—" This time Zénobe interrupted himself. "...that you are anything but an extremely intelligent woman. They would do so at their peril, that is all I have to say."

The Empress smiled at Zénobe.

"The reviews have come in," continued Zénobe. "The appraisals have poured forth from very high echelons, and all concur that you are, that you are... of paramount intelligence. You are the equal of Voltaire, *madame.*"

"Oh, he told me frequently that I was superior to him in intelligence... and in talent!"

Zénobe became red-faced again. "Of course, you are. Your plays are magnificent."

"Oh, now we've descended into flattery and cajolery. You had a very good teacher in Voltaire. You don't need to speak this way, *monsieur* de Bosquet. I expect only sincerity from you, like I expected from *monsieur* Diderot. Sincerity is a breath of fresh air for me. I need it to live. I receive it so rarely from those around me. Understood, my handsome companion? I need you to continue being sincere, come what may. You know that I will never punish you for your, shall we say, frequent indiscretions. I know you are young, although a full-grown man! But one of the things I love about you is your youth and purity. You've not had time to grow complacent and allow a thousand compromises to sap your spirit or harden your heart. Cynicism has found no place in your virtuous spirit to inject its resentful venom. I need your vigor and your sincerity, *monsieur* de Bosquet, so please do not disappoint me."

"I will do my best, *madame.* And thank you, for your assessment of me. It is the best compliment I have ever had from anyone."

"Ah, you have made me happy again. It is therefore time to change the subject. I am sure you've noticed that box placed next to you."

"Indeed I have, Your Majesty, but courtesy warranted that I wait until you mentioned it."

Zénobe looked down at the box, then at Catherine's impassive expression which gave him no incentive to either reach for the box or to ask her about the box. Instead he reached for his teacup and had a sip of tea.

Catherine finally had to ask, "Aren't you just a little bit curious?"

"About the tea?" asked Zénobe. "Is it from India?"

Catherine answered, "Why, I've no idea where the tea comes from. I am convinced that Russia has its own tea plantations, somewhere, in the south, I'm sure. Most probably in the south, yes. I'll have to ask to find out."

Catherine could not contain herself for one more minute.

"Aren't you curious about the box?" she asked.

"Ah," said Zénobe, as if officially recognizing the existence of the box so close to him. "Yes, *madame*, one can say that I am a bit curious about this box. It looks beautiful. May I pick it up?"

"Yes, of course. It's for you!"

Zénobe picked up the box carefully and admired its smooth, lustrous qualities. Its honey and brown swirls were a testament to nature's beauty. On one corner there was a dramatic line of light beige. He observed that on the bottom there was an imprint of a double-headed eagle, the symbol of Russian hegemony. As he brought the box closer to his eyes, his nose captured the scent emanating from the wood. Astounded, he brought the box right to his flaring nostrils and inhaled deeply and longingly. He had never experienced such an exquisite perfume.

Catherine smiled like at a child who discovers something novel. "It's cedar," she said. "Now that is Russian."

"It's a haunting fragrance," said Zénobe. "It is rich and dark and redolent of a forest, of smoke drifting from some faraway hearth, of cool air warmed by the sun, the tree enchanted by its rays, the sap in the wood energized by the life penetrating into its bark. This is the essence of an entire forest which I hold in my hand!"

Catherine was amused by Zénobe's description.

"Perhaps just of a little forest," she answered, using his last name, *bosquet*."

He smiled and continued to turn the box around admiringly.

"Aren't you tempted to open it?"

"You mean there's more to this?"

"If you thought the container itself was remarkable, wait until you see what is inside."

Zénobe carefully took the box and its lid in separate hands and pulled them apart gently.

Inside, nestled in the soft folds of red velvet, was a ring of yellow gold set with a single faceted jewel the size of his little fingernail, but much deeper and heavier. Even in the relative darkness inside the box the ghostly gemstone was emitting beams of light into Zénobe's eyes. As he removed it, it flashed radiance from its myriad of facets, gleaming with cold light but looking as if it should be hot to the touch.

Catherine could not contain herself. "It's a diamond, you see."

Zénobe could not say a word as he gazed into the very center of this micro-universe. He realized his mouth was gaping and he quickly closed it, but he thought he felt his eyes get bigger as they were infused with the shimmering sparkle of this mere stone. His only experience with anything remotely similar to this is when Candide and his valet Cacambo discover that the ground of El Dorado is covered with pebbles of precious gems and nuggets of gold. Now he could understand their attraction to rocks on the ground. He was brought back to reality by Catherine's laughter.

"You are definitely not like any man I've given a diamond to before. First of all, nobody's admired the box like you have, and when they see the ring, they emit some suitable sound of admiration before they plop the thing right around their finger. Only you have stared at the gem as if you've never seen a diamond before."

Zénobe wanted to answer that he hadn't, but felt it was more diplomatic to say, "I've never seen one so beautiful as this!" He was breathless. But then he had a thought that brought his breath back quickly and his words even faster.

"But, *ma chère dame*, this is no trinket. I fear that your generosity is a thousand times more grand than my worthiness. I fear—"

An imperial hand raised put a stop to Zénobe's speech.

"Do not finish that sentence. You risk my displeasure and you will do so at..." Her own sentence remained unfinished. "It is not polite," she continued with a less regal voice, "to risk my displeasure."

Zénobe bowed his head and said nothing.

"Here, *mon ami*, give me your hand."

She took the ring from him and placed the ring on his finger. She saw the hair on Zénobe's phalanges and the thicker hair on his wrist escaping from within his sleeve. His nails were a healthy pink and well-groomed. She held on to his warm hand and it was her turn to admire a thing of beauty.

"Look how splendid this ring looks on your hand!" she exclaimed. "Every time you look at it, you will remember your friendship with Catherine. Wherever you go, near or far, a part of me goes with you."

Even though Catherine was looking at his hand and not into his eyes, Zénobe felt a deep emotion from the words she was saying to him. She sounded sincere, and friendship with a queen sounded grand. It was because of Voltaire that Zénobe had risen enough in society to deserve the friendship of a queen. His eyes took on a sheen that reflected the light of the numerous candles in the room.

When Catherine's gaze finally left his hand, she was shocked by the beauty of Zénobe's pale blue eyes shimmering as brightly as the diamond. She herself was touched, and she responded emotion for emotion, sentiment for sentiment. They stared into each other's eyes for a long time, enjoying the quiet union of amity, of a close companionship between two people who are surprised to find a similar soul in the world, with whom they can share and feel at ease, and know that they are not alone.

A Simulated Circumstance

After four afternoons of visiting the Empress, Zénobe was beginning to tell her ladies-in-waiting apart. One of them was a countess who stood out from the others because her French was flawless. The others, like their mistress Catherine, revealed their foreignness by keeping a Germanic lilt, or a Russian tendency to pronounce the 'l' liquid and flat, or the inability to pronounce the guttural French 'r'. They all spoke French fluently, but one could spot them from across the room as linguistic infiltrators, using the French language as a proxy to their own. That is, all save for Anna Stepanovna Protasova, the Empress's first maid-of-honor and daughter of Senator Stepan Feodorovich Protasov and Anisya Nikitishna, née Orlova, and thus cousin of the Orlov brothers, favorites of Catherine.

The second or third day, when Anna Stepanovna and Zénobe were in the anteroom awaiting Catherine's arrival, Zénobe addressed the countess directly for the first time.

"You know," he said generously, "in Versailles you could stand in for an authentic French lady-in-waiting. You have no accent at all. Marie Antoinette has a German accent, and her two sisters-in-law Marie Joséphine de Savoie and Marie Thérèse de Savoie have an Italian accent. But you would fit right in with all the duchesses and countesses of the French court. You could pass for an authentic French lady."

"But am I as beautiful as your sisters?" asked Anna Stepanovna with a sly smile. Apparently she was one who believed that the two Savoy princesses and Zénobe shared the same father, Victor Amédée, *duc* de Savoie and King of Sardaigne.

Zénobe jumped to his riposte. "Indeed, milady! Absolutely, you are! Without a question. Actually… No! I must say with all veracity that you are even more beautiful. Why, just your cheekbones would shame them into submission. Besides, Marie Joséphine has a moustache."

Anna Stepanovna laughed freely with unbounded mirth, enhancing her beauty with a dimple in each lovely cheek and flashing her straight, white teeth. Catherine's arrival put a stop to their conversation.

On the fifth afternoon visit to Catherine's apartments, it was the countess alone who was waiting for him with the tea and vodka. None of the other ladies was present.

"Her Imperial Highness sends her regrets. She cannot be here today. She was brusquely called away on official business. She hopes that you do not mind if I take over the duties of hostess."

Zénobe hesitated a second too long. "Of course, I do not mind," he said. "Is Her Royal Majesty still in the palace?"

"I believe Her Royal Majesty is still in the palace. Somewhere in the palace. You know, the palace is very big! Most probably she is at her study where she grants audiences to diplomats and official people, or maybe in the Great Hall,[121] if the occasion calls for something a little more… uhm, ceremonious. She certainly is no longer in this wing, in her personal apartments. She apparently took the other ladies with her because I'm all there is. I have been left all alone, but we did not want you to be disappointed since we knew you were coming over for tea and… and… and other refreshments."

She laughed as she poured vodka into a small crystal glass.

"Her Majesty is oftentimes called away at the last minute on official obligations," she continued. "A queen's work is never done. There are always intrusions, interruptions, interventions… I believe that one of her generals arrived bearing news from Turkey. Yes, I heard that the occasion was military in nature. The Turks have not rested since their defeat and are constantly lurking around in the least likely of places! They constantly need to be observed. Russian spies are sent everywhere! They go to where the Turks go. Not a single action of the Turkish army is undertaken that Her Imperial Majesty does not find out about in a few days. She is aware of all that happens in her domains, from here east to Siberia and from here south to the Crimea. But when the generals come, it is completely haphazard. There is no way to exercise control over that. They come and go where duty sends them. But please, do not worry. I am here and shall be most happy to act on behalf of the queen as your hostess. Her Majesty trusts me enough that she frequently allows me to play hostess in her stead."[122] [123]

Zénobe was disappointed but could not let on that he was. He had organized a series of topics with which to entertain the queen. He had no idea which subjects to broach with the countess so he decided to let her chose the themes of their conversation. He did not have to wait too long because Anna Stepanovna kept up a happy prattle that touched on everything from the Turks to social etiquette to riding.

"Oh, I'm sorry, not riding. Writing."

"Yes, that's it. Writing on paper with a quill. Not riding on a horse with a… with a horse."

All Zénobe had to do was incline his head to agree or frown a bit to look questioning or doubtful. She asked questions which required only a «Oui, merci» or a «Non, merci». His longest answer in their conversation was when he said, «Je ne suis pas sûr, mademoiselle.»

When Zénobe heard a noise in the boudoir next door, Anna Stepanovna increased the speed and volume of her speech. He felt coerced to interrupt her to say, "I wonder if that is Her Highness returning?"

Anna Stepanovna leapt to the door and opened it enough to thrust her head inside.

"No, just as I thought. Nobody's there. They're all gone to the throne room."

---

121   Anna Stepanovna is referring to the Hall of Audience, officially known as St. George's Hall, the Winter Palace's main throne room.

122   Zénobe unfortunately did not know to what extent Countess Protasova functioned as her mistress's representative. History knows her as the «*éprouveuse*», or «tester» who would «try out» would-be suitors before they were delivered to Catherine. A doctor would examine the young men as well before they could be approved for the Queen.

123   [From the author] *Herr* Ralph, perhaps the reader might be interested in another historical fact. Anna Stepanovna replaced another countess, Praskovya Aleksandrovna Bruce, as official *éprouveuse*. But Countess Bruce lost her job when Catherine found her in the throes of testing the official Imperial lover Rimsky-Korsakof *after* he had been approved as royal favorite. He also lost his job. This is why Zénobe dropped into Catherine's life just at the right time, between royal favorites. Well, perhaps at the wrong time.

"Perhaps we could make our way there, if you think Her Majesty wouldn't mind."

"Oh, she would. She would. Indeed she would. Mightily! It is official business, you see. It is a general, I believe, who appeared unexpectedly. Perhaps one of her spies. This, you see, would be confidential in nature, this meeting with one of her military people. They would speak about the Turks, you know. You know the Turks? We're not at war with the Turks now, but we were until recently. And apparently they want to recuperate what was taken from them. You know, recapture it. The Crimea, for instance. Everybody wants the Crimea! They say the coast there is beautiful. That is why Her Majesty keeps an eye on the Turks. Through her generals, with spies, lots of spies. Everywhere there are spies. They come to report directly to her."

"Are the other ladies-in-waiting privy to this information?"

"No, of course not… They are not. They stay in the anteroom to the throne room. Excuse me, the Hall of Audience. They cannot hear the information that comes in. It is only for the ears of Her Imperial Highness, no one else."

Anna Stepanovna pressed her hands to her ears to dramatize the inability of the ladies-in-waiting to hear official spy reports.

She walked back to the sofa and went to the tea table.

"More tea? More vodka?" she asked.

"Oh, no, thank you. You are a marvelous hostess, and you acquit yourself superbly as proxy to her Royal Highness. I could ask for nothing more!"

Anna Stepanovna returned to the sofa they had been sharing, but this time deposited herself right next to him. Her arm touched his while she said smilingly, "But if you wanted to, would you?"

"Would I what?" he asked politely, truly out of ignorance.

"Would you ask for more, if you could?" came the reply.

"Ask for more? I would ask for more? *Mademoiselle*, I am wholly satisfied, what with this stupendous tea, this smooth intense vodka and these lovely cakes that come in all flavors and colors. If I eat anymore I will not be hungry for supper!" he said, ending in a laugh which sounded sufficiently plausible to his own ears.

The countess sighed happily. "Does this vodka not liberate your fancy?" (The word she used in French was «*fantaisie*».)

"My fancy? I… I suppose my fancy… my fancy… is satisfied with these lovely refreshments. I certainly could ask for nothing more, *mademoiselle*. You have attended to everything superbly."

Zénobe denoted the tea table with everything on it and used the inertial energy of the movement of his arm to gain six inches of distance between him and the countess.

She lost no time in closing the gap again. Now Zénobe was all the way at the end of the sofa with nowhere else to go.

"I'm implying…" she continued, "that if you were to think of something else that I might provide you with…" With these words there was an accompanying gesture of her dainty manicured hand which landed gracefully on Zénobe's knee. "Whatever your imagination can come up with, not necessarily a tidbit for eating, but perhaps just as delicious…" Anna Stepanovna's face was suddenly within inches of his own. "A delicious kiss, for instance? A kiss for dessert?"

Her other hand came up to his face and caressed his cheek. Zénobe felt her warm breath on his lips and before he knew it she was kissing him with a dainty little tongue attempting to part his lips.

Instead of closing his eyes, Zénobe opened them wide with astonishment. He had already experienced something similar to this with *madame* de Polignac in the streets of Paris and he certainly did not need the same lesson once again. The novelty of sex with a woman had worn off, and he did not want to partake of what was sure to follow. Moreover, he was convinced that there was somebody in the next room. Perhaps he and Anna Stepanovna were being observed. Perhaps it was the queen herself who was doing the observing. Did not the countess say that Catherine sent her spies everywhere? Well, why not here in her own private rooms? Zénobe's mind soared above and beyond this thorough kiss he was receiving. He could not keep from thinking that this was a part of the scheme of seduction that Catherine had been attempting since the second day they had met. Since the queen herself had not been successful, she had sent a delegate to simulate a regal seduction. It was an attempt to garner vicarious knowledge, a sort of knowing through effigy, seeking useful material in an indirect, virtual fashion. He was the subject being studied and tested, like a bug under a magnifying glass.

Zénobe did not play his part well in this play. Out of courtesy, he could not spit out the countess's tongue away from his mouth, but he arched his back away from her as much as possible and held his palms facing out to her in a mute request for her to stop what she was doing. It did not take her long to realize that this young man did not want to perform the role she was foisting onto him. She was immediately miffed, then mortified, then offended, and Zénobe saw all these emotions playing about her face in quick succession. He felt he had to do the courteous thing, as a foreigner who was enjoying the hospitality of the monarch, and said, with all the combined seriousness, sincerity, and tenderness that he could muster, "*Ma belle dame*, the respect and esteem in which I hold you precludes any act of concupiscence with you. Please do not mistake my reticence: you are indeed beautiful, as I said before, you are radiantly appealing, intoxicating, even, but unfortunately I do not love you or covet you in a carnal way. You are the paragon of beauty that must be admired from afar, esteemed for your loveliness and grace. To take you physically would be to sully you and dishonor your virtue. I cannot do it, but must behave towards you with rectitude and probity."

Zénobe thought that Joseph Andrews himself could not have expressed it better.

Anna Stepanovna seemed to be mollified, yet disappointment was written liberally all over her face. She reviewed the scene of her failed seduction with dismay, refusing all the while to look at her recalcitrant partner in the eyes. With a toss of her head and an impulsive lunge lacking in grace and refinement, she reached over his knees to the tea table, grabbed a cake with her fingers and stuffed it into her mouth. A moustache of powdered sugar appeared over her upper lip, and when some of the *crème fraîche* filling overflowed from her lips she licked it back up with her tongue helped along with her sticky fingers.

Not sure of what to do, Zénobe, in order to accompany the countess, also picked up one of the cakes and took a nibble, but in a more fastidious manner. He was in awe of this woman, could admire her courage, and sympathized with her discomfiture. Women of her class probably never met with such a lack of success. He smiled at her with a mixture of sympathy and what he felt to be gratitude, for having tried to extend the queen's hospitality. But the countess continued to avoid his gaze and instead took her ire out on the pastries.

Absconding to the Summer Palace

After the failed seduction, Catherine the Great decided to whisk Zénobe away from society, away from the court at the Winter Palace, and away even from his fellow librarian Wagnière, whom she suspected as having sway over the lad. She knew that the morality of protestants was of an immovable rectitude with no room for minor exceptions. God! They even thought that thinking about sinning was a sin! If that were true, why, she would be a constant sinner!

But before she could get away from Saint Petersburg, she had to tend to the business of politics and international diplomacy and confrontation with the muslims from Turkey. War was coming; it was unavoidable. Yet, a monarch did not have to be in a hurry to confront it. It would come all on its own. She did not see the need to hasten its inevitability. Moreover, she had other affairs of state to supervise, and she wanted the docket free and clear for a few days. She wanted to take one of Voltaire's librarians to the imperial country estate of Tsarskoe Selo where the philosopher's books had been deposited. They would retrieve them and eventually put them up on the shelves of her private study in the Oval Room of the Winter Palace where they would be more accessible.

It was convenient that Wagnière was not up to the task. By now, he was walking everywhere by himself, although he still complained of fatigue and aches in his joints. This was not the librarian that Catherine wished to isolate from humanity. She had decided that her next court favorite would be Zénobe de Bosquet, of Haute Savoie, Turin and Sardinia. She was convinced that he would make a splendid favorite. She kept thinking of the Russian word for "preferred man": временщик (pronounced 'vryemyenshtchik'). Its translation was more like "man of the hour" and she hoped he would like to remain in Saint Petersburg indefinitely in the role of imperial court escort, permanent timely person. It was still only a hope, for he was proving to be a tough nut to crack. Why had he not been in her bed by the second day? Anna Stepanovna had not fared any better. Catherine felt that a few days of isolation under her charming influence would have this wild bird eating out of her hand.

They left on their excursion on a clear, sunny, and cold morning, leaving the sprawling, white and muted city behind them. It was a ride that took only a couple of hours, depending on the depth of the snow. Today, it was deep. On the way, Catherine spoke of her love of books. She had spent her years as a lonely princess reading—devouring—Locke, Voltaire, Diderot, Rousseau, all alone in her room, with no one to share the philosophers' ideas. Her husband, the future tsar Peter III, dull and vacuous, went out of his way to shun her. He cared only for the society of sycophant friends who dominated him through flattery and used him to enrich themselves and gain power, and who used gossip against his foreign-born wife. They whispered in his ear: what is the use of a tsarina who reads books? There is something wicked and twisted and bizarre about her. She prefers to stay alone in her room. They said that this unnatural wife was a recluse, a misanthrope, who spent her days plotting against her husband and incubating untoward aspirations of her own. They knew with certainty that she was a danger to him, for she was an upstart woman with a head full of odd ideas, foreign ideas, treacherous ideas, ideas which would bring about his downfall and the subversion of everything that was dear to Russian hearts. She had to be eliminated. Peter planned to put her permanently in a nunnery.

It was precisely that, when Peter did become tsar after the death of the empress Elizabeth, when he began preparations to have her locked up in a convent, that a desperate Catherine decided that she needed to take control of her life. It was the easiest coup she had ever encountered in her history books, although not deprived completely of danger or fear. She had friends, many friends who disliked Peter, who identified Peter as someone easily duped by those who wished to wield influence. But Peter's pro-Prussian stance, his friendship with Frederick II and his antipathy for the Russian Orthodox Church, made him many enemies who easily came to the aid of Catherine during her hour of need. The deed was done in a few days, Catherine rose to the position of imperial power, and her husband's descended to utter impotence. In a week he was dead, overindulgently murdered by some of Catherine's truest, most devoted, friends, the Orlov brothers, of whom one, Gregory, had been her lover for years and had even fathered her child. These last details Catherine kept secret from Zénobe.

Catherine had become Empress of Russia as an act of defiance against her husband, an attempt of independence and self-preservation. Peter had been too stupid to rule. She could orchestrate a much better enterprise, with enlightened ideas behind her. With the aid of the philosophers who published books, she had hopes and faith that her administration would effectuate the changes that Russia needed to undergo in order to become a nation worthy of the first category. It was of course daunting to dare to change a land still immersed in feudal stagnation and run by uneducated—even illiterate—aristocrats who could not live their lives without serfs. Russian society was still overseen by Orthodox clerics who were also staunchly opposed to any change whatsoever. Relieving them of their possessions had been one of the best things Catherine ever did. Were not the ecclesiastics descendants of Jesus? Were they not supposed to mimic him in his directive to embrace poverty? Well, she had an idea that would help them to do just that. Forthwith church properties became part of the state.

It was good to be empress. She commanded, and changes occurred. She commanded that torture cease in the interrogation of alleged criminals. She had read her Beccaria and her Montesquieu. Torture did not work. Those who were tortured, anxious for the pain to stop, would say whatever the clergy wanted to hear, and would confess even to crimes of which they had not been accused. But the followers of Christ were too inculcated in medieval ways of thinking; they would have kept torturing until the end of days. That was another of her best moves for progress. She was proud of that one. She had the proof in her books, her treasured books, which opened her mind and made her see. Her Russian subjects were children who needed to be educated, but children often do not see the benefits of such education. Catherine's work was still not done. "Would it ever?" she asked Zénobe rhetorically.

During her tutelage as princess and accompanying her in her progress as she became queen, there was an emissary of the Enlightenment whose ideas came sailing in right through her door, in the shape of even more books. Not just any books they were, but books that were banned and burned elsewhere in Europe. But now these books from her favorite philosopher, Voltaire, were here! These were his own books whose margins he had filled with his ideas and reactions to what he was reading. Catherine thanked Zénobe a hundred times for having protected Voltaire's library during their trajectory through dangerous terrain. Zénobe couldn't help but emphasize the danger, exaggerate the ferocity of the ruffians who had stopped Wagnière and him on the road outside Bassum, and paint the vivid emotions they had felt during the storm that tossed their boat upon the sea. Voltaire's books could have been stolen by marauders, burned in a pyre or thrown down a ravine, confiscated by Frederick, or sunk to the bottom of the sea! The empress shut her eyes and shuddered.

For Catherine, Zénobe was that bright and courageous intellect who had brought her these precious books, along with the universal knowledge encased within their pages. As Zénobe spoke, Catherine thought that he himself was like a richly-bound book, telling stories and conveying concepts and theories too exciting to acknowledge in solitude. This is why she desired to keep him close to her so that she could enjoy discourse with him, while sipping her afternoon tea, and savor explosive new ideas with him. Savor him, as well, for he was easy on the eyes, virile and assertive, and he had called Voltaire his friend. What more could an empress want? But the answer to this question she kept guardedly from him. All Zénobe knew was that they would be arriving at Tsarskoe Selo in a few minutes where they would spend the day gathering the crates of books of the Voltarian library and placing them within easy reach of workers who would then load them up in a wagon for the trip back to Saint Petersburg the following day. As far as Zénobe knew, they would be spending only one night at the summer estate. This is what he had told Wagnière.

But as soon as they arrived at the palace, instead of going directly to where the books were being housed, his hostess took him on a tour of the palace to see the apartments that she had appropriated for herself. No one accompanied them. As they passed from room to room, Zénobe realized that the library was going to have to wait. The tour started in the White Dining Room, with its walls covered with white silk and ornamented with wooden gilt carvings modeled in the rococo style. Its furniture was gilt in the style of Louis XVI and was also covered with white silk. Tall mirrors along the wall were raised on slabs of gray marble. Near a window stood a bronze group denoting the rape of the Sabines. On tables were artistically arranged a series of Japanese and Chinese porcelain of the XVI and XVII centuries. At the end of the room against the wall stood two magnificent chests of drawers and a spectacular desk between them. Two inscriptions had been carved into the chests: on the left one, "The laws of the Great Empress Catherine II" and on the right one, "For the prosperity of all loyal subjects."

Catherine waited until Zénobe was sufficiently impressed before they left the White Dining Room.

The room adjacent was the Amber Room with its walls covered entirely in amber, a gift from the Prussian king Frederick William I to Peter the Great, who had not known what to do with such a magnificent treasure. It was Peter's daughter, the Empress Elizabeth, who had used it to create this magnificent room. Inserted into the plain amber walls were four mosaic pictures in rich frames of carved amber, depicting allegories of the five human senses. To lighten the room, the furniture was painted white and covered in yellow silk. Near the windows standing like sentinels were a series of vitrines holding small amber bibelots, snuff boxes, caskets, chess-men, and the like. A huge clock ornamented a wall, made by Causard of Paris of bronze and representing a tree with branches, leaves, and flowers in porcelain. Zénobe's mouth was agape and Catherine smiled.

The following room was the Portrait Room; the one after that, the Green Room with Pillars; then the Crimson Room with Pillars; followed by the Pink Drawing Room; then, after the Big Hall, another set of rooms: the First Antechamber, the Third Antechamber, the Arabesque Room, the Lyon Room (called thusly for the yellow brocade from Lyon that covered the walls), the Chinese Hall, the Light-Blue Study, the Glass Study, the Glass Loggia, Catherine's Dressing Room, the Passage Room, the Waiting-Women's Room, Catherine's Marble Bath, then, at last, Catherine's Boudoir.

But the tour did not end there. On the other side of Catherine's Boudoir, began another series of rooms put to her use: the Agate Room, the First Study, the Round Dressing-Room (which was really oval), the Jasper Study, after which they returned anew to the Big Hall (Zénobe did not know how), then the Cupola Room, and—finally!— Catherine's Library. Zénobe espied the crates of Voltaire's library strewn in a corner, one of them open and its books dispersed onto the nearest shelves.

But they could not linger in the library for by that time it was way past dinnertime. Their afternoon meal was laid out in the Grotto, also known as the Morning Hall, a few minutes' walk behind the palace on the other side of Catherine's private gardens. It was still called the Grotto because Elizabeth had adorned the walls with 210,000 large shells and seventeen and a half poods of smaller ones.[124] As soon as she could, Catherine had had the shells pulled down from the walls and a sober design of squares and rectangles put up instead. Sometimes the Grotto was also called the Hall of Antiques because that is where Catherine decided to place her growing collection of art and statuary. Indeed, the first statue that greeted Zénobe as they walked into the hall was Houdon's statue of the seated Voltaire, naked but for a Grecian robe draping his body in a negligent fashion. Zénobe's eyes teared up and this was too much for Catherine. She grabbed the boy and in her grief embraced him tightly.

"I feel that he is still in the world," she said.

"He is," was Zénobe's response. "His influence was so vast, so ubiquitous. He will remain among us forever."

"Indeed he will, *mon ami*, indeed he will."

With that, they sat down to dinner, served by only two liveried footmen, who vanished as soon as everything was placed on the table at once, including a dessert of fruit compote slathered in *crème fraîche*. The silence was total and Zénobe could hear the sound of their chewing. After so much time at the Winter Palace, the silence was also eerie surrounded as they were by hundreds of statues and hundreds of portraits on the walls. Zénobe felt that they were not alone. They were being watched by the unblinking eyes of a multitude of historical luminaries who, by their very presence, made Zénobe curtail his conversation to polite niceties and formal platitudes. It was of no matter, because Catherine kept talking about the changes and restorations being made to Tsarskoe

124 A pood was a unit of mass equal to 40 funt, the Russian pound. The pood is approximately the equivalent of 16.38 kilograms, or 36.11 pounds. There were thus 286.65 kg, or 632 pounds of small shells.

Selo, including her efforts to keep costs down. Her predecessor Elizabeth had been careless about the quality of construction and a major part of the work entailed taking down and replacing structural components before any embellishments could be made.

"If only things had been done right in the first place!" lamented the Empress.

"A stitch in time saves nine!" offered Zénobe.

"I know how to stitch," said Catherine.

"I do, too," countered Zénobe.

"I know the running stitch, the back stitch, the cross stitch, the split stitch, the broken chain stitch, French knots—"

"I don't know French knots!"

"I shall teach you. It's ever so easy!"

This was representative of their conversation during dinner. Nothing dangerous or dramatic, in view of their mute ogling audience, although the presence of Voltaire made them exchange the following observations:

"Voltaire had to use such a great variety of *noms de plume* and *noms de guerre* on his publications, to throw the censors off the track," observed Catherine.

"Surely he had to. Otherwise he would have had a permanent room in the Bastille!" answered Zénobe.

They left it at that.

After dinner they walked a couple of minutes to the edge of her private gardens. With great pride, Catherine wanted to show Zénobe her beloved "child": the town of Sophia, whose church and bigger buildings were visible from their vantage point through the naked trees.

"You are building a village?"

"Yes, I am," she responded with a beaming smile. "And it is coming along splendidly!"

"It looks beautiful," observed Zénobe.

"It has a school for boys, it has a school for girls. It has a hospital. It has a town hall for gatherings and festivities. It has a park for the children to play in. It has a huge cistern for clean water. It has a row of commercial buildings for the townsfolk to purchase their supplies and foodstuffs. On this street there can be found the cobbler, the cutler, the leather tanner, the barber, the weaver and rope maker, the apothecary, in short, all the trades that people will use, within walking distance of their homes."

"A bookstore as well?" asked Zénobe.

Catherine's enthusiasm deflated a bit. "No, no bookstore. But the children have plenty of books at school!"

"What about their parents? What do they get to read?"

"The children are learning to read. But the parents never did."

Zénobe looked sad.

"*Monsieur* de Bosquet!" said Catherine dramatically. "This is the first generation that is beginning to learn how to read and write and calculate with arithmetic. Do not expect miracles quite yet. This is Russia. We have a lot of catching up to do. Now do you see why Diderot was disappointed? He kept asking me these extremely specific questions, like how many types of crops are grown on Russian farms and how many hectares are devoted to each one? How many monasteries and convents do we have? What is the population of priests, monk and nuns? Is that number going up or down? What is the condition of Russian Jews? Types of exports and imports? Laws regulating the commerce of grains? Taxes on the distillation of alcohol; the cultivation of tobacco; the production of oil, honey and furs; the existence of tariffs on merchandise, etc. I could not answer him! He thought I was being evasive. The truth was that we did not know the answers to his questions. We had never even thought to ask those questions of ourselves. What was the need? Only now are we getting around to asking them. Only now, after his visit, do we see the benefit of asking these types of questions. At the very beginning, I had thought his questions impertinent and disruptive. Now I realize their value. But we are still far away from being able to answer them with any degree of certainty."

Zénobe knew that his friend Diderot had returned to France deeply disillusioned. But the fact that Catherine had invited the philosopher to even make the voyage and spend time with her, the fact that Catherine had also bought his library,[125] all this was a sign that Catherine's mind was active and curious and willing to drag Russia into the modern era. That it was a woman doing it was a direct indictment of all male monarchs in the world who refused to bring their nations into contemporary modes of production. Catherine was truly an "enlightened monarch" and deserved to be praised for her efforts.

Zénobe spoke sincerely when he said to the empress, "Your Majesty should be proud of all that she has done for her people. It was your people and no one else who gave you the designation of "Great" which they also gave to your predecessor Peter. This was not done in error; it was not done lightly; it was not done for future accomplishments. They gave you that name for your past achievements and present efforts, to praise your care and concern for your people, and to tell the rest of the world of their happiness in having you as their queen. You think that there are plans afoot among the French to call Louis the XVI 'great'? He's a bumbling idiot, even when he does the right thing for France! You think that the English will bestow anytime soon the adjective 'great' to George III? When he's not behaving like a raving maniac he wastes lives and fortune on retaining possession of the American colonies when, clearly, the colonials want nothing to do with him. Do you think the Spanish will reward their monarch, Charles III, with the name of 'great'? Yes, he wishes to forbid bullfighting and he did manage to throw the British out of the Falkland Islands, but his people do not support those poor bulls and the British navy came back with an even bigger force. So, you see, Your Imperial Highness, only you have the strength of your convictions, only you can convince your armies of the rightness of your wars, and only you wish sincerely to put a halt to the wars and bring peace and prosperity to your people. And now you have built a utopia that has escaped from its architectural plans and that now exists in the world and others can see it and emulate it."

Catherine was beaming.

"You always seem to know exactly what to say, *monsieur* de Bosquet. You make me very happy, and one of my greatest hopes is that you will remain by my side as one of my advisors as I continue to govern. I wish to offer you the post of Honorary Chamberlain to the Empress."

Zénobe groaned inwardly. He had been in this position before when the *marquis* de Villette had offered him the very same post of chamberlain. At least this time, he knew what the duties of a chamberlain entailed. He wanted none of it.

He bowed from the waist and said nothing.

---

125   Catherine generously allowed Diderot to keep his library until such a time that she would be able to take custody of it, upon his death.

Catherine snapped back, "Is there nothing I can do, nothing I can offer you, that will convince you to stay on in Saint Petersburg? In my mind I explore other possibilities, but the post of chamberlain seems ready-made for your character and temperament. You would have political influence, your own bureau, your own retinue, your own suite of rooms in the palace. Your stipend will be whatever you want it to be, your personal palace can be wherever in Russia you want it to be, with an ample domain and a plethora of serfs. You want a river to run through it, a lake or a mountain on it, a château on the warm Crimean coast, an ice palace in Siberia? You have only to say it, and it will be done."

"Your Imperial Majesty, you do me too much honor, and I swear to you that I wish to act in an honorable way. You desire to place much responsibility on my shoulders; I yearn for nothing more than to comport myself responsibly. You believe that I may have influence over others; I must convince myself that this influence would be beneficial to those over whom I hold sway."

"With me guiding you, your influence will be beneficial."

"But what if you and I disagree on a point of policy or in the way that the policy is being put to practice, what then?"

"But we will not disagree. We will discuss the matter until we see eye to eye."

"Two individuals will never see eye to eye on one hundred percent of subjects. There will come a time when we do disagree and we cannot come to satisfactory terms of a compromise. What then?"

"Well, I am certain that you would yield to the opinion of your empress."

"Then, you would insist that I come to terms of a compromise with myself, with my conscience, with my own opinion."

"I will… I will convince you of the rectitude of my decision. My generals and I all agree all the time with the proper strategies and procedures."

"I am sure that you trust their expertise and that you follow their proposals, not the other way around."

"This is true!" she exclaimed. "There is always a chance that you will convince me of the rectitude of your own opinion. I am not rigid in my thinking. If the Enlightenment has taught me anything it is always to remain willing to consider new ideas, or new ways of thinking about old ideas. Our relationship will be one of debate, contention, heated argument leading to appeasement and concord."

"Your Highness makes it sound as if we were two nations wishing to halt their combat and seek peace between them."

"Individuals are like nations! We each of us, and each country, have our ambitions and our fears, our desires and our faults, our crazy whims and our rational volition. Somewhere between all these conflicting vectors there is enough space, between two people, between two states, to craft an immediate truce, and to work on a lasting peace. Sometimes compromise is the best solution, because permanent discord is no way to live."

She beckoned him to return to the palace with her, then said, "Let us not pursue this subject any longer. We shall return to the warmth and coziness of the library. I am patient enough for you to… to… mull over what I have said, and make a decision."

Zénobe offered the empress his arm and the two of them walked back, carefully, over the garden muffled in snow and the steps covered in ice.

They took a different path on the way back and in the distance Zénobe observed an unusual monument.

"What's that?" he asked.

Catherine looked in the direction of his gaze and said, "Oh, yes! Let us go take a closer look at it. I spend many happy, and sad, moments there, in absolute solitude. Whenever I go there, everyone knows not to bother me."

As they approached, Zénobe saw a sort of arbor in the shape of a four-sided granite pyramid. At the sides stood four small columns made of marble, behind which lay three slabs, also of marble. As they walked around this beautiful and elegant architecture, Zénobe saw names engraved on the stone and was relieved to note that they were not in Cyrillic. "Sir Tom Anderson"; "Zémore"; "Duchesse," Zénobe read out loud. "Who were they? he asked.

"They were the best companions I ever had, who never were greedy to obtain power or wealth at my expense, who never betrayed me, asked for nothing more than to be with me and be satisfied, and happy, only that. They were my English greyhounds, my favorites, who were more kind, more grateful, more loving than ever a human could be. Their love for me, and my love for them, was strong and true, and with them by my side, I felt I needed no human companionship. They always made me laugh with their antics, and with their devotion they made me bitter to think that we humans do not even come close to understanding loyalty, companionship, constancy."

Catherine's eyes were by this time overflowing with tears. Zénobe did not know how to console her but felt instinctively that he should stand close to her and silently mourn with her.

"Do you like the pyramid?" asked Catherine. "It is a replica of the one at Kew, which in turn emulates the sepulchral monument of Sestius in Rome."

"It is beautiful," admired Zénobe. "It must be even more so in the spring when these vines are in flower."

"It is phenomenally beautiful. The vine is honeysuckle. The blossoms fill the air with an otherworldly scent and you can suck the sweet nectar from the stems of the flowers."

Zénobe read out loud the inscription under one of the names.

Here lies Zémire and the Graces in mourning
Should throw flowers on her grave;
The gods, witness of her tenderness,
Should have rewarded her fidelity
With the gift of immortality,
So that she might for ever remain next to her mistress.[126]

"Those verses were written by the *comte* de Ségur, my French ambassador," explained Catherine. "He understood, he sympathized, he captured my sentiments for my Zémire."

As they slowly walked back to the palace in silent meditation, Zénobe felt that nothing else before this would have tempted him to remain in Russia as Catherine's chamberlain and paramour. But now he thought that anybody who had this much love for animals must indeed be a great person.

---

126   In the original French: *Ici gît Zémire, et les grâces en deuil / Doivent jeter des fleurs sur son cercueil; / Les dieux, témoins de sa tendresse / Devroient à sa fidélité / Le don de l'immortalité, / Pour qu'elle fût toujours auprès de sa maîtresse.*

The Difficulty of Historical Novels

The trouble with writing an historical novel with any chance of success lies in the choice of facts that the writer decides to foist onto his reader. The reader's credulity is like a gossamer spider's web: it will stretch up to a point, before it tears into tatters. If a monarch and her friend spend the afternoon ambling about the rose garden of Tsarskoe Selo in the middle of winter, as Catherine did with Zénobe, it challenges the reader's imagination almost to the point of disbelief. Why would the two of them have gone out there in the first place, in the dead of winter? There was nothing to see! The rose bushes had been cut down to the ground and covered with mulch, the allées and parterres were invisible under feet of snow, the daedalus left no evidence of its existence. Only an empress of Catherine's stature could have had enough weight in her whimsy to have had the snow swept back by the bemused gardeners in order to provide the solitary couple with enough space for their promenade. They were in an amphitheater of sorts, a crater of soft white with the snow pushed up high on the sides like a giant saucer. No one was around.

It was so cold! Zénobe had never felt such cold. The mountains of Savoy could kill an unprotected man overnight. Here the chill would extinguish the warmth of life in less than an hour. What were they doing out here in the empress's private gardens of Tsarskoe Selo?

"I absolutely love to come out here in the winter!" exclaimed the empress. "The opportunities are few when I can be all alone. Don't get me wrong, they're watching, standing guard by the windows. But nobody wants to come out!" Catherine cocked her ear to the sky. "Listen to the silence," she said with a smile. "As much as I love music, and at times, the din of social hubbub, I do love silence."

Indeed, even the air was still. There was no living thing around them from which noise could emanate, not a bird, not a serf. The solitude was liberating. Zénobe ran ahead a few steps with arms outstretched to the metallic gray sky and gave a holler, whirling in circles as he gamboled.

Catherine laughed at his antics. "There is nobody around to tell us how foolish we are!"

"Foolish? Am I being foolish?" Zénobe replied.

"It is not quite the decorum and fastidious deference required by the Court," observed the empress.

Zénobe laughed, then whooped again. "I'll show you deference! I'll show you decorum!"

After a few more turns and twists that looked like a silly cross between ballet arabesques and fencing lunges, whirling out in a growing spiral with Catherine as its focus, Zénobe ran back to her and hurled himself to his knees in front of her.

"Your Imperial Highness, I thank you from the bottom of my heart for showing me the beauty of your gardens."

Catherine laughed. "You nitwit! One cannot even tell that there are gardens underneath all this snow!"

Zénobe stood up and looked all around. "This is beauty! This is serenity! This is silence! This is whiteness!"

"You are not in your right mind!" said Catherine as she continued to laugh. Only a small part of her face was visible amongst all the fur coats, stoles, and scarves that enveloped her. A hat perched on her head and a muff encasing her hands finished the portrait of a cold queen warmed by the antics of her companion.

"*Madame*, could I please have the honor of a dance with Your Royal Majesty?"

Catherine shrieked with mirth. "You are daft, I knew it! From the very first moment I saw you I knew it!"

But she allowed Zénobe to place a hand behind her back and to retrieve a gloved hand from her muff. While he hummed the tune of a German *contredanse* he had heard recently, they swayed and chasséd to the melody of a hundred imagined musicians, violinists, cellists and oboists, moving over the fluff of snow which they kicked up with their steps.

Zénobe was enveloped in coats and scarves as well, but was hat- and wigless. Catherine enjoyed watching his straight black hair sway back and forth over his shoulders as he maneuvered the intricate steps of the dance. From their laughing mouths puffs of white vapor expanded in volume and frequency as the dance became more strenuous. It was true that nobody was there to see how foolishly they were acting, unless they were still watching at the windows, but their dance was rather graceful and nimble. Catherine was a superb dancer, having danced her first steps as soon as she could walk. Zénobe had only recently begun to dance, but he saw the art as an extension of fencing: in both forms of movement he had to keep his body centered and balanced and his extremities free to show some flair. Only the head movements were different: rigid and even for fencing, but for dancing he could angle it into the forward movements then angle it back when he retreated.

When the dance was over Catherine said, "Oh, now I feel warm and tingly all over! *Monsieur*, you dance very well."

"And you, *madame*!"

"You learned to dance in Turin or in Paris?"

"In neither of those two places, *madame*. I learned to dance, only quite recently, in Potsdam."[127]

"What do you mean, in Potsdam? In the court of Frederick?"

"The very same. Frederick excels at many talents, martial, musical, poetical, a-a-a-a-a-and terpsichorean."

"But isn't there a severe paucity of ladies at Frederick's court? If we are to believe the reports, there are, I believe, no ladies at Frederick's court."

---

127   The seat of Prussian government, Frederick the Great's palace of Sans Souci.

"Such is the reality and I am here to verify it, but *madame*, one does not need ladies to perform these steps while listening to music."

"Well, where is the amusement in that, then?"

"The amusement is in the performance of the dance steps, in time to the cadence of the music. Very frequently, Wagnière was my partner when we practiced. He has always been spry, and he will be again when he recovers fully from his illness."

Catherine surveyed the horizons of snow, before she posed her next question.

"Did you enjoy being at Frederick's court?"

Zénobe thought about this query for a few moments, then answered slowly, as if his thoughts on this subject were newly nascent.

"Wagnière and I were in Potsdam under duress. Frederick's border patrol had found us and brought us to Sans Souci, and while we were not precisely prisoners, we were obliged to be his guests. Not that His Highness turned out to be imperious (he was in effect, rather charming a host); yet we were not free to exercise our own volition. He did not let us go until he himself had to depart for the war front. To answer your question, enjoyment can only be fulfilled when one is free to chose it."

"Then, one can say that the King of Prussia stole that time away from me, when you should already have been here. Tell me, did he ask to see Voltaire's library? Did he insist on confiscating his correspondence with Voltaire?"

"Not at all. He didn't even mention Voltaire's library. I imagine that he believed that his correspondence with Voltaire had already been made public during all the years of its duration. What advantage could he have received had he kept those letters?"

"None, I suppose. But tell me, my young friend. Did Frederick... Did the King of Prussia... Bless me, God, I do not know how to choose my words to frame this next question."

"I believe I can ask it for you," said Zénobe.

"You can? How the devil do you know what I want to say?"

"You seem to be discomfited by this question, therefore there can be only one possibility. You wish to know if His Royal Highness ever asked me for an association of a more intimate kind."

"You surmised it correctly and expressed it discreetly. But forgive me for asking. Frederick is known for his dalliances with men. I thought perhaps that he... that you... I mean..."

"The answer is no, *madame*. There passed between the Prussian monarch and me nothing more intimate than conversation. He also serenaded me with his flute and played compositions that I found to be novel and highly entertaining. His comportment was admirable and exemplary, as befits a king of such standing and bearing."

Catherine sighed. "I always thought it a bit uncanny that Voltaire had such a friendship with Frederick."

"Voltaire loved those especially who were on the cusp of divergence from the norm. Voltaire, the philosopher, despised uniformity so much that he befriended those who were different, who were at odds with the majority, who were unique. He himself was different to the point of being a thorn in the side of the Church and of the State—"

"This is something I know," interrupted Catherine. "I just don't know how I would act around Frederick. He does not like women. Perhaps he would not even like me! He set up his own wife in her own palace and never visits her, and never invites her to visit him. What kind of marriage is that? Not only is it a *mariage en blanc*, it is a *mariage de loin!*"[128]

"It was a *mariage d'état*, like all the unions of European monarchs. This arrangement of marriage is so taken for granted that no prince or princess has the presence of mind to put up a fuss. You all go to the altar like sheep and marry a person who has been chosen for you by outside forces, without your blessing, without your permission."

Catherine was astounded by such an impertinent statement, but when she weighed it for veracity, she did not find it wanting.

"What you say is true, my young man. I hope that you never have to marry for the sake of convenience or diplomacy. But let's change the subject from something dull and distasteful to something enticing and delicious: I instructed the kitchen staff to have hot chocolate prepared for us when we come back in."

Zénobe was astounded. "Chocolate? In Russia?"

"Why, *monsieur*," scolded the empress, "we are not in some remote or isolated hinterland! We are fully a part of Europe! As a matter of fact, the war with Turkey has brought us many products from warmer lands. We have no penury of coffee or tea in Russia, and now chocolate is on the tables of many of the nobles."

"But does not war interrupt the chains of supply?"

"Well, yes, but in some cases it dislodges others and knocks them into our favor. So what, if the cocoa beans were meant for England? They can scrounge around for another source. All is fair in love and war."

"All is fair in love and war," repeated Zénobe. His mouth remained open for he still had something else to say, but he waited for a dramatic pause before he dared state to the queen, "Which is why you asked *madame la comtesse* Stepanovna to seduce me."

Catherine's expression was at first an attempt at innocence, an incipient ploy to deny all allegations. But in view of Zénobe's strong intellect and intuition, she relinquished such a cowardly reaction with a shrug of her shoulders and a lift of her head to the sky, as if to say, God is watching.

"I should have guessed that you of all people would see through our play-acting and discern our true intentions. *Madame la comtesse* Stepanovna has always been instrumental to me. She has helped me avert many fiascos, though not all of them. With her preceding me, she initializes relationships in a, how shall I put it, cleaner fashion. She has rejected outright many a ruffian, or a delinquent. She weeds out the inefficient, the impotent, the maladroit, the conceited, the weird. What she approves of usually works out for me. Of course, Anna Stepanovna cannot weed out the scheming or the ambitious. Intimate proximity to me sometimes brings out unwanted aspirations in my lovers, that is, those who think that they have the right to clamor for political power. But I did not rid myself of a tyrannical husband only to saddle myself with a new master. No! No! My ideal mate must be subservient, amenable to my wishes. He must be available constantly, but remain discretely in the background. Accessible, but invisible."

"*Ma chère impératrice*," said Zénobe while inclining his torso towards her to belie his familiar tone. He even put a hand to his heart. "Did you think that I could ever be such a man who would allow himself to become owned and used in such a manner?"

"I suppose not, *mon ami*," responded the queen with a disconsolate look. "With your over-sized sense of dignity and your gift of self-awareness, you could never fall into a

---

128 *Mariage en blanc* = marriage without consummation; *mariage de loin* = marriage from afar. In the next sentence: *mariage d'état* = marriage of state.

situation where your precious freedom was being circumscribed in any way. A whore closes her eyes while she is being used; she opens them to see the lucre she has been paid. I see your point, *monsieur* de Bosquet. Even a man can see when he is in danger of being exploited, even if it's only for a moment. Yet, *monsieur*, my intentions were pure, perhaps not as pure as a Ficino or a Petrarca would pretend to be,[129] but as pure as I can get my heart to express its feelings, its emotions. You see, my philosophical friend, my handsome Voltairian kindred spirit, every now and then I feel that my heart beats heavy with love for you. As the French and English say, I have 'fallen in love' with you. I do not agree with this idiomatic expression. I feel it should be 'rising up' in love with you. I'm ascending, not falling, and you are the subject of my love."

Zénobe was startled by this candid confession.

"*Madame*, as Voltaire loved you and appreciated you, so do I. You are no tyrant whose own unruly scruples lead her to a debauchery of authority and chaos of governing. You are a sovereign with a conscience and with the volition to rule well, to endow her countrymen with the fairness and the goodness to live up to their potential. You are indeed the Enlightened Monarch as Voltaire described you. How could I not love you in the same way he loved you? How could I not put you on the same pedestal that he put you on?"

"Your words fill me with sadness, *monsieur* de Bosquet. I would not want you to love Catherine the empress. I would prefer that you love Catherine the woman."

"The heart, *madame*, cannot be governed. The mind may be altered, tempered, coaxed into tender feelings of companionship, amity, sharing of mutual concerns. But the heart remains proudly isolated and indifferent even before the most lovable of subjects. When it does not love… When it does not love, nothing can make it change. In spite of all forces and energies thrown upon it, in spite of all pitiable looks and acts of despair stomped on it, in spite of lovely words to cajole and implore it, the heart listens not to love's enemy, reason, not even to reality. Try as you will to awaken its sympathy or compassion, it will not stir. The heart travels alone, oftentimes in a different direction from the mind."

Zénobe took Catherine's hand.

"I do not love you the way you want me to love you. But I offer you my incessant friendship, my faithful service, my undying gratitude. This, I believe, may be a true foundation of a relationship between us. How could I ever reject this wondrous love that you as a woman offer me?"

Zénobe then, instinctively, did a most horrible thing. In another context it would have brought him a few days in the stockade. He switched from the formal *vous* to the familiar *tu* as he addressed Her Royal Highness, Empress of Russia. It meant that he was speaking to the woman, and not to the queen.

"I do not wish to offend thee, and while I have great respect and admiration for thee, I do not love thee the way you want me to love thee."

Catherine responded in turn, also dropping the formal address. "Thou dost not offend me, my beautiful friend [*mon bel ami*], but these tears that I shed are evidence of the pain that thou dost cause me. I ask thee to give me time, time for my mind to come to terms with what my heart wants but cannot have. I need thee to include

---

129   Marsilio Ficino and Francesco Petrarca were Italian Renaissance writers who wrote of the importance of 'platonic love' in which the moral and the spiritual take precedence over the corporeal and
mundane.

patience with thy friendship and service, so that I may subdue my unruly heart, and bring peace to my soul."

Catherine smiled through her tears. By this time, Zénobe was weeping, too, in sympathy.

"Ruling over thy immense realm," he said, "may not be as difficult as ruling over thy heart."

Catherine laughed. "I cannot help thinking of Corneille. *C'est Vénus toute entière attachée à sa proie.*"[130]

Zénobe smiled in recognition and nodded his head.

"Well, then," said the queen. "Help me to pry Venus's fangs off my heart and send her back to Mount Olympus."

"It will be my pleasure," said Zénobe. "What sayest thou if we go in and warm ourselves with hot chocolate? Then, perhaps, we shall go to the library there to seek those books that will be like a balm for thy heart. There is much consolation, much wisdom, to be had from books. You yourself know this. [Zénobe returned to the formal *vous.*] Remember those years when you were a lonely princess. Reading in solitude was your only pleasure. I do not need to tell you about the benefits of reading: distract the mind, feed the spirit, and give time to the heart to heal itself."

As they went in, Zénobe gave one last look around and said, "This is beautiful! Like Rousseau himself said, Nature, too, can be like a balm for the soul. Nature will also help the heart to heal."

Catherine smiled, even though tears still ran down her cheeks.

After they had seen to Voltaire's books, then taken an early supper with plenty of wine, and after Zénobe had spent all evening soothing a queen's self-esteem and comforting a woman's heart, Catherine had become jovial once again.

They had repaired to the Amber room where desserts, coffee and liquors had been laid out for them, but they were alone.

"My darling Zénobe," exclaimed the Sémiramis of the North with a mischievous laugh. "Open your mouth!" Just in case the young man thought he had another choice, she added, "I command it!"

Dutifully, Zénobe opened his mouth and angled his head back. From across the salon, over the back of the chair she had just vacated, came sailing a catapulted projectile towards a seated Zénobe. It was a brandy-soaked cherry and it hit him on his lower lip, bouncing away from him but he managed to catch it mid-air and promptly popped it into his mouth.

---

130 From Corneille's play *Phèdre*, in which the eponymous heroine plays the role of the quintessential victim of love who cannot free herself from the tyranny of her emotions. It is love that is consuming her; she is being devoured by it. "It is Venus entire clutching hard at her prey."

"Oh, that is not fair! The use of hands is not allowed!" said the Queen. "Spit that one out!"

"Too late," said Zénobe, opening his mouth and his hands to show that there was nothing there.

Catherine made a noise of disappointment. "Oh, no! What did you do with the pit?"

"Swallowed it," came the reply.

"But it'll sprout in your stomach. You'll have a tree grow inside you!"

Zénobe laughed. "I'll be like Daphne chased by Apollo and turned into a tree."

"Here comes another one," warned Catherine. "Get ready, here it comes!"

Another cherry followed, Zénobe's bright blue eyes fastened intensely on its arc. At the last second he had to bring his torso forward to catch the cherry squarely in his mouth.

"*Bravo, mon beau*! Excellent reflexes. Wonderful use of the neck muscles!"

"Oh!" exclaimed Zénobe as if he were Christopher Columbus seeing the New World for the very first time. "I have never seen this, an empress behaving badly!"

She laughed with such delight that it was only with difficulty that she managed to bring two glasses of brandy back to her seat. "Here, my kind gentleman, take it before I drop it!"

"Ah, *madame*, another glass, this time of brandy. Thank you very much, but I am afraid it will dull my intellect and I will have nothing intelligent to speak about."

"Oh, you'll still have plenty to speak about, *mignon*, intellect dulled and all. But I need to tell you of a decision I have made."

"Oh, no… a decision?" asked Zénobe, already jumping to the conclusion that an empress's decision would be detrimental to his fate.

"No, listen to me. It is a wise and just decision. Here it is: I have decided to offer you, even though you do not seem to be enthralled by it, the position of Vice-Chamberlain of the court, under the supervision of Count Andrei Shuvalov who has been my chamberlain for a while, but he could use the help of a competent and erudite deputy. You could start as soon as you have successfully acquitted yourself of your librarian duties."

When Zénobe said nothing, Catherine asked, "Well, what do you think? Are you not in the least bit tempted to serve my court as a vice-chamberlain?"

Zénobe was of course, again, remembering the very same offer of employment that he had received from the *marquis* de Villette, although in that case it was to have become a full chamberlain. Now it was vice-chamberlain to the Empress of all the Russias. He simply had no desire to be anybody's chamberlain. Why was Catherine being obtuse and refusing to understand that he wished to return to France? Then the thought entered swiftly into his mind that he had never told Catherine that he had a pressing engagement in France: André. Nostalgia for André came flooding into him, images of André seeping into his mind and memories of his love for André overwhelming his heart. Thinking of his friend on his farm in Normandy brought tears to his eyes. He decided to use these tears in his response to Catherine.

"Your Imperial Highness, I am touched by your kindness, by your generosity, by your faith in my abilities. But I cannot remain in Russia. I must return home."

"But, Zénobe! The priests will get you as soon as you cross the border into any one of those catholic lands. You are safe here! I will protect you!"

"My work… my work with the *philosophes* awaits. *Messieurs* Condorcet and Diderot and I must continue working on our objective to sap the influence of the Church so it does no more harm. We need to undermine the Church's primacy with the Crown, and to continue to empower the common people who also deserve to pursue happiness and success. With the priests and the aristocrats bearing down on them, they will never obtain their freedom!"

"But Russian serfs also need their champion!"

"Excuse me, Your Imperial Highness, but I must be truthful here. Russian serfs are way too ignorant and illiterate to accept, or even be willing to consider, the values of the Enlightenment. The ambition to free themselves from slavery has been beaten out of them. For far too long they have been crushed into submission, and they only respect their tyrannical masters who discipline them with physical abuse. Will Russians ever be ready for self-determination and democratic principles? French peasants, at least, according to their noble masters, are becoming insolent and insubordinate in their dealings with the ruling class. This is proof that their defiance is becoming stronger and that the ability of the aristocrats to govern them is fast losing its sway. The conceit and dominance of the aristos is slowly being rejected. All because Voltaire taught the plebeians to think for themselves, and not to continue believing in what the priests and the lords tell them. What the rebels in America have done, the peasants and the workers in France must now do. They must use the courage of the revolutionaries and the spirit of the *philosophes* to create a new society for themselves. Why should they continue to be the only ones to work and to be taxed and to be humiliated in the bargain. Enough! What was given freely is now retained. More than half of their production used to be given to the priests and the aristos. Why? The feudal accords are no longer valid; they never were. The workers in France are just now waking up to that conclusion. The feudal accords are not valid here in Russia, either. But the serfs are too ingenuous and ignorant to undertake a crusade for progress."

Catherine closed the circle. "And the Russian nobles are too entrenched in their ruthless mentality and in their violence against the serfs. Believe me, I tried, but the virulence of their opposition to the smallest, most basic, of advances put an immediate stop to my tampering of the sacred laws of sovereign and country."

After a full minute had elapsed, Catherine spoke again. "I understand, *monsieur* de Bosquet. I understand your desire to assist our dear friend Voltaire, who dedicated his whole life to relieving the miserable existence of the downtrodden and to give them hope for a future where fairness and justice rule society. This so-called holy alliance of Church and State must be dispelled forthwith. Your philosopher friends have been saying this for so long; the revolutionaries in America are saying it with action. You must go where the prospects are better. Russia is far too intransigent. Russians will always want an autocrat to rule over them. At the very least, I am not cruel. The French, I think, are ready for a radical alteration of their society. '*Écrasez l'Infâme*' is on everybody's lips. Mine, too. But I am bound to this country, even though it was not mine and I did not choose it. It chose me. Now, I must see to it that I bring as much progress to my adoptive people as I can."

Zénobe set his glass on the low table in front of him and sat up in his chair. "I can still help you, even from afar," he proposed. "We are both fighting on the same side, and for the same aims. Together, we can support each other, with the help of our mutual friends. And I promise to return, one day. Who knows, maybe with Diderot. Maybe with Condorcet, or Grimm, or d'Holbach. We have but to establish a league of Enlightenment, one that is made up of common interests and of promoting liberty to those who do not have it. We shall be on the winning side of history, away from despotism and slavery.

Voltaire's work is far from done. As a matter of fact, I would say that it is only just now beginning. He provided the theory; we must establish the practice."

Catherine sighed. "But in the bargain, I must lose you. Life is cruel. We must forever struggle to bring advances to others, but we must leave ourselves behind. Self-abnegation has never been one of my stronger suits."

With great impatience Zénobe jumped to his feet. "Look around you, my queen. Does this…" With his arms splayed out he indicated their surroundings in the Amber room. "Does this look like one who is even close to rejecting self-abnegation? I regretfully must inform you that this splendor and excess have a price."

He strode to the nearest wall and plucked a piece of amber from its spot at the base of a sconce.

Catherine gasped. "This is not mine," she exclaimed. "I had nothing to do with it. The amber was a gift from Frederick William to Peter.[131] He did not make any use of it, but the tsarina Elizabeth loved it and had it put up in this room. It was she who was a spendthrift, not I. Here, in this one room, she outdid herself. I, at least, am more circumspect when it comes to money. I really do not care much for this room. There is an excessive amount of amber; I feel I am drowning in honey."

Zénobe looked at the piece in his hand. His eyes scrutinized it, but from Catherine's vantage point she observed that he was admiring it. Then he scrunched up his eyes and brought the golden piece of amber closer to his eyes.

"There is something inside it!" he exclaimed.

"Amber often does enclose little curiosities," Catherine responded. "What is in that one?"

"It looks like a cockroach. But behind it, and arrayed in a semi-circle, is a group of tiny dots."

"Go to that desk," suggested Catherine. "You will find a magnifying glass in the top drawer."

Zénobe went to the desk and took the magnifying glass. His blue eye looked huge as he directed it at the contents of the piece of amber.

"Oh, my lord!" he cried out. "Oh, my dear lord!"

"Well, what is it?" Catherine asked with impatience. "What do you see?"

"Each of those little dots is a tiny cockroach."

She put out a hand to see for herself. Zénobe brought her the piece of amber and the magnifying glass.

After examining the amber, Catherine glanced at Zénobe with empathy. "Poor creature. It was a mother. She was caught by the tree resin and in the throes of her death struggle she released her egg case just at the moment that her babies hatched."

They both peered through the magnifying glass.

"Yes," she said. "That is precisely what happened. It is like her egg case exploded and the poor little ones landed in the resin behind her. No one escaped."

---

131   Frederick the Great's father, Frederick William I, gave the amber to Peter the Great in 1716. Peter's daughter, Empress Elizabeth, had the amber installed at the Catherine Palace, the summer home of the Russian tsars and tsarinas. It is estimated that the Amber Room contained about 13,000 lbs of the fossilized tree resin. It was looted during World War II by the Germans who took their booty to Königsberg, in other words, back to Prussia, but the heavy bombing by the Royal Air Force, followed by the shelling from the Red Army, may have destroyed the treasure. There are reports that the amber was placed in a German submarine which was promptly torpedoed and sunk, or that it was placed in a silver mine or sunk into a lagoon. The Amber Room in Tsarskoe Selo today is a complete reconstruction from the original plans.

Zénobe was horrified. "We are witnesses to a small tragedy that happened long ago."

"Such is the vision of the gods. One day they will catch us in the throes of our own death struggle."

"Only there are no gods. They are but an extension of our own longing to be powerful enough to determine our own destiny. Yet, we are swept away by larger forces over which we have no control. If we think we do, it is only a fantasy on our part."

"This is true," said Catherine. "We are but a reed in a storm. But we are a reed that knows how to bend. We are a thinking reed."

"Thank you, *madame* Pascal," answered Zénobe. But let us not be as somber and desolate as he. We have more brandy to drink, have we not?"

"Now we drink Porto wine!" Catherine said excitedly.

"Porto wine? From Portugal? How in heaven do you get that all the way here?"

"*Monsieur* de Bosquet! You still seem to think that we are at the antipodes of civilization! We get Porto from vessels that ply the seas and traverse mighty distances to get it all the way to us up here. Before you sit back down, would you do the honors of liberating that wine from its bottle there? Yes, that one, to your right."

The cork gave a pleasant pop when he removed it. The wine was sweet and potent. Neither one of them wished to end their private soirée and repair to their bedrooms. It was nearly midnight when Catherine gave a little yawn.

Bidding Her Imperial Majesty a good night, Zénobe said that he was looking forward to organizing the crates of Voltaire's books that were to follow them back to Saint Petersburg on the following day.

"Or perhaps on the next," said the queen. "I have some business to attend to, but you may go ahead and see that the library will be ready for removal."

Zénobe kissed Catherine's hand and she swept away from the room.

One more day at Tsarskoe Selo, said Zénobe to himself. Why is she lingering here?

A snippet of an answer should have occurred to him when a gentleman appeared at the doorway opposite the one where the tsarina had just exited.

"*Bonsoir, monsieur,*" he said in heavily accented French. "I am arrived here to place you in your boudoir. If you will please follow my steps."

This was the first courtier Zénobe had seen since first arriving at the palace on the previous day. Everything up to now had been arranged to simulate solitude.

Zénobe would not have harbored any misgivings whatsoever, save for one telling detail. This gentleman who had been sent to conduct him to his bedroom was handsome, very handsome. He was almost as tall as Zénobe, well dressed in a Russian gentleman's attire, wearing a wig that could have come straight from Paris. He moved as if he had spent time in a regiment, with his head held high, his posture straight, his back broad, his pelvis slender.

When they arrived in Zénobe's room, the gentleman smiled and said to him, "Her Imperial Majesty wishes me also to assist to you tomorrow for your duties with the books. I shall return this coming morning at nine o'clock, if this is allowable by you."

Zénobe realized that this was a question and blurted out, "*Oui, monsieur, absolument.* That will be perfect."

The gentleman clicked his heels and bade Zénobe a good night.

"Wait, please," called Zénobe after him. "What is your name?"

"My name is Andrei Olegovich Dém***,[132] at your service," he answered, and for the first time, he smiled.

As he left, Zénobe sighed. Dear Lord, he said to himself. Another André.

---

132   This family still exists in Russia and elsewhere. Out of propriety and discretion, the family will anonymous remain.

An Empress in Love

The reader might perhaps believe, at this moment of the narrative as we approach the end of Zénobe's sojourn in Russia, that she is being made to swallow a bill of goods and to think that her hair is being pulled. An empress falling in love with a former peasant? Well, Zénobe had metamorphosed into a learned gentleman because of the contents of his mind. His residual innocence and naiveté made the contents of his heart overflow with kindness and deference, and Catherine, a lonely queen who sought to rule over men's hearts, not minds, found an affable, charming young man with whom she could be herself. His Swedish officer's uniform and the fashionable—and expensive—wig that Maurel had procured for him, managed to complete the metamorphosis. There is no need to think that the wool is being pulled over anybody's eyes. One has only to examine the historical evidence. Catherine II had a confidant, Melchior Grimm, with whom she corresponded and to whom she poured out her heart and soul. He was German, like her, and a brother *philosophe* to Voltaire and Diderot. Catherine was grateful to receive from him both counsel and sympathy.[133]

A small bundle of letters from Catherine exists, dated from January 8th to February 16th, all in the hand of the Empress herself,[134] addressed to Melchior Grimm in Paris. Through the vagaries of history and the cultural exchanges between nations, this particular bundle of letters eventually ended up in the possession, and jurisdiction, of the Russian National Library which also houses the 6,814 books of Voltaire's Library, over 2,000 of which display marginalia written in the philosopher's own hand. Since as of this writing, diplomatic relations between Russia and the West remain strained, it would be difficult, of not impossible, for a researcher to request access to these letters, to say nothing of Voltaire's library. Verification of these letters would of necessity have to wait for a subsequent glasnost. However, it will probably not be in the near future that Western researchers will be allowed to examine them. The Russians themselves, of course, can examine them with ease.

It is indeed sad to realize that the verisimilitude of a novel rests on the amity, or enmity, between nations. In the interim, the parts of Catherine's letters that were published previously and that are pertinent to our story are now presented. Perhaps

---

133 Friedrich Melchior, baron von Grimm, 1723-1807, was born in Regensburg but lived most of his life in Paris. In 1773 and 1778 he visited Catherine in Saint Petersburg, where the Empress made him, along with Diderot, a member of the Russian Academy of Sciences. He and Catherine corresponded until her death.

134 This means that she did not dictate the letters to a secretary, ostensibly to keep her missives secret.

this will be enough to assuage the reader's curiosity and give assurance of the trust-worthiness of the novel in her hands.

All of Catherine's letters to Grimm begin with the place in which she wrote them, either the Winter Palace or Tsarskoe Selo, the date, and the greeting, 'to *Monsieur le philosophe*'. There is a strong indication that the 'Pyrrhus, king of Epirus' of her letters is none other than Zénobe himself.

> This letter will perhaps resemble the gossip that takes place at Tsarskoe Selo, and any idiot who might read it before you did might find it indecent that people as grave as you and I are would write such extravagant letters.

> It is true, that sometimes I am the victim of insomnia and of anguish.

> I have at times hours of weakness and at others hours of force; it stems from an intermittent fever, but it is more in the moral sense than in the physical.

> I am overwhelmed: today I received two of your letters, two from the King of Prussia, three from the King of Sweden. At least they help to distract my mind from other things.

> I have just received Franklin's medallion; now there is a big head. I will send you one of Pyrrhus, king of Epirus, and you will say: now there's a beautiful head, a Grecian physiognomy, Grecian propor-tions. There's a figure that our sculptors know nothing about; I shall demonstrate that many perspectives of nature in which the sculptors do not believe, really do exist, when nature is perfect to such a degree. Oh, sir! It is such a beautiful thing! You will thank me for it one day.

> There is none but Pyrrhus, king of Epirus, that all sculptors should sculpt, all painters should paint and all poets laud.

> Infatuated, infatuated! You know that this term is not appropriate when speaking of Pyrrhus, king of Epirus, the challenge of painters, the despair of sculptors. It is admiration, *monsieur*, it is enthusiasm, that the masterpieces of nature inspire. When Pyrrhus appears in the room, all take notice; when he speaks, all listen. Never does Pyrrhus make a gesture or a movement that is not noble or graceful. He shines

like the sun and spreads his splendor all around him. None of that is effeminate, but rather manly, and one would not have it any other way. In a word, it is Pyrrhus, king of Epirus; all is in harmony; there is no single thing missing; it is the effect of precious gifts accumulated by nature in its beauty, where art has nothing to do with it and the contrived is a thousand miles away.

The luxury of beautiful and cute but useless things gains in importance from day to day, and Pyrrhus, king of Epirus, too, and everything that surrounds him also takes a form analogous to his physiognomy. Know that he is the antipode of the gloomy and the somber, and the fusion of the winsome, the graceful and the elegant.

Tell me only that Pyrrhus is handsome, that his countenance is noble and proud, and know that if you were to hear him speak, how he speaks and what he speaks about would leave you in awe, in tears, weeping with wonderment and emotion.

Pyrrhus is leaving. He desires to go back whence he came. How can it be possible for my heart to retract to its original dimensions and my sentiment to dry up like grains of sand in a desert? His look is still as proud and as impish as always. How can I efface it from my mind and still manage to hold on to my peacefulness? You philosophers have not yet found a way to separate ourselves from our follies, to divorce ourselves from our fantasies and to break the hold of our illusions. Shame on you! You would be doing the world a favor were you to teach us how to live in the world of the ephemeral and the phantasmagoric, for such is the world of love.

Temptation

A ndrei Olegovich D***ov was so obliging, so very charming, that Zénobe was quite predisposed to forgive him for mangling the French language to such a degree. He was also beautiful. His salient feature was a pair of dark-brown eyes over which floated his eyebrows that looked like the black upturned wings of a rapacious bird soaring against a milky-white sky. His nose was perfectly formed and his lips delineated as if by an artist, his philtrum deep and exquisite. A dimple in the center of his chin completed the picture, and it was all Zénobe could do not to stare at him.

This morning, promptly at nine o'clock as he had promised, Andrei Olegovich had returned to Zénobe's room, carrying a silver tray with steaming hot coffee and cakes, milk, bread, butter, and some elliptical items called *syrniki*.[135] He lay everything out on a small table by the window whose curtains he had opened to let in the light of day.

Zénobe felt awkward eating in front of Andrei Olegovich and invited him to share his breakfast.

"I eat already, this morning early," he answered.

"Well, why don't you at least sit with me and have some coffee? I do not like the idea of you having to wait on me."

" 'Wait on me'? What this mean?"

"It means you having to serve me. I'd rather you sit when I sit. We sit together, yes?"

"Oh, this not possible. You French gentleman. You guest of Her Imperial Highness. I just Russian gentleman. I supposed to wait upon you."

"Wait *on* you."

"Wait on you, yes." After a smile of embarrassment, Andrei Olegovich said, "French difficult. Russian much easier."

This made Zénobe laugh. "Oh, no! Russian is very difficult. French is easy as pie."[136]

"Pie is easy?" asked Andrei Olegovich.

"I really have no idea. I've never made it!"

They both laughed at the irrationality of language.

---

135 Сырники are a sort of pancake, mixed with quark (curdled milk), flour, eggs, and sugar. Fried in oil, the outside is crisp while the center stays creamy. They may be garnished with cream, apple sauce, marmalade or honey.

136 Zénobe used a French expression, *simple comme bonjour*, which literally means "simple as good day." In case the reader is curious about the original French in this conversation, it went on like this:

«*Oh, non! Le russe est très difficile. Le français est simple comme bonjour.*»

«*Le bonjour est simple?*»

«*Certes, je n'ai aucune idée. Je ne l'ai jamais tenté!*»

His Russian host sat down hesitantly, but in a chair five feet away. Zénobe gestured toward the chair by the table opposite his. Andrei Olegovich changed seats.

"Here, have some coffee," offered Zénobe. "It is piping hot!"

"Hot, like pipe?"

"Something like that."

"But that is your coffee cup, *monsieur.*"

"We haven't another one. I told you, we can share. There is enough coffee in the pot for a regiment."

Andrei Olegovich laughed at Zénobe's hyperbole. "I send for other soldiers?" he joked.

"No, no," answered Zénobe. "I was exaggerating. We'll just keep it for the two of us."

Andrei Olegovich took a sip of the coffee and burned his lip.

"I told you it was hot!" said Zénobe. "Are you all right?"

"Yes, I am. But my lip is not." Andrei Olegovich laughed while pretending to be in pain.

"Here, have a… have a… What did you call these?"

"They are *syrniki.*"

"*Syrniki.* I'll have one, too. *Gott in Himmel!*," Zénobe exclaimed, thinking that German would be halfway to Russian. "This is very good. Delicious!"

Andrei Olegovich smiled as Zénobe passed him a *syrniki.* When Andrei Olegovich smiled, his whole face brightened and became even handsomer. He bit into the *syrniki* and part of the creamy center squirted onto the corner of his mouth. It took all of Zénobe's will power not to reach over the table and lick it off.

Immediately after breakfast, Zénobe started working on the crates of books with Andrei Olegovich's help. They did not see Catherine at all that day, and they were left to their own devices.

With the exception of one of the crates, the rest were all still sealed so there was nothing to do but remove them from the library and stack them by a side entrance where a wagon would be picking them up. Instead of loading them up on a garden wheelbarrow that had been provided for them and risk gouging the parquetry of the floors, they each took a side and carried the heavy chests bodily. Whoever had opened that single crate had begun to place the books on a bookshelf. Zénobe stood by the bookshelf and pulled down the books which he handed one by one to Andrei Olegovich as he crouched by the crate. Zénobe couldn't help, however, announcing a short description of each book.

"This is the book that got Voltaire into so much trouble with the king. He had to flee from France for this one."

"This is the book that Voltaire never admitted to having written. It is still on the Church's list of prohibited books."

"This is the book that Voltaire published with his mistress, the *marquise* du Châtelet. It is about Newton and his laws of physics."

"This is the book that Voltaire wrote in praise of Louis XIV. Not that it helped him with Louis XV."

Eventually Andrei Olegovich observed, "Voltaire not afraid to write. His quill same as foil, sharp attack to enemies."

"That's right. He wrote to attack his enemies. He wrote to protect their victims, to protect humanity."

"Great man, Voltaire. I like him."

Zénobe quickly looked over the books remaining in the bookcase until he found what he was looking for.

"Here, this one is for you to keep."

"Book for me?"

"Yes, it is quite all right. We have numerous copies of this edition. It is Voltaire's *Philosophical Dictionary*. We even allowed a German bandit to take a copy.[137] It is very typical of what he wrote, and you will find it very useful, and very entertaining."

"Thank you, *monsieur*. I will put it by my bedside. I read, make my French better, learn about Voltaire."

They finished that last crate in a couple of hours. Between the two of them they took it to join the others.

Zénobe slapped his hands as if removing dust and said, "*Eh, bien, voilà!* We're done. Now what shall we do?"

Andrei Olegovich shrugged his shoulders. "What you want to do?"

Zénobe had an idea. "Shall we go find out what Catherine is doing? Is she in the palace?"

The Russian quickly overruled this suggestion. "Catherine occupied, official… ah, official…"

"Official business?"

"*Da, da*, official business. She in palace, but cannot see."

"You mean, she cannot be seen."

"*Ya dumayu, moy frantsuzki ochen plahoy!*[138] My French language very bad! I see passive voice, but I not know how form passive voice. Russian not have verb *to be*."

"Russian doesn't have the verb *to be*? One needs the verb *to be* to form the passive voice! So, tell me, Andrei Olegovich, what does Hamlet say in Russian, when he says, 'To be or not to be?' "

"He says Быть или не быть. Russian have infinitive *to be*, but no conjugation in present tense."

"Oh, what a strange language! Why don't we go to my room so you can continue teaching me this strange new language?"

Andrei Olegovich laughed at this. "Russian maybe strange, but not new. Very old. Russian very old."

"Can you teach me the Cyrillic alphabet as well?"

"Yes, very happily! Cyrillic alphabet very easy. Orthography very easy in Russian. French orthography impossible!"

---

137 Zénobe must have forgotten that the book given to the highwayman was the *Henriade,* not the *Dictionnaire philosophique.*

138 Я думаю, мой французский очень плохой.

They laughed at the irrationality of French orthography. Foreign languages were difficult, even impossible, especially when one was a novice. And yet, communication was being made between the two young men, in the form of laughter, in the form of eye movements, of gazes and furtive glances, light touches of the hand on an arm or shoulder. The words they used, banal, hard to spell, at times erroneous, sewn together with inaccurate syntax, and pronounced unintelligibly with awkward tongues, had nothing to do with the ineffable empathy being conveyed, with great success. Their unnameable feelings, their interior thoughts, their inchoate longings, were developing enigmatically into exterior recognition, into an unmentionable understanding.

Laughing and jesting in the hallways, they eventually made it to Zénobe's boudoir where they spent the rest of the afternoon comparing French and Russian linguistics, teaching each other language skills, and helping each other to pronounce difficult sounds of each other's tongues. They didn't, of course, become fluent in just a few hours, but they earned plaudits from each other in their efforts to be avid learners, to surpass each other in their earnest desire to communicate. Youth has such impatience when it comes time to know another person, and any linguistic barrier that may have existed between Zénobe and his Russian friend Andrei Olegovich was quickly overcome. Their exertions for proficiency were so strenuous, their vocalizations so spirited, their acquisition of lexicological vernacular so vigorous, that in time they quieted down and fell asleep on Zénobe's big bed.

They were so profoundly asleep that they were not at all aware of Catherine who opened the door and came sailing into the room to see if Zénobe was available to have supper with her.

January 16, 1779, evening, & the following morning

The Queen is Not Amused

W hat Catherine observed inside Zénobe's boudoir can be surmised from her reaction: she was distraught, but did not vocalize her feelings for fear of awakening Zénobe and Andrei Olegovich. She slowly backed away from the bed on tiptoes until her back hit the wall. She fumbled for the doorknob and quietly let herself out.

The kitchen staff received orders not to serve supper in the Amber Room. They were not to serve supper at all; the queen was not hungry. This made them quite happy for then they could eat it all themselves: *caille à la Stanislas*, quail stuffed with foie gras, in the manner that the deposed king of Poland liked it; beet salad, cabbage rolls, and cauliflower with potatoes. They especially loved the dessert they had made, *pastila*,[139] a peasant dish but which they embellished with a chocolate-vodka sauce. They enjoyed it so much that the thought did not cross their mind to wonder if their empress was indisposed or occupied with state affairs or simply not hungry.

But Catherine was not indisposed. She was seething. Indeed she was very occupied, mentally occupied, thinking of the ways in which she could punish the two young men she had found asleep in bed. Andrei Olegovich was easy. She would simply send him back to his parents in Tula and banish him forever from her court. His family, the De***ovs, ennobled by Peter for their wealth in having founded metal foundries, would not care if she sent him back to them. Andrei Olegovich was something like tenth in line of familial primogeniture and therefore had no future anyway. She had found out that being her favorite was nowhere in his future.

What would she do to Zénobe, however?

Banishment did not seem satisfactory enough. He wanted to go back home to France, anyway, so banishing him would be a reward!

Banishment to Siberia was a possibility. Geographically farther away from France, it would be well deserved, but he might find a way to escape.

She could throw him in jail here in Saint Petersburg, for a few years. That would be enough time to deflate his self-esteem. Zénobe thought of himself as Voltaire's heir, and thus important to society. Nobody was that important to society.

However, thoughts of Voltaire brought to her mind the times that Voltaire himself had twice been thrown into prison. It had not been for faults of his own; it had been

---

139   In the Cyrillic alphabet: пастила, made of egg whites, sugar or honey, and fruit purée, with a light, foamy consistency that melts in the mouth, leaving traces of apple, quince or berries.

because a French aristocrat had been miffed by Voltaire's disrespect, later because the government, in collusion with the Church, could not tolerate his writings.

But here, tonight, in this case, a young man had demonstrated a serious lapse in moral comportment. All the more injurious, it was a young man whom she was grooming to become her favorite. She had poured her sentiment into this plan, but in the end, he had rejected all her attempts to tame him, to bring him into her dominion, and then, this is how he had repaid her generosity. She had caught him in bed with another man!

All night long, Catherine was in the clutches of her own imagination: thoughts of Frederick the Great flashed through her mind, and she saw the Prussian monarch seducing, and corrupting, her future favorite. She saw Zénobe, falling under the influence of the evil king, a young, impressionable, innocent and noble boy, descending into depravity and malevolence. A young man without blemish, accepting the wicked ways of the evil tyrant. But perhaps he had been an unwilling victim?

She would wage war on Frederick who deserved to be obliterated from the face of the earth, who was wicked and bellicose and responsible for hundreds of thousands of deaths, including his very own people.

Then Catherine began to weep and spent an hour or two sympathizing with Zénobe's innocence. He had been seduced! He had been ravaged! The Devil himself had enticed him to go down the road of wickedness!

Well, Catherine was stronger than the Devil. She would save Zénobe from the villainy of degeneracy. She would bring him back to virtue, to robust moral health. She would take him to bed and teach him about righteousness and propriety. She would straighten him out.

These thoughts of hope and happy endings brought some peace into her heart, and drowsiness into her mind. She fell asleep shortly before dawn, and slept until noon.

Zénobe and Andrei Olegovich were up at eight and, after washing and dressing, reported to the library where they thought that Catherine would be appearing to give them final instructions. Since neither the queen nor a subordinate appeared, they found books in the stacks that they could peruse while waiting. Hunger made Andrei Olegovich go to the kitchens to have breakfast brought to them, which was promptly done. They ate, read, and discussed their favorite books. Zénobe was of course better read than Andrei Olegovich, but the young Russian said that he was partial to German literature, and especially loved Goethe. Zénobe told him about the afternoon he had spent with Goethe in November, and his friend was duly impressed.

Eventually a footman arrived and gave instruction to Andrei Olegovich that his presence was required elsewhere. He left the room, and Zénobe never saw him again.

The queen came into the library a few minutes later. Zénobe immediately knew that something was amiss. Catherine's face was red and puffy, from lack of sleep, perhaps, or because she had been weeping. Her eyes were damp, so perhaps she had been weeping.

Zénobe sprang to his feet in order to greet her, but, following court protocol, waited for Catherine to be the first to speak.

First she sat down on a sofa and gestured to Zénobe to come sit by her. He complied. He could see that she was making an effort to compose her features and quell her emotions. He dared not speak first, even if it was to ask about her well-being. The silence was becoming unbearable so he cleared his throat in preparation to speak.

But she cut him off. Monsieur de Bosquet," she said, and stopped. A few seconds later, she tried again. "*Monsieur* de Bosquet... I wish to ask you a few questions."

"Of course, Your Imperial Highness. It is proper."

"What did you and Andrei Olegovich do last night?"

Zénobe understood immediately what Catherine's disconcertion was all about. He attributed it to spies having told her about his private activities with Andrei Olegovich. He decided to be intentionally obtuse.

"Last night? Before or after supper?"

"After supper."

"Let's see..."

Zénobe realized that he and Andrei Olegovich had had no supper the previous evening. They had slept through it.

"Well... since we were deprived of your Royal Highness's presence, we adjourned to my boudoir and gave each other lessons in our respective languages. I for one have a great desire to learn the Russian language."

"Why didn't you go to the library for that?"

"We had been in the library, Your Highness, all day long. We went to my boudoir because we did not want to appropriate access to other rooms in the palace without express permission from you. But you were inaccessible, lamentably for us, and I didn't see that I was usurping the authorization to repair to my room. I am a guest here, and I would not consider it proper for me to roam the halls without approval, either from you or from one of your representatives."

"Once in your boudoir, what did the two of you do?"

"As I said, we tutored each other, I in French, and Andrei Olegovich in Russian."

"But what did you do, physically?"

"We wrote, on pieces of paper, the conjugations of verbs, the spelling of difficult vocabulary, the Cyrillic alphabet... Those papers should still be in my room and it is of course your prerogative to view them."

"What did the two of you do in bed?"

"That is where we were writing. The little round table in the room was too small to lay out all our papers, so we used the bed as our center of language activity."

"Why did your remove your clothing, if all you were doing was trading vocabulary?"

"In order to be more comfortable. But we only removed our coats and boots. The rest of our attire we were still wearing. Andrei Olegovich is my friend, but I would not feel comfortable being partly disrobed in front of him."

"Did you become physical with him?"

"Physical? Physical in what way?"

"Did you embrace him, or kiss him, or... or... or... or..."

"Or touch him in ways that would be construed as inappropriate or lacking in decorum?"

"Yes. Yes. Did you do any of that?"

"Well, one of our vocabulary games was to learn the parts of the body. So for some of these words, particularly when we were verifying our ability to memorize the words, we would point to each other's body parts. I imagine that at times our finger might have made contact with the other's body, but it was only the major parts that are always in full view. I still don't know the Russian word for penis."

Catherine made a petulant movement as if to rise up out of her seat. But she remained on the sofa.

"Then why, why were the two of you embracing when I walked into your room last night?"

"We were embracing!"

"Yes, you were, my friend. I saw you with these very eyes."

"I know how to say that in Russian. It's глаз!"

"That's just one eye. The plural is глазá!»[140] But don't change the subject!"

"I remember being cold. Sometime during the night, I climbed under the sheets."

"This is true," said Catherine. "You were under the sheets. Andrei Olegovich was on top of them."

"Aha! So you see, we were not in direct contact. Simply Andrei Olegovich became cold sometime during the night and, in his sleep, embraced me for warmth. But he didn't really know what he was doing. He was asleep! Haven't you ever done strange things while you were asleep?"

Catherine thought about it for a while and finally responded, "No, I cannot say that I ever have. Maybe once in a while I have lost the book that I was reading prior to falling asleep, and then later I find it deep within the folds of the blankets."

"So you see, sometimes we lose sight of… of… the things that surround us while we are asleep, and then in the movements of sleep, of which we remain totally unaware, we reconfigure our position with them, we alter the arrangement of these things on the bed, and in the morning we wake up with everything in a new position. Obviously, Andrei Olegovich must have awakened first and moved away from me, because I had no idea that we had been in a position of embrace. This all happened under the state of slumber while we were unaware and not in control of our body's movements, and therefore it all remained innocent."

Catherine stared into Zénobe's eyes as if looking for a sense of veracity at the very center of his soul.

"Is this true, *monsieur* de Bosquet? I like you so much that I want very much to believe you. But last night…"

"As I said, whatever position you might have found us in, it was unintentional. It was below the cusp of observation, for we were deeply asleep. After all those language lessons, our brains were fatigued, and our slumber profound. How can one be deemed guilty of having done something that was not done out of volition, indeed that could not have been deliberate. It was done in innocence, out of being tired and cold."

Catherine seemed to have calmed down. She bit her lower lip and gave an audible sigh.

"*Madame*," Zénobe asked. "Did you send Andrei Olegovich to me in the same manner you sent countess Anna Stepanovna, and for the same reason?"

"I do not know what you are asking me. I did not 'send' Andrei Olegovich to you. He is Anna Stepanovna's relation. It was she who asked him to come. In any case, Anna

---

140   Pronounced 'glas' and 'glə-sá.'

Stepanovna is a woman, so she would be able to ascertain certain qualities about you. Andrei Olegovich is a man. What possible information could I get from him that would have pertinent significance?"

She rose from her seat and so did Zénobe.

"It is time to leave Tsarskoe Selo. We shall leave in a few hours. See to it that all the crates of Voltaire's books are safely placed in the wagon that will transport them to Saint Petersburg."

"Yes, Your Imperial Highness, I will."

"The wagon may leave for the Winter Palace as soon as the crates are loaded. We shall follow it soon."

Zénobe went back to his boudoir to pick up his clothing and saw on the little round table that Andrei Olegovich had left his copy of Voltaire's *Dictionnaire philosophique*. With sadness he picked it up and packed it with the rest of his possessions. He was sorry not to have a way to send it to Andrei Olegovich D***dov. But he had no idea where he lived, and thought it imprudent to make inquiries. He was also sorry not to be able to say goodbye to him. As he turned toward the door with his traveling bag, he glanced over at the bed. It had been made and all the little slips of paper had been gathered and placed in a small stack on the bedspread. His look was wistful and forlorn. He remembered what had gone on in that bed, the fervent passion, the lustful zeal, even heartfelt affection. Nobody had a right to know what went on in that bed the previous evening and much of the night, not even Catherine. It had been a night shared between two young men who deserved their privacy and who deserved to be left alone. They certainly did not deserve to suffer the indignity of being judged by others who were entirely ignorant of the miracle that they had shared. Catherine could send her interrogations to the devil. She was just one more person, albeit an empress, but she could keep her judgments to herself.

Zénobe could not agree more with Catherine. It was time to leave Tsarskoe Selo. He decided to go a step further: it was time to leave Russia.

Final Addendum

Last Days of January into February, 1779
Departure

I t was good to be empress. She commanded, her subjects obeyed, things got done, progress ensued.

But what about commanding someone who was not her subject, someone who owed her no allegiance? How could she force a foreigner to do her bidding? Moreover, how could she force anyone to fall in love with her? Love was outside the realm of decree and entreaty, exempt from plea and litigation, unrestrained by claim or petition. Love could not be governed.

Zénobe was a subject of the King of Sardinia. Catherine had no extradition treaty with Victor Amadeus III that would allow her to keep his son under her jurisdiction, even if it were just a bastard son. She knew that Victor Amadeus' relationship with Zénobe was fraught with conflict, perhaps they were even estranged, due to his wayward son's anti-religious opinions. Still, kings became peeved if their offspring were held by a foreign power without their consent. That is one of the reasons why she had tried to keep Zénobe entirely without duress, entice him without pressure. The lengths to which she succeeded in softening her command and belying her dominion were futile. As much as she tried to gild the cage, the independent young man was as unresponsive as he was indifferent, although he was polite enough to show his gratitude and sympathetic enough to show concern for her emotional well-being.

In the end, Catherine gave in to the temptation offered by Zénobe, weak and tenuous though it was. She had to accept his version of the events that had transpired in his bedroom, the one he and Andrei Olegovich occupied together on the evening and night of January 16-17. His explanations, couched in the familiar tone of rationality, evidence, and conclusion, brought relief to her overwrought nerves. This boy, a protégé of Voltaire, spoke convincingly of the hours the two young men spent in the exchange of foreign language lessons. She had, after all, seen the bits of paper on which were written different types of vocabulary: square shapes of paper for conjugated verbs, circles for declined adjectives, triangles for nouns, in both French and Russian. That the two boys had been so meticulous about their parts of speech went far in bringing the balm of relief to her shaken trust of Zénobe. Never had loose nouns, adjectives and verbs gone so far in helping her to make sense of an event to which she had not been an eyewitness.

This boy, who had interrupted her life, had brought her Voltaire's books, some of them, no, most of them which had in the same manner interrupted her life by interrupting her thinking, sweeping her away by their dire message, sweeping her old thinking away and replacing it with new ways of thinking. The best of them had changed her views forever: *Les Lettres philosophiques*; *Le Traité sur la tolérance*; even *Candide, ou l'optimisme*, simple as that story had been. Such books are unusual in that they make one new, as if waking up for the first time with different ideas in one's head. Zénobe himself had done that to her, presenting himself as a simple librarian who had no ambitions of political power. Yet that loathsome image seared into her retinas of the two boys embracing in bed was not a thought easily shaken off. Zénobe and Andrei Olegovich asleep together, separated by only a few folds of sheets and blankets, with French verbs and Russian adjectives littered pell-mell on and about their recumbent bodies, that was not a sight to be seen every day! What Zénobe said in their defense did possess elements of undeniable truth, a truth that her own memory served to confirm. She did remember that the two boys were dressed, even though Zénobe was partly covered by the sheets and blankets. Andrei Olegovich wore no coat but he still had the rest of his clothing on, including his black shoes.

In the end, Catherine let herself become convinced of the innocence of the two boys, not by the preponderance of Zénobe's logical explanations or by the strength of his evidence, not for her love of reason and logic, but because of the distaste with which she contemplated a horrendous thought. It was much easier to be convinced of the rectitude of Zénobe's evidential claims that he and Andrei Olegovich had spent the night immersed in language learning. Learning a new language, indeed, learning one that is written in a different alphabet, is cumbersome and tiring. The memory is simultaneously assailed by the myriad components of lingual[141] and lexicological complexity: pronunciation, grammar, orthography, true meaning, and metaphorical meaning. The mind reels and is quickly fatigued. Sleep cannot but follow very soon. It all made sense, it felt right, and her mind rose to the rationality of this version like a rose stretches towards the sun and leaves the dark and sordid mud underneath. When Catherine, as a little girl, had fears, she preferred to do battle on them with her natural optimism, like in Voltaire's novel *Candide*, where optimism is tempered with the steel of logic. In order to be thought of as enlightened, a queen had to direct all her thinking to the dynamic process of reason. She was not about to put an end to her habits of thinking. She thought that Zénobe could not have been foolish enough to have consorted with another man because he would not have dared to displease the queen and risk her wrath. In turn, he would not have risked her wrath because he was a righteous man and knew the parameters of virtuous comportment. And finally, she knew Zénobe to be as naïve and innocent as Candide who, when the young baron, the brother of his beloved Cunégonde, starts to seduce him, runs him through with the blade of his sword.[142] The fusion of Zénobe and Candide in Catherine's mind sealed her persuasion. The virtuous Joseph Andrews also, perhaps, played a role in tipping the scale towards Zénobe's innocence. Zénobe, the hero of this novel, was blameless of any unworthy accusations. He could not be guilty of abhorrent proclivities or deplorable behavior. After all, Catherine had spent more than a week with the young man. She had seen nothing dark or unwholesome about him. Catherine knew herself to

---

141   The term 'linguistic' had yet to be invented. It will appear first, in German, in 1824.

142   Perhaps Catherine is right in her interpretation of this crucial scene, but there are others who believe that Candide runs his sword through the baron because the aristocrat still insists that Candide, a mere commoner, cannot harbor the ambition to marry his sister Cunégonde.

be an expert in human character. She would have caught the slightest deviance no matter how deeply held in Zénobe's heart. He could not have succeeded in hiding this particular sordid detail, that he secretly was drawn to intimate congress with men. She would have seen it, or felt it; in some way she was sure she would have identified it. Her faith in her ability to read people, especially in the case of Zénobe's sweet and fraternal proximity to Candide, allowed her to put all distasteful speculations aside. A new tactic of thought overwhelmed her: she loved Zénobe; she could never have loved a vile and wicked man who was diabolically debased. Zénobe was nothing if not lovable. His soul was transparent. His behavior was absolutely virile. Catherine knew who he was. She knew what type of man he was. He was, in effect, too good. He believed deeply in virtue, so deeply that he rejected illicit relations with her, to her everlasting detriment.

The rationality of her mind proved victorious when she realized that she had to let him go. He was not the type of man to be trapped in a gilded cage. He was master of his own destiny, and Catherine could respect such a man.

A final thought bourgeoned into her mind. Perhaps she had been too hasty in sending Andrei Olegovich back to his parents' estate in Tula. She could very easily invent a reason to have him brought back.

In the meantime, on the other side of the palace, Zénobe was also lost in thought. He had walked back to the bed to pick up the stack of language notes for he truly was interested in learning Russian. Glancing at the bed he realized how keen he had been on learning about his Russian teacher. Andrei Olegovich had been an attentive and delightful host, and an amenable pupil to Zénobe's French lessons. They had rather enjoyed the body parts game as they both struggled tooth and nail to wrap their tongues around impossible articulations. There was hardly any difference in the pronunciation between *oreille* and *orteil*![143] Andrei Olegovich confused *cœur* and *corps*, much to the delight of Zénobe. "*Je t'aime de tout mon corps,*" was uproarious. The «ы» sound in Russian sounded so funny that it had Zénobe in stitches. For Zénobe it was a vowel from hell that unbelievably was produced in the throat and he could not imitate it. His efforts to produce it made Andrei Olegovich remark, "You sound like forest monster from Ural Mountains." More laughter ensued when Andrei Olegovich could not get the guttural French «r» to work, or the «u». Hands came up to guide the jaw and the lips to facilitate these foreign sounds, mouths were already rounded to say either «ы» or «u», and the «r» led to a natural purring once the kissing started. During the heavy petting, strangely enough, the bilingual utterances came to a halt and were replaced by universal and ineffable glottal emanations that can best be described as sighs, grunts, moans, whispers and growls. My god! Andrei Olegovich had a beautiful face. Zénobe

---

143 *Oreille* = ear; *orteil* = toe. Next sentence: *cœur* = heart; *corps* = body. The following sentence means, "I love you with all my body."

wanted to taste that tongue that said «ы» so easily; Andrei Olegovich wanted to feel with his lips the vibrations of Zénobe's throat as he trilled a prolonged «г». He couldn't pronounce it himself, however, for his own r's were trilled next to his front teeth. No amount of work on Zénobe's part would make the Russian's r's descend into his throat. But they did enjoy the efforts. The discovery of a new language is an exciting adventure, akin to exploring a new land or reading an amazing new book, or getting to know an intriguing new person. A new world opens up, and we enter with mouth agape. Zénobe remembered that he did learn the Russian word for 'penis': it was член.[144]

Zénobe took a last nostalgic look at the bed, stuffed the language lessons into his pocket, and slowly left the room. As he closed the door behind him, he thanked the gods of destiny that he had had the prescience to insist that they both get dressed again. He remembered the scene in the *marquis* de Villette's boudoir where he and André had been caught in bed without a stitch on. The Russian Andrei understood the wisdom of this and had complied, even putting his shoes back on.

While walking through the halls of Tsarskoe Selo, Zénobe pondered: How the devil could I have thought that an Empress, a Queen, a woman Head of State, for all the evidence I had been given which demonstrated her enlightened ways of viewing the world, in the end not show her true feelings and not prove to me that she possessed all along the despotism of a soul corrupted by power! That she should doubt him, accuse him of horrible things, think of him, if even for a moment, as a monster of vice and iniquity!

Yet, how Voltaire had extolled Catherine's virtues! In all his letters to her and about her, he mentions her unwavering love for fairness, for justice, for rational thinking in the aid of ruling a nation. Truly this was a modern kind of miracle, where instead of a tyrant there stood at the apogee of political authority a steadfast human who thought of herself, not as a usurper of her subjects's power, but as a leader who believed in the dignity of everybody's volition, who could see their motives and actions through a universal code of conduct, and who would therefore judge them through the wisdom of her mind and the mercy of her heart.

Where is the mercy of her heart now? thought Zénobe. Catherine may be Queen, but she has no sway over my heart or over my private life. Her true colors I can now identify and I see her for who she is, a despot who wants to rule over what goes on in my mind and a tyrant who dares to judge me for what is in my heart. My sentiments have no master, not even myself! If I allow them free rein, it is because the actions and reactions that they create within me are benign in nature, even virtuous, for they express love for one's fellow man and that in and of itself can only ever be a good thing.

She attacks my honor! How dare this Queen or any other, cast aspersions, foment calumny, and decry as mine this guilt of a crime so heinous, so despicable, yet whose only legitimacy is traced back to the biblical inanity of the tradition and intolerance of an ignorant tribe of Levites? Where is Catherine's extolled enlightenment now? She has never derived statutes or edicts from the bible; why is she guilty of it here?

The fact that I am not her subject and therefore untouchable must grate excessively on Catherine's pride as she flails about in a doomed attempt to find a dénouement to this tragedy. Here now, is the crux of Catherine's problem, and mine. Ah, spurned, cast-out woman, her heart turns to stone and will not seek rational redress in the appeasement of her harried soul! All she sees is tinged with her fury; she desires ardently to cast

---

144   Pronounced chlyen, or /tʃljen/, using the International Phonetic Alphabet.

me into her dungeons in an effort to seek retribution and solace. I vow not to give her such satisfaction, for her whole attitude is feudal: were I her vassal who has betrayed his Queen, my fate would be sealed. But she is not my Queen and I am not her vassal. Still, she would have me molder in prison for the rest of my life. That, according to Catherine, is punishment swift and just.

An entire life sacrificed, a person's desires, ambitions, passions, along with his will to live and to be happy, everything thrown out in order to balance the wrath of a scorned woman.

She will not get the satisfaction of sitting in judgment over me for my conscience is out of her bounds. Moreover, my crime is no crime at all. My only error was to have trusted Catherine at all.

Oh, the inconstancy of a woman, feeble in her rationalizations, influenced so readily by her emotions, piqued to the quick by her suffering pride. I should have lain with her and gotten it over with! Wagnière would have understood that it would have been the most expedient thing to do, rather than now face the smoldering of the dragon. Something tells me, however, that the Empress would not have been satisfied with just one or two or four nights of my amorous services. She would have wanted me forever, another addition to her Italian Greyhounds, and then I would never have been able to extricate myself.

It is better that I did not lie with her. Even if she is angry. Let her steep in her anger. Her emotions have run away with her ability to think rationally. I shall continue to press on and attempt to influence her with my infallible logic and show her, prove to her beyond a shadow of a doubt, that I was not unfaithful to her, and that her whole conclusion, of my culpability of both crime and sin for alleged actions taken with another man, is a fallacy conjured up by her unstable faculties of observation. What she calls unassailable proof, that Andrei Olegovich was embracing me, is a spurious misjudgment. And even if he had been embracing me, such an innocent event to occur on a cold night, while we were both sound asleep, could never be embellished to suggest that anything evil had gone on that evening.

How can something so innocent, so loving, so virtuous, ever be painted in the tawdry colors of a sordid and wicked congress? I am sorry I will never get to see Andrei Olegovich ever again. He was a great friend, inimitably handsome, and a peerless language teacher. I shall miss his Russian lessons; I shall miss even his atrocious Russian accent in French. It would serve Catherine right were I to go out of my way to seek him out. I believe he said his family is from Tula, wherever that is.

But I better not augment her pique. Nor will it do to disparage her for her emotions. I have already wasted too much time assailing her irrationality. There comes a time to act, and to act incisively. One accepts the situation, wraps the shreds of one's honor about one, and seeks a methodical solution to the problem. It just takes a little bit of courage. The problem is that she cannot govern her feelings which have run away with her power to use logical thought. The solution is that I will use the balm of reason on her, and hope for the best. How many times has reason been of succor to me? It is the only force on earth that will tamp down wild human emotions, not with the brute force of tyranny, but by the liberating force of understanding, of acceptance, and of realization.

The length of the hallways in Tsarskoe Selo allowed Zénobe an abundance of time to engage in such meditative meanderings. Obviously, he could not gauge the extent to which his own emotions were affected by Catherine's accusations. He had committed no crime. But he had committed something that by others is construed as a crime. His honor was besmirched with false accusations, yet he was blind to the truth of those accusations only because he found his conduct to be quite honorable. In the end, his conscience was at peace, abetted by his powers of reasoning. As he climbed the steps into the royal *berline* to join the empress, he worried that he would have to continue to elucidate, all the way to Saint Petersburg, his excuses and justifications. He could not know that she had already figured out a solution to their problem by the use of her own rationalizations. Not a word was said about untoward nocturnal activities and there was no further mention of Andrei Olegovich. Instead, Catherine and Zénobe spoke about their mounting excitement to see Voltaire's books about to find their permanent home.

Without qualm, without hesitation, that very same afternoon in Saint Petersburg, Catherine presided, in the Throne Room, over a hastily arranged ceremony to appoint Zénobe de Bosquet Chamberlain of the Realm. But since the young man remained adamant about leaving, he was to become Roaming Chamberlain of the Realm, or Chamberlain-at-large, an appointment that came with the request that he report to her at regular intervals. This post came with an annual salary of five thousand rubles, which she presented to him ten years in advance. She also decreed him a Russian Count, complete with papers of nobility. Had he stayed in Russia, he would also have received a palace and two thousand peasants. She gave him diplomatic papers, and a passport, to see him through all borders; new military uniforms with the colors of her regiments (he couldn't tell what they were since he was color-blind); a trunkload of aristocratic evening attire; and a magnificent *berline* with six horses. Zénobe responded that this vehicle would attract too much attention; four horses would be sufficient. Catherine told him to get used to the attention; he was destined for greatness. Even the archbishop of Paris himself, Christophe de Beaumont, would never dare to stop an official diplomat's *berline* with six, so Zénobe would have the wherewithal to visit Paris with impunity. She also gave him letters of introduction to Grimm, her correspondent in Paris, and instructions to Grimm to re-introduce Zénobe to the other *philosophes* under his new identity. Catherine's last gift to him was her portrait in gold miniature, surrounded by 100 small diamonds, with a large ruby in the shape of a teardrop encrusted at the top of the frame. The precious stones shone like the Milky Way.

The diplomatic papers, the documents of nobility, and the passport all revealed a new name with which Catherine had baptized Zénobe. From now on he would be known as Зеноб Теофилович Роща, pronounced Zenob Teofílovich Rósha, *rósha* being the Russian word for *bosquet*, or little forest.[145]

"But my father's name was not Théophile," commented Zénobe on the patronymic.

"It is of no consequence," answered Catherine. "I want this part of your name to protect you. I know that you are an atheist, but I am not."

Zénobe accepted. From now on he would be known as "the son of the beloved of god."

---

145   The transliteration of this Russian name will become, in French, Zénobe Théophile Rochas.

Of course, all of these gifts, all of this adulation coming from Her Imperial Highness, roused the suspicions of Zénobe's fellow librarian, Wagnière, who spent days glancing at him with naked accusation. Even though they worked for hours together during the day to place Voltaire's books on Catherine's shelves, they could not contend with having conversations of a private nature for there were always other people around and the empress herself could appear at any moment. She would drop by majestically into her private study in the Oval Room of the Winter Palace and observe the progress the two were making. Wagnière and Zénobe were placing the books just as they had been in Voltaire's library in Ferney. Catherine would linger before the bookcases, caress the books, remove one to view its title page, and maybe take it with her to read.

"I am in book heaven," she told them one day with genuine excitement. "These books transfer an energy to me; I feel alive; almost as if I were being introduced to a future lover. I feel an energy here," she said, pressing her fist to her heart. "It is an energy that can move mountains, my friends. But what am I saying? You are already convinced of this, since you are, after all, Voltaire's librarians."

The day came, however, when the last book was placed on the last shelf. Catherine said goodbye to Wagnière in the library, thanking him profusely for all he had done for her and bestowing on him a yearly pension for life.[146] As for Zénobe, she asked him to come into her private rooms in order to say goodbye to him for she knew that she would weep.

"Thank you..." began Zénobe.

"Thank you..." said the empress at the same time.

They both laughed.

"You first," said Zénobe with a deep bow.

"No, no, you first, my dear Rósha."

Zénobe took one of Catherine's hands and bowed low again to kiss it.

"I do not have the words to thank you for all you have done for me. Your generosity and your beneficence leave me speechless."

"Well, this is truly the first time I see you lacking for words," she said with a smile on her face.

"It is not because words don't exist... But they fall short, far short, of reality. I need to tell you that I, too, am very sad to say good-bye."

"So, then, stay, my beautiful Little Forest (*Petite Forêt*). Stay with me and let me be kind to you. Be my companion and... and... But no, I see by the light of your eyes that there is something out there... out there, in the world, that draws you away from me, away from Russia. We have covered this ground before, so let us not repeat ourselves. My heart cannot take any more. You must leave and I must stay, and my wounded heart must accept the sad reality and begin its period of convalescence. *Petit* Zénobe, it is my sincere hope that I see you again one day. Embrace me now, before you go."

Zénobe embraced her and held her in her arms, prepared to do so for as long as she wanted. But it only lasted for a few seconds. She broke the embrace, saying, "Oh, the 'what ifs' and the 'what might have beens' are thoughts that haunt our minds and terrorize our hearts. We must be strong and relinquish them, drive them from our thoughts, so that we may find peace once again. Go in peace, my kindred

---

146   Catherine continued to pay Wagnière a yearly pension of 1,500 *livres* for the rest of his life, whereas Voltaire had bequeathed to his indispensable secretary an annuity of 400 *livres*.

spirit (*mon âme sœur*), find joy and satisfaction elsewhere, but think of me once in a while. Write to me. Keep me apprised of events and public sentiment in France."

Zénobe promised to conscientiously acquit himself of his duties as Chamberlain-at-large, wherever he went. He surprised himself when tears started to fall copiously down his cheeks. His parting words to her were, "*Vous êtes mon âme sœur,*" pronounced with sweet emotion and an added touch of sudden realization that they were, indeed, kindred spirits, which pleased the empress.

Zénobe could not help realizing that the date of their departure from Saint Petersburg, February 10th, was the anniversary of his entry into Paris the year before. What a difference a year has made, he marveled. From being lost, destitute, bereft of all solace, to this, friend of philosophers and kings and empresses, an authentic aristo, with enough money to be independent and to try to do some good in the world.

It wasn't until after they had left the imperial premises, in Zénobe's impressive new *berline* and six, headed west and for home, that Wagnière exploded in curiosity and allegation.

Zénobe remained calm for his conscience was at peace.

"*Cher* Wagnière," he told his companion and fellow librarian. "You may think whatever you claim to be appropriate and sound, but nothing, absolutely nothing, happened between the empress and me."

Without a word, Wagnière gestured to the sumptuous appointments of the interior of their *berline*.

"Well," countered Zénobe. "Her Imperial Majesty gave you a yearly pension for life. What did you have to do to deserve that?"

"You know very well what I did to deserve that. I accompanied Voltaire's library on a perilous journey, defending it from marauders, protecting it from the elements, risking my very life to deliver it all the way to Saint Petersburg. That is what I did."

"Well," responded Zénobe. "I did the same thing, since we were in this exploit together, but, it is true, I might have done a bit more for Catherine than you did. However, as much as your unbridled imagination may entertain certain occurrences, I never did anything with her that might make me feel ashamed, or that might make you think that I was unfaithful to my dear André. Not with her, not with a single one of her ladies-in-waiting, not with any residents of Her Royal Highness's retinue."

Zénobe hesitated to look into Wagnière eyes and discern to what length he believed him. He stole a glance. He observed a persisting glint of skepticism in the depths of his gaze.

"I think that what I gave her was much better than what you think, anyway. For the time we were here, I gave her companionship, intelligent conversation, new concepts, rational discourse. Ours was a dialogue mutually agreeable, entertaining, and we both came to know each other rather well. There was no need to tumble into bed with her. It was not necessary. So you see, *cher* Wagnière, there is no need for you to worry about the state of my soul and the possibility of me going to hell for having committed the carnal sins of concupiscence and fornication."

Wagnière might have been appeased, but others, especially those who have been following the plot of the young man's deeds and conduct, might beg to differ. Did Zénobe truly forget all about his one-night incident with the beautiful Russian aristocrat, Andrei Olegovich Démidoff,[147] or did he intentionally hide it from the protestant Wagnière? To what extent does the interplay between memory and conscience begin to encroach on the veracity of the events that transpired?

Such is the opaqueness of life that the novel attempts to disperse. It was Stendhal who likened the novel to the mirror of life that reflects both the muck and the divine of human existence, the evil and the saintliness of men and women. More than a mirror that faithfully reflects the images which fall upon it, the novel is a discerning eye that never closes, that sees all, and that hides nothing. People forget, dissemble, stretch the truth or truncate it, but the novel follows them inexhaustibly and demands to discover the veracity of their deeds and of their sentiments.

---

147   I thought we were this last name hiding.

www.ingramcontent.com/pod-product-compliance
Lightning Source LLC
Chambersburg PA
CBHW031937130726
47905CB00008BA/2479